A Death by Any Other Name

TESSA ARLEN

A Death by Any Other Name

MINOTAUR BOOKS
A THOMAS DUNNE BOOK
NEW YORK

A THOMAS DUNNE BOOK FOR MINOTAUR BOOKS.
An imprint of St. Martin's Publishing Group.

www.thomasdunnebooks.com
www.minotaurbooks.com

Library of Congress Cataloging-in-Publication Data

Names: Arlen, Tessa, author.
Title: A death by any other name / Tessa Arlen.
Description: First edition. | New York : Minotaur Books, 2017. | Series: Lady
    Montfort mystery series ; 3
Identifiers: LCCN 2016043778| ISBN 9781250101426 (hardcover) |
    ISBN 9781250101433 (e-book)
Subjects: LCSH: Countesses—Fiction. | Murder—Investigation—Fiction. |
    Upper class—England—London—Fiction. | Great Britain—History—
    Edward VII, 1901–1910—Fiction. | BISAC: FICTION / Mystery &
    Detective / Traditional British. | FICTION / Mystery & Detective /
    Historical. | FICTION / Mystery & Detective / Women Sleuths. |
    GSAFD: Historical fiction. | Mystery fiction.
Classification: LCC PS3601.R5445 D42 2017 | DDC 813/.6—dc23
LC record available at https://lccn.loc.gov/2016043778

Our books may be purchased in bulk for promotional, educational, or business use. Please contact your local bookseller or the Macmillan Corporate and Premium Sales Department at 1-800-221-7945, extension 5442, or by e-mail at MacmillanSpecialMarkets@macmillan.com.

First Edition: March 2017

10 9 8 7 6 5 4 3 2 1

To Flossie and Dud, with thanks and love

Acknowledgments

Many, many thanks to my family for their continued support and love—you are all of you so generous in so many ways.

On Bainbridge Island, thanks to my local indie bookstore Eagle Harbor Book Company and to Channie and Barry Peters of What's Up Bainbridge—community support is vital to a writer.

As always I have to thank my clear-sighted and hardworking literary agent, Kevan Lyon. *A Death by Any Other Name* involved many at Thomas Dunne/Minotaur and my thanks go to Anne Brewer, Peter J. Wolverton, Emma Stein, and Jennifer Donovan on the editing side; to Shailyn Tavella for her bright ideas in PR, and to David Rotstein's art department for this wonderful cover in a shade of delicious peacock blue.

There are many in the talented authors' group I belong to who have been particularly generous: Susanna Calkins, Nancy Herriman, Anna Loan-Wilsey, Alyssa Maxwell, Meg Mims, Sharon Pisacreta, Vicki Thompson, and Ashley Weaver. Together we bolster each other when things are miserable, cheer each other on when they go well, and help each other out with all sorts of odd things that writers of historical mystery simply have to know.

And last, to every one of you who connect with me on Twitter and Facebook, who read my blogs and who take the time to tell me how much you enjoy the company of Clementine and Jackson—thank you.

Characters

Iyntwood House at Haversham in Buckinghamshire, England
Ralph Cuthbert Talbot: the Earl of Montfort and loving husband to Lady Montfort

Clementine, Elizabeth Talbot: the Countess of Montfort and amateur sleuth

*Mrs. Edith Jackson: Lord Montfort's housekeeper and Lady Montfort's fellow sleuth

Miss Gertrude Jekyll: celebrated plantswoman, artist, and garden designer

Mr. George Hollyoak: the butler

Miss Edna Pettigrew: Lady Montfort's personal maid

*Mrs. Mable Thwaite: the cook

*Mrs. Beryl Armitage: Hyde Castle's ex-cook and bearer of interesting news

---

*Cooks and housekeepers were referred to as Mrs. out of respect, even if they were unmarried.

ix

Hyde Castle at Bishop's Hever in Buckinghamshire, England

Mr. Roger Haldane: the master of Hyde Castle and manufacturer of Haldane's Hearty Stew

Mrs. Maud Haldane: long-suffering wife to Mr. Haldane and chairwoman of the Hyde Rose Society, a group of amateur rosarians

Mrs. Albertine Bartholomew: a plant collector from France

Mr. Rupert Bartholomew: rosarian and manufacturer of Bartholomew's Bully Beef

Mr. Finley Urquhart: an elderly rosarian with a wide interest in herbal lore, witchcraft, and the occult

Mrs. Amelia Lovell: rosarian and close friend of Mrs. Haldane

Mr. Clive Wickham: rosarian and magistrate at the Court of Assizes

Mrs. Dorothy Wickham: a flirtatious young wife addicted to romance novels

Mr. Ernest Stafford: landscape designer, ex-student of Gertrude Jekyll, working at Hyde Castle

Mr. Evans: the butler

Charles: the footman

Mrs. Walker: the housekeeper

Colonel Morris Valentine: chief constable for Buckinghamshire

A Death by Any Other Name

Chapter One

Coming home after a holiday is almost as enjoyable as the holiday itself, Edith Jackson thought as she surveyed the familiar comfort of her bedroom and parlor, her eyes lingering over beloved objects that she had collected over the years. Here it all was, just as she had left it: her small library in one corner, a pretty writing bureau by the window that she had been given by Mr. Hollyoak, the butler, to celebrate her appointment from first housemaid to housekeeper ten years ago. She sat down in a deeply cushioned wing chair, a present to herself four years ago: a fireside chair that offered deep comfort for long winter afternoons with a good book. However humble or simple these simple objects appeared to be, they nevertheless made her homecoming a welcome one.

She pulled her canvas rucksack across the carpet toward her and carefully took from its place, between her nightie and a pair of heavy woolen stockings, a slightly creased watercolor of the magnificent view from Stanage Edge in Derbyshire painted by her friend Emily Biggs. She propped the painting up on the mantelpiece, tilting it so it would be visible from her armchair and then sat back down to enjoy it. Considering that there had been a stiff breeze blowing when she had set up her easel, Emily had done quite a good job of capturing the immensity of the peak district in northern England with its gritstone cliffs, outcrops of boulders and wide, ever-changing skies.

As Mrs. Jackson gazed at Emily's painting she realized how much she would miss her friend's outgoing company and good-natured disposition. Their walking holiday of the hills and dales of Derbyshire, with its open prospects, had given each day a sense of endless liberty—a pleasant contrast to the often claustrophobic life they led in service to families of consequence. Emily Biggs, the niece of the Talbot family's old nanny, worked as a governess to Sir Stanley Pritchard's three youngest daughters at neighboring Northwood. Mrs. Jackson felt more than a little sympathy for Emily, as Sir Stanley ruled his household with a rod of iron and had an unpredictable temper; a man wholly unlike the Earl of Montfort, whose grand Elizabethan house, Iyntwood, Mrs. Jackson was proud to call home as its housekeeper.

But however placid the atmosphere at Iyntwood, Mrs. Jackson's holiday in the north of England had been a particularly welcome break; she rarely strayed from the earl's principal country seat, unless she was required to make the occasional trip up to the Talbot family's London house if her ladyship had need of her particular help. She sighed as she got up from the chair to finish her packing. Lady Montfort in the last two years had developed what could only be described as a rather intrusive desire to involve herself in other people's problems. Not the usual sort of problems that beset gently bred women of the aristocracy, such as whom their daughters should marry or whether their sons should be discouraged from indulging their passion for aeroplanes and fast motorcars. Mrs. Jackson's expression became somber as she remembered the last two rather unorthodox demands made on her time in what she privately referred to as "plain old interfering" in matters best left to the police.

She stowed her walking boots and empty rucksack at the back of the wardrobe. Lady Montfort's investigation last winter into the murder of a guest at a dinner party to celebrate the birthday of the First Lord of the Admiralty, Mr. Winston Churchill, had certainly started out as a polite "inquiry," as her ladyship liked to refer to their interfering. But it had almost backfired on them, quite dangerously for her ladyship, before they had pieced together the identity of the murderer.

Ah well, the English aristocracy are not without their eccentricities, she thought as she closed the wardrobe door. At least Lady Montfort did not involve herself in the outrageous antics of the suffragette movement like the assertively outspoken Lady Constance Lytton, the middle-aged, unmarried daughter of the Earl of Lytton who had spent the last five years escalating her fight for the franchise from setting light to the occasional post-box to instigating a one-hundred-woman-strong hunger strike in Liverpool Prison, which had brought untold humiliation to her family. And neither did Lady Montfort design highly unsuitable underclothing like that embarrassing Lady Duff-Gordon with her fancy London salon, Madame Lucile, in Hanover Square. Everyone knew it was unsuitable for the wife of an aristocrat to earn her own living—a fact made quite clear by the Court of St. James when Sir Cosmo Duff-Gordon was informed that he would not be permitted to present his entrepreneurial wife at court. Mrs. Jackson gave her mackintosh a good shake before hanging it up on a peg by her parlor door. No, there were never any unconventional and awkward displays from Lady Montfort, she had that at least to be thankful for. Her ladyship conducted her inquires with tact and quiet good manners as befitted her place in society.

Her unpacking complete, Mrs. Jackson washed her face and hands and walked through into her comfortable and well-furnished parlor where a tea tray had been left ready for her by the third housemaid. She had the rest of the afternoon to settle herself before she tackled whatever situations had blown up in her absence belowstairs—perhaps she might run over the household accounts after she finished her tea.

It took disciplined organization and considerable forethought to maintain a house as grand as Iyntwood and Mrs. Jackson was curious and a little nervous as to how the butler had managed without her. Mr. Hollyoak was without doubt their leader in the servants' hall, but it was the housekeeper's industrious and conscientious attention to the many details that an establishment of this size and importance required that made her an invaluable second-in-command, and she had a particular flair for organizing important occasions.

She opened her parlor window to the warm afternoon air and, hungry from her long railway journey home, sat down at the table in anticipation of a nice cup of tea and some hot buttered toast. But no sooner had she lifted the teapot than there came a knock on her parlor door. Before she could call out a reluctant summons to enter, it opened and Iyntwood's cook put her head around it into the room. *But I've only been back for less than an hour,* Mrs. Jackson thought with exasperation as she noticed that Mrs. Thwaite's long face was wearing a particularly peevish expression. Any expectation that she might have an hour or two to herself, to savor her homecoming, evaporated with the steam of the teakettle. In Mrs. Jackson's experience, Mrs. Thwaite liked to get her version of any unpleasant event in first—usually because she was responsible for most of the tiffs that took place belowstairs at Iyntwood. And true to form, Mrs. Thwaite waded in with her usual asperity.

"So you're back then and not before time," the cook said, as if Mrs. Jackson had escaped from Iyntwood, been tracked down, and marched home in disgrace. "I hope you enjoyed yourself up there in Derbyshire, climbing up and down them hills all day." Her curious eyes came to rest on Mrs. Jackson's rosy cheeks and lightly sunburned nose, which gave her large gray eyes an even greater clarity and depth of color. "Looks like you had good weather for it then." This was said with marked criticism to one who had been self-indulgent enough to enjoy the luxury of sunshine.

"It was a most enjoyable interlude, thank you, Mrs. Thwaite, but I am glad to be back." She politely waited for what was coming next as she poured herself a cup of tea.

"You've no idea what's been going on here while you were away, have you? Well, I am here to tell you it's been *quite* a to-do." Cook's tone became more conciliatory as she sidled into the room with her head tilted to one side like a sly parrot scuttling along its perch. "I think Mr. Hollyoak is losing his marbles, I really do."

The housekeeper did not respond to this disrespectful description of the state of the butler's mental health as it was apparent that she was about to be caught up in one of the many power struggles between Iyntwood's cook and its butler. It was an unequal struggle since the butler held complete sway over his dominions belowstairs, but Mrs. Thwaite was by nature a woman of considerable thrust and was not afraid to provoke a minor border skirmish now and then.

Uninvited, she sat her bony bottom down on a chair and folded her arms expectantly under her nonexistent bosom, and Mrs. Jackson understood that she was being invited to adjudicate in the age-old feud between cook and butler, which was dormant if she was vigilant but had obviously flared up in her absence. She fixed her tranquil gaze on Mrs. Thwaite's face as she sipped her tea. To invite further information from Cook was unnecessary, as it would be forthcoming anyway, but she would not encourage her in the mistaken belief that she was her confederate in whatever state of affairs now existed in the servants' hall.

"Frustration doesn't begin to describe the last week in this house, Mrs. Jackson. All caused by a certain person who is determined to undermine my status, causing me great embarrassment in front of my staff." She was referring to three kitchen maids and one scullery maid, all of whom worked directly under, what she often referred to as, her purview. The cook guarded her lofty status belowstairs—no one crossed her without thinking twice about it. No one except the housekeeper, and from long experience Mrs. Jackson picked her battles where the cook was concerned.

She guessed at the cause of the disagreement that must have raged throughout the servants' hall. Mr. Hollyoak had probably refused to allow Cook to use the telephone to place her orders with local tradesmen, Fortnum & Mason, Harrods, and the Billingsgate fishmonger in London. It was an old battle that had been fought many times over the past two years. The instrument was in the butler's pantry and might be used only by Mr. Hollyoak and Mrs. Jackson. It was a simple enough rule and understood by all as immutable. No doubt in the housekeeper's absence Mrs. Thwaite had assumed that as acting second-in-command belowstairs, with temporary authority over the pantries and larders, she would also have access to the thrilling power of the telephone and its sophisticated place in their domestic world.

She listened in impassive silence to complaints and threats, which ended with the cook lifting her large red hands to her face in what Mrs. Jackson recognized as pretended despair. She noticed Mrs. Thwaite's bright little eyes regarding her through her fingers to judge the effect of her suffering at the hands of the butler and felt a wave of sympathy for her old comrade

Mr. Hollyoak. She could only imagine how draining her time away had been for him.

"Now, Mrs. Thwaite, it is a shame that you have upset yourself over this business. But, as you know, it is Mr. Hollyoak's responsibility to order grocery items and other food supplies when I am not here to do it for him. I hope you have not made things difficult between you, because . . ." she lifted a hand to halt the flow of explanations that started to spill from the cook's lips, " I was particularly banking on your being Mr. Hollyoak's right hand whilst I was away and not—"

"He wouldn't *let* me be his right hand, Mrs. Jackson." Mrs. Thwaite could barely contain her indignation. "Wouldn't even *let* me lift the earpiece of the tele—"

"And being his right hand meant that you also followed his orders, just as you would if I were here, don't you see? Now, I will talk to Mr. Hollyoak and explain to him that your intention was only to help him, and I am sure everything will sort itself out in the next day or two." *If you will only let it,* she added to herself.

With this she got up and went to the door, opening it wide for the cook to pass through ahead of her. "I have yet to meet with her ladyship."

"She is presently taking her tea with that Miss Jekyll, the gardening woman, in the rose garden," Mrs. Thwaite informed her as she stumped ahead of her down the back stairs to the servants' hall.

"So, we have just the one guest then. What are you planning for their dinner?" And she respectfully listened to the cook's menu for six courses, all of which sounded quite delectable and made her only too conscious that she was more than ready for her supper.

———

Clementine Elizabeth Talbot, the Countess of Montfort, was seated under a bower of fragrant, white climbing roses. An illustrated book, *Roses for English Gardens,* by the renowned horticulturist and plantswoman Gertrude Jekyll, lay open on her lap, and a pencil and notebook were on the table in front of her. She lifted her head to observe a majestic procession coming across the terrace toward her. Hollyoak was proceeding at a measured pace followed by his under-butler, Wilson, and first footman, James, each bearing the wherewithal for afternoon tea. She slipped a letter from their middle daughter, Althea, to mark her place in a chapter titled "Roses for Converting Ugliness to Beauty" and sat back in her chair with her eyes closed.

What are we to do about a young woman whose only interest in life is to travel? Althea's letter was full of enthusiastic descriptions of her sailing expedition with her uncle Clarendon and older married cousin Betsy Twickenham around the fjords of Norway. Clementine had noted with resignation from her letter that Althea was hoping to sail on to the Baltic with them before returning home: "Well in time, Mama, I promise you, to come with you and Papa to Wethergill for the start of the grouse-shooting season on the twelfth of August." Althea was already a month overdue for her return home. *Why are young women these days so determinedly independent?* she asked herself with more than just a little irritation. *I was married and a mother by the time I was nineteen.*

Clementine was anticipating with pleasure the gathering of her three adult children for the Talbots' annual trip to Inverness for the start of the Glorious Twelfth. Their elder daughter, Verity, would be joining them from her home in Paris and bringing her two little boys. Clementine smiled at the thought of her grandsons, it had been nearly six months since she had last seen them. Lord Montfort and their son,

Harry, would take off to spend long hours with their guests on the grouse moors, leaving Clementine, her two daughters, and her grandchildren to spend long, uninterrupted, happy days with close friends away from the obligations of the estate.

The warm summer air carrying the drowsy and hypnotic sound of late-afternoon birdsong was now accompanied by the soft chink of china and the rattle of teaspoons as Hollyoak and his attendants set about laying the table with the reverence that such ceremonies required.

Clementine opened her eyes and observed a short, rounded figure whose shape somewhat resembled a large onion, wearing a wide-brimmed hat, approaching at an energetic pace. She closed the book on Althea's letter and laid aside her plans for the family visit to the Highlands of Scotland.

"Ah, tea," Miss Jekyll said. "Gardening on a warm afternoon is such thirsty work." She peeled off a pair of heavy leather gardening gloves and dropped them onto the lawn beside her chair. "I am glad to say that Mr. Thrower's valiant fight to save the rose garden has been victorious, Lady Montfort. Not a sign of black spot anywhere; everything is thriving and quite healthy. He must be careful to spray again in autumn and again, to be on the safe side, early next year, before things start to sprout. But a capital job though, you have to admit it all looks quite splendid." She turned to survey the immaculate rose garden stretching before them in formal beds that spilled a profusion of blooms in ivory, buffs, golds, reds, carmines, and pinks onto the smooth grass pathways intersecting each parterre.

"When Thrower appeared at the end of April holding a leafless rose stem in one hand and a handful of black-and-yellow leaves in the other, I must admit I was close to panic." Clementine would not forget the shock of seeing leaves that had unfurled in the first warm days of spring with the glossy gleam of vigorous health, curled and discolored two weeks later with a virulent case of black spot. Without hesitation she had written to Gertrude Jekyll begging for her help. "I can't thank you enough, Miss Jekyll, for coming to our rescue. Once one rose goes down with the disease, you live in dread that it will spread to the others before you have a chance to treat them." And knowing what was expected of her, Clementine did not keep her guest waiting but sat forward on the edge of her lawn chair to pour tea.

She was well aware how lucky she was that Miss Jekyll, old friend and very distant neighbor, was prepared to motor up from Surrey to spend a couple of days pottering around her gardens as their guest at Iyntwood. And knowing how much Gertrude Jekyll enjoyed her food, Clementine had been careful to instruct her cook to be lavish; Miss Jekyll's time was much sought after. Clementine smiled as she thought that asking Gertrude Jekyll to come and advise her head gardener on cures for rose diseases was rather like asking the late King Edward to pop over and give some instruction to the butler on what port to lay down in the cellar.

Miss Jekyll, now comfortably seated in a wide lawn chair, fixed expectant eyes on a Victoria sponge cake sandwiched with raspberry jam and thick yellow cream adorning the middle of the table on its crystal cake stand. And the two women fell into the most satisfying of topics, that of roses: the best breeds to cultivate and the benefits of different fertilizers.

They were interrupted by the arrival of Lord Montfort, who came across the terrace toward them, followed by his dogs. Ralph Cuthbert Talbot, the Earl of Montfort, was a calmly mannered man, with the habitual leisurely air of the landed aristocrat. In looking up to greet her husband, Clementine noticed his preoccupied expression and suspected that all was not quite well in his world.

"Lovely afternoon . . ." He put an affectionate hand on his wife's shoulder. "Just heard from Harry; he wrote to say that he will join us at Wethergill, but only for a couple of weeks; he and Tom Sopwith are hard at work on testing a new aeroplane design." Their eyes briefly met over Miss Jekyll's head.

Oh, dear, she thought, careful to keep any concern to herself, for any mention of their only son's fascination with flight and exploring new innovations in aeroplane design with his engineering friend at Mr. Sopwith's aeroplane manufactory always stirred a little anxiety in Clementine's maternal bosom. Last winter Harry had been offered a commission by the First Lord of the Admiralty, Winston Churchill, to join the new Royal Naval Air Service and had added the rank of captain to his traditional title: Viscount Lord Haversham. "I am so glad he can get away," was her response to this news; there was no need to burden their guest with their family problems. "Miss Jekyll has just been congratulating us on the success of our fight to save the roses from black spot."

Gertrude Jekyll laughed and lifted her second cup of tea to her lips. "Yes indeed, Lord Montfort, as you can see, the garden is certainly at its best." Her dark brown eyes shone with health and good humor behind wire-rimmed spectacles. *How old is she now?* thought Clementine as she gazed at Gertrude Jekyll's large, tanned face deeply lined from exposure to all weathers. *She must be in her seventies and she has twice the energy of a woman half her age.*

Underneath her serviceable straw hat Miss Jekyll's hair was quite gray, but her large, strong hands held her teacup with light delicacy and her movements were brisk and assured; there was no indication from her vital good health and abundant energy that this little tub of a woman had any intention of slowing down the tempo of her busy and purposeful life. She neatly wolfed down a couple of sandwiches as if by sleight of hand,

and, with her mouth full, she nodded an enthusiastic "Yes," to Hollyoak's proffered slice of cake.

Lord Montfort set down his cup and dropped a hand to offer the last bite of his sandwich to the dog lying closest to him, causing the heads of the other two lying on the grass at his feet to lift in immediate expectation. He reached for two more sandwiches, so as to avoid hurt feelings, and said in his quiet and unemphatic way, "I'm afraid I heard quite the most depressing news this afternoon." He had their instant attention. "Emperor Franz Joseph of Austria has just declared war on Serbia. Apparently he does not believe that the Serbian government made a sufficient attempt to comply with his request to deal effectively with their anti-Austrian rebels. I was praying this wouldn't happen after the assassination of his nephew in Sarajevo but, unfortunately, it has."

"I heard that his demands were wholly unreasonable." Gertrude Jekyll's profession kept her busy at the country houses of Britain's top families in government, so she was well informed. "And what about the German kaiser? You can be *sure* he's backing the emperor." She put down her half-eaten piece of cake. This was indeed grave news.

"The situation is just about as bad as it can possibly be. Serbia complied with the Austrian government's demands the best they could—but they refused to have an Austrian police force maintain law and order in their country. So Austria has declared war. This means, almost inevitably, that Russia will rumble to her feet in defense of Serbia and in defiance of Austria and, if so, it would be impossible for Germany and France to refrain from lending a hand to one side or the other. So at the moment we are in measurable, or imaginable, distance of a real disaster in Europe."

"But we would not involve ourselves, surely?" Clementine felt a ripple of alarm as she reluctantly left the serene world of gardening and roses to join a greater one that suffered far more threats in this complicated day and age than simple black spot. "Surely it's just a storm in a teacup?" she asked hopefully, lifting her cup to her lips and taking a sip of China tea.

The ominous word *war* hung in the soft afternoon air. If Britain was pulled into war, Harry and his group of pilots would take off in their ridiculous flying machines to do something he often referred to jubilantly as "air reconnaissance." She glanced at her husband's serious face, no wonder he had looked so tired when he'd walked across the terrace to join them. "Surely it's just Austrian bluster in response to what happened in Sarajevo? Isn't *that* what everyone is saying?" She managed to remain calm as she said this, but underneath her polite suggestion alarm bells rang. Althea, sailing toward the Baltic Sea, was probably already putting ashore somewhere in Estonia. *Oh good heavens above, they simply must put about and come home now;* her fingers tightened on the fragile handle of the cup she was holding and she carefully set it down in its saucer on the table. It was out of the question that Althea continue on with this ridiculous junket if there was unrest in Europe. And she would write immediately to Verity and tell her to consider extending her month's stay in England until this falling-out in Europe was well and truly over.

Her husband sensed her alarm and hastened to reassure: "I have telegraphed to Clarendon to advise him to turnabout and head for home—with our daughter onboard, no matter how persuasive she is about exploring the Baltic. There is probably no real need to curtail their yachting holiday, but we should play it safe." Clementine blessed her husband's unruffled and farsighted view, and his ability to put a firm foot down where Althea's gadding-about was concerned and only prayed that her cousin Clarendon had the strength of character not to be persuaded otherwise by their strong-minded daughter.

Having reassured his wife of their daughter's imminent arrival home, Lord Montfort returned to the possible crisis in Europe. "I hope it is a minor storm, but the assassination of Franz Ferdinand has given the Austrians the excuse they were looking for to bring Serbia fully under their control. And now we must all sit back and wait to see how things roll out from here." His wife noticed that he did not add *And pray they roll out smoothly,* because she was quite aware that prayer would not help in this particular instance.

Chapter Two

Mrs. Jackson discovered that she was not to be given the opportunity to ease her way back into the rhythm of her working day after her holiday. Early the following morning, once she had quieted Mrs. Thwaite's vociferous complaints and soothed Mr. Hollyoak's injured dignity, she was on her way to the linen press to check the inventory when she was stopped by the first housemaid.

"Mrs. Jackson, there is a woman at the scullery door asking for you. She said she wanted a quick word, if you have the time." Agnes's round, pretty face expressed the deepest curiosity for Mrs. Jackson's visitor.

"And did she say who she was and why she was here, Agnes?" And then a sigh as the housemaid replied, "I'm sorry I forgot to ask her name, Mrs. Jackson, but she's quite a respectable sort and she said it was urgent."

A caller belowstairs who was not known to the Iyntwood servants might be the bearer of interesting news. The working day was long and often monotonous and, as Mrs. Jackson knew only too well, any interruption would be greeted with hopeful enthusiasm by maids and footmen alike.

"Very well, tell her I will be along in a moment, and next time please take the trouble to find out a little more before interrupting me." Her ten-day absence had evidently been a holiday for everyone belowstairs, she thought as she took off her black apron.

The woman who was waiting for her at the scullery door was not known to her, but she was, as Agnes had said, a respectable person. Mrs. Jackson's glance took in her serviceable summer coat of reasonable quality, her hat tidy and suitable, and her darned but clean gloves despite the heat of the late July morning. It took less than a minute for the housekeeper to assess her visitor's status and background: a middle-aged working woman from the respectable upper-servant class, or perhaps the wife of a farmer with a small holding.

"Good afternoon, I am Mrs. Jackson, you asked for me?" She walked through the scullery door and out into the courtyard, leaving the door ajar behind her. No stranger, no matter how respectable he or she might appear to be, was invited into the house even belowstairs.

The woman hesitated. There was a slight air of tension about her and Mrs. Jackson suspected that she had come to ask a favor, and one that she was not quite sure would be well received. To keep their conversation from being overheard by the kitchen maids, who were all crowded into the scullery and peering through its windows, she walked her visitor a little way out into the kitchen courtyard, and sat down next to her on a bench under the shade of the mulberry tree.

"Thank you for seeing me, Mrs. Jackson. You don't know me, but my name is Beryl Armitage and my brother is Walter Armitage, who works here as a dairyman on his lordship's estate." Mrs. Jackson instantly recognized the familial similarity between brother and sister. Mrs. Armitage was stout of body and limb, with a sturdy strength about her. She had a round shiny face, a cascade of chins, and her deep-set blue eyes were clear and met Mrs. Jackson's with the honest hope that surely help was in the offing. She couldn't imagine why the dairyman's sister was here to see her and she waited for Mrs. Armitage to state the reason for her visit.

"I am, or rather I was, the cook over at Hyde Castle near Bishop's Hever, Mrs. Jackson. I am here to ask for her ladyship's help in getting to the bottom of something that happened at Hyde Castle and has been bothering me for some time." Now that she had revealed that she was in need of help, Mrs. Armitage paused as if asking permission to continue. And the housekeeper gave it with a nod of her head.

"It's like this, Mrs. Jackson. Almost five months ago now, in early spring, the third of March it was, Mrs. Haldane had a group of friends staying at the castle and, all of a sudden like, one of them got sick and died. An accidental death, the doctor said it was. He said that Mr. Bartholomew, for that was the gentleman's name, had died from food poisoning, most probably from a tainted dish of kedgeree at breakfast. To make a long story short, I was turned away without notice and with no reference." It was evident that Hyde Castle's former cook was still upset by the incident as her eyes filled with tears before they were quickly blinked away.

Mrs. Jackson said nothing, knowing that there was more to come, but she tilted her head in sympathetic encouragement.

"The reason why I have come here, Mrs. Jackson, is that I don't believe it was accidental food poisoning at all. For I had some of that kedgeree myself before it went upstairs to the dining room. I believe Mr. Bartholomew's death was planned by someone in the house and that he was . . ." Mrs. Armitage's anxious eyes regarded her as she faltered, and then said with a rush of determination: "I am here to report a murder, Mrs. Jackson, the murder of Mr. Bartholomew."

Mrs. Armitage's words sounded overloud in the quiet courtyard and Mrs. Jackson half turned to the open door of the scullery. She got up from the bench and went to close it. And when she returned she took a moment before she replied, "Have you been to the police about what you suspect, Mrs. Armitage?"

"No," the woman confessed, "indeed I have not. I am sure the police would disbelieve me. The doctor said Mr. Bartholomew died of food poisoning from something *I* prepared. And that was what was decided at the inquest too, even though I told them I had tasted the kedgeree, before it was sent upstairs, with no ill effects whatsoever. I am sure that the police would think I was just trying it on if I was to go to them with a story contrary to what the inquest had decided. Mr. Haldane is a very rich man, influential, so to speak." She left it to Mrs. Jackson to see the futility of going to the police when Mr. Haldane had sacked her and had a death certificate clearly stating the cause of Mr. Bartholmew's accidental death to be as a result of her negligence.

Mrs. Jackson sat for a moment in thought. If a hand holding a red flag had appeared from behind the mulberry tree and started waving it she would not have been surprised. "But I don't quite understand why you are telling *me* all of this," she said, and she smiled because she didn't want to appear callous as the poor woman was now perspiring freely even though they were sitting in the shade.

Recounting the story of her hopeless predicament had caused Mrs. Armitage's shoulders to slump in despair as she stared down at the toes of her sensible boots peeking out from the hem of her serviceable, navy blue skirt.

"Just a moment, please, Mrs. Armitage." Mrs. Jackson got up from the bench, walked back to the scullery, shooed a crowd of kitchen, house, and scullery maids back to work, and returned with a glass of water. Mrs. Armitage took a grateful sip and then went back to explaining the reason she was bothering Mrs. Jackson with her strange request.

"There is a gentleman working for Mrs. Haldane who said that you and Lady Montfort might be able to help me. He is known to both of you, he says. His name is Mr. Stafford and he sends his respects."

Mr. Stafford? Mrs. Jackson was so taken aback at the mention of his name that she stared at Mrs. Armitage in uncomprehending surprise. How on earth had Mr. Stafford become involved in this unhappy situation? And why had he, in turn, involved Lady Montfort? After a moment's pause she guessed the answer. Mr. Stafford had worked for the Talbot family for the past eighteen months in designing and establishing Lady Montfort's new sunken garden and planning an extension to the rose garden. He was a capable and likable man, a bit too outward in his manner, perhaps, but highly regarded by both Lord and Lady Montfort, and, if she was honest, by herself as well. Mrs. Jackson's rather stern expression softened as she remembered how particularly sympathetic and helpful he had been during that ugly business a summer ago over the murder of Lord Montfort's troublesome nephew. What a mess it had been until her ladyship had involved herself in the puzzling events surrounding that nasty boy's death. Well, it hadn't ended too badly after all, they had between them sorted things out, but Mr. Stafford had been most generous with his time in helping her look at people's behaviors in a different way from that traditionally expected of position and duty. As a result, they had become quite good friends. She remembered the last time they had met, and then resolutely pushed to one side the memory of a pleasant afternoon spent at Kew Gardens. Mr. Stafford's work took him all over the country and her life was here at Iyntwood, so she had not expected to hear from him again.

But it was not really a surprise that his name had cropped up in offering Mrs. Armitage a possible solution to her problem by recommending she confide in Lady Montfort. *Well, I suppose the very least I can do is listen to the rest of this poor woman's story,* she thought.

"Mrs. Armitage, I think it would be a good idea to begin at the beginning. Start with the day Mr. Bartholomew died and go on from there, if you wouldn't mind." And she sat back to listen.

Mrs. Armitage breathed out her thanks in a gust of relief and visibly pulled herself together by squaring her shoulders. Then she took a deep breath and began her story.

"There were just five guests staying at Hyde Castle in March. All of them belong to Mrs. Haldane's little club. They call themselves the Hyde Rose Society, it's a sort of hobby they have. They get together every three months or so and talk about their roses. They have all been coming to the house now for at least ten years. Mr. Bartholomew was part of this group and a very nice man he was, too. He liked his food, and particularly enjoyed a good breakfast. Whenever he came to stay I always made sure to include a kedgeree on the breakfast sideboard as it was one of his favorites." Mrs. Armitage almost smiled. "On this particular morning I ate a small portion of the kedgeree before it went up. It was a good one, nice and spicy with smoky flavors. Mr. Bartholomew was always first in the dining room, and the footman said that on that morning he made a good breakfast and enjoyed a full plateful of the kedgeree, and that when he finished his first plate, he had taken a second helping but had not finished it. Halfway through his second helping, so the footman told me, Mr. Bartholomew said he felt in need of some fresh air and decided to go for a morning's constitutional before the group got together for their first talk of the day.

"Well, just as I was getting luncheon together there was such a commotion. The butler, Mr. Evans, came running down the back stairs and said that there had been an accident and that one of the guests was in the orangery, unconscious, and that the doctor had been called. It was that poor Mr. Bartholomew. Of course I didn't hear the details until later that afternoon. He had been found a few hours after breakfast by one of the head gardener's boys, Johnny Masters; he'd only been with us about a year, poor little lad, as he's only fourteen. Anyway, Johnny went into the orangery to sweep up dead leaves and water the trees in there, and in the corner he found Mr. Bartholomew." Mrs. Armitage stopped and sipped a little water. She took a handkerchief from her coat pocket, wiped her forehead, and dabbed her upper lip. Catching Mrs. Jackson's eye, she said, "It still gives me the shivers to remember this part." She recovered herself with another sip of water before she continued.

"Mr. Bartholomew was out cold when poor Johnny found him. He was lying in a pool . . . of . . ." Mrs. Jackson closed her eyes and shook her head. "Well, he had been very ill, very ill indeed. Poor Johnny was horrified. He cried out for help, and Pete Wainwright, who was working outside, came running in, that's how loud the lad's cry had been—Pete later told me that Johnny's face was ashen and he could barely speak, he just pointed to the far corner of the orangery to where the body was lying." Another sip of water.

"Pete said that he had never seen such a mess in all his life. He said the smell was awful. And that the gentleman . . ." Mrs. Jackson put a hand on the older woman's arm. "There is no need to describe every little thing, Mrs. Armitage, it will only distress you."

"Yes, you are right about that, Mrs. Jackson, you certainly are. It was distressing; is distressing still, the poor man. Well, Pete and Johnny turned Mr. Bartholomew over, he was lying facedown in . . . And they said the look on his face made their blood run cold. It was quite clear to both of them that he was dead, and had died in the most terrible agony."

"And then the doctor was called?" Mrs. Jackson gently prodded, as Mrs. Armitage had gone very quiet and was staring into her empty water glass as if at a loss as to how to continue.

"Yes, Dr. Arbuthnot arrived about an hour later. Made his examination and then went into Mr. Haldane's study, where he wrote up a death certificate. He said Mr. Bartholomew had died of food poisoning because the haddock I used in the kedgeree was off. As if I would use tainted fish." The worst of her story over, Mrs. Armitage allowed herself to be affronted.

"The following day there was an inquest and they agreed with the doctor's report. That afternoon, Mrs. Haldane sent for me and Mr. Evans, the butler. She was in a terrible state as Mr. Bartholomew had been an old and close friend. She handed me an envelope with two weeks' wages and told me to pack my bags and be gone by the next morning, and that until I left the house I was not to go into the kitchen. Nor was I to talk to any of the other servants, except the butler. Mr. Evans was as horrified as I was. We both pleaded with Mrs. Haldane to reconsider. Mr. Evans stood up for me wonderfully he did, said I was reliable and responsible and very careful with the storing of perishables such as fish. But it was no good. Mr. Haldane came into the room and shouted at me to get out. He was very upset; he shouted at all of us: Mrs. Haldane, Mr. Evans, and of course me. Mr. Bartholomew was his greatest and oldest friend, he said, and I had as good as killed him."

The cook bent her head and applied her already damp hanky to her eyes. Mrs. Jackson gave her a minute or two and then asked, "You felt no ill effects at all from eating the kedgeree? Did you tell them you had sampled a portion?"

"No ill effects whatsoever. Mind you, I certainly didn't eat a huge plate and a half of the stuff—Mr. Bartholomew was a great trencherman, loved his food, especially his breakfast. And yes, Mrs. Jackson, I told them at the inquest quite plainly that I had eaten some of the kedgeree with no ill effects, and I also told them that two pigs had eaten the remainder of Mr. Bartholmew's portion, left on his plate and scraped into the kitchen slop bucket, and had also died . . . both of them."

"And there was no kedgeree left in the chafing dish on the sideboard?"

"No, there was none left at all, just a few grains of rice, which of course went down the drain when the dish was washed."

Mrs. Jackson considered as she sat quietly upright on the bench, her hands folded in her lap.

"How can I help you, Mrs. Armitage? Unfortunately, we have no need of a cook here, as we already have one. I could perhaps make some inquiries." She was playing for time because she knew what was coming next.

"No one will take me on, Mrs. Jackson, not without a reference. I gave up a good position to go to Hyde Castle, and even after many years there I do not have enough put by for my old age quite yet. I don't know what is to become of me." She bent her head and held her breath until she had mastered her emotions. "I have to clear my good name, you see, to regain my reputation, it's the only way. I have to prove that Mr. Bartholomew was poisoned on purpose—murdered."

The red flag was waving frantically now as Mrs. Jackson waited for the inevitable. "And then I bumped into Mr. Stafford at Market Wingley last week, what a nice sympathetic gentleman he is. He said that you are a very clever woman and that you had got to the bottom of a very nasty situation here at Iyntwood that involved the death of someone at the house, and that Lady Montfort had saved the life of an important gentleman in the government. He said that you and her ladyship worked together and I should ask you both to help me. I thought about what he said all last night and decided to take a chance. That is why I am here." Mrs. Armitage sat back on the bench, her upturned palms in front of her in the age-old gesture, *I am in your hands, please help me,* a gesture that made Mrs. Jackson feel quite uncomfortable.

"I am not sure what you mean, Mrs. Armitage. Or what Mr. Stafford could have been thinking of to say such a thing. Lady Montfort is not a private detective, as you seem to think she is. It is out of the question for her to become involved in an inquiry into the death of someone who was a perfect stranger to her, especially since there has been an inquest." Glancing at Mrs. Armitage, she saw the despair in her eyes and added, "But she *might* speak to the Market Wingley constabulary on your behalf and help you in that way. They will listen to you *if* Lady Montfort is prepared to speak to them." She was thinking of Colonel Valentine, the chief constable for the county, who was a personal friend of both Lord and Lady Montfort.

"Mrs. Jackson, I am begging you, please ask her ladyship to intervene. If I don't clear my name I don't know what will become of me. I can't stay with my brother and his family for much longer, his cottage only has two bedrooms and they have five children. I am running through my savings, and I had hoped to work for at least another twelve years for my retirement. The way things are going I will be destitute by the time I'm sixty. I am begging you to at least talk to Lady Montfort. Mr. Stafford said she was a kind woman."

Meaning I suppose that I am not, thought Mrs. Jackson, feeling quite horribly trapped.

She stood up. "You are staying in the village, Mrs. Armitage?"

"Yes I am, on Green Lane, 12 Green Lane."

"Very well. I will talk to Lady Montfort, but only on the

condition that you promise me that you will abide by her decision, no matter what it is."

And with tears of gratitude running down her face, Mrs. Armitage grasped Mrs. Jackson's right hand in her two large hot ones and said she would do anything Lady Montfort suggested—anything at all.

Chapter Three

"Poor creature," said Lady Montfort when Mrs. Jackson finished her account of Mrs. Armitage's visit. "It sounds a little bit like this Mr. Bartholomew died of a surfeit of lampreys."

"Lampreys, m'lady?"

"King Henry I, Jackson, was a reasonably healthy monarch who died one night after he had overindulged at the dinner table; he ate an entire dish of lampreys or what we would call eels. His sudden death, leaving his daughter Mathilda to inherit the throne, was the start of a civil war in England called the Anarchy."

"I see, m'lady." Mrs. Jackson decided to let this one go, as she had no wish to bog things down with a history lesson.

"And what is she like, this Mrs. Armitage?"

"She is a respectable woman, m'lady. Neatly dressed, spoke nicely, and was respectful." Mrs. Jackson thought of Mrs. Thwaite bashing pots and pans around downstairs in Iyntwood's kitchen and wished that their cook had as much self-restraint as Mrs. Armitage had. "She is the sister of Mr. Armitage, the dairyman, and is staying with his family in Green Lane. I told her that I would ask you for your advice on how she should proceed. But I think," she tried not to sound too emphatic, as her opinion had not been asked for, "that she should go directly to the police with her story. Clearly something was not right about what happened at the castle."

"Do you, Jackson? Think she should go to the police, I mean. Why should she do that? I wonder. It is five months since the death of Mr. Bartholomew. There was a death certificate and the inquest clearly agreed on a verdict of accidental death. I can't imagine the police being enthusiastic about going round and banging on Mr. Haldane's door and asking him about murder. Do you believe her story? Yes, I can see you do."

What Mrs. Jackson was thinking, and what she most certainly would not say, was that this was Mrs. Armitage's business and not theirs. The whole situation smacked of interfering and meddling as far as she was concerned. She could see where they were headed and was careful not to encourage anything that might lead to their involvement in what looked like the worst sort of a muddle. She had so many reasons why they should not involve themselves that if she had been asked—and she wouldn't be—she would have been hard pressed to know where to start. But an answer was required of her and so she said, "If Mrs. Armitage feels that an injustice has been done, then she has a *duty* to go to the police, m'lady. She has no other choice." She thought perhaps that sounded a bit too hard on a woman who had been dealt an unfair blow and now stood to lose everything, so she reluctantly added, "And perhaps we might help her find a new situation in London."

"Yes, I had thought of that too, Jackson, and of course we should most certainly look into that, at the very least. But I think Mrs. Armitage was asking for something else. She said she wanted her name cleared. The poor woman has lost all respect and she naturally wants her reputation as a cook to remain unblemished. I can hardly blame her. And I also have a duty, if there has been an injustice, to do what I can to help."

This is a new one, Mrs. Jackson thought. *We never took the*

A DEATH by ANY OTHER NAME

moral high ground with the other two investigations. Now people were turning up at Iyntwood's scullery door requesting help, as if Lady Montfort and Mrs. Jackson were a couple of private investigators who had just put a well-worded advertisement in the local newspaper.

"I wish I knew more about these Haldanes. Do you know anything about them, Jackson? No? They are new to the county, aren't they?" She meant of course that they were not an old family. *And if we don't know who these Haldanes are, all the more reason not to get involved,* thought Mrs. Jackson.

She was determined to say nothing more on the subject. She had fulfilled her promise to Mrs. Armitage. But a feeling of unease was beginning to build within her upright body, and even though her handsome face betrayed nothing of the kind, she felt distinct consternation as she observed her ladyship sitting on the edge of her chair looking eager.

When she had come into the room earlier, her ladyship had been delighted to welcome her home and to hear all about her walking tour in Derbyshire with the old Talbot nanny's niece, Emily Biggs. And then Mrs. Jackson had told her of Mrs. Armitage's visit, and her eyes had positively lit up. She had leaned forward in that way she had when she was intensely interested in something. *Too interested by far,* Mrs. Jackson thought as she scanned her ladyship's intent face.

"I wonder if I should have a little talk with Mrs. Armitage." It wasn't a question; her ladyship was halfway to making a decision.

Mrs. Jackson's heart sank. *Oh Lord help us all,* she said to herself, as she dropped her eyes to stare in dismay at the central medallion of the oriental carpet in Lady Montfort's sitting room. *She can't possibly be thinking . . . ?*

But her ladyship *was* thinking, and thinking hard. It was evident from the frown on her face and the lightly tapping

29

fingers on the arm of her chair. And then, having come to some sort of conclusion, she clapped her hands lightly together. "Here is what we will do. I think it would be a good idea for me to have a little talk with this Mrs. Armitage, so ask her to come back after luncheon this afternoon. And in the meantime I will do what I can to find out a bit more about the Haldanes. I think Mr. Haldane bought Hyde Castle several years ago. What does he do for a living? Someone did tell me. I think I heard he is a manufacturer of some sort with pots of money. And I think I met Mrs. Haldane briefly, about a year ago at the Bishop's Hever vicarage tea party, and for the life of me I can't remember much about the woman, other than she was tall and she loves to garden. And now it would seem that our old friend Mr. Stafford has taken a commission to do some garden design for the Haldanes. Oh good heavens!" A bright smile transformed Lady Montfort's lovely face from frowning concentration to elation no doubt at her own brilliance, and she jumped to her feet. "I expect Miss Jekyll knows something about them, especially if Mrs. Haldane has engaged Miss Jekyll's old student Mr. Stafford. Yes, I will sound out Miss Jekyll. But before anything else I think I might just write and reintroduce myself to this keen gardener, Mrs. Haldane, and let her know that Miss Jekyll is staying with us."

Mrs. Jackson left Lady Montfort busily writing away at her desk and went downstairs to send the hall boy over to the village to bring back Hyde Castle's erstwhile cook, and to come to terms with the fact that there was no doubt Mrs. Armitage would not be encouraged to go to the police with her tale of murder. *I hope to goodness she doesn't intend to make a habit of this sort of thing,* she thought as she shut herself in the linen room and opened her inventory ledger, and then realized the futility of worrying about something that had already happened.

The following morning, Lord Montfort arrived in his wife's bedroom as Clementine was sitting up in bed eating her breakfast. He sat down on the edge of her bed and shared a cup of tea with her as she buttered him a piece of toast.

"No need to worry about Althea, darling. I received a reply to my telegraph to Clarendon care of the Port of Tallinn in Estonia. They arrived there a couple of days ago. Clarendon says they are sailing for home today and they will dock at Southampton on the first of August, so we will have Althea with us a day or so after that."

Clementine's shoulders came down a notch. "Thank goodness you caught them before they moved on. Absolutely no more exploring for Althea for a while I think."

"I don't want you to get steamed-up about this Serbian business, darling. We will carry on as usual until we need to think otherwise. Let us not get in a state about Verity either; I am quite sure that if the situation worsens in Europe she will continue her stay with us—at least until all this fuss dies down. Etienne is a generous man about how much time his wife spends with us."

Her husband's apparent lack of concern banished all anxiety and Clementine spent a most satisfactory morning with her head gardener, Mr. Thrower, as, together with Miss Jekyll, they wandered up and down the herbaceous borders that led from the west terrace down to the lake and made plans for new plantings in the autumn. After which Clementine and Miss Jekyll walked down to the new sunken garden to enjoy a picnic luncheon from a hamper brought down for them by a footman. Lord Montfort joined them, and they all reclined on cushions on a rug spread out under the shade of a rapidly maturing birch grove to enjoy the delights of a meal taken alfresco. The sunken garden was still in its infancy, and when they had all sung the praises of the marvels wrought by Mr. Stafford, who two years ago had started the business of transforming an old flint quarry into this mountain valley garden in miniature, they settled down to enjoy their picnic.

"Mr. Stafford has always had a wonderful eye for composition." Miss Jekyll took a sip from her glass of hock and turned to survey the scene created by her old student. She waved a chicken leg in the direction of the southwest corner of the garden. "He is a very talented young man."

"Mr. Stafford has actually taken a commission at the Haldanes' at Hyde Castle at Bishop's Hever. I have no idea what they have in mind, perhaps you know?" Clementine said in what she hoped sounded like an artless question.

Miss Jekyll nodded. "Ah yes, he wrote to me. Mr. Haldane is extremely rich and his wife is a passionate gardener. I have never met them of course." Miss Jekyll was not a snob, but at her time of life she had the pick of the crop and that did not include the arrivistes in society unless they were very well connected and blessed with enough humility to be completely guided by her. "Mr. Stafford is draining an old pond, having it dug out and reshaped, and is going to transform it into an ornamental lake with what Mrs. Haldane refers to as a 'vista.'" Miss Jekyll laughed; she had to deal with grandiose garden schemes from the unenlightened every day of the week.

Lord Montfort, who was finishing the last of his cold chicken, said with his mouth full, "Haldane made a packet in manufacturing food: Haldane's Hearty Stew, he calls it. It comes in tins. Incredible to think anyone would want to eat stew from a tin, but it seems people will eat anything these days if it comes in ready-made form. Sadly it seems we are rapidly relinquishing skills we have taken centuries to acquire just for the sake of ease. Anyway, I remember when he bought Hyde Castle several years ago now. There is not much of the original castle left of course; it was in near ruins when Rigby took it in hand in the 1860s. It was popular then to live in a castle and the Rigby family was large and prosperous so they incorporated the old castle into a new building in the baronial style, bristling with turrets and crenellations. When they lost nearly everything in the panic of 1893, overinvested in American railways apparently, he had to sell off all their land. There was a tenant in the house for a while and then it was sold to Haldane. He spent a good deal of money bringing it up-to-date. I am told that there are parts of the original building that date back to the 1500s. I know Anne of Cleves was supposed to have spent a week or so there while her marriage to Henry VIII was being annulled—before she was established at Hever—the Rigbys were always very proud of that part of the castle's history."

"What's he like, do you know?" Clementine asked, and both Lord Montfort and Miss Jekyll said in unison, "A self-made man," and laughed. And Lord Montfort added, "Supposed to be a decent enough chap, but as hard as nails."

Clementine, who was presiding over their picnic, having sent off the footman, offered her husband a peach and insisted that Miss Jekyll try a delicious little meringue crushed into fresh raspberries with a dollop of cream.

"Funnily enough I had a letter from Mrs. Haldane this morning, such a very polite letter." Clementine did not mention that the letter had been written on pink, rose-scented writing paper in lavender ink and that it had been in reply to her letter sent yesterday introducing herself as a fellow gardening enthusiast and inviting herself over to Hyde Castle for a few days. To make sure of her welcome she had included the offer of an additional guest to Hyde Castle, that of the famous Miss Jekyll. "Apparently Mrs. Haldane is the chairman of an amateur rose society, the members of which are staying with her this month. Mrs. Haldane was wondering if we"—she nodded to include Miss Jekyll in the invitation—"might have the time to run over there later this afternoon and join them for a couple of days. She must have found out that you're our guest, and you can imagine what a privilege it would be for her to introduce you to her friends. There are some notable amateur rosarians among them apparently. What do you think, Miss Jekyll, shall I say yes? It might be fun." As she laid her carefully conceived plan before them, she suffered only a minor pang of conscience. Miss Jekyll was pressed all the time to address groups of zealous amateur horticulturalists, and being a practical and confident woman with not enough hours in her day, she had no trouble at all in saying a polite but firm "no." But for the next couple of days Miss Jekyll's time belonged to her, as her husband would pay Miss Jekyll's very substantial bill for services rendered to Iyntwood's extensive gardens. So if Clementine wanted to pop over to Hyde Castle then Miss Jekyll would go with her. And to Clementine's relief she said as much, but with one proviso.

"I am sure it will be an interesting occasion. Apparently one of their members was recognized by the Royal Horticultural Society for his tea rose. It might be an interesting little jaunt, though I have an appointment next week with the Duke of Wendover and I must go home to Munstead before I set off for Devon. So, yes I would be happy to accompany you, but it is imperative that I leave the day after tomorrow as planned. I do hope you understand my stay will have to be limited, Lady Montfort."

Clementine said she most certainly did and that she would reply in the affirmative to Mrs. Haldane to expect all three of them tomorrow afternoon.

"All three of you, my dear?" Her husband had risen to his feet and was brushing away crumbs with his napkin, preparatory to leaving them. He bent over to help her up from her place on the rug, and she found herself gazing into his eyes as they searched her face. "Who else is going with you?"

"Well, I thought I would take Mrs. Jackson with me because Pettigrew has been seriously under the weather all week with a summer cold."

"Ah yes, Miss Pettigrew's cold, how unfortunate. But how long do you expect to stay?" He was still holding her hands in his and Clementine gently pulled hers away.

"I can only imagine that I will leave when Miss Jekyll does, when they have finished with their rose symposium. They all sound so expert; it will be an education for me."

"Oh, it most certainly will," said her husband. "I am sure you will find the new owners of Hyde Castle fascinating company, and you must tell me what tinned beef stew tastes like." He started to laugh and Clementine had the slightly unsettled feeling that she was being laughed at and that in some way Lord Montfort had accurately guessed the real reason for her visit to Hyde Castle, though how he would know of Mrs. Armitage and the accidental death of Mr. Bartholomew she couldn't imagine.

Chapter Four

"There you are, Jackson, come on in and let's put our heads together," Lady Montfort greeted her as she stepped over the threshold of her ladyship's sitting room and sat down in the chair indicated to her ladyship's right.

As she had walked up the back stairs in answer to Lady Montfort's summons, Mrs. Jackson was well aware of the direction that things had taken since their last conversation. Mrs. Armitage had come up to the house yesterday afternoon and Lady Montfort had spent over an hour in conversation with her. And before the good woman left she had come by the scullery door and taken the time to ask for her before she left. Then with complete sincerity Mrs. Armitage had expressed her gratitude, with much fervent nodding as she stood before Mrs. Jackson, her hands clasped earnestly before her and her eyes misty with emotion.

"What a gracious and kind soul her ladyship is, Mrs. Jackson. How lucky you are to work for the quality. Her ladyship was tact itself. You are all so fortunate to work for such a thoughtful and considerate employer, indeed you are. I have told her ladyship my story, and she has promised to do all she can to help me. Thank you, thank you so very much."

"And you are quite prepared to abide with Lady Montfort's

decision on the matter, Mrs. Armitage?" Mrs. Jackson's fate it seemed was decided: there would be another "inquiry," which meant more sneaking about and asking prying questions. "I am indeed, Mrs. Jackson, I said as much to her ladyship, God bless her." And with that she trudged off up the drive toward Haversham village, which lay on the far side of Iyntwood's park.

Now, as she sat straight-backed in her chair in Lady Montfort's sitting room, Mrs. Jackson opened her notebook and waited.

"Ah yes, Jackson, glad to see you have come prepared, but I don't have time to share all I have learned with you right now." Lady Montfort beamed at her and flipped open her own notebook. Mrs. Jackson saw, to her dismay, that at least four pages were covered in handwriting, in list form it seemed, each item neatly numbered.

"I will brief you on what I have discovered from Mrs. Armitage, and it is all very interesting, as we drive over to Hyde Castle this afternoon with Miss Jekyll."

Hold on just a moment—this afternoon, with Miss Jekyll? These exclamations rang loudly in her head as her face expressed bland interest. *As usual, Edith, you are of course the very last to know.*

"I simply cannot undertake an inquiry into the events surrounding Mr. Bartholomew's unfortunate death without your help, Jackson. My inquiries can only be made among family and friends at Hyde Castle, but I need you to find out more about what was happening belowstairs when Mr. Bartholomew ate his last breakfast. So I think it best for you to accompany me as my companion, which will give you access to both upstairs and downstairs." She smiled, looking altogether very pleased with herself. "I have received a reply to my letter to Mrs. Haldane; she is enchanted with the idea of meeting Miss Jekyll, and she is expecting us today in time for tea. So you had better go and pack, as we must leave in about an hour."

Mrs. Jackson could think of nothing to say to this, and after all what was there to say? Once her ladyship made a decision, she acted on it. There were no half measures, no opportunities given to voice possible pitfalls. She closed her notebook and stood up.

"Miss Pettigrew . . ." she started to refer to Lady Montfort's personal maid, who always accompanied her ladyship on her visits away from Iyntwood. "So unwell it would be wrong to take her. She has insisted on packing for me, dear Pettigrew, but then I told her she must remain here where she can enjoy a complete rest. I have instructed Mrs. Thwaite to give her plenty of nourishing chicken soup for her head cold. And Mr. Hollyoak says he can certainly spare you for a few days. So, Jackson, you have about thirty minutes to get yourself ready."

"But, m'lady . . ."

"No, Jackson, there is absolutely no need to worry about the maiding part. You can dress my hair simply; this will not be a formal gathering, and I must be careful not to be too grand. And for the rest of the time we will have such fun finding out what happened in that house when Mr. Bartholomew ate all the kedgeree for breakfast. Now, off you go. I can brief you in the motorcar, as Miss Jekyll will be driving herself to Hyde Castle."

And Mrs. Jackson was sent from the room feeling a little flustered and at the same time experiencing what was becoming a familiar little flutter of delight that they would be starting out on their third investigation together.

Comfortably installed in Iyntwood's Daimler as it made its way down the drive, Lady Montfort took the opportunity to inform her housekeeper across from her.

"What I suspect we have here, Jackson, is a straightforward

case of Mr. Haldane preventing any form of an official investigation right from the start. That is if Mrs. Armitage is to be believed, and she appears to be a straightforward sort of person: capable no doubt, respectable certainly, and I suspect without enough imagination to make up a story."

"Yes, m'lady, there seems nothing slipshod or careless about Mrs. Armitage, whereas the investigation seems to have been both of those things."

"Exactly. You will be pleased to hear that Mr. Evans, the butler at Hyde Castle, is a good friend of Mrs. Armitage. He was very upset about her removal and is willing to help us—or rather you—with the part of our inquiry belowstairs to find out a little more about what actually happened on the day Mr. Bartholomew died."

"Does he know we are investigating the situation, m'lady?"

"He knows that we are coming to Hyde Castle to make some discreet discoveries. Mrs. Armitage wrote to him yesterday evening so he will have had her letter by the time we arrive. It will be of immense help to have someone in the house on our side, but he is the only one in the house who knows the true purpose of our visit." She opened her notebook and smoothed its pages down flat before she continued.

"Apparently the Bartholomews and the Haldanes were old friends. Mr. Bartholomew was part of Mrs. Haldane's coterie of rose breeders and he was also a close business friend of her husband. Mr. Bartholomew's wife, who is a horticulturalist, but not actually part of this Hyde Rose Society, was not at the house when her husband died, but traveling in the Orient. She is a plant collector and goes away on specimen-gathering expeditions every year with her brother." Lady Montfort glanced down at her notes. "As to Mr. Bartholomew: he was apparently an early riser, often the first into the dining room in the morning as he particularly enjoyed his breakfast and was, according to the cook, a hearty eater. On the morning of his death he ate breakfast alone in the dining room attended by the footman, Charles, and the butler, Mr. Evans. And if he was murdered by someone putting poison into the kedgeree, which is what Mrs. Armitage suspects happened, then of course anyone staying in the house had the opportunity to bring this about. Sir Arthur Conan Doyle once said that murder by poison is the ultimate premeditated crime, so we must have our wits about us. This inquiry promises to be a challenge."

She flipped her notebook shut, but kept a finger in place, in case she might need to refer to her notes again. And Mrs. Jackson remembered that whenever Lady Montfort wanted to forestall any arguments in the process she intended to take with an investigation, she always cited Sir Arthur Conan Doyle as if she had just had a conversation with him on the telephone.

"Mrs. Armitage told me that Mr. Bartholomew had two helpings of kedgeree, but the remains of the second helping were still on his plate when he left the dining room for his walk. This was taken downstairs to the scullery and scraped into the slop bucket for the pigs, two of which died as a result of eating it. Now why this was not made more of at the inquest I cannot imagine."

Mrs. Jackson had heard most of this firsthand from Mrs. Armitage but something she had been told about pigs flashed into her mind. "I thought, m'lady, that pigs have such a strong digestive system they could eat practically anything and thrive. I can't imagine that tainted haddock would have presented a problem for two healthy pigs. But I wonder, are they able to withstand a powerful poison like arsenic or strychnine?"

"I am rather ignorant about pigs. But it is a good point and one most likely ignored at the inquest." Her ladyship opened her notebook and appeared to write a few lines about pigs.

"Mrs. Armitage told me she ate some of the kedgeree before

41

it went up to the dining room, or at least she sampled it, another point that she said was not made much of during the inquest, m'lady. I have a feeling she probably ate quite a sizable portion and yet suffered no ill effects whatsoever." The last of Mrs. Jackson's reluctance ebbed away. *This might,* she thought, *be quite an interesting investigation after all.*

"Well exactly, Jackson. Did the coroner's court miss this important point because she underplayed how much she ate, or was it because it was heavily influenced by a rich man, determined to establish accidental death?" It was clear that Lady Montfort did not care very much for the inquest.

"And perhaps, m'lady, we should find out exactly how many people had access to the dining room just before breakfast was taken up, and did anyone come into the room when Mr. Bartholomew was eating his breakfast?" Mrs. Jackson industriously made notes.

Satisfied that she had briefed her housekeeper, Clementine had a moment or two to speculate on the prudence of their mission and, above all, for her own curiosity's sake, how Mrs. Armitage had chosen them to act on their behalf.

"Jackson, as a matter of interest, why do you think Mr. Stafford recommended Mrs. Armitage come to us? I wonder why he thought that I might be able to help?" Clementine thought she might know the answer, but she was curious to see what Mrs. Jackson would say.

Her housekeeper roused herself from contemplating the hedgerows along the wayside and looked almost embarrassed at this question. They had come to a complete stop. The lane along which they were traveling was full of sheep, which were being driven down the narrow country road ahead of them by a shepherd and his two dogs. She could hear the chauffeur muttering with irritation under his breath.

"When he was engaged to work on the sunken garden,

m'lady . . . when Mr. Mallory was murdered, he made some very interesting observations about Violet's situation as a new maid at the house. I think," she looked down at her gloved hands folded quietly in her lap, "he was . . . quite aware . . ." She looked out the window at the herd of sheep pressed up against the sides of the motorcar and fell silent. Clementine could hear the chauffeur arguing with the shepherd.

"Do you think he guessed about our involvement in solving that particular little problem, Jackson?" Clementine saw her housekeeper's ears redden a little at the tips. She felt almost ashamed for putting Mrs. Jackson on the spot.

"Yes, I think he did, m'lady. He is a very observant man and quite aware of people and their little ways."

People and their little ways . . . Clementine could imagine that Mr. Stafford would be more than able to understand people's little ways quite astutely. Like Miss Jekyll, it was important that he understand the vagaries of human nature, as the success of his job depended on his giving his clients what they believed they wanted without sacrificing the integrity of his creations.

"It wouldn't surprise me in the least, Jackson, if the entire population of Little Buffenden, Haversham, and Cryer's Breech knew we had a hand in that one. Gossip spreads so quickly among our villages. They just don't say anything about it . . . to us."

Did Jackson find gossip about their doings troubling? Did she mind being involved in her inquiries? She had fleetingly pondered this before. Over the past two years her relationship with her housekeeper had changed. There was still the outward formality of mistress and servant that would probably always remain the same. But a comfortable ease had sprung up between them, and they had developed a new sort of respect for each other. Now, for some reason, she was curious as to whether Mrs. Jackson actually wished to be involved in what had after all become her new hobby.

Her housekeeper had never expressed any enthusiasm whatsoever in being asked to help her with their last two inquiries—even though she had been instrumental in their success. But she had been quick to draw her attention to Mrs. Armitage's plight most probably out of a sense of duty, and not, sadly, because she was curious about what had happened at Hyde Castle. It was often rather difficult to gauge how Jackson felt about so many things; her professional role, it seemed, governed her most strictly. Ralph, on the other hand, was fully aware of why she was popping over to Hyde Castle and had had no trouble in telling her how he felt about it last night.

"Clemmy, there is absolutely no need to pretend that you want to go and spend time with these wretched Haldanes. They will bore you to death. I can only suppose you are interested in what happened to that guest of theirs who was reported to have died of food poisoning while he was staying with them. I am afraid you are in for a disappointment, the inquest was quite clear—it was an accident." He was laughing as he got into bed and lay down next to her. But she had said nothing as she turned her head on her pillow and they looked into each other's eyes: she, measuring exactly how much disapproval she could hear in his voice for what he imagined she was up to; he, she imagined as he looked at her with that kindly and affectionate smile on his face, trying to gauge the strength of her determination to interfere in what was already a judicial fait accompli.

"Not saying? Darling, you know I am putty in your hands—always have been—you can tell me surely?" He lifted his hand and stroked the hair off her forehead. "I know I have an eccentric wife"—he gave her a kiss—"who finds people and their murderous tendencies quite fascinating." Another kiss, and

Clementine smiled. "And who has developed a taste for pitting her clever brain against the odds. Your secret is quite safe with me."

Her husband's appreciation of her quick wits and her original cast of mind did not always extend to his indulgence where her inquiries were concerned. He was even more disapproving of her involving their housekeeper. The Talbot family had occupied this corner of Buckingham and Oxfordshire for centuries; their arable farmland stretched in every direction from the country town of Market Wingley and provided a still rather feudal livelihood for countless tenant farmers. Ralph took his duty to those who depended on him most seriously—too seriously, Clementine often thought, as her husband struggled with the burdens of owning land in this new and progressive century. And it was her job first and foremost to conduct herself always as a countess and not as a carefree Mrs. Talbot.

"What secret?" she asked and widened her eyes in pretended innocence, thinking that she was rather lucky that her husband did not view her just as an elegantly dressed, well-mannered appendage to his life, but clearly appreciated her for who she was. *As long as I don't let down the side,* she reminded herself. *As long as I maintain the status quo.*

Ralph gathered her into his arms.

"That you dearly love a good puzzle—some people play charades and other silly parlor games to pass the time. But my wife likes to solve mysteries." She relaxed. He was on board then, but there would be a stipulation, of this she was quite sure. Ralph might indulge her, but there was a limit. "And . . ." *Ah, here it is.* "You must promise me that if you find that things were not quite as they should have been, you will be prudent and call in Colonel Valentine." He was referring to the chief constable for the county.

"Of course I will, *if* I happen to turn up anything of suspicious interest. All I wish to do is help clear the name of a woman who might have been wrongly accused, and who has lost her living."

"Then we must do what we can for her if you find she was blamed unfairly and is in need of our help," her husband had replied in a rather dismissive tone; he was often badgered by those dissatisfied with legal judgment on their lot in the county. "But I often find myself wishing that you would restrict your acts of charity to visiting the sick and in-need on the estate and not providing all comers with the benefit of your detecting abilities."

Later, in the motorcar, sitting across from her newly appointed paid companion, Clementine decided that she had to accept her husband's reluctance that she busy herself in other people's business, just as she had to accept that her housekeeper was with her today because it was her job to serve the Talbot family, and that if Mrs. Jackson did not care for the task she would never have brought up the subject of Mrs. Armitage in the first place.

Chapter Five

Oh good Lord above, have we arrived at Balmoral? Mrs. Jackson thought as they drove through a pair of aggressively grand wrought-iron-and-gilt gates that marked the entrance to Hyde Castle. The Daimler continued on, up a long, straight drive through a small park to a tall, square stone house with pointed turrets at each corner and a crenellated parapet. It was a strangely overdone entrance, thought Mrs. Jackson, as she knew that there was no estate. The land had been sold off to pay the Rigby family's debts long before Mr. Haldane had bought the castle, and the massive entrance gates that so portentously heralded their arrival were only to a modest park of some fifteen acres, which included the castle and its gardens.

She was a little anxious about her role as a companion to Lady Montfort. She would be staying in the house as a minor guest, a paid appendage to her mistress, and would either eat her meals in her room or be invited to the occasional dinner or luncheon with the family. Any trips she made to the servants' hall would be on errands for her mistress and she certainly would not be expected to eat belowstairs. But should she get out of the motorcar with her ladyship as it pulled up outside the entrance to the house, or should she remain in it to continue to the servants' hall entrance with their luggage? Thankfully, her ladyship must have sensed her unease because she nodded for Mrs. Jackson to join her on the drive.

The butler, Mr. Evans, was waiting for them on the threshold of his master's house. Her first impression was that he was in his middle thirties; a tall man, with broad shoulders and impeccable bearing. His thick, dark brown hair was cut close, his arms were relaxed at his sides, and his gaze was fixed somewhere above their heads. He was at first glance a representative example of the well-trained upper servant. The man came down the steps to welcome them and she had a better opportunity to consider the only person at Hyde Castle who was willing to help them in their inquiry. It was evident that Mr. Evans was a prepossessing man; his features were well proportioned, but it was his eyes that were the most arresting feature of his face, they were large, well-shaped, and expressive and softened his large nose and strong jaw.

She found the fact that the butler was willing to help them with their inquiry rather strange; in her experience, upper servants were loyal to their masters before anyone else, but as she had become aware in recent years, this was not always the case these days. She wondered why Mr. Haldane's butler was willing to assist them in disproving that the cook had been sacked by his master for the negligent performance of her duties. She couldn't imagine that Mr. Hollyoak would be so disloyal to a family he served, but then Mr. Hollyoak was from an older generation and the family he worked for was far more august than the Haldanes.

"Good afternoon, m'lady. Miss Jekyll arrived ahead of you and has already gone up to her room." The butler's voice was low and pleasant, his manner correct—he did not seek eye contact—and his greeting was conventional and appropriate. Mrs. Jackson couldn't fault his demeanor. So it was almost impossible for her to understand why she felt such immediate antipathy for the man.

They followed him up the steps through the double, nail-studded oak doors into a large wood-paneled hall with a wide oak staircase and a heavily carved and ornamented balustrade leading up to the two floors above them. The exterior of the castle might look very much like a drawing of a castle in a child's picture book, but inside it was simply another Victorian country house. *How disappointing*, thought Mrs. Jackson. *I had so wanted to sleep the night in an ancient castle.*

She had not been quite sure what to expect of the Haldanes' country house, as she did not run around the countryside with Lady Montfort on her many excursions to visit friends. That was Edna Pettigrew's job as her ladyship's maid; housekeepers stayed at home and ran things. So she was naturally curious as to what sort of house a man with "pots of money" but no name would own. And it was evident that there was lots of money to be had from the manufacture of tinned beef stew, for the castle was furnished in luxurious style; and from the little she had seen as they got down from the motor, the gardens that stretched out around the house were perfectly maintained.

"Mrs. Haldane is waiting for you in the rose drawing room; her other guests will be coming up from the garden in just a few moments to join her for tea in the library." The butler led them cross the hall and into a room with pink silk damask walls and cluttered with so much furniture, little tables and cabinets full of porcelain collections, that Mrs. Jackson immediately pulled in her skirt so that she didn't inadvertently brush anything to the ground. The room was opulently appointed and gleamed with the gloss of recently acquired luxury, displaying none of the warm patina of old wood and the antiquarian collections that furnished Iyntwood.

Mrs. Haldane was standing alone by the windows looking

out across the well-kept lawns on the south side of the house. She was a tall woman, dressed in a pale pastel shade of aquamarine more suited to a woman of younger years. Two large, anxious eyes regarded them with considerable apprehension from a lined face framed by ornately dressed graying blond hair. The words *fading into middle age* struck Mrs. Jackson as apt in describing Mrs. Haldane. In her younger years she would have been a pretty woman, but there was overall something so insipid about her appearance that it was impossible to imagine that she had ever glowed with the radiant health of youth.

Mrs. Haldane came toward them across the room, her hand stretched out in greeting to Lady Montfort. The contrast between the two women was marked. They were probably about the same age, and there all similarity ended. Lady Montfort's skin was firm and unlined, and her glossy, bay-brown hair and brilliant dark eyes radiated vitality and purpose. Her figure was supple and still quite slender and she moved with the vigor and grace of younger years in her elegant afternoon dress and coat with her smart hat perched fashionably forward above her forehead. She made Mrs. Haldane look blowsy and tired, like an overblown rose at the end of summer, Mrs. Jackson thought as she watched the two women greet each other.

"Lady M-M-Montford, I am Maud Haldane, so very pleased to meet you. How kind of you to come to our s-s-symposium and how generous of you to bring Miss Jekyll. We are indeed honored."

I have no doubt you are, thought Mrs. Jackson. Although she had no interest in gardens, she knew Miss Jekyll's worth to those who tirelessly coaxed the earth to produce a profusion of flowers and shrubs in a weed-free but romantically natural state. Was Mrs. Haldane nervous of meeting her ladyship or was that a habitual stutter?

Lady Montfort was cordial and quite at ease. "How very

kind of you to invite us, Mrs. Haldane." She turned to her housekeeper. "My companion, Mrs. Edith Jackson." And Mrs. Haldane obediently walked to Mrs. Jackson and put her hand in hers and Mrs. Jackson gave it a gentle shake or two.

"May I call you Edith?" The pale blue eyes fixed themselves earnestly on her face. Mrs. Jackson was appalled; she glanced at her ladyship, who was looking out of the window, her eyes shining in delight. "By all means, Mrs. Haldane," she managed.

"No, please call me Maud. Everyone does. We d-d-do not stand on ceremony at Hyde Castle."

More's the pity then, thought Mrs. Jackson, wondering how she was going to cope with such a startling disregard for civilized convention. *Would all the Haldanes' guests be as informal and presumptuous as Mrs. Haldane?* The use of her Christian name by a complete stranger made her feel most uncomfortable.

"I expect you would like to freshen up a bit before tea time." Mrs. Haldane could barely bring herself to look at Lady Montfort directly and appeared to be far more comfortable in addressing Mrs. Jackson. *She is overwhelmed to have a countess in her house,* Mrs. Jackson accurately assessed and felt immediate sympathy for the woman. She felt ill at ease herself masquerading as a paid companion when her rightful place was below stairs as a working woman and not standing around in a drawing room talking about tea.

As the butler stepped forward to take them up to their rooms, the door to the drawing room opened and a large, middle-aged man came into the room. While he was not exactly tall, he more than made up for it with breadth of shoulder and girth. Mrs. Jackson realized it was Mr. Haldane, for it was without doubt the master of the house who came barreling into his drawing room, causing his butler to hastily step to one side, hands outstretched, his big fleshy face wreathed in smiles, and then seeing that there were two women in the drawing room with his wife, he stopped and looked to her for an introduction.

"Lady M-M-Montford, may I present my husband, Roger Haldane?"

Lady Montfort turned toward the man, her face composed in polite greeting, but Mr. Haldane rounded on his wife and said abruptly, "Montfort with a *T,* Maud, not Montford. Lady Montfort will wonder if you are aware she is the Countess of Montfort." And he barked out a laugh as he tried to seize Lady Montfort's hand in both of his large paws.

He has fingers just like pork sausages, thought Mrs. Jackson as she viewed his familiarity with her ladyship with distaste.

"Hullo-how-are-you, Mr. Haldane." Lady Montfort, in the flat monotone she used when she was offended, neatly avoided being grasped by the hand and turned to Mrs. Jackson. "And this is Mrs. Jackson, my companion. We are very much looking forward to meeting the Hyde Rose Society." She stood her ground, and Mrs. Jackson marveled at her poise in the face of this big red-faced man who squared up to her like a pugilist about to take a swing.

He barked out another too-loud laugh, barely glancing at the paid companion, and closed the gap between himself and Lady Montfort. He was so close he could have effortlessly engulfed her in his arms.

"I know how you ladies love your flowers," he boomed in what he evidently fancied was the hearty manner of the country squire. "Pretty ladies always love their pretty flowers." Another series of barks. "It is an honor to have you in my house, Lady Montfort. Met your husband a few years ago at a local magistrates' meeting." And then, turning to his wife, he chided her as if she were a girl who had wandered down from the schoolroom. "What are you thinking, my dear, you haven't even offered Lady Montfort so much as a cup of tea." He smiled as he scolded, precipitating his wife into simpering apologies, which he cut off with a custodial and heavy hand on her shoulder.

"My dear," he said. "Busy day ahead of me, but I will look forward to meeting your guests at dinner." And with that he turned and strode from the room. Lady Montfort had the sort of expression on her face that Mrs. Jackson had seen when her ladyship caught naughty boys teasing the smallest and most easily intimidated little girl of the group in the nursery.

As Mrs. Jackson watched Mr. Haldane's broad back disappear through the door she noticed that however well cut his tweed Norfolk jacket, it was the most disconcerting shade of what was often referred to as a heather mixture. This particular blend had relied on the lavender hues a little too heavily, she thought. She also noticed with distaste that his fat, red neck bulged over the back of his shirt collar.

Mrs. Haldane had been reduced to a quaking state of indecision by her husband's interruption and his jocular admonishments about the lack of tea.

"I d-do hope you don't think I have forgotten about tea," she said, her anxious eyes begging to be forgiven. "W-we will be taking tea in the library just as soon has you have had a chance to freshen up a little, if that is all right with you both. Or of course we could take tea now if you would p-prefer."

"How kind of you, Mrs. Haldane. We will join you momentarily in the library." Her comfortable manner had its effect on Mrs. Haldane, for she visibly relaxed and turned to her butler to show them to their rooms.

And off they went, shepherded out of the room and up the staircase to the third floor of the house, to a wide landing where the butler turned and led them down a corridor to two rooms at its end. He opened the first door, and they stood on the threshold of a room that looked east onto perfectly groomed herbaceous borders and the side of the great lawn that stretched away toward a grove of trees at its far end. The room was beautifully appointed and sumptuously furnished with wood paneling and some heavy tapestries hanging from ceiling to floor on the far wall at the window end. There was a door in the right-hand wall and the butler opened it to reveal Mrs. Jackson's corner room, which was opulently furnished with a splendid view of the drive and the towering gilded wrought-iron gates that they had driven through just moments ago.

"Quickly, Jackson, let's leave the unpacking until later, and wash our hands. I am dying to meet the rest of these people, and it seems that Mrs. Haldane has quite taken to you already."

"Do I come down to tea with you, m'lady?" Mrs. Jackson had opened Lady Montfort's large trunk and was lifting out her beautifully packed gowns, each rustling in layers of tissue paper. She prayed she would be able to return the trunk to Pettigrew as equally well packed, or there would be head-shakings and little *tuts* for days.

"Oh yes, Jackson, please do. Unless you would prefer otherwise, I think it a good idea for you to join us for all the meals here. And I hope you do not mind if I call you Edith." Lady Montfort's eyes were shining with merriment.

"Not at all, my lady. Apparently, everyone else is."

Tea was being served to a talkative gathering in the library as Mrs. Jackson and Lady Montfort rejoined their hostess. Some half a dozen people were grouped around the short figure of Miss Jekyll, all chattering gaily and, in the case of the ladies, fluttering and crying out their praises at the wonders she had wrought in the gardens of some of England's most beautiful country houses.

A young woman with golden curls done up in a ribbon and wearing a fashionable afternoon dress said with enthusiasm, "Actually, my husband and I live in Hampshire quite near to Upton Grey. We have been lucky enough to see the garden you designed several years ago. And what a wonderful . . ."

A much older man standing by her side interrupted her, the way fathers do when their daughters exhibit a little too much eagerness. Clementine was surprised at the mutinous look the golden-haired girl cast in his direction. "I practiced law with a cousin of the owner of Upton Grey," he explained to those not fortunate enough to have his connections. "We spent quite a few days at Upton last summer. Miss Jekyll's use of color in her garden designs is so harmonious with nature."

It was Mrs. Haldane who quietly interrupted the rhapsodies of the group gathered around Miss Jekyll and said in her hesitant and gentle voice, "Lady Montfort, may I present the Hyde Rose Society's most notable members?" Clementine noticed that among her friends their hostess appeared to be more at ease, as her stammer was not evident and there was almost a lively quality to her. *So it's only her husband that makes her behave as if she is a complete ninny,* she thought.

The chatter stopped immediately and curious eyes turned to Clementine and Mrs. Jackson standing in the middle of the library saying "yes, please" to a cup of tea and "no, thank you" to a large tray of elaborate sandwiches and decorative cakes.

"And her ladyship's companion and friend Mrs. Edith Jackson," Mrs. Haldane added, walking over to Mrs. Jackson's side and putting a tentative hand on her arm as she indicated a chair and waved at her footman to offer her something to eat.

"Now, where to begin with my introductions?" And with a fluttery, self-conscious laugh Mrs. Haldane continued, "Lady Montfort, may I present Mrs. Dorothy Wickham?" The young woman with the golden curls bowed her head to Clementine;

she was the youngest of the group, with pink cheeks, large, rather protuberant blue eyes, and a shot-away chin, who said, "How lovely and pleased to meet you," rather breathlessly, and then, turning to the older man at her side, "My husband, Mr. Clive Wickham," and the gentleman bowed.

Clementine thought he looked a little irritated, maybe because he had been interrupted in the middle of his explanation about how well he knew the owner of Upton Grey. Or perhaps he was always irritable, she thought, as she took in his long serious face, small tight mouth, and fussy little mustache. He was of below-average height with a slight stoop to his shoulders and had the look of a pedant who complained endlessly about small missed details, and who knew the departure and arrival times of all the trains at his local railway station. She had caught his reference to the law. Yes, he would be a punctilious lawyer. Interesting that a man of quite senior years should have such an extraordinarily young wife; Mrs. Wickham was surely in her early twenties, whereas Mr. Wickham was well settled into his fifties.

Mrs. Haldane continued with her introductions in a rather haphazard but charming way as she extended a hand to each of her friends in turn, regardless of gender, age, or social standing.

"My dear friend Mrs. Amelia Lovell," and a neatly dressed, pleasant-faced woman who was eating a cucumber sandwich nodded gravely and said, "Pleased to meet you, Lady Montfort, Mrs. Jackson. Miss Jekyll says your rose gardens at Iyntwood are renowned for their rare specimens." Clementine appreciated the quiet dignity of her greeting. Mrs. Lovell was probably about the same age as Mrs. Haldane, but here all similarities ended. Mrs. Lovell was a well-built, heavy-shouldered woman who neither fluttered nor overwhelmed, nor bragged, but sat center-sofa in such a composed manner that Clementine was quite impressed. She noticed that Mrs. Lovell took an interest in what was going on around her with no apparent desire to overpower the conversation. *A listener, rather than a talker,* Clementine decided.

"And one of our most gifted rose breeders," Mrs. Haldane said as she turned to a man of frail build seated in a large wing chair, whereupon Mr. Wickham bristled a little and laughed as if Mrs. Haldane had a made a mistake, which caused her to stammer. "I sh-should say *one* of our *many* gifted rosarians—Mr. Finley Urquhart." And a bent, little man got up from his chair, allowing the soft cashmere shawl that was draped across his gray-trousered knees to slip to the floor. He bowed first to Lady Montfort and then to Mrs. Jackson. He had the bushy, white side-whiskers of the late Victorian gentleman and wore a pair of silver-framed spectacles perched on the bridge of his nose, which gave him a schoolmasterly appearance, until she noticed that on his head was a round, plum-velvet pillbox hat heavily embroidered with mauve heartsease and yellow primroses. When he spoke it was with the gentle and precise enunciation of a Scot raised in the refined drawing rooms of Edinburgh. "How delightful," he said, his bright little eyes shining behind polished lenses as he looked from one to the other of them with interest. "How very delightful; am I right in understanding, Leddy Montfort, that you are also something of a rosarian yerself?"

Clementine warmed to this dapper gentleman and his benign good manners, and crossed the room to pick up his cashmere shawl. As he sat down she draped it over his bony knees and noticed with pleasure that he had laid aside an embroidery frame on which he was stitching an enchanting pattern of tiny little roses and their buds in shades of carmine red and pink.

"Oh, oh, oh, how could I have forgotten?" Poor Mrs. Haldane was not having a successful afternoon, it seemed, for the door had opened and an elegant woman entered the room.

"Dear Albertine, how remiss of me I should have sent Evans to tell you that tea was being served in the library. Lady Montfort, may I present Mrs. Albertine Bartholomew?"

"No, it is I who should apologize for being so late to tea, Maud. Good afternoon, Lady Montfort." Mrs. Bartholomew gave a polite nod to Mrs. Jackson and turned to take a proffered cup of tea from the footman. She was a tall woman, but not quite as tall as Mrs. Haldane, her thick, dark hair dressed in a simple style at the nape of her neck. She was not exactly pretty, Clementine thought, but she had an arresting quality and moved with grace and elegance. Her dress in the dove gray of late mourning had the sort of style that is always equated with the perfect lines adopted by the well-dressed Frenchwoman with a considerable income at her disposal. She was without a doubt, thought Clementine, as she noticed the cut of Mrs. Bartholomew's walking suit, the most distinguished-looking woman in the room.

Clementine gazed across the room at Mr. Bartholomew's widow of five months as she sat herself down next to Mr. Wickham, whose bad-tempered face almost creased into a smile as he pulled his chair close so that they might talk without being interrupted.

How strange, she thought. *I had not imagined that the late Mr. Bartholomew's wife would be French.* And, not wanting to betray her curiosity for the very French Mrs. Bartholomew, she turned her attention to Mr. Urquhart, who in his gentle voice was bullying the footman to make sure that his tea-time crumpet was served: "Very hot, with all the butter carefully melted, and cut up into wee pieces."

"Such a disaster, this messy business of eating hot buttered crumpets at tea time, but I am so partial to them." Mr. Urquhart lifted a delicate porcelain cup to his lips, sipped, and then winced. "Oh dear me no, I think this must be India tea that has steeped too long." He held the cup on its saucer out to the footman. "Charles, make me a fresh cup, please, less strong and with not as much milk." And to Clementine by way of an explanation: "One can never be too careful about the strength of Darjeeling tea, otherwise it becomes too acerbic," and to the footman who was hovering over him: "Yes, Charles, I will take a scone, no cream but plenty of butter, and if the strawberry jam is homemade I will take some of that. And if you are offering me cucumber sandwiches take them away, cucumber is ruinous for my poor system."

And with his tea-time rations organized he turned his attention to Clementine and asked about her rose garden. "Miss Jekyll says your rose garden has one of the most interesting collections of old Damask, China, and Bourbon roses in the south of England." And like all keen gardeners, Clementine was not only too happy to answer his every question with as much detail as she could provide.

As they were finishing their tea Mrs. Haldane came over to Mrs. Jackson and sat down on a little chair to her right.

"Edith, I understand from Lady Montfort that you are wonderfully efficient and have organized so many of her entertainments at Iyntwood."

"Yes indeed, Mrs. Haldane, the Talbot family hold two balls every year and it is my responsibility to organize them. If there is anything I can do to make myself useful here, you have only to ask."

"Everyone calls me Maud," Mrs. Haldane said with a trace of her earlier coy manner. "And yes, there is perhaps something you could help me with. I am arranging for Miss Jekyll to give us a little talk after dinner and she has, I believe, brought with her an easel on which to display some illustrations of her wonderful landscape designs, as well as some of her beautiful watercolor paintings of her gardens at Munstead. Would you be kind enough to direct the efforts of my butler and footman in setting up in the Salon Vert, so that we can be comfortable there, after dinner, for her informal talk?"

Mrs. Jackson said she would be delighted to, and mentally congratulated Lady Montfort on having already created a useful opportunity for her to meet the butler, who was standing with a particularly bland expression on his face, being careful not to look in the direction of Lady Montfort and Mrs. Jackson, as he directed the footman to serve tea.

"It is not too much of an imposition, is it? After all, you have had a long journey today. Are you sure you are not too tired? You would tell me, wouldn't you?" Having asked her favor and having been reassured that it would be granted, Mrs. Haldane was now preparing herself for a rebuff. And Mrs. Jackson, who always found it irritating when someone asked her for her help and then tried to talk her out of saying yes, cut short Mrs. Haldane's breathless trembling at her presumptuousness. "I would be very happy to help you. In fact I would enjoy it." She was careful not to use Mrs. Haldane's Christian name because to call this woman Maud would make her feel most uncomfortable.

"Very well then, I will tell Mr. Evans that you will meet him in the Salon Vert at half past six. Would that give you enough time to instruct him before joining us for dinner?"

Mrs. Jackson said it would and that if it would not be inconvenient she would be taking dinner in her room. "Miss Jekyll has asked me to organize the rose competition that she will be judging tomorrow," she explained. "I must give some thought to that."

"You are? Oh dear, we have loaded you down. I am so sorry.

Thank you so much, how kind you are. I will have to spend some time this evening finding a little prize for Miss Jekyll to award for first place." And she laid a limp hand on Mrs. Jackson's arm. "I am so delighted you have come to my house, Edith. I know we are going to be great friends."

And Mrs. Jackson's rather cool manner melted a little, because there was something so simple and well-meaning about this poor woman's desire for approval.

Chapter Six

"Good heavens, Jackson, I have to have a few minutes to myself to take it all in. What a very intriguing group of people." Lady Montfort was laughing as they gained the sanctuary of their rooms after tea.

"I noticed that Mrs. Haldane was chatting away to you. Poor creature, I think she is easily intimidated, not surprising with that overwhelming husband." She caught herself and looked a little guilty at having criticized their host to her housekeeper, who with her customary deference was standing in front of the door to her bedroom. "What did *you* think of them all?"

Mrs. Jackson hesitated; she had been asking herself this since they had left the library after tea and come up to their rooms. If they were back at Iyntwood she would never have dreamed of offering her opinion of Lord Montfort's guests to her ladyship, even if she had been asked. And anyway she would have been spared that embarrassment because her ladyship would never have dreamed of asking. There was a distinct lack of formality about the Haldanes' guests that was puzzling. Mrs. Jackson was used to the polite arrogance with which the English aristocracy treated their servants. But there was a marked difference in behavior with this particular group, who exhibited such open frankness that it seemed as if every thought that came into their heads was uttered without consideration for how it was heard. And their host's manners were, as pointed out by her ladyship, overpowering and, to her mind, uncouth.

"I think Mr. Haldane has rather an unfortunate manner," she said. "But Mrs. Haldane seems to be a decent sort, m'lady."

"He is both obsequious and boorish, a most unattractive combination. But she is rather a dear, if she could only stop apologizing. What about the lawyer?"

"The lawyer, m'lady?"

"Yes, Mr. Wickham is a lawyer, or is it a solicitor? I can never really tell the difference, and he is also a magistrate, the elderly Scotsman, Mr. Urquhart, told me."

"I thought he looked quite annoyed with everyone—except perhaps Miss Jekyll, whom he wants to impress."

"Mr. Wickham was quite discourteous to his wife. What is wrong with these men? They are perfectly horrid, except for that dear little Scotsman with his embroidery, his precise manners, and his passion for buttered crumpets." Lady Montfort laughed. "So, has Mrs. Haldane asked her favor yet, Jackson?"

"Yes; I am to go downstairs to meet with the butler in the green salon, or the Salon Vert as it is referred to, m'lady. We are going to organize the room for Miss Jekyll's talk after dinner and make arrangements for the rose judging tomorrow morning before luncheon. So, if you will excuse me, m'lady, I think I had better be on my way downstairs. Is there anything I can do for you before I leave?"

"No, thank you, Jackson. Please be back here in time to help me dress for dinner. I am not sure I can struggle into that"— she pointed to a mousseline silk evening dress that she had taken out of the wardrobe and thrown across her bed— "without some help."

"Certainly, m'lady. I will be back by half past six." And with that, Mrs. Jackson went into her own room and shut the door, where she leaned up against it for a few minutes and closed her eyes, trying to find her equilibrium in this new world in which she found herself as a guest in a grand house.

The strangeness of her situation was difficult enough. But she was now to go downstairs and direct the efforts of Mr. Evans and his footman and the thought of it filled her with unease. She was more than capable of organizing any social event; her skills lay in her ability to put together, with impeccable timing, evenings of understated elegance. She had a creative flair for making drawing rooms and salons look their best with the placement of furniture and the right flowers to welcome large numbers of guests. But there was something about the butler: *What is it about him that makes me feel unsure and awkward?* she asked herself. *He is quite correct in his manner, far more so than Mr. Haldane.* If master and servant stood next to each other, Mr. Haldane, the master of the house, would be mistaken for the odd-job man who worked for Mr. Evans, the butler. But there was something about the man that made Mrs. Jackson reluctant to spend time alone with him.

The strangeness of her situation and her antipathy to the butler were not all that was worrying her. Sooner or later she would bump into Mr. Stafford, and however much she had enjoyed his company the last time they had met, she had avoided all communication with him since then. She sat down at the ornate dressing table and looked at herself in the large gilt-edged looking glass as she tidied her hair.

There was no conscious vanity in Mrs. Jackson's appraisal of herself. She did not recognize that her features were even and classically proportioned, that her large, clear gray eyes shone with health and energy, and that her mouth was well-shaped and full-lipped. The only imperfections were the two vertical lines between her eyebrows, worn there by a habitual frown of concentration, and her tendency to compress her mouth into a thin line when she was annoyed. Given time, these marks would etch themselves fully into her face and mark her as a typical spinster, unloved and alone in the world. Today they merely gave her face character.

You will be able to write a book about this one day, Edith, she told the young woman in the looking glass, *considering all the pickles her ladyship involves you in. And as for that Evans, he is just a servant to a family in trade, so there is no need to be uneasy about him.*

She got up from her seat, searched for her notebook and pencil, and left her room by the door that led into the corridor to go downstairs and find the butler.

"Yes, that should work very well." Mr. Evans stood away from the easel in front of the fireplace at the top of the salon and turned in a tight circle with his forefinger placed on his lips to assess the setup of the room for possible faults. "I think everyone will have a perfect view of whatever she is showing them. And as you say, it is important that they can leave their chairs and come over to the easel, without squeezing past each other, to take a look at her drawings when she has finished with her talk."

She had suggested they arrange the room's comfortable upholstered chairs and sofas in three clusters of three in a loose semicircle around the easel, with a little table in the middle of each grouping for Mrs. Haldane's guests to put down their glasses of wine. When all had been arranged, she had asked Mr. Evans if the rosarians had brought specimens of their roses with them.

"Yes, they have indeed; the conservatory is full of them." He walked over to the closed double doors that led into the great glass-paned room attached to the outside of the house and waved to the crowd of trees and flowers thriving in its interior. Every gesture he made when he was not in waiting was large and had a flourish to it, she noticed.

"Might a few of them be gathered and put here next to the easel?"

"Yes, if we dare to cut them." He laughed for the first time and Mrs. Jackson caught a glimpse of large, white, even teeth. His natural laughter made the man appear years younger and less studiedly flamboyant in his manner. "If you wish to put roses in here, then I would suggest you walk out to the rose garden. There are plenty of blooms there you may cut. I will send Charles up with some secateurs and gloves. He will also show you to Mrs. Haldane's garden room, where you may arrange them."

"Will Mr. Haldane join the gathering?" she asked.

"No, he will not, Mrs. Jackson. These are Mrs. Haldane's friends, not his." He said this as if he personally had forbidden Mr. Haldane to attend, and once again she sensed the butler's dislike for his master and regard for his mistress.

"Oh, then we need to remove a chair, we have one too many."

"No, we do not, Mrs. Jackson; Mrs. Haldane particularly wants her landscape designer to come up to the house for this talk. I believe he trained with Miss Jekyll and whatever she has to say might be helpful to his work here."

She felt alarmed only for a few seconds. *This is why I feel so out of sorts*, she thought, *this is why I am feeling on edge and unsure*. She was both dreading and looking forward to seeing Mr. Stafford again. She lifted her eyes and found the butler's intense gaze fixed on her face, and he immediately averted his eyes. *He is probably waiting for me to bring up this business of Mrs. Armitage,* she thought.

"Mrs. Armitage . . ." she said in a low tone and then stopped as he lifted a hand to silence her and turned to the footman.

"Thank you, Charles, that will be all for now. Go downstairs and set up trays for coffee and ratafia biscuits. Mr. Urquhart and Mr. Wickham will join the ladies immediately after dinner, so please make sure we have port wineglasses on a separate tray." And Charles, without a backward glance, left them alone together.

"Yes, Mrs. Jackson, we must indeed talk about this very unfortunate business of Mrs. Armitage. What will become of her, do you think?"

"I think her ladyship will find Mrs. Armitage a position in London, Mr. Evans. I hope she is a good cook."

"The finest." This was said with such simple conviction that it made Mrs. Jackson lose some of her aversion to his rather florid manner. "She brought refinement to the dishes she prepared that far outshone anything I have had from French chefs in more prestigious establishments." Then his showy manner reasserted itself: "You must understand, Mrs. Jackson, I worked for Lord Carmichael at Reaches for many years." His large, dark eyes were fixed on her face as if waiting for confirmation that she was impressed. She said nothing. "And before that I trained as a footman in this very house when the Rigby family owned it. This was of course just before they lost their fortune and had to give up this lovely house. So I remember Hyde Castle as it was in its gracious days and I am familiar with how an establishment like this should be run for a family of quality, and also for the standard of food that should be served to them." He stopped and stared at her as if waiting for her to acknowledge his credentials before continuing. Her face remained impassive as she nodded for him to continue. "Mrs. Armitage also worked for the Rigby family; she was a kitchen maid, training up to become a cook." He smiled, and then to her surprise he said, "Mrs. Armitage's talents were completely wasted on the boorish individual who now owns this lovely old house." Another pause before he concluded rather dramatically, "In my opinion, Mrs. Jackson, our wonderful old traditions and our great families are rapidly becoming a thing of the past. I dread to imagine the future. Being in service is certainly not the same as it used to be in the old days, especially if we work for the likes of Mr. Haldane."

Good grief, thought Mrs. Jackson, *it doesn't get more honest or outspoken than that.* She felt her cheeks color a little. There was a palpable animosity radiating from the butler. His face was without expression, but his eyes were blazing with the intensity of his meaning. She felt quite uncomfortable by this outward expression of emotion. In all her working life she had never heard an upper servant be quite so contemptuous of his master in such a dramatic manner. *Why does he continue here if he dislikes his employer so much? Good butlers are hard to come by; it would be easy for him to find another place.*

"Mrs. Armitage did not use tainted fish in her kedgeree, Mrs. Jackson, I can assure you of that. She is a careful and conscientious woman and took pride in her work. Mr. Bartholomew was maliciously poisoned by someone staying in this house on the day he died, I am quite convinced of it. Mrs. Armitage was used as a scapegoat by someone callous and unprincipled enough to ruthlessly eliminate someone he called his friend. The doctor's death certificate was a cooked-up lie and the inquest was a sham. And as a result, a hardworking woman was accused of being so slovenly in her work that she caused a man's death." To Mrs. Jackson's acute discomfort, the butler demonstrated his outrage: his eyebrows had practically disappeared into his hairline, and his arms were stretched out on either side of him, palms upward, as if he were appealing for justice to a higher authority than the British legal system.

As he struggled to regain his understanding of a world without integrity, he shook his head and turned abruptly away to straighten a chair just behind him.

He means Mr. Haldane; he believes Mr. Haldane murdered Mr. Bartholomew by poison. Mrs. Jackson swallowed down her rising anxiety; the butler's exhibition of his passionate dislike for the man he worked for was not only disturbing, it was distasteful.

As if sensing her disquiet, he drew in a slow breath and continued more calmly. "Unfortunately, as I am quite sure you understand, this is the busiest hour of my day so I may not spend any more time with you. But I would like to invite you to tea tomorrow, belowstairs; we will be joined by Mrs. Walker, our housekeeper and, incidentally, she does not know the reason why you and her ladyship are our guests here. And afterwards I would be happy to answer any questions that you might have, so that justice can at last be brought to bear." And on this rather dramatic note, the tall man turned and walked from the room, leaving Mrs. Jackson staring at the empty chairs that awaited the happy group of rosarians, so eager for their innovative lecture on garden design and color harmony, and for her to be reunited with her old friend Mr. Stafford.

To Clementine's surprise, dinner turned out to be a far more interesting occasion than she had anticipated. After Mrs. Jackson had buttoned her into her evening dress and demonstrated her competence in dressing her hair, she came downstairs to the rose drawing room to find the company gathered in an excited group, all of them talking at once.

"Good evening, Lady Montfort," said Miss Jekyll, turning as she came into the room. "Awfully bad news, I am afraid. The situation worsens in Europe. It seems that Mother Russia is rumbling to her feet in defense of her ally, Serbia." Miss Jekyll's pleasant face was wrinkled in concern. "The Russian ambassador to London has just announced that if Austria does not back down with her intention to go to war with Serbia, then Russia will come to Serbia's aid. Lord Montfort was right: the situation has grown into more than just a little tiff between neighboring countries."

What is the date today? Is Althea still sailing home from the Baltic Sea? Her hand hidden in the folds of her skirt, she counted off the days on her fingers with her thumb. It was the thirty-first, and her shoulders relaxed; the *Bon Adventure* would dock in Southampton tomorrow.

"Without doubt Germany will declare on Russia, without doubt. And I hope they do. What Europe needs is a good housecleaning. Time we swept away all the degeneracy that is weakening Europe. We have to sweep away the scourge of socialism and trade unions, the unruly Irish and women who believe they are educated enough to vote, before it is too late. Too late I tell you." Like all men whose emotions led their intellect, Mr. Wickham reiterated his stronger statements at least twice. *It's as if he is trying to convince himself,* thought Clementine.

"Nay, surely not, my dear Clive; we don't want that kind of upheaval in our world." But Mr. Urquhart's gentle Scots accent was drowned completely by a braying voice from the doorway, and there was Mr. Haldane, clad in white tie and tails that made him look even more strangely disproportionate than he had looked in his violently hued country tweeds.

"Oh yes, there will be war, make no mistake. This is simply the beginning and tomorrow will bring us more news. Now, my dear . . ." He turned to his wife, who was hiding behind the chair of her friend Mrs. Lovell, whose expression bore such a strong resemblance to Clementine's kind but no-nonsense nanny that she was not surprised when Mr. Haldane's dictatorial tone was dropped abruptly as he acknowledged Clementine before addressing his wife again. "Tell Evans to bring my dinner to me in my study. I will be very busy indeed for the next few days." He rubbed his large, clumsy hands together in pleasure and Clementine supposed that Britain's being drawn into a European war held some useful significance for him.

"Will you perhaps join us for . . . ?"

Mr. Haldane threw up his arm in dismissal of her invitation and Mrs. Haldane tittered nervously as if she were a silly little girl for even making any suggestion at all. Her husband swung away from her and, drawing ferociously on his cigar, marched to the door, leaving his flustered wife to wring her hands and girlishly exclaim over her now-unbalanced seating for dinner.

Mr. Wickham made an attempt to reclaim his usurped position. "I have no doubt at all that Germany has an agreement with Austria, and if Russia doesn't modify her aggression toward Austria then Germany will show her hand in the next few days." But no one was listening; Mrs. Haldane's friends were gathered around her to reassure their hostess that her dinner party would not be ruined.

"Oh, we will make do, Maud," Mrs. Bartholomew did her best to reassure. "Miss Jekyll can preside from one end and I will take your husband's place. You can call me Albert." She laughed at the masculine version of her pretty name.

Clementine heard a sigh of relief from Mr. Urquhart, who had sidled up behind her as Mr. Haldane and Mr. Wickham had explained the European crisis to them. She turned to find him gazing at her from behind his round spectacles.

"Dear Leddy Montfort." He smiled gently. "We are at least spared Roger's bellicose opinions on war for the rest of the evening. I do so hope the cook has remembered to provide me

with steamed fish; there is so much red meat served in this
house, and it has a very costive effect."

Clementine, grateful that she would not have to sit next to
her host for dinner, was disappointed that she was taken in to
dinner by Mr. Wickham instead of gentlemanly Mr. Urquhart, where he proceeded to enumerate all the reasons why his
hybrid tea roses would be found growing in every single suburban English garden for decades to come. His tedious pom-
posity had a rather stupefying effect on her and she was heartily
grateful to turn to Mrs. Bartholomew to balance out his tire-
some lecture on the dangers of grafting roses.

"I understand from Mrs. Haldane that you are a plant collector, Mrs. Bartholomew."

"Yes, that is correct." There was the faintest trace of an accent in Mrs. Bartholomew's otherwise flawless English. She
had an attractive voice, low in pitch, and her slight French accent was charming. "Every year I try to visit either China or
Japan. Earlier this spring I was in the Hubei province of China."

"That must have been a wonderful experience."

"It was. Travel conditions are often difficult. We were in the
west of the province, where the only access in and out of the
area is by the river. The Hubei mountain region is full of deep
ravines so when we were collecting we had to climb steep ele-
vations all day. But it is a very beautiful part of China and there
are some exceptional specimens to be found." *This would explain why you look so immensely fit,* Clementine thought as she
noticed the woman's smooth, firm neck and shoulders and her
supple and athletic grace.

"And did you find any interesting new specimens?"

"Yes, we collected some wonderful new species of 'osta and

'ydrangea." The only indication that English was not her native language was that she habitually did not pronounce her aitches. "It is a plantsman's paradise if you can tolerate the climate. In the spring season it often rains for days on end, then when the river floods it can be quite dangerous. Living conditions in the villages are primitive by our standards." A slight Gallic shrug to her shoulders as Mrs. Bartholomew dismissed the danger and discomfort she had faced daily.

"What a fascinating trip it must have been. How long were you away?" Clementine hoped she didn't sound too nosy.

"From the day we left France to the day we returned was nearly four months. I travel with my brother. He is the real plantsman; I am just there to assist." She must have been gone about four weeks when her husband died, Clementine thought, mentally counting back through the months. Would Mrs. Bartholomew have been in the Hubei province on the third of March and was this why she had not returned home to England sooner? *I must find an atlas,* she thought, *I have no idea where the wretched Hubei province is.*

"Is it safe to travel in China?" she asked.

"Oh, do you mean the Wuchang Uprising and so forth?" Another slightly dismissive shrug. "But that was three years ago. Things became a good deal more violent when Emperor Puyi was forced to abdicate and then President Sun Yat-sen was kicked out. That was a terrible time for China. We made our collecting expeditions to Japan in those years. But now it is quite safe to travel in the republic. The people are most hospitable and we are always made very welcome." She smiled as she shook her head as if things like revolutions were an inconvenient part of her daily life to be tolerated along with mosquitoes and damp clothes.

"How exciting it would be to visit distant lands and explore such incredible places. But you must have felt quite cut off from the world." Clementine pushed a little more, hoping that Mrs. Bartholomew would reveal her whereabouts at the time of her husband's death and lament how inaccessible she had been when her husband's friends had tried to contact her with the devastating news that he had died.

But Mrs. Bartholomew merely gave her another polite smile. "Yes, the west of Hubei is very remote and several days' journey from Shanghai, which is a most cosmopolitan city. Shanghai is often referred to as the Paris of the Orient. But I simply cannot understand why; it is a particularly unpleasant, vice-ridden rat hole." This candid observation made Clementine almost choke with laughter on her fish; the last time she and her husband had been in Paris he told her daily he couldn't wait to leave and had used the same words to describe the French capital.

Evidently Mrs. Bartholomew was a reserved woman, because she made no attempt to continue their conversation as soon as Clementine stopped asking her questions. She fell silent, eating her turbot with precise, unhurried movements, rarely sipping wine from her glass.

A massive roast sirloin was carried in with some ceremony and carved at the sideboard, and generous slices of meat were served. Before Clementine turned back to talk to Mr. Wickham she noticed Mr. Urquhart shudder and wave away the footman's proffered slice of rare beef. Reaching for a water glass, he hurriedly produced an enameled Regency pillbox. *Goodness me,* thought Clementine, *he is taking his medicine at the dinner table. Just the sight of beef has a ruinous effect on his system.* And she smiled at the eccentricities of the dedicated valetudinarian as she turned back to Mr. Wickham, who was ready with more information for her on the business of rose breeding. Clementine was equally as ready for him. She fixed an unwavering gaze on his face and nodded her head at intervals as she listened in to the happy chatter on her left between Mrs. Haldane and Mrs. Bartholomew. *They are the best of friends,* Clementine realized; *they must have known each other for years.* Mrs. Bartholomew's natural reserve had disappeared completely and Mrs. Haldane sounded almost lively.

Mrs. Jackson ate an early dinner in her room and then went downstairs to the conservatory, which opened off the green salon. It was attached to the outside wall of the room, an incongruous Victorian addition to the castle's adopted medieval style. Hexagonal in shape, its considerable height was capable of housing several ornamental palms. A pair of lead-framed glass doors opened inward from the salon into its humid interior, and an identical pair opened outward onto the terrace.

When Mrs. Jackson walked into the conservatory she was immediately engulfed in the warm, clinging air of the great glass room. There was something breathless and claustrophobic in its suffocating heat and she felt oppressed by the rare tropical specimens towering above her and the riotous foliage and orchids crowding its transparent walls. In the center of the heated floor was a collection of deep wicker chairs with chintz cushions. She automatically counted them and found there to be more than enough to seat the Hyde Rose Society as they waited for their roses to be judged by Miss Jekyll.

On a long, low trestle table were a collection of large, unglazed terra-cotta pots displaying the proud offerings of the Hyde rosarians. Mrs. Jackson was not a gardener but she knew that the still, damp heat of the conservatory was not one that made any rose particularly happy for long, and she wondered why the competition would take place in such an unlikely location. *It must be because Mr. Urquhart feels the cold,* she thought, remembering the elderly man's cashmere shawl even though the July weather was particularly warm.

She studied the roses on the table before her. She had never appreciated hybrid tea roses. She found them artificial and stiff, with their long, straight, thick stalks. They reminded her of the sort of scentless roses sold in florists' shops. She walked along the table, glancing at the metal labels proudly proclaiming the name of the rose contained in each pot. Bending down, she read: Court Scarlet, Maiden's Blush, Lovely Amelia. Her hand came up to her mouth and her eyes disappeared into delighted crescents of suppressed laughter. From behind her hand came a snort of muffled derision. Every rose on the table perfectly represented its creator. The only rosarian she had not yet met, nor ever would, was the breeder of Bartholomew's Golden Girl, a splendid specimen of incomparable rich yellow with a scent as sweet and as delicate as ripe apples that was set slightly apart at the bottom of the table.

Still smiling, she turned away from the trestle table to find that she was no longer alone in the conservatory. A man was standing in the shadow of the doorway watching her as she had inspected the roses. She was so taken by surprise that she jumped.

Chapter Seven

"Do roses usually inspire laughter, or is it just *these* unfortunate specimens?" The figure in the doorway walked into the light of the conservatory.

"Not usually, but I think I can tell which of the Hyde amateur rose breeders was responsible for producing each of these, just by the names."

"Yes, I am sure you can. What artificial things they are." Mr. Stafford's face was disapproving.

"The roses or the people who bred them?"

"I don't know the individuals, but their roses are quite ugly. You know, hybrid tea roses only thrive with masses of well-rotted manure. Hopefully most of them will contract one of the many rose diseases that inflict grafted roses and disappear altogether. The only decent specimen here is Golden Girl and this other white rose next to it." He walked over to the white rose that had the look of an old English double Damask. "The color is a pure, dense milk white. So hard to achieve." He bent to inhale. "There is a subtlety to its scent—almost like apple blossom." His expression was so serious it made her nervous.

"Mr. Bartholomew's new rose."

"Yes."

"Like him, then?" she asked, smiling.

"Never met him." He walked back along the table of roses toward her and now he was smiling, too. "Yes, actually I did see him once from a distance. He was overweight, his hair was too long, and he looked like a bit of a softy. How are you, Mrs. Jackson?" The last time they had met he had called her Edith.

"I am very well. Thank you for recommending our services to Mrs. Armitage." She had meant to sound sarcastic; but she found herself far too pleased to be talking to him to be bothered with the irritation she had felt when Mrs. Armitage had mentioned him as the reason for her visit.

"I thought an interesting accidental death in the house of a neighbor might appeal to you. It seemed to be the only way to see you again, after I was dropped from your list of correspondents." She glanced up at him to see if he was annoyed with her, but he didn't appear to be. And she wasn't sure herself why she had stopped writing to him.

"I am sorry, Mr. Stafford, it was rude of me not to reply to your last letter. There was so much to plan for Christmas and we were late getting back to Iyntwood. I couldn't believe how behind I was with preparations for the season." He would have no idea how demanding her job was; how long her working day was when there was a grand occasion to celebrate at Iyntwood.

Both of us depend on pleasing those we serve, she thought. *He surely understands how demanding my job is.*

"So Lady Montfort does not think that Mr. Bartholomew was a victim of accidental food poisoning?"

She wasn't sure she wanted Mr. Stafford to know too much about this rather unsavory part of her job, but now it seemed she had no choice.

"I think her ladyship is more interested in helping Mrs. Armitage clear her name. So this is what we are here to do—to find out a little bit more about that day. Luckily Mrs. Armitage's friend Mr. Evans is prepared to help us."

"Ah yes, Evans. He's a bit of a rum cove, don't you think?" She caught the flash of his smile in the gathering dusk of the conservatory.

She laughed at the "rum cove."

"I have never quite understood what that meant," she said.

"It means that he is a bit of a rogue," came his quick reply, and his smile widened.

"Oh, not to be trusted then?"

"I think you must think very carefully about what he is up to. I am sure what he says is quite believable; there just might be a bit of a gap between what he says and then what he thinks. And I have nothing to base this on except my sense of the type of man he is. You don't think he is just a little theatrical?" He was laughing now and he lifted his right hand and ran it back across his head from forehead to crown in a parody of the butler smoothing his sleek, well-barbered hair. His invitation to laugh at the florid manners of the butler dispelled the last of her apprehension about their meeting.

"I don't know if he is a rogue, but he *is* a very strange man. And he, evidently," she lowered her voice, "dislikes his employer."

Mr. Stafford nodded. "Yes, Mr. Haldane is a bit of a domestic tyrant but underneath I think he is quite a decent sort. He has been very fair in his dealings with me, and he certainly wants to give his wife what she wants. Mrs. Haldane is a kind woman and she loves her gardens."

The thought of Mrs. Haldane's winsome and girlish manner to her unpleasant husband came into Mrs. Jackson's head. It was sometimes difficult for her to ask questions directly about the behavior of others, so she waited, hoping that Mr. Stafford would reveal more. He laughed as if he knew what she was thinking and obliged her.

"She is his second wife; she was the governess to Mr. Haldane's only child, his daughter. Then the first Mrs. Haldane died during her confinement with their second child. The present Mrs. Haldane was barely twenty when she married Mr. Haldane, about fifteen years ago now."

She still thinks she is just a young woman, thought Mrs. Jackson, recalling the pale pastel frilly afternoon dress. "They seem to be rather an odd pair," she said, gently pushing for more information.

The doors into the salon opened to admit Mrs. Haldane and her guests. Miss Jekyll noticed them in the conservatory and came straight in to greet her old student, Mr. Stafford.

"Ernest," she said with evident pleasure. "How very nice to see you here. I have to leave tomorrow after luncheon, but I want to see what you are doing for the Haldanes. Your preliminary sketches looked most promising and I like your idea for limbing the trees at the south end of the lake to open up a view to distant hills. "

She nodded to Mrs. Jackson and kept her face turned away from the garish display of roses on the trestle table behind her. Mrs. Jackson suspected that Miss Jekyll did not approve of hybrid tea roses any more than Mr. Stafford did. She was amused at how deferential he was toward his old teacher. He looked almost ridiculously pleased at her approval of his design for Mrs. Haldane's lake and it was clear he wanted to show her his work here at Hyde Castle.

"I am surprised to find you here, Miss Jekyll," he said, acknowledging her exulted status as one of the country's most sought-after garden designers.

"Lady Montfort was invited to come here for the symposium and she asked me to accompany her. She is such a generous woman to her neighbors." Mrs. Jackson breathed a sigh of relief. Well, here, at last, was someone who did not know the real reason for their visit.

They were interrupted by the exuberant chatter of the Hyde Rose Society as they accepted glasses of port and sat themselves down in their chairs, all eyes turned expectantly toward the conservatory, willing Miss Jekyll to come in and pay attention to them.

"Ernest, I am going talk to Mrs. Haldane's friends about color harmony. It is something that I am hoping will be useful to these nice, diligent people in helping them produce lessstrident specimens." She half glanced at the offensive crowd of blooms on the table as she turned and walked back into the Salon Vert.

As the rosarians gathered for Miss Jekyll's talk, Clementine found herself spirited away from the core of the group by Mr. Urquhart. She willingly allowed herself to be led to three chairs grouped together toward the back of the room. She wanted information from Mr. Urquhart, and to make sure they were not joined by anyone else, she beckoned her housekeeper over to sit on her other side. And then, as Miss Jekyll finished her talk on the importance of *subtle* colors that exist in harmony with one another in the design of any garden, she laid a detaining hand on his forearm.

"I have heard so much about your charming roses Maiden's Blush and Cupid. I can't wait for tomorrow's competition. Do you have one every year?" The elderly man quivered with happiness at her compliment and assured her that his offerings, although pretty, were prey to many afflictions. He listed them all with enthusiasm as he sipped a small glass of oloroso and nibbled a ratafia biscuit.

"Oh, my dear Leddy Montfort, the powdery mildew can wreak havoc with Maiden's Blush—all my fault I assure you. And as to leaf wilt . . ." He shuddered and sipped his sherry.

Clementine decided that she liked this courteous man with his fastidious manners and his passion for hypochondria, which seemed extended even to his beloved roses, and exclaimed in sympathy for his afflicted progenies.

"So you see, Maiden's Blush is perhaps not destined to remain in the world very long, poor girl, and as for the dear Cupid, it is quite an astonishment to me that she has not already expired." He dolefully shook his head as if he were mourning members of his close family. Clementine imagined delicate spinster sisters with gentle dispositions languishing in quiet rooms fed on a diet of tea cakes and weak milky tea to coax them to cling to life.

Mr. Urquhart produced three small ornamental pillboxes and took samples from each one, carefully sipping them down with sherry.

"I do hope you are not unwell, Mr. Urquhart," she said, hoping to draw him away from his invalid roses and into the world of humankind.

"My dear Leddy Montfort, the trials of dyspepsia, I am simply never free from them. I was silly enough to eat some of the soup at dinner tonight, and I immediately knew it was a mistake. The broth was more than likely made with onions . . . ruinous, quite ruinous to the nervous system." He patted the corner of his mouth with a napkin and slipped his pillboxes into the pockets of his buff velvet waistcoat, which was intricately embroidered in shades of blue.

"Ah yes, dyspepsia, such a trial to the constitution," she commiserated.

"Indeed it is, and Mrs. Haldane's new cook lacks all refinement. It's meat, meat, and meat in this house. I have to bring my own little supplies of biscuits and shortbread when I visit just to keep me going throughout the day. The only meal I can really trust myself to enjoy is at tea time. Of course"—he glanced around—"you know that Mr. Haldane was once a butcher, which explains all the great haunches of beef and mutton we must struggle through. And they unfortunately sacked their last cook, a wonderful woman with the lightest touch, who produced such deliciously delicate food."

"Sacked her?" Clementine pretended horror. "Why sack a good cook? A good cook is so terribly hard to come by."

"They say she poisoned a guest here earlier this year. Absolute twaddle, if you don't mind my saying so. The woman was an artist, the man who died a glutton. Roger was embarrassed that his friend ate himself to death in his house, and made poor Maud get rid of her cook." Mr. Urquhart's outrage was clearly expressed in his need for another pill. With trembling fingers he produced a chased silver box.

"A compound of slippery elm and mustard powder," he informed her as he swallowed two tiny pale-yellow tablets and took another sip of sherry. "Balances acid in the system," he further explained.

"I must remember that," Clementine said. "Lord Montfort suffers tremendously from an unbalanced system." She didn't feel the slightest guilt at denigrating her husband's robust health, but she felt Mrs. Jackson stir at her side.

"But tell me about this terrible thing that happened here in the spring. How upsetting it must have been for you all," she coaxed, her eyes wide in invitation, an addicted gossip.

"It was indeed quite terrible." Finley closed his eyes at the memory. "If I tell you it was a catastrophe, Leddy Montfort, it would be no exaggeration. Poor Rupert came down early one morning and ate his usual more-than-ample breakfast. I am afraid he overate shamelessly, but then all Rupert's appetites were abundant. Well, after his breakfast he went out for a walk and died most horribly in an outhouse somewhere in the grounds. And most likely from a gastric eruption; his terrible gluttony had killed him." Clementine looked regretful and shook her head. But Mr. Urquhart was not quite finished. He gave her a knowing look, and Mrs. Jackson leaned farther in as he lowered his voice.

"Poor Rupert was addicted to *all* the earthly pleasures." Clementine shook her head as she heard of these mortal excesses. "Yes, I am afraid he was rather weak where life's human passions are concerned. All of the dear leddies here"—he looked in turn to the motherly Mrs. Lovell in conversation with Miss Jekyll, the bobbing curls of the pretty Mrs. Wickham as she chattered away to Mr. Stafford, and the submissively bowed head of Mrs. Haldane nodding politely as Mr. Wickham irritably discoursed on improper procedures in root grafting to her and the elegant Mrs. Bartholomew—"were quite obsessed with him and he had them all in such a tizzy. *And* poor Maud had to replace all her young and pretty housemaids with staid, solid country women of more mature years. Yes, Albertine was a saint—a complete saint where her husband's self-indulgence was concerned."

"It is not unusual for some gentlemen to feel they have to cast their net wide," Clementine offered from her worldly perspective. Her smile was that of a woman who understood these things, and it was all the elderly man needed to rush in with more information.

"I would not have been at all surprised if Clive or Roger had taken Rupert out to the woodshed and horsewhipped him—that was how much he upset the husbands in this house," he said, and at Clementine's look of surprise at such eighteenth-century methods of dealing with affronts to masculine dignity, he continued. "However much Amelia loves her dear friend Maud, at one time there was such jealousy between them that we none of us could concentrate on our work. Every time we gathered together it was the same exhausting repertoire: tears, interminable moody silences, and sulking in corners. And naughty Rupert behaving as if he was oblivious to all of it. It was then that he enticed Dorothy into some indiscretion or other. Clive, of course, put a stop to that one very quickly, but he never forgave Rupert."

"And Mr. Haldane, how did Mr. Haldane react?"

Mr. Urquhart tutted and waved the footman over to fill his empty glass. And in the short silence that followed, he polished his spectacles and fitted them more firmly on the bridge of his nose so that he could better judge how far to go with his gossip by the expression on the faces of both "leddies" to his left.

"Roger Haldane," he announced in a conspiratorial whisper as he took a sip of sherry, his eyes fixed on Clementine's face for emphasis, "is quite *besotted* with his wife. He has been ever since the day she came to work here as governess to his daughter, what was it now?—sixteen years ago." He turned to Mrs. Jackson to make sure she was included. "Maud was little more than a girl herself then, of course. Then the first Mrs. Haldane died and Roger married Maud within the year." He sipped and became thoughtful.

Clementine gently prodded with her customary tact: "He evidently cares for his wife very much." She did not catch Mrs. Jackson's eye as she said this. "It is hard when a husband cares so much for a faithless wife," she suggested.

"Oh dear me, *no*, Leddy Montfort, absolutely *not*. Maud was not faithless with Rupert; it is not in her nature, she is a most constant wife. But Maud and Rupert were the greatest of friends and no doubt she was very fond of him. But, you see, Rupert was *interested* in her and sought her out. They spent hours planning the genetics of her new roses, though as I am sure you must have realized, Maud is a dabbler and not a breeder in any sense of the word, really." He paused and sipped, searching perhaps for the right word, but it evidently eluded him. "Of course, Roger became aware that Maud was *always* with Rupert—off in the greenhouses trying to find the perfect growing medium for his seeds. And Roger was quite beside himself with jealousy, poor man. Everyone thinks that Roger and Rupert were the greatest of friends, but they were not. They were silent enemies." He hastily looked around and his voice sank into the deepest whisper. "They were business competitors first of all, d'ye see? Roger made his money the hard way, but Rupert inherited a very successful business from his uncle and held a government contract that Roger coveted. Then when handsome Rupert paid attention to Roger's wife it was really the last straw. They fought most terribly just before Christmas— most terribly. All of us expected Roger to drag Rupert from the house and shoot him at dawn. It was quite awful." And Mr. Urquhart, exhausted from recounting this piece of history, fell back against the cushions of his chair and took solace in the glass. "It was the most terrible scene I have ever witnessed in my life and it was only Albertine who saved the day."

"Mrs. Bartholomew?" Mrs. Jackson leaned forward to peer around Clementine at the elderly Scotsman.

"Yes, my dear Edith, Mrs. Bartholomew." Mr. Urquhart craned his neck so that he could see her face. "*She* told Roger that he was behaving like a schoolboy. That Rupert liked and admired Maud but did not seek to . . . seek to . . . that there was nothing improper. Of course Roger backed down somewhat, but he has never forgotten or forgiven. Poor Maud, she is so adored by Roger. I don't know if you have noticed that he has rather an overshadowing effect on her, though. Of course it comes from his being her senior in so many years and she is one of the most obliging and sweet-natured of women. Her time spent with Rupert was simply a pleasant alternative to all of that . . ." he groped for the right word and Mrs. Jackson quickly supplied it.

"Bullying?"

"Yes, I suppose that is true about Roger. He is so *very* masterful."

"And Mrs. Bartholomew?" Clementine asked as she watched a very serious discussion taking place on the other side of the room among Mrs. Bartholomew, Mrs. Lovell, and Miss Jekyll. "How did she feel about her husband's enjoyment in the company of her women friends?"

"Ah, Albertine, what a wonder she is. She always managed Rupert perfectly. He was lost without her. It was only when she went off on her long planting trips with her brother that Rupert got himself into a pickle. But she certainly soothed Roger's jealous heart, albeit temporarily. Every man needs an Albertine in his life," he ended, smiling wistfully as if his own behavior where women were concerned, if left unguarded, could be as divisive and unscrupulous as that of Mr. Bartholomew.

To Clementine's annoyance, they were interrupted at this point by Mrs. Lovell, who had broken away from Miss Jekyll and come across the room toward them.

"I think it is time I said good night to everyone," she said. "It is almost eleven o'clock and I simply have to be fresh for tomorrow. I am so gratified that we will be judged this year by a *true* plantswoman. The things Miss Jekyll has accomplished at Munstead are a horticultural revolution."

"Amelia, we are judged soundly and fairly every year and always by someone who knows of what they speak." His smile was kindly, but his tone was strict. It certainly made the stately Mrs. Lovell hesitate before she spoke.

"I wonder if keeping the roses in the conservatory is perhaps not a particularly good idea. It is very hot and humid in there."

"For a mere two days? Oh my dear Amelia, you worry unnecessarily. I can tell you that they are quite happy basking in the conservatory. Henry Bennett believed that a little heat was particularly efficacious for strengthening certain strains of roses, he told me so himself last week."

"Henry Bennett?" Clementine was puzzled. The name was familiar. Was Mr. Urquhart perhaps referring to *the* Henry Bennett, whose hybrid tea rose Mrs. John Laing had graced every suburban garden in the home counties at one time or another?

"Yes, the great rose breeder Henry Bennett, the father of the hybrid tea rose. His crosses between tea roses and perpetuals gave us the pedigree hybrids of today," answered Mrs. Lovell. "He bred the beautiful rose Lady Mary Fitzwilliam." She referred to a particularly heavy-headed rose in a hideous pink that managed, unfortunately, to bloom all summer long.

"But isn't he . . ." Clementine hesitated before saying, "dead?" *How on earth could this funny little man converse with someone who surely died years ago?*

"Yes, indeed, Lady Montfort." Mrs. Lovell smiled at Mr. Urquhart and he twinkled back at her. "Henry Bennett died almost twenty-five years ago, but Finley talks to him regularly, don't you, dear?" They laughed together as if Mrs. Lovell had made a tremendous joke.

And with that Mrs. Lovell wished them good night and left the room and Mr. Urquhart bent toward the two ladies on his left to whisper, "Ah, dear, dear me. Poor Amelia, try as hard as she might, every rose she develops looks exactly like the last one. She had some minor success with her first rose, Lovely Amelia, it was favorably mentioned in the *Rose Breeder's Gazette,* but since then every single specimen has been exactly the same: in petal count, in color, and she has never managed to produce a rose with any scent at all. They all sadly smell quite . . . sterile." His eyes regarded them sadly from behind his spectacles as he sighed and signaled to the footman. "Charles, I am ready to retire now. Please ask Sanders to bring up my peppermint tea in exactly half an hour." Rising to his feet, he executed a charming little bow to them both. "My dear Leddy Montfort and Edith, how happy I am you have come to join us. Maud is so hoping you will both become a part of our modest little group, for we understand the Iyntwood rose gardens are quite exquisite. I wish I could spend longer with you, but I fear I am in for a restless night."

"We will see you at breakfast, Mr. Urquhart," Clementine said.

"Ah no, I am afraid not. I always take my breakfast in my room. Then I must spend some time with my dear girls to get them ready for Miss Jekyll."

And will you be speaking to Henry Bennett about them, too? thought Clementine as she turned to her housekeeper and saw that Mrs. Jackson's eyes were sparkling with glee. She laughed and said under her breath, "Do you think he is perhaps a Theosophist, Jackson?"

Chapter Eight

Clementine awoke in the small hours. Was it her covert reason for coming to Hyde Castle that had awoken her with a feeling of distinct unease, or was there something here, close to her, that was of malevolent intent? She lay very still in her bed and listened.

Hyde Castle, with is mongrel architectural styles built to encompass an older structure, was a hotchpotch of rooms scattered upstairs and down, connected by long stone corridors, odd flights of stairs sometimes leading to other corridors and then surprising the visitor by opening into a mundanely modern, overly furnished sitting room. It was a confusing building to navigate during the broad light of day, but at night it had the allure of a haunted abbey portrayed in eighteenth-century gothic novels. This contrived gloomy gothic charm did not make Clementine feel anxious about sleeping alone—this was hardly the Castle of Otranto—and Clementine was well acquainted with the eccentricities of buildings far more ancient than Hyde Castle.

But something had awoken her. She strained her ears in the dark. Silence. She held her breath and listened. All was as quiet as a church on a Monday afternoon. *It must have been the call of an owl, or a mouse hurrying back to its nest in the wainscoting.*

She lay quite still in her bed and stared into the implacable blackness, her ears straining to a silence so profound that they started to ring. *Relax*, she instructed, *it's nothing at all, these extremely odd people are making you jumpy.* She turned on her side, rearranged her pillows, and closed her eyes preparatory to sinking back into sleep.

And just as she was drifting off she heard the sound that had no doubt awoken her. Most definitely this was not a mouse or an owl, it was a most human sound. On the still night air she briefly heard a thin, high wail, like that of a child—a frightened child. She sat up in her bed and stared once more into the dark. Silence, and again she held her breath. And then came again, a high, distant cry, cut off so abruptly that she was quite prepared to believe that her heightened senses had imagined it. The cry had not come from her bedroom window thrown open to the night air. And it was certainly not the wind wuthering against the tall stone walls of the house, as it was a particularly calm night.

She reached for the light on the table next to her bed and switched it on as she swung her legs over its edge and groped for her dressing gown. Even though parts of the castle had the studied appearance of the fifteenth century, Mr. Haldane had thoroughly modernized it. Electricity lit the long, dark, crooked corridors and hot water poured obediently into huge bathtubs in the bathrooms that she imagined adjoined every bedroom.

The sound came again, but a little fainter this time. *If I go exploring,* thought Clementine, *I will probably meet the Hyde Castle ghost. It must have been installed along with the plumbing.* She put on her dressing gown and walked silently across her room on bare feet in the direction that she fancied the cry had come from. The southeast wall of her room was hung with heavy tapestries and she pulled the first a little to one side and felt along the wall. Her palm lightly scraped along the surface of undressed, closely mortared stone. She thought that she was staying in the newest part of the house, but this wall had the feel of ancient stone hewn hundreds of years ago. The tips of her reaching fingers brushed up against the beveled edge of wood. Here the old part of the wall ended, or did it? She lightly passed her hand over the linen-fold of oak paneling, and her knowledgeable touch informed her that it was hand-planed from an age older than the smooth, wallpapered walls of the rest of her room. *This is part of the ruined castle they incorporated into the new building,* she thought. *Perhaps I am going to meet a ghost after all.* But why disguise something as beautiful as a medieval stone wall and paneling with these dreadful faux tapestries? She pulled the wall-hanging to one side and slid behind it. Half of the wall was stone, the rest paneled. She laid her ear against the wood and listened.

She heard the faint, soft scrabble of mice; the unmistakable tick and shift of old timber rafters and joists as they settled on ancient foundations; the rhythmic and comforting thump of her pulse and the quiet inhalation and exhalation of her breath—and a long, sobbing cry.

Facing the wall, she shuffled along it, an ear close to its surface, feeling ahead as she went. Her right hand bumped up against the jamb of a door, and slid effortlessly over its stile. Reflexively her hand dropped to the door's handle, and closed around the cold iron ball of the doorknob. She turned it to the right. With her shoulder pressed against it, the heavy door swung silently away from her. She held it open, just wide enough to put her head around to listen. It was dark on the other side of the door, and at this moment her courage wavered in the dark night as she contemplated the black void before her.

Should she return to her room and wake Jackson and then perhaps with the aid of Jackson's torch they might see into this room that opened so clandestinely from hers? Was it a closet, perhaps, or another room? Standing on the threshold of the black space, she craned her head forward. And then around her feet she felt a cool draft of air, which lifted the hem of her light silk dressing gown and stirred a wisp of hair that had fallen across her face. She pushed her hair out of her eyes and waited. It was cold in this room, if that was what it was. It smelled dry with the fustiness of places that are not used and she sensed that she was standing in the doorway of a corridor. She could see, just a little ahead of her, a gray patch of light. She took one tentative step forward, spreading her arms wide on either side of her body. Fingertips touched rough stone. Yes, she had been right, it was a corridor. And just as she took another step she heard again the cry that had awoken her, short and sharp before it fell to a sobbing murmur. Was it her imagination or did she hear the responding tones of a deeper voice? Surely someone was crying in the dark of the night and whoever it was, was not alone.

She slid a foot forward and her bare toes found smooth wide flagstone. She took another step and turned; the door to her room was still open. She could see a glimmer of comforting light coming from around the edges of the tapestry.

Just a few steps along this corridor—I can turn back at any time. I can even see my room from here. Now she extended her arms in front of her as she advanced slowly forward, step-by-step: five paces. The dim light became a little brighter as she rounded a bend in the corridor. Here was a single small casement window with leaded panes, which allowed the light she had seen from the doorway to her room. She put her nose to the thick glass panes and stared out into the night. A three-quarter moon was high in the sky, its silvery beams lighting her uplifted face. The casement window was ill fitting and she felt a substantial draft filtering into the corridor from around its edges. She peered down the length of the corridor and saw that there were no doors along its walls, but she could just about see the end, twenty feet ahead. With her arms reaching out to the walls on either side of her, she went forward. She felt with her toe a shallow step of stone, then another of smooth polished boards. In front of her was a closed door. She turned her head and put her ear against the heavy oak panel.

Silence, except for her own breath and leaping pulse. Very carefully she placed her hand on the iron curve of the door handle and, pushing down, heard the muted click of the spring-loaded mechanism releasing the latch. She pushed, but the door did not move. Was it locked? She stepped back and pulled and the door opened inward. She steadied its swing and put her head around it. She saw a wide corridor, with only two doors, one at the bottom to her right, the other almost directly in front of her. It was lit with electric sconces, and before her on the floor was a bright Turkish rug on the well-polished wood boards; flowers had been arranged on a small table, a landscape hanging on the wall behind it. There was the reassuring scent of fresh flowers and beeswax common in well-kept houses. Clementine breathed a deep sigh of relief at the sight of this pleasantly commonplace corridor.

What had she expected to find when she opened this door? A dusty forgotten chamber, with bare boards and mismatched furniture? A narrow iron bed on which tossed the body of a gaunt creature with masses of tangled hair and, off in the corner in the light of an oil lamp, the large figure of a woman keeping watch through the night? In her short walk down the stone corridor she had half believed that this door would open into a secret room on the fourth floor of Thornfield: the attic room that housed Mr. Rochester's insane Creole wife and her guardian, Grace Poole, whose occasional bouts of inebriation enabled the violent Bertha to range the house at night and set fire to people in their beds. Is this what her overwrought imagination had prepared her for when she had so daringly opened the door? *Yes,* she had to admit to herself, *it was.*

The stone corridor, most probably used by the housemaids to go from one side of the house to the other when they were cleaning this floor, had taken her from the guest rooms of the house to the wing where the family slept. Hadn't the butler pointed out the family's wing when he had turned right at the top of the wide landing? Conscious that she was trespassing and embarrassed with herself for creeping down the corridor in the first place when she should be in her bed, she stepped back, preparatory to closing the door, and heard a long, low sob so clearly and so near that she realized it came from behind the door across the corridor. There was such despair in the lament that Clementine felt an overwhelming desire to rush to the woman's aid. And from behind the door, in response, she heard a low, insistent rumble, the words muffled and vague. She stepped lightly across the corridor, conscious as she did so that she was breaking all conventions that bind polite guests in the houses of friends and, even more significantly, complete strangers when someone has kindly extended an invitation. She allowed this moment of self-admonishment to give her pause for the space of several seconds before she pressed her ear against the door and listened.

The low, breathy sobs continued and above them came a male voice, almost conciliatory in tone. Ah, she drew a breath; someone had come to this tragic woman's aid. The voice was so low that the words were indistinguishable, it rumbled on and then abruptly changed, lifted in volume and tone, and she heard, "Disappointed," quite clearly, and as the voice rose in pitch, "... and then you make me lose my temper ..." was plainly audible as Mr. Haldane's reproving tone became angrier. There was a gasp, and a woman's voice cried out in pain and entreaty. Clementine pulled back in horror.

Oh dear God, what am I doing? I am eavesdropping on the Haldanes. She turned and fled back through the door she had come through, closing it behind her, and with her arms outstretched in front of her, she tiptoed down the two steps, felt flagstone under her feet, and as fast as she could made her way back toward the glimmer of light at the end of the corridor. She pulled her bedroom door open wide and stepped cross the threshold into her room, closing it behind her. Feeling below its handle, she found a key and turned it in the lock. *That is what you should have done when you found this door,* she quite angrily told herself, *instead of creeping around the Haldanes' house like a spy.*

But, oh what a relief to be back in her room with the door into that terrible corridor firmly locked. She slid out from behind the tapestry and found herself staring at her own reflection in the looking glass over the dressing table. Her face was white, her eyes wide, and her bedtime plait swung as she turned and cast a guilty glance at the tapestry that concealed the passageway to the Haldanes' private wing of the house. She was across her room in a flash and, climbing into the high, wide bed, she slid her feet down under the sheets and put her hands over both ears to prevent herself from hearing the wails of Mrs. Haldane's suffering at the hands of her husband.

How on earth can I sleep when I have just broken all the rules of good manners and in return have been taught a sharp lesson, thought Clementine as she lay back against her pillows and tried to come to terms with what she had just done and, even more shocking, with what she had just heard.

The apologetic pale face of Mrs. Haldane, with her watery pale blue eyes and soft, fading blond hair, stared at her reproachfully, and over the woman's shoulder Clementine saw the red leathery face of Mr. Haldane, his frown belligerent as he accused her of a serious breach of good manners in a house she had been invited to visit.

She closed her eyes to block out these images and at the same time reached out a hand for the book she was reading. She would read herself to sleep and when she awoke it would be to a bright sunny day and she would forget the sobbing, fearful cries and the angry voices of the Haldanes. Her eyes remained fixed on the page but she found she couldn't make sense of a single word.

Mr. Haldane is one of those terrible men who dominate and mistreat their wives, she thought. Mrs. Haldane's cry of despair kept echoing in her head. *How can she live with a man who is so brutishly cruel?* And then she remembered what Mr. Urquhart had said just hours before, when he had been indulging in a cozy little gossip about his friend Mrs. Haldane: "Poor Maud, she is so adored by Roger. I don't know if you have noticed that he has rather an overshadowing effect on her."

An overshadowing effect on her? What a shattering understatement. What she had overheard was a man who not only socially overpowered his wife but was both physically and verbally violent to her. For surely the cries she had heard, the sobbing and the entreaties, were the response of a woman who has either been forcibly restrained or cruelly punished. Clementine accepted that sleep would be impossible—she was far too disturbed—but more than that she was angry. And the more she dwelled on the bullying she had just overheard, the angrier she became. Anger was welcome, it washed away her sense of shame at being a sneak. She was so angry she could hardly stay in her bed. She wanted to leap up and dress herself, go to the Haldanes' room, open the door, and command the man to leave his wife alone. *No, I actually want to brain the brute with a poker.*

Mr. Haldane was the sort of man who believed it his right to possess his wife, to control her every deed and thought and to require her to serve him—as if she were an indentured servant, without the freedom to leave and find another job. It made complete sense to her in this moment that Mrs. Haldane had found comfort and friendship in the company of Mr. Bartholomew, and that if her husband had found out he would have punished her and killed her friend.

Clementine pulled her notebook out from under her pillow and started to write. She would have to be very careful not to arouse suspicion with what she intended to find out. The thought of that angry, violent man turning on her made her heart beat furiously, as she wrote, *Where was Roger Haldane on the morning that Rupert Bartholomew ate his poisoned breakfast?*

Chapter Nine

Lady Montfort and Mrs. Jackson had decided to go down to breakfast together to familiarize themselves with the room in which Mr. Bartholomew had eaten his last meal. As they descended the wide staircase into the hall, Mrs. Jackson wondered if she would have any appetite at all for breakfast in this house, but as they arrived in the dining room she was reassured by the beautifully appointed room with its well-polished mahogany table set with fine china and silver. Sunlight streaming in through windows fell on vases of simple summer flowers arranged in the center of the table. Even more reassuring was the sight of the sideboard with its familiar row of well-polished silver chafing dishes, which every country house in England set out to greet its guests each morning. The silver dishes glinted in the morning light, each offering the glories of a well-cooked and bountiful breakfast that had been the tradition of hearty English country squires down through the ages. The only difference in this modern century was that there was no small-ale on offer, but the delightful aroma of fresh coffee.

Miss Jekyll, already seated at the table, was tucking into a buttered kipper and two poached eggs, with a rack of toast awaiting her attention to her right. There was a purposeful and rather grim expression on Miss Jekyll's face. And was it Mrs. Jackson's imagination or did she send a rather reproachful look in Lady Montfort's direction as they walked into the room? *She is probably not looking forward to this rose-judging business,* Mrs. Jackson thought, *and given the overly competitive nature of the individuals involved, I don't blame her one bit.*

She lifted the lids of the chafing dishes on the sideboard and noticed that there was no kedgeree among the many offerings. She helped herself to a sausage, some mushrooms, and a grilled tomato, then sat down next to Miss Jekyll, who was already in conversation with Lady Montfort as her ladyship sipped her tea and nibbled toast and marmalade. She noticed, in the bright light of morning, that her ladyship's face was strained and tired and that she was barely listening to what Miss Jekyll was saying to her.

"That won't be enough to fuel you for the day," Mrs. Lovell said, her plate piled with eggs, bacon, and kidneys, as she lowered her newspaper and gave Lady Montfort's lean breakfast a critical once-over. Her ladyship merely smiled and sipped her tea, her tired eyes politely fixed on Miss Jekyll's face as she listened to her opinions on the overuse of statuary, urns, and fountains in the naturally designed garden. "Excessive use of these objects ruins the aesthetic balance of a well-planned landscape and simply designed gardens, as they clutter the lines of sight," she pronounced and, judging by her creased forehead, it was clear that Hyde Castle's owner was guilty of sprinkling the terrain with far too many objets d'art.

Mrs. Lovell put her newspaper to one side and said to Mrs. Jackson, "I do hope you were not put off by Mr. Urquhart talking about his conversations with the long-dead Henry Bennett." Her round plain face was wrinkled in concern that her friend might be thought a crackpot. And Mrs. Jackson smiled in what she hoped was encouragement as she poured milk into her tea and picked up her knife and fork. The sausage, she noticed with approval, was absolutely delicious, simply bursting with flavor. She made a silent vow to visit Hyde Castle's dining room every morning for breakfast.

"Finley has many eccentricities, but he is a very dear man, and would not harm a fly," Mrs. Lovell pursued, her large breakfast left untouched on her plate. "But he truly believes that we can converse with the spirit world." She picked up her knife and fork but made no attempt to eat as she watched Mrs. Jackson's face, no doubt hoping for signs of disbelief. "It is quite a harmless preoccupation, I assure you. It is not as if he dabbles in the occult."

The occult? The words conjured up images of the Hellfire Club. Mrs. Jackson had to look away and bite the inside of her lips so that she did not smile at the image of Mr. Urquhart luring tender young virgins up to the West Wycombe caves where a group of elderly Regency roués lay in wait as they took snuff and flicked specks of dust off their impeccable Honiton lace cuffs. She shook her head in incomprehension as she took another bite of heavenly pork sausage and wondered if it would be greedy to help herself to another one. Images of an uneaten plate of kedgeree came to mind and she decided against a second helping.

"I was not joking last night when I said he consulted the long-dead Henry Bennett on the procedures for breeding roses," Mrs. Lovell explained, her eyes watchful, her manner alert to how her words were received. "Of course Maud, being the kind soul she is, obliged him in a little séance years ago. That is until Clive put a stop to it. He said that sort of thing was against all the tenets of the Anglican faith, but Clive can be very judgmental." She laughed. "I just wanted you to understand that Finley only calls on benevolent spirits." She lowered her voice. "Sometimes I am almost tempted to ask him to talk to Henry Bennett about *my* roses." She sighed at the frustrations she evidently experienced in producing the perfect rose. "Once one has had a little success with breeding a good specimen, it is terribly hard to produce another that does not replicate the first one. I am hoping that Miss Jekyll will be able to offer some helpful advice."

"I am very much looking forward to seeing *your* roses." Mrs. Jackson decided she had heard enough of Mr. Urquhart's fascination with table turning and Ouija boards. She rather agreed with Mr. Wickham that contacting the spirit world was sacrilegious. "What is the name of *your* rose, Mrs. Lovell?"

"I have two," Mrs. Lovell corrected. "Lovely Amelia is my very first pink tea rose. And Lovell's Beauty is the rose I am working on at the moment. We are nearly there, but a rose-breeder's work is never done." She smiled, and Mrs. Jackson thought what a well-meaning individual she was. It must have been quite a task for her to help keep the peace with the touchy Mr. Wickham, the aggressive Mr. Haldane, and the apparently flirtatious Mr. Bartholomew causing havoc among the ladies. But for the life of her she could not imagine this kindly woman being jealous of Mrs. Haldane's crush on the late Mr. Bartholomew.

"And Mrs. Haldane's roses?" she asked innocently, quite aware that there was no specimen on view from Mrs. Haldane in the conservatory.

"Excuse me a moment, Mrs. Jackson, I have just remembered to arrange for the roses to be moved from the conservatory, before they all expire in the heat. Charles . . ." She gave detailed instructions to the footman to arrange for the head gardener to move the trestle table out onto the terrace, and after all her orders had been repeated faithfully back to her, she turned to Mrs. Jackson to explain her reasoning.

"It is a lovely morning; there is absolutely no need for us all to be confined in the heat of that conservatory on such a delightful summer's day," she said, with an almost indulgent smile for the elderly man. "Finley will wrap up warmly and we will all enjoy the beauties of the day.

"I am so sorry to have interrupted you, now where were we? Ah, yes, you were asking about Maud's roses. Dear Maud has so far not produced a specimen that she wishes to share with us. She is still a novice and, to her credit, does not take risks or shortcuts but is patient to learn her craft. But when Maud produces a specimen I expect the world will most certainly sit up and take notice." She ended quite passionately, making Mrs. Jackson wonder again at Mr. Urquhart's gossip that Mrs. Haldane and Mrs. Lovell had been at each other's throats over the irresistible Mr. Bartholomew. *Perhaps now that Mr. Bartholomew is no longer around to cause trouble between them, their friendship has regained its original happy state,* she thought as she regarded the earnest face before her.

"Maud is a selfless woman," Mrs. Lovell continued. "She is generous-hearted and sympathetic. I respect her loyalty to a husband who is sometimes a little selfish where she is concerned." For a moment Mrs. Jackson thought that perhaps Mrs. Lovell was going to say more on the subject of Mr. Haldane, but clearly she felt she had said enough about her host. She patted her mouth with her napkin and put it down next to her plate. The footman came over to pull her chair back from the table as she stood up.

"Now I must go and get my roses ready for Miss Jekyll." And she left the room.

Mrs. Jackson decided that she rather approved of Mrs. Lovell. But she was not entirely sure that Mr. Urquhart had the relationship between Mrs. Haldane and this kindly woman quite right; she simply could not imagine Mrs. Lovell being jealous of Mrs. Haldane, and it was quite clear that she valued their friendship and was Mrs. Haldane's loyal friend.

After breakfast, Mrs. Jackson, in the company of Miss Jekyll and Lady Montfort, spent a pleasant hour inspecting the large, irregular crater that Mr. Stafford had made in the middle of what had once been a smooth south-facing lawn. And when they had finished exclaiming about long views, perspective, and the simplicity of a well-balanced landscape, Miss Jekyll took Lady Montfort off to the shrubbery on their walk back to the house, leaving Mrs. Jackson to walk with Mr. Stafford.

"I feel rather stupid, but I don't understand how you create a lake," Mrs. Jackson said to Mr. Stafford as they crossed what remained of the lawn and made their way to the flight of stone steps leading up to the rose garden and from there to the terrace of the castle.

"Oh, you simply dam a small stream, or deepen and widen a pond that is spring-fed, as I am doing. But it is a protracted business."

"And very expensive?" Her Lancashire prudence about money never left her, even working as she did for a rich man who spared nothing to gratify his wife's often rather grandiose garden plans.

"Terribly expensive." He laughed. "But Mr. Haldane can well afford it. And if there is to be war then he will be still richer, if he can persuade the government to give him a contract for supplying the army with his tinned beef stew."

Mrs. Jackson shuddered at the thought of opening a tin of stew. "How can men go into battle with nothing but that sort of stuff in their stomachs?" Her disgust made him laugh again.

"Because it's convenient. What do you imagine the army ate

when it went into battle, before there were tinned rations? I promise you, army victuals have always been unpleasant and frequently scarce; more often than not, men fought on empty stomachs after a day of marching."

But she didn't hear him, as she was thinking that if Mr. Haldane had coveted Mr. Bartholomew's lucrative government contract and was jealous of his romantic friendship with his wife, then here were two very strong motives for his getting rid of his friend.

"What was the name of Mr. Bartholomew's tinned beef?" she asked.

"Bartholomew's Bully Beef; it was what we all ate in the Boer War. It was awful stuff, a lump of beef fat and gristle, with turnips. Eat it hot or cold, it said on the tin. But you had better try to eat it hot, because cold it was lethal. Mr. Bartholomew increased his fortune considerably through the Boer Wars with his tinned rations, and he was still under contract to the government when he died. But now the contract is open to new vendors."

"I didn't know you fought in the Boer War," Mrs. Jackson said, thinking he was surely far too young and also that it was interesting that on Mr. Bartholomew's death a plum contract was now available.

"I was, for a mercifully short time, at the very end. I was at the relief of Ladysmith in 1900 with Lord Dundonald, to my everlasting shame. I was shot through the shoulder, a flesh wound, so I was back in England when they rounded up the Boers, burned their farms, imprisoned their women and children in camps and then, when they were broken and defeated, shipped the men off to different parts of our glorious empire. Later I found out that most of those men died when they were transported." She glanced up and saw how grim his face was. This was a different account of the Boer War from the one that Iyntwood's butler, Mr. Hollyoak, loved to tell. "Did we really do all of that to the Boers?" she asked.

"Yes, we really did all of that to the Afrikaner men, women, and children—we took everything they had from them and when they had nothing left, took their dignity and the lives of their families. War brutalizes men. It doesn't take much to strip away the thin veneer of civilization and expose our barbarity." She was struck by his thoughtful understanding of human nature. *It is true,* she thought, *it doesn't take much to push a man, or woman, to do the most terrible things if they believe the lives of those they love and protect are threatened, or,* she thought of that lucrative contract, *are motivated by greed.*

She stopped and they stood looking out across the crater toward the distant hills; she tried to imagine it brimming with placid blue water, its scarred outline softened by mossy banks and trees shading its edges. It would be a beautiful prospect when it was finished. She could easily see from this distance that the lake would fit quite perfectly into the shallow valley. She realized that she appreciated the ornamental landscape in much the same way she appreciated a well-appointed and beautifully furnished room. Miss Jekyll had said in her lecture yesterday that a garden was like a house, it had several rooms, and that each had its own particular identity.

"Do you think we will go to war?" she asked the silent man standing next to her, gazing down over his carefully thought-out contribution to the immaculate grounds they found themselves in.

"Our Foreign Secretary, Sir Edward Grey, is trying to set up a meeting to negotiate for peace in Europe—I hope it is not too late. War accomplishes nothing in the long run. At the very least it creates a muddle for future generations to deal with and at worst it destroys civilization. But I fear there will always be wars; it is part of man's nature." And then, perhaps hearing how grim he sounded, he added in a different tone of voice altogether, "I would much rather discover who might have murdered Mr. Bartholomew with you."

She did not dare look at him when he said this, but she felt the hairs on her neck prickle in delight and she had to force herself to say quite matter-of-factly, "So you think he was murdered, then?"

"I have no idea, but it would be interesting to find out, don't you think?" She risked a glance at his face and felt her throat tighten. He was smiling at her with such a tender expression, his brown eyes in the morning sunlight were bright with good humor, and she could see the flecks of gold in the irises, like tiny splinters of barley sugar.

"Yes," she agreed. "It would be interesting to find out."

Clementine's walk into the garden in the early-morning sunlight in the company of practical and straightforward people whom she liked and trusted was a tonic after the miseries of her night. She had not yet spoken to Mrs. Jackson about what she had overheard last night. Part of her was reluctant to share this information. Mr. Haldane's bullying behavior was outrageous, but she felt that her corridor-creeping had been both dishonorable and ill bred. *As soon as the right moment occurs I will ask her what she thinks about what I overheard,* she said to herself, still feeling acute embarrassment at admitting to anyone that she had eavesdropped on her host.

As she and Miss Jekyll broke free of the path through the shrubbery and approached the flagstone terrace, Clementine was conscious of an atmosphere of tension mounting among the members of the Hyde Rose Society. As they walked up the wide, shallow stone steps to the long trestle table set out in front of the conservatory and covered in a heavy dark cloth—the better to display the specimens to be judged—the chatter ceased among the competitors and they fell into a watchful silence.

The pots of roses were separated into four distinct groups with each of their nervous creators standing behind them.

"Oh dear." Miss Jekyll's plain, round face expressed reluctance and Clementine felt guilty for having involved her. "I am sure they will be most awfully annoyed with me when I have finished with them."

"Perhaps leniency is the best approach," Clementine suggested, and Miss Jekyll turned a disapproving face toward her. "I don't think I need to let them off that easily, Lady Montfort. As serious rose breeders they need to know that they have produced some specimens that will be a blight on the rose world unless they are told of their deficiencies; except perhaps for Mr. Bartholomew's Golden Girl and his other white rose. In the end all that will be bruised will be their egos, and it is not the ego that should be considered here but the interests of horticultural science." She took a deep breath and strode forward purposefully toward the now-silent group.

Mrs. Wickham and Mrs. Haldane, both dressed in white cotton voile dresses and wearing ornate hats covered in silk roses, were standing side-by-side, sharing a lacy sunshade. Clementine had not yet seen Mrs. Haldane this morning and was surprised that after her night of suffering, she appeared to be quite normal in her unsuitably ornate dress. Standing next to Mrs. Wickham and Mrs. Haldane, Mrs. Jackson's handsome face glowing from the exertion of her early-morning walk in contrast to the two pale ones beside her, made Clementine almost catch her breath. *But there is something else going on here too,* she thought, for as Mrs. Jackson turned her head to listen to something Mr. Stafford had just said to her, Clementine perceived in the angle of the way they were standing, a little apart from the group and even from each other, that they were wholly wrapped-up in their conversation and completely oblivious to the others standing around them. The look on her housekeeper's face was, as usual, quite composed and yet there was a distinct gleam in her eye as she responded to what Mr. Stafford had said and then she gave a quick smile as she nodded her head and the smile almost broke into a laugh. *Great heavens, Jackson is certainly very pleased to have met up with Mr. Stafford again. I wonder . . .*

But what she wondered at would have to wait for a moment or two because in her forthright and no-nonsense way Miss Jekyll was addressing the three savagely red roses that were the proud contribution to the world of the tea rose by Mr. Wickham.

"From seed, Mr. Wickham?" Miss Jekyll's gruff voice reached all of them easily.

"Yes, the first two are crosses from . . ." and Clive irritably gave the lineage of his Clive's Red, Wickham's Justice, and the brash Court Scarlet. As Miss Jekyll continued to discuss Mr. Wickham's roses, Mrs. Wickham broke away from Mrs. Haldane, sidled up to Clementine and with a self-conscious, girlish laugh said, "Clive worships his roses. He is far more interested in them than anything or anyone else." Another little laugh and Clementine nodded and smiled without taking her eyes off Miss Jekyll in conversation with Mr. Wickham, but turned her right shoulder a little to invite more confidences.

"But I don't expect him to win," Mrs. Wickham said with the conviction of the enlightened. "One does not spend one's life married to a rosarian without being made aware of the many problems they grapple with when producing a new strain." Again the affected laugh, but Clementine nodded in agreement to encourage more information.

"Clive's roses are very demanding," she said. "They need masses of rich fertilizer to thrive and unfortunately Clive's Red suffers from root canker, discovered too late and passed on to the other roses." She spoke with happy enthusiasm, as if every failure along the way that caused Mr. Wickham a sleepless night was a gift to her.

They were certainly quite the most oppressively horrid shade of red Clementine had ever beheld in a rose, more like the color of brick than the rich and deep hues that make the true red rose so breathtaking. Miss Jekyll evidently agreed because she was delivering a little lecture on the importance of clear reds and passed over Court Scarlet and Wickham's Justice.

"Told you so," muttered Mrs. Wickham. "The only rose here worth its salt is Golden Girl." She sighed.

"Mr. Bartholomew's rose?" Clementine prompted.

"Yes; the scent is exquisite, the petals beautifully formed, the leaves glossy and bright, and its stem is strong and straight. Golden Girl is more like a . . ." She racked her brain, stuck for the term she was seeking.

"Old Garden Rose?" supplied Clementine.

"No, the French one."

"Ah, the Bourbon Rose." Clementine, who had been impressed with the young woman's knowledge, now realized that she was merely parroting a higher authority. Mrs. Lovell? No, it was probably her old flame Mr. Bartholomew talking about his own specimens.

"Yes, that's it, the Bourbon Rose—Rupert's garden at Fairview is full of old roses. It seems he admired everything that was French," she added rather sadly.

Does this absurd young woman still fancy herself in love with Mr. Bartholomew? thought Clementine. *I can't say I am surprised; her husband is such a tetchy little worm. What misery it would be to be shackled to a man who believed his role in life was always to correct.*

Miss Jekyll had moved on and was now in discussion with Mrs. Lovell, who was standing with her head bowed to accept her verdict. Mr. Urquhart was quite right, both Lovely Amelia and Lovell's Beauty were identical in shape and color, a particularly flat, rather pasty pink that put Clementine in mind of her Wood's Cherry Tooth Powder, and, if Mr. Urquhart was to be believed, had no scent whatsoever. Miss Jekyll's voice, pitched low for Mrs. Lovell's benefit only, was inaudible to the group craning their necks to hear what she had to say.

"No scent," Mrs. Wickham informed. "I don't think Miss Jekyll is particularly impressed with Mrs. Lovell's roses. But they are healthy. Extraordinarily vigorous and only prone to powdery mildew if the weather is particularly warm and wet, and since this is England . . ." She laughed again and her husband looked up at her and frowned.

Miss Jekyll's conference with Mrs. Lovell was involved and Clementine noticed that Mrs. Lovell did not look particularly crushed. She nodded earnestly at Miss Jekyll's suggestions and jotted down little notes on the back of an envelope, then thanked her at the end.

"Now this will be interesting." A sly little giggle as Miss Jekyll moved on to Mr. Urquhart. *Really the girl is quite treacherous,* thought Clementine, wishing she had not encouraged her to be so outspoken, *and she is behaving abominably.*

Mr. Urquhart was dressed for a chilly day. He was wearing a well-tailored frock coat and a silk tricot wrapped up high and tight around his neck. Gray suede gloves and a cashmere shawl carefully draped over his shoulders had been donned in case any draft should permeate his outer barrier of worsted wool and silk.

No wonder he wanted to have the competition in the conservatory, thought Clementine, noticing the old man shiver. *This fresh air must be playing havoc with the balance of his system, poor old thing.* It was difficult for her to see Mr. Urquhart's expression as his face was obscured by the shadow of his tall, silk top hat. But it seemed to Clementine that Mr. Urquhart was doing all the talking and Miss Jekyll all the nodding as she stared down at the pretty roses in their pots. To Clementine's horror she noticed that their leaves were a little yellow.

"Maiden's Blush and Cupid." Clementine's face flushed with annoyance as Mrs. Wickham's clear young voice rang across the terrace. She turned with her forefinger uplifted in the traditional admonishment reserved for the very young or the ill-mannered, but not quickly enough to silence Mrs. Wickham's opinion.

"Of course their scent is quite delightful. Oh, if only they had leaves." She tittered, and Clementine, as she stared across the terrace to the far horizon, wondered if it was possible that this unfortunate young woman could possibly have been drinking. Her eyes were unnaturally bright, and her voice was extraordinarily loud. She glanced at Mrs. Wickham out of the corner of her eye and realized why she was commentating on the roses in such a pronounced fashion. After everything she said she glanced at Mr. Stafford, standing next to Mrs. Jackson, to see if she had his attention. *What a little flirt,* thought Clementine. *Every group has its resident coquette and this young woman certainly sees herself as the adored member of the Hyde Rose Society.*

"I like Mr. Urquhart's roses," said Clementine rather repressively, because she did. They reminded her of the delicate Noisette roses of her first season in London. She had worn a coronet of Old Blush roses in her hair for her first ball, very like the pretty pink-tinted roses in Mr. Urquhart's pots. "They are so pretty and natural and the color is quite delightful, the softest tint of dawn." She hoped she had silenced the girl, but she hadn't.

"But unfortunately no foliage, isn't *that* rather important?" A pert laugh as Mrs. Wickham glanced over at the only man under forty standing on the terrace.

"But of course there are leaves," Clementine persisted. "And I am quite sure that Mr. Urquhart will succeed in strengthening his strain." She kept her voice as pleasant as she could but she caught the young woman's eye and frowned at her. Mrs. Wickham bit her lip, like a scolded child.

Having delivered her correction, Clementine turned back to the group around the table, thinking as she did so that if only this young woman would leave the nursery and take her place in the adult world, perhaps her husband would take her more seriously and she wouldn't have to behave quite so outrageously for attention.

It was now Mrs. Bartholomew's turn to receive the expert opinion of Miss Jekyll on her late husband's roses. She stepped forward and gravely listened to Miss Jekyll's praise for Golden Girl. *The yellow is quite charming*, thought Clementine. *There is such richness and depth to its color. It looks fabulously robust. And his unnamed white rose is quite perfect.*

"Rupert really understood the art of breeding roses," said Mrs. Wickham, clearly anxious to regain Clementine's good opinion. "Golden Girl's scent is quite wonderful. I have no idea how he managed to contrive a rose with such a heavenly scent." Despite the positive words of praise, Mrs. Wickham's voice was still too loud. Her husband glared at her from over the top of his garish rose hedge, his annoyance palpable.

Miss Jekyll's final remarks to the Hyde Rose Society and their exhibits were not a surprise to anyone. She opened her verdict by saying that she had given her notes to each of them to assist in their furthering the difficult business of producing a strain of hybrid teas that were primarily disease-free. And then she placed the roses in order of merit.

Clementine had always disliked active competition; she held her husband's distaste for men who counted their bag at the end of a day's shooting and compared their numbers with those brought down by others. She found it hard to look at the Hyde Rose Society's exhibitors as they waited for the results of their impromptu contest like a pack of hungry wolves as they fastened their eyes on the particularly plump and earnest rabbit who had so thoughtfully judged their offerings.

"Given the difficulty of your quest to produce the best tea rose possible, I am happy to say that the late Mr. Bartholomew has certainly achieved sterling results." Miss Jekyll turned to Mrs. Bartholomew, who bowed her head with a smile of thanks. And Mrs. Wickham, who was standing in front of the group, clapped her hands together with a little cry of joy.

"And despite his *serious* problems with yellowing leaves, I believe this could be corrected with more iron in your potting mixture, Mr. Urquhart. Maiden's Blush and Cupid embody everything we seek in a hybrid. Their color is subtle, harmonious with nature, and pleasing, their shape quite delightful, and what is more, you have contrived to produce blooms with a most delicate and pretty scent." Mr. Urquhart bowed with an expression of such exultant triumph on his face that Clementine had to look away.

"Now this leaves Mrs. Lovell and Mr. Wickham in a direct tie." An exclamation from Mrs. Wickham interrupted her momentarily as the young woman turned to her husband and said, "At least it is a *tie*, darling."

Miss Jekyll continued as if Mrs. Wickham had not uttered a word. "Both of your specimens are quite healthy, this is a tremendous start. But color and scent are areas to work on. And

I hope that my notes to both of you will be of some help in furthering your strains. I am sure I will see a tremendous improvement next year."

"In my opinion, Rupert's new white rose is actually perfect," said Mrs. Wickham. Her voice cut across the group on the terrace and heads turned in her direction. "And I hope it is named after him, as it should be." There was a hysterical note in her voice and Clementine saw tears spring into her eyes.

Mrs. Haldane, looking extremely distressed, said, "Dorothy, c-come now. Of course, you know it will be . . ." and walked over to lay a restraining hand on the young woman's arm.

"I don't, though, because Albertine . . ." Mrs. Wickham cried, jerking her arm away. "Rupert was working so hard to perfect his white rose. He was so proud of it, it *must* be named after him." And, pulling a handkerchief from her pocket, she ran from the terrace.

All eyes immediately turned from Mrs. Wickham's tempestuous exit back to Mr. Wickham standing to attention behind his roses. His hands were clasped behind his straight back, his mouth pulled into a tight line of disapproval. He neither looked at his friends nor turned his head to his departing wife, but stared down at Court Scarlet. But the expression on his face was tight and angry, and Mrs. Jackson looked across the terrace to meet Clementine's astonished gaze and she raised her eyebrows as if to say, *What on earth was that about?*

Chapter Ten

"Jackson, I am utterly overwhelmed by these people, I simply can't make out what is going on." Lady Montfort was sitting by the window of her bedroom looking more than a little pensive. "It seems to me that too much information too soon can rather make one's head swim. Have you had a chance to make head or tail of it all?"

Mrs. Jackson hesitated; her experience of the world was extraordinarily limited. For the first time in her life she was a guest within a great house, rather than a servant below its stairs, and it was taking all of her concentration to maintain a level of behavior that would not discredit her mistress. She suspected that her ladyship, whose life had been as correspondingly narrow and protected as her own, was completely at a loss as to how to cope with this outpouring of opinion, not to mention the competitive jealousy so publicly demonstrated by the Hyde Rose Society.

People of Lady Montfort's station might keenly experience similar emotions as those they had just seen betrayed on the terrace, but they simply did not reveal them. In polite society emotion of any kind must be kept firmly under wraps. And there was certainly no public display of self-indulgence tolerated among the Talbots' servants. It simply was not done. The

British middle classes, she decided, were as a foreign people who inhabited a distant land and spoke an entirely different language. But one thing she understood quite unequivocally was that all the quirks and foibles found in human nature were universal. No matter if one was king, commoner, or tinned-beef-stew manufacturer: hopes, fears, and jealousies were felt deeply no matter what background one came from.

"I would say that they are a most unhappy group of people, m'lady—except perhaps for Mr. Urquhart and Mrs. Lovell. And certainly all this gossipy information is rather confusing. To help me make sense of it, I have written up some notes. Shall I read them to you, m'lady?" And she turned as if to leave the room.

"Oh, if only you would, Jackson. Thank goodness for your practical and level head. The more I go through everything I have been told, the more muddled I become. I can't believe we have only been here twenty-four hours, it feels more like as many days." She laughed as she said this; perhaps embarrassed, her housekeeper suspected, that she had succumbed to voicing her own complaints. "I was wondering just now if perhaps we have taken on more than we can manage."

Her ladyship's face was tired and it had occurred to Mrs. Jackson more than once this morning that she seemed almost despondent. On two occasions during their walk to the lake she had noticed that she had looked almost depressed, saddened even. *Something else must have happened that she is not telling me about,* she thought. *She seemed to be coping quite well with all of them last night. Perhaps it's all this talk of war.*

"After luncheon Miss Jekyll will make her getaway. The poor woman will probably never forgive me for involving her in this farce of a symposium. Goodness me, how striving they all are with their desire to compete and be awarded prizes—so unattractive. I was thinking that when Miss Jekyll leaves, this gives us a perfect excuse to go too. Even though Maud—oh my goodness they have got me at it too—*Mrs.* Haldane, has begged me to stay until the end of the week. But the thought of it fills me with dread. I think it best if we call it a day, Jackson, I really do. We can find Mrs. Armitage a post in London quite easily. There is surely no need for us to try to prove that one of these strange people actually murdered Mr. Bartholomew."

Mrs. Jackson, who had been on her way to her room for her notes, stood in the doorway and waited for further instructions, but none came so she said, "Of course, m'lady. I will start packing before you go down to luncheon. Then we will be ready to leave with Miss Jekyll after luncheon."

"And before we have to eat dinner with that dreadful Mr. Haldane." Lady Montfort shuddered and Mrs. Jackson guessed that it was the presence of the master of the house that was making her ladyship want to run for the safety of Iyntwood.

"I am not sure that I can bear any more talk of war in that horribly triumphant way he has. And the sight of his poor drooping wife's anxiety that she might say the wrong thing." Her eyes, as she stared across the room to the tapestry at the far end of the room, were particularly troubled. "I have come across some unpleasant men in my life, Jackson, but no one as despicably coarse as Mr. Haldane. It makes my heart wrench for that wretched woman as I watch her trying to gauge his mood and say the right thing. I wouldn't be surprised if he poisoned Bartholomew. I really wouldn't."

Good grief, thought Mrs. Jackson, *what is she on about? Mr. Haldane is certainly rather uncouth, and he is possibly a bit of a bully to his rather feeble wife. But Mrs. Haldane does not seem to be particularly wretched and her husband provides very lavishly for her.* Nevertheless, she obliged by summing up her thoughts on the master of the house based on the two things she had been told about him.

"He was jealous of his wife's friendship with Mr. Bartholomew, apparently, m'lady, and if we are to go to war, he will probably secure a government contract for his tinned beef now that Mr. Bartholomew is dead and his business in disarray. So Mr. Haldane has most certainly gained by Mr. Bartholomew's death."

"Do you really think so, Jackson? Do you really think he might have killed Bartholomew?" Lady Montfort was sitting very straight in her chair, and she turned her head and fixed her gaze intently on her housekeeper's face as she sought her opinion.

Mrs. Jackson realized that their going or staying depended on her answer. If they left now, she could go back to Iyntwood and get on with her abandoned duties. There was much to do to ready the family for their journey north to Inverness. Certainly Mr. Hollyoak would resent her being absent at such a time, and it was not fair to make him struggle on alone when she had only just returned from her summer holiday. But there again, she was intrigued by this group of ill-assorted people, and she had spent such a pleasant morning renewing her acquaintance with Mr. Stafford, and their most pleasant reunion was perhaps the most puzzling part of the dilemma she faced.

"If Mr. Bartholomew was murdered, m'lady, and we still can't be sure he was, then with what I know at this moment, I would pick Mr. Haldane as my favorite suspect." She said this firmly and met her ladyship's eye as she thought, *You have as good as sealed your fate for the next few days, my girl.*

"Give me your reasons, Jackson. Read me your notes." And Lady Montfort reached for her own leather-bound notebook and searched on the table for her pencil, and Mrs. Jackson walked into her room and returned again with her neatly written thoughts.

"Very well, m'lady. Number one: Mr. Haldane, according to

Mr. Urquhart and Mrs. Lovell, is very jealous of his wife. Mr. Urquhart said she had a close friendship with Mr. Bartholomew, which made her husband extremely angry. And both the butler and Mr. Stafford have said that he is a 'petty domestic tyrant.'" She quoted the last part and watched her ladyship write it down in her notebook.

"And, according to a conversation I had with Mr. Stafford, Mr. Bartholomew's death was most useful to Mr. Haldane's business. He was quite clear on this point." Again she watched her ladyship write this down before she lifted her head. "How would Mr. Stafford know this, do you think, Jackson?"

"He said that when he first started here Mr. Haldane would wander down occasionally to see what Mr. Stafford was doing. He said that Mr. Haldane found the business of making a lake fascinating and that they had one or two conversations about Mr. Haldane's business, and his hope of gaining a government contract for his stew." Mrs. Jackson faltered, having had no reason of her own to doubt Mr. Stafford's opinion.

"I have most definitely been made aware of the bullying. But I had no idea about the business connection."

"Mr. Stafford told me that Mr. Haldane belongs to a group of businessmen whose sole aim is to secure government contracts in the event of there being a European war."

"Mr. Stafford told you all this? My goodness, he is a mine of information. What sort of businesses, did he say?"

"Two of Mr. Haldane's friends make canvas rucksacks, kit bags, and tents, m'lady. Another makes bars of chocolate. Chocolate bars wrapped in tin foil, portable energy, Mr. Stafford says Mr. Haldane called it." Mrs. Jackson laughed at the idea that soldiers on the march would do so much more effectively if they all had bars of chocolate in their pockets.

Lady Montfort evidently saw the funny side of this too, and they both shook their heads at soldiers being rewarded like schoolchildren. "My goodness, what a strange world we live in," said Lady Montfort, her good humor almost restored. "Go on, Jackson, you have been very busy."

"My second suspect is Mr. Wickham. After that scene on the terrace just now, he was visibly angry when his wife carried on in that way about Mr. Bartholomew's roses. She is the worst kind of flirt." Mrs. Jackson thought of all the young and pretty housemaids she had known in her time, and their flirtations with the footmen. There was always one young woman who had to have every man in the servants' hall running after her. Luckily their troublemaking did not last long, and when they had set everyone belowstairs on edge, they went on their way to conquer other households, leaving a wake of ill feeling that took weeks to disappear. She had not been slow to see how often Mrs. Wickham had glanced over to see how her observations were received by Mr. Stafford. "If Mr. Wickham suspected that his wife had a . . . romantic . . ."

"An affair, Jackson, we need to be clear that this young woman might well have had a relationship outside of marriage with Mr. Bartholomew, not just romantic daydreaming and silly flirtations, but an adulterous affair." Mrs. Jackson's eyes strayed to the other side of the room at this uncomfortably plain language.

"Very well, m'lady, an affair, then, with Mr. Bartholomew. Perhaps Mr. Wickham felt that enough was enough and he decided to do away with him. And there is something else that makes me feel that Mr. Wickham does not have a particularly strong grip on reality: his attitude to his roses."

"Oh good heavens, you have hit it bang on the nose as usual." Lady Montfort leaned forward. "These people are completely batty about their roses. Can you believe how competitive and jealous they are? I thought Mr. Wickham was going to curl up and cry when Miss Jekyll praised Golden Girl to the high heavens, after evidently doling out some stringent advice for his hideous Court Scarlet. The only one of them who took Miss Jekyll's criticism of her dreadful roses on the chin was Mrs. Lovell. But go on, Jackson, I interrupted you."

"Not at all, m'lady, you clarified exactly what I was thinking. If Mr. Wickham knew that his wife was making a fool of herself with Mr. Bartholomew, and Mr. Bartholomew's rose is praised as being superior to his, which the entire group of them were saying long before Miss Jekyll's arrival, then all I can think is that there are two reasons why Mr. Wickham would want Mr. Bartholomew out of the way." She paused, somewhat out of breath, and realized that her ladyship was out of the doldrums and was scribbling away in her book with all her customary enthusiasm and energy.

She looked up from her writing and said, "Now then, Jackson, what on earth do you make of Mr. Urquhart's bit of gossip last night that Mrs. Haldane and Miss Lovell were both so infatuated with Mr. Bartholomew that their jealousy made it most uncomfortable for the group when they gathered here?"

Mrs. Jackson turned over several pages to find what she had written. It was not much. But she had felt that Mrs. Lovell seemed to be far more protective toward Mrs. Haldane than envious of her. At breakfast this morning she had expressed approval of her; she was her champion rather than her competitor.

"I am not too sure about that, m'lady. I think Mr. Urquhart might have misinterpreted what he saw. It seems to me that Mrs. Lovell is a very close friend of Mrs. Haldane, and that she dislikes the way her husband condescends to her. Mrs. Lovell strikes me as being a very solid and practical woman; I can't imagine her forming a romantic attachment to a married man. She doesn't appear to have a flighty bone in her body. Whereas I can see that Mrs. Haldane might be easily swayed by another man's attentions, and as for Mrs. Wickham, she is . . ." She stopped, stuck for the word, and Lady Montfort laughed and said, "She is a committed flirt, she simply can't help herself, and I don't think she is particularly bright. It's all emotion and passion with that young woman, very dangerous."

"Yes, m'lady, whereas Mrs. Lovell has her feet firmly on the ground. I like the way she took her criticism of her ugly roses from Miss Jekyll. I liked her dignity." She then repeated her breakfast conversation with Mrs. Lovell and, in particular, how Mrs. Lovell believed that Mrs. Haldane would surprise the world one day with her ability to breed a great rose.

"I see what you mean, Jackson. Well done, you picked up on that one nicely. Yes, perhaps Mr. Urquhart was exaggerating in his opinion of their jealousy. We must bear in mind with this group that what they reveal about themselves and each other is merely their point of view. It is important we rely on our own intuition and observations too. And it is Miss Lovell, by the way, isn't it?"

"I believe it is Mrs. Lovell, m'lady. She was married many years ago and is now a wealthy widow."

Then she glanced at the fob watch she had pinned to her blouse and said, "If I am to pack before luncheon, m'lady, I should start straightaway. And I must remember to tell the butler that I will not be taking tea with them this afternoon."

"Oh, let's give it another day, shall we, Jackson? I mean, after all, what can be so terrible about having dinner with Mr. Haldane?" But as she said this her voice trailed off at the end, and Mrs. Jackson watched her withdraw as if the very thought of Mr. Haldane was more than she could tolerate.

Miss Jekyll left almost immediately after luncheon. Clementine stood in the drive and watched her motor-car disappear down the road at an alarming rate. *Oh dear,* she thought as she turned and walked back into the oppressive gloom of the castle's baronial hall, *I hope I have not ruined a friendship by bringing Miss Jekyll to Hyde Castle.*

Luncheon had been a hurried and joyless affair. The food had been quite delicious, and after her restless night Clementine found she was extraordinarily hungry. But the delights of a delicious cream-of-leek soup had been refused as too rich by Mr. Urquhart, whose happy mood after the results of the rose competition had turned to one of sour irritation as the soup was put before him. He fretted and complained about disorders of the system and plaintively asked the butler to provide an alternative to superbly grilled lamb cutlets. Used to the chatty enjoyment of those gathered around her own table, where it was considered ill mannered even to remark on the food they were eating, it was torture to Clementine to listen to his catalog of likes and dislikes. Mrs. Haldane had evidently guessed that he was behaving poorly in Clementine's eyes because she leaned toward her a little and said, "I am dreadfully afraid that poor Finley is feeling quite unwell today." And Mrs. Wickham, who had heard her remark, chipped in, "He is simply upset because his beloved roses were acknowledged to suffer from leaf wilt. There is nothing more unattractive than a pink rose with sickly yellow leaves." And then she peeked to see if he had heard her.

This exchange had been so unpleasant that Clementine had been unable even to look across the table at Miss Jekyll, who was talking quietly with Mrs. Jackson about the merits of a well-organized cutting garden.

Mr. Wickham had obviously had a falling-out with his wife because he ignored any remark she addressed to him. He ate his meal in silence. Every mouthful was snapped off his fork and it was possible to hear his jaws working away from where Clementine was sitting.

The only person at the table who was at ease was Mrs. Haldane. Clementine wondered if the accusations and brutality that she had heard last night were commonplace in her life. Was what she had heard a habitual disagreement between husband and wife, a pattern established over the years where Mrs. Haldane's response was to sob if her husband criticized her? She knew women who said they employed this tactic to their advantage, but she suspected that Mrs. Haldane was not the type. No, that was not what she had heard; what she believed she had heard was Mr. Haldane being not only verbally but physically cruel to his wife. But one would never guess, looking at this woman in the stark light of day with her friends gathered around her, that she had begged and pleaded with her husband last night and then sobbed in broken despair. Her hostess looked up from her plate and caught her eye and Clementine realized that she had been staring at her and said the first thing that came into her head.

"Is Mr. Haldane interested in roses?" At the mention of her husband's name the woman's eyes darted about the room as if she would find him standing in a dark corner, critically observing her behavior.

"What? Oh n-no, not at all, Lady Montfort. He doesn't have the luxury of time for little hobbies." She laughed, a nervous, joyless sound, and Clementine felt even more awkward and embarrassed. *I seem to be losing my manners completely in this house,* she thought, feeling quite wretched. *I don't think I have any talent for this sort of thing at all.*

Chapter Eleven

It was balm to the soul, Mrs. Jackson decided, to be among working people who offered one another such quiet respect and behaved with such restrained decorum. Mr. Evans ran a well-disciplined servants' hall whose members evidently got on well enough with one another and observed the differences in their rank with good-humored deference. After the butler had introduced her to the senior members of the servants' hall he opened the door of the housekeeper's parlor, where they were to take tea with Mrs. Walker.

"Mrs. Jackson, may I present our housekeeper, Mrs. Walker?" The angular woman, her graying hair pulled into a tight knot stuck through with bent hairpins, rose to her feet and bobbed her head as she regarded Mrs. Jackson with polite but marked curiosity.

"Mrs. Jackson is companion to the Countess of Montfort," Mr. Evans continued rather pompously. "We will not be seeing much of her belowstairs." A self-conscious laugh as if he had secured a prize for them for tea today. "But it is important that you know who she is in case she needs any help from us in making her ladyship's visit here a comfortable and welcoming one." He made a little bow and pulled out a chair, and Mrs. Jackson found herself seated at the tea table, which was laid with pretty china and enough food to feed the entire servants' hall.

There were three kinds of sandwiches, a solid Dundee cake, and jam tarts—an abundant meal indeed even for upper servants, thought Mrs. Jackson as she sipped her tea. They were waited on by the third housemaid, a plain-faced middle-aged village woman who, though lacking the finesse usual in a housemaid to a grand country house, was reasonably deft and well trained in her work.

As Mrs. Jackson had expected, conversation was restricted to the weather and the possibility of war between Germany and Russia.

"I wouldn't presume to give an opinion with what is going on in the world today. I leave that sort of thing to the menfolk and people like the master. But I don't really think these troubles in Europe are our business. Let them all get on with it, I say. We should stay out of it," Mrs. Walker said as she poured tea.

"Perhaps the Russian czar will come to his senses," Mrs. Jackson offered.

"Willy and Nikki," Mrs. Walker continued, referring to the Kaiser and Czar Nicholas as if they were upstairs on the nursery floor of the house, "have always been very jealous of His Majesty. If only the old king were still with us to keep the peace in Europe between his nephews. King Edward would never have put up with this sort of carry-on."

The European crises, summed up in the comfortable parlance of the nursery, where naughty boys were sent to bed without their bread and milk for supper and everyone said their prayers kneeling at the foot of their bed, caused a round of head nodding as sandwiches and cakes were eaten and tea was sipped.

Mrs. Jackson felt that she had bided her time long enough to introduce the age-old discussion that rang out in many a housekeeper's parlor and butler's pantry: that of the problem of finding, and keeping, a good cook.

"Mrs. Haldane keeps a very nice table, Mr. Evans." Mrs. Jackson decided it was time to turn to the subject of Mrs. Armitage. "Your cook must be congratulated. Has she been with you long?"

Mr. Evans turned his dark eyes toward her and gave an ahem sort of cough, as if warning her that this conversation might be kept for later. But Mrs. Jackson was curious to hear if she could what the housekeeper had to say about the sacking of the last cook.

"Mrs. Slocomb is indeed a very capable individual, Mrs. Jackson, and is doing her best to fit into a servants' hall that has been established for many years; she has been with us just a few months," Mrs. Walker said, and glanced across the tea table to the butler, who lowered his head to indicate that he would not take part in this discussion and perhaps the housekeeper shouldn't either. "We are very lucky at Hyde Castle, you see, most of the women servants are about my age." She smiled at the butler, who was at least a dozen years her junior. "But regardless of our ages, we have worked together for many years, so we are like family to each other. Our third housemaid is a cousin of mine, and Mrs. Haldane's personal maid is the eldest sister of one of our gardeners. Charles, the footman, is my sister's son. Such a bright lad with ever such nice manners." She beamed with pride. The footman, Charles, Mrs. Jackson recalled, was a presentable young man, obviously intelligent and determined to do his best.

"Charles could have gone to the grammar school, but there was no money to be had for that kind of an education. But he is a great reader is Charles and he collects stamps, just like His Majesty." She nodded to affirm that her nephew had the same taste in hobbies as the king. "Mr. Urquhart, such a kind gentleman, gives Charles all his stamps from foreign places, so he has a growing collection."

Now that she had opened up on the subject, Mrs. Walker was most informative. "Our previous cook, Mrs. Armitage, was not only a gifted cook, but as calm and unflappable as you could wish for in the kitchen. Unfortunately she no longer works here." And she tucked her chin down into her neck and frowned in disapproval into her teacup.

"That is a shame. I expect she retired?" Mrs. Jackson said, refusing to look at the butler, who sighed rather audibly. But Mrs. Jackson was having none of that; she would not be silenced. *This is my investigation,* she thought, *and if I want to talk to the housekeeper about the sacking of Mrs. Armitage, he can like it or lump it.*

"Oh no, she did not retire, Mrs. Jackson," Mrs. Walker burst out. "She was sacked, and sacked for no good reason. It was a terrible thing. The poor woman was let go without a shilling, except her wages. Mr. Haldane," she practically spat their master's name, "got it into his head that she had poisoned one of his guests and gave her notice. It was a coldhearted and shameful thing to do to a working woman who put her heart and soul into her job." There was a moment of silence and then the butler announced that he would speak by clearing his throat.

"There was no possibility whatsoever that Mrs. Armitage could have accidentally poisoned anyone, Mrs. Jackson. It was thought at the time, not by those of us downstairs, of course, that she had used tainted haddock in the kedgeree she made for breakfast one morning. I have no choice I suppose but to reveal the facts, as they have already been made a subject for discussion." A long-suffering sigh as he ran his hand over his smooth head, and Mrs. Jackson saw Mr. Stafford's perfect imitation of the gesture and had to bite the inside of her lip to avoid laughing. "The haddock arrived the previous day, a beautiful piece it was, and the cook placed it in the new refrigerated storage that Mr. Haldane had installed in the larder last year. And what a useful invention it has proved to be. It prevents the spoilage of both dairy and meat foods most efficiently. Now we really do not want to burden you with the sad business of our last cook's dismissal." He laughed and gave a meaningful look to Mrs. Walker with evident disapproval, which was completely ignored by the housekeeper as she clearly had much more to say on the subject. So he coughed and consulted his waistcoat pocket watch and she obediently rose to her feet with exclamations of things that must be done before dinner and what a treat it had been to meet a companion to a real countess.

Mrs. Walker was so determined to make her feel welcome that she clasped Mrs. Jackson's hand in both of hers and said, "So very nice to meet you, ma'am. Now you know where to find us if you have a spare moment for a chat, and if you should need anything at all just pop down here and ask for me." And with that, she left to go about her working day, leaving Mrs. Jackson and Mr. Evans alone together.

"What a pleasant interlude." The butler smiled at her as he pulled her chair back for her. "Let us take a little walk into the kitchen courtyard so I can help you with your inquiries, before I have to oversee preparations for this evening's dinner."

They stopped on the way to inspect the refrigeration system, in which Mrs. Jackson took a genuine interest as she had heard of the benefits of this innovation and hoped to convince Mr. Hollyoak that he should talk to Lord Montfort about buying one for Iyntwood's kitchens. When Mr. Evans opened the door of the refrigerated pantry to a blast of icy air, she immediately decided to step up all efforts to have a similar model installed belowstairs at Iyntwood.

"My goodness, Mr. Evans, how wonderfully cold it is. Like

many old houses, we have blocks of ice on the larder floors to keep our perishables fresh. This would make things so much easier. How does it run?"

"It is powered by gas, Mrs. Jackson, and that is the extent of my knowledge." He swung the door closed and secured the catch. "Of course Mr. Haldane uses refrigeration in his factories for the meat, which is why we have this wonderful invention. It is a godsend, Mrs. Jackson, a perfect godsend, especially in a summer as warm as the one we are having this year. There is absolutely no doubt in my mind that the haddock Mrs. Armitage used in that kedgeree was as fresh as it could possibly be."

The butler led the way up the main corridor toward the scullery door, which he opened for her.

Once they were outside in the large kitchen courtyard, he quickly ducked around the corner into a covered passageway, which ran between the outer kitchen wall and the entrance to the dairy, where he came to an abrupt halt. And Mrs. Jackson found herself in near darkness, and quite uncomfortably close to the towering figure of the butler.

Why on earth could we not have stayed in the larder and finished our conversation there? she asked herself as she sensed the butler's tall, broad-shouldered frame looming over her in the confined space of the passageway. In order to demonstrate that this secretive meeting was for the butler to give her information, she stepped away from him and walked back to the entrance to the passageway before she spoke, making sure that her voice was neutral and her tone formal. "You mentioned yesterday that you thought the doctor's death certificate was a cooked-up lie. What makes you think this?"

If the butler guessed that looming over her in semidarkness had made her uneasy he gave no sign at all but answered her quite readily, in a low undertone, bending his head toward her ear in such a conspiratorial manner that she felt immensely irritated.

"I think Dr. Arbuthnot was called in to give a death certificate for Mrs. Bartholomew because he is an old friend of Mr. Haldane. It was Dr. Arbuthnot who administered to the first Mrs. Haldane during a very difficult confinement. And it was Dr. Arbuthnot who was so drunk that night that he might have been responsible for the death of both mother and unborn child." In the half-light she sensed that his dark, brooding eyes were fixed on her face, and she felt a little shiver of dislike. *There is something very odd about this man's demeanor,* she thought. This hole-in-the-corner choice of meeting place made her think of furtive scullery maids sneaking out to meet their followers. And she sensed that the butler's choice of this concealed place to talk demonstrated a complete lack of respect and propriety. She felt such distaste for the man that it was probably this that made her sound distinctly sniffy as she asked the butler to continue.

"I believe, though I have no proof, that Mr. Haldane called in a favor when he specifically asked for Dr. Arbuthnot to come to the house when Mr. Bartholomew was found dead. I suspect that Mr. Haldane wanted a verdict of accidental food poisoning so that there would be no further investigation. Now, of course it might have been Mr. Bartholomew's gluttony that killed him; I understand that his health was not particularly good . . ." a pause for effect, "or, that he was murdered by poison by someone staying in the house."

"How did you know his health was not good?"

"Well, I suppose I don't. He was not a particularly active man . . . he rarely moved a muscle if he could help it."

"What kind of man was he?" she asked, having formed many different opinions in the last twenty-four hours. "You say he was a glutton—was he grossly obese?"

"No, he was not obese. On the contrary, he was a nice-looking man, very tall of course, well over six feet and large-framed. In his youth he might have been quite an athlete, but he enjoyed the pleasures of the table and he was no longer an active man, as I have said, so as he approached his middle years he was perhaps—er, softening a little."

He paused again and, annoyed by these long silences, she said, "Yes, please go on." She didn't want him to stop talking, didn't want there to be silence between them in this ill-lit, narrowly confined place.

"He was quite a well-setup man with thick, wavy brown hair that he wore unfashionably long and a luxuriant and well-kept mustache. He was always dressed well, with never a hair out of place . . . a complete gentleman and one who attracted the attention of the ladies," the butler finished with a note of approval. *A well-kept mustache and never a hair out of place does not necessarily mean that Mr. Bartholomew was a gentleman, but it certainly describes a man who would appeal to a certain type of woman,* Mrs. Jackson thought, feeling the same sort of dislike for men who "attracted the attention of the ladies" as she felt toward Mr. Evans.

"Was he pleasant to the staff?" She remembered Mr. Urquhart's remark about pretty maids.

"Oh yes, he had very nice manners. He got on well with everyone"—he cleared his throat—"especially the fairer sex," and a playful little laugh as if she would also find Mr. Bartholomew attractive. Mrs. Jackson felt another stab of dislike. Mr. Haldane might bark at his wife and be a bit of a blustering lout, but he evidently did not fawn over and run after other men's wives.

"And Mr. Haldane, did he get on with Mr. Bartholomew?" She kept her tone cool and neutral.

"Mr. Haldane is unfortunately a very difficult man, Mrs.

Jackson. He is not a very likable individual, not popular—except perhaps with his wife. He married Mrs. Haldane when she was about twenty. She was such a pretty young lady then. Gentle, quiet, and one of the kindest women I know or ever had the privilege of working for. Not a lady by birth, you understand, but a gentlewoman nonetheless." His loyalty to Mrs. Haldane softened the expression on Mrs. Jackson's face for a moment, and it was as if the butler sensed it. He drew nearer and continued softly, "I was working here as a very young second footman when the first Mrs. Haldane died, not long after Mr. Haldane bought the castle. One of the reasons I stayed on was because Mrs. Haldane is such a kind and decent woman."

He was far too close; she could almost feel his breath on her cheek. Reflexively she straightened her back and lifted her hands, palms out, to ward him off. "Would you step back please, Mr. Evans?" And when he complied, "There now, that's better." She turned away from him and walked out from the entrance to the passageway into the courtyard. The sunlight fell on her face and she breathed more easily out in the open space of the yard. Mr. Evans joined her and stood at a respectful distance, his hands at his sides, the picture of the perfect butler. The contrast in his demeanor now that they were no longer in the darkened and cramped space of the passageway was almost absurd. *He just tried it on with me,* thought Mrs. Jackson. *He was testing to see what I would do, what a low trick.* Mr. Evans was the sort of cowardly male who waylaid young housemaids in dark corridors and inched up to them, watching closely to see their reaction so he might take advantage: a light touch to the upper arm, an absentminded pat on the bottom, or perhaps the more tender approach: smoothing a tendril of hair off a young forehead. She stared the butler down with a frown on her face, allowing him to see that she knew his type, that she was neither interested in him nor willing to be the focus of his attentions. It certainly had its effect: he straightened up and took another step backward, his manner immediately deferential. *Ah yes,* thought Mrs. Jackson, *I know your type all right, Mr. Evans, no wonder there are no young maids in this house.*

"Was Mrs. Haldane close to Mr. Bartholomew in a way that would cause her some trouble with her husband?" She didn't really want to ask this question of a man who obviously had no sense of decorum, so she held herself stiffly upright and kept the expression on her face stern.

The butler smiled at her. He had evidently played this game often enough to understand that she was not interested in him, and his tone as he replied was appeasing. "Mrs. Haldane was very fond of Mr. Bartholomew. And perhaps she felt tenderness for him, because he was a genuinely sympathetic man." He said this, she thought, as if emphasizing that he was this sort of man himself. "He was a very different man from her husband, and this is perhaps why Mrs. Haldane sought Mr. Bartholomew's company a little too often. But I can assure you, and as butler I would know, there was nothing improper between the two of them. Unfortunately, Mr. Haldane was obviously quite convinced otherwise. So you can imagine that this gave him a good reason to dislike Mr. Bartholomew, and he made this clear on several occasions. At one time he was so angry with what he perceived was improper conduct between the two of them that he threatened violence to Mr. Bartholomew. Not that anyone in the house was aware of this—their quarrel took place by the old dog kennels." He threw out a long arm and gesticulated with a large, well-kept hand in the direction of the outbuildings on the other side of the kitchen garden that made up the stables and coach house.

"And what about Mrs. Wickham, was she interested in Mr. Bartholomew?"

"Mrs. Wickham naturally admired Mr. Bartholomew, as I said, he was a ladies' man, and you have seen how Mr. Wickham treats her. But there was nothing between them." His voice was quite dismissive and he offered no further comment on the giddy Mrs. Wickham. Which was odd, thought Mrs. Jackson, because Mrs. Wickham's behavior on the terrace that morning would have led anyone to believe that she had cared for Mr. Bartholomew rather too much.

"What can you tell me about Mrs. Lovell?" she asked.

"Mrs. Lovell is a very respectable woman. She is a close and loyal friend to Mrs. Haldane. She has a very calming influence on the group." *So, nothing more than that?* thought Mrs. Jackson. *He has shared so much information about the Haldanes and Mr. Bartholomew and now he clams up about Mrs. Wickham and Mrs. Lovell. Am I being steered to suspect Mr. Haldane of murdering Mr. Bartholomew?*

"And Mr. Urquhart?" She wanted to be done with their interview; even in the open she found the man's manner repellent.

The butler laughed. "Mr. Urquhart is a gentleman of the old school, quite harmless unless you take away his toasted tea cake. And before you ask, I have nothing but the deepest respect for Mrs. Bartholomew." He smiled, showing his large, perfect, and even white teeth, and into her mind sprang the image of the wolf in the fairytale who had waylaid the girl in a dark wood, looming out of the trees to stand too close and offer help.

"Oh really?" she replied coldly. "Now why is that?"

"Mrs. Bartholomew is an intelligent woman. She understood her husband very well, she knew he was harmless, and she managed him with tact and affection. He was lost without her when she went off on her trips."

"So what do *you* think happened here, Mr. Evans, on the day that Mr. Bartholomew died?"

"I wish I knew, Mrs. Jackson, I really do." The butler seemed to exhibit genuine concern now that she had touched on the reason for her questions. "It was a terrible thing to see Mrs. Armitage made a scapegoat in such a cruel way. I know the kedgeree was not spoiled—it could not possibly have been—but as to whether Mr. Bartholomew was murdered by poison, or simply died from a heart attack from his many excesses, it is not possible for me to say, of course. But I certainly had strong suspicions at the time that there was foul play. And Mrs. Armitage was convinced that Mr. Bartholomew was murdered."

Mrs. Jackson thought for a moment or two. From what they had learned so far from both Mr. Urquhart and the butler, there seemed to be motive enough for both Mr. Haldane and Mr. Wickham to have wanted Mr. Bartholomew dead. But she did not take that to mean they had murdered him.

"How did Mrs. Bartholomew react when Mr. Bartholomew involved himself romantically with other women?" she asked, thinking of the fury of women scorned.

"She was rarely here, Mrs. Jackson, when Mr. Bartholomew came to visit. Mrs. Bartholomew was gone for four months out of the year, most years. Her brother is René Barbier, a very well-known horticulturist in France. When she visited Hyde Castle with her husband Mrs. Bartholomew appeared to have a restraining influence where her husband's many little weaknesses were concerned. He adored her, despite his flirtations, and he always behaved himself properly when she was around."

"Thank you, Mr. Evans, you have been most helpful. Lady Montfort would like you to write, to the best of your memory, where everyone was on the morning that Mr. Bartholomew died. Would you include in your list everyone in the house, both upstairs and down? It would be most useful to her." And she walked out into the middle of the courtyard just as Mr. Stafford rounded the corner from the drive.

"Good afternoon, Mrs. Jackson." Mr. Stafford offered the barest nod of his head in greeting to the butler. "The head gardener gave me the key to the orangery and I have been waiting there for you. Did you not get my message?"

"Oh dear," said the butler, smiling at Mrs. Jackson. "I was so wrapped up in our interesting conversation, I quite forgot to pass on Mr. Stafford's invitation to show you and Lady Montfort the orangery. How forgetful of me." And Mrs. Jackson, to her embarrassment and annoyance, blushed as if the time she had spent with the butler had not been quite aboveboard.

Clementine, on her way to the drawing room for tea, said good afternoon to Mrs. Wickham as the young woman came in through the front door of the house. "You must be looking for your companion, Lady Montfort." Mrs. Wickham gave her such a knowing look that Clementine stopped.

"Actually I wasn't looking for Mrs. Jackson," she said, rather puzzled.

Mrs. Wickham's soft girlish pout had quite disappeared; her lips were thin and compressed and her expression conveyed, thought Clementine, that in some way she felt insulted or perhaps slighted. Into her mind came an image of an Anglican missionary that Clementine had met years ago, at the vicarage garden fete, who had talked about "rescuing the unclad and immodest heathen of Africa from godlessness." Her face had worn the same look of disapproval as Mrs. Wickham's did now.

Before Clementine could continue on in to tea, Mrs. Wickham asked, "Is your companion part of your family, Lady Montfort?"

Ah, so it is Mrs. Jackson who has upset this rather ridiculous young woman.

To Lady Montfort's further irritation, Mrs. Bartholomew wandered out of the green salon and strolled across the hall toward the drawing room, where she waited in the doorway, her head turned slightly toward them. Clementine felt a momentary flash of apprehension. She wisely did not reply to the young woman's remark, but waited for more from Mrs. Wickham.

"I am sure it is none of my business . . ." Mrs. Wickham started to backpedal, or at least tried to give the impression that she was doing so. But Clementine decided that there was a point being made here and politely waited to hear what it was.

"I rarely repeat gossip." Clementine smiled. *Why is it that those who enjoy the titillating buzz of rumor always declare their aversion to gossip before they indulge themselves?* "Our fellow guests are rather addicted to a little chinwag now and then, I'm afraid, and they have mentioned that Mrs. Jackson seems to have formed an attachment to Mrs. Haldane's landscape gardener in a surprisingly short time—I passed this off as harmless tittle-tattle, of course."

"Of course," murmured Clementine, glancing at Mrs. Bartholomew, whose head was inclined in their direction, even if she was still facing forward into the drawing room.

"I was in the herb garden just now picking some chamomile for Finley and I was quite surprised to see Mrs. Jackson and Mr. Stafford coming out of the orangery . . . there was something . . . not quite . . ."

Clementine lifted an admonishing hand, and set about putting an end to this unpleasant chatter.

"Mrs. Wickham, how kind of you to take the trouble to tell me this. I can understand your evident concern, but there is absolutely no need to worry yourself. Mr. Stafford is known not only to Mrs. Jackson and Miss Jekyll, but also to me. Lord Montfort and I count him as a friend of the family."

She watched Mrs. Wickham's cheeks redden and her eyes slide away, no doubt searching for an exit; the one into the drawing room was blocked by Mrs. Bartholomew, who made no attempt to move, and Clementine had the corridor to the library and the salon covered.

Mrs. Wickham apologized and said, as the malicious do when they have just tried to cause trouble, that her concern was kindly meant. And Clementine acknowledged her apology with the aloof dignity that her mother-in-law, the dowager Countess of Montfort, would have applauded.

"Will you join us for tea, Mrs. Wickham?" she said in what she hoped was an affable tone of voice.

"Not this afternoon, Lady Montfort. I have a headache." And Mrs. Wickham turned and made for the only exit available to her—the staircase—leaving Clementine perplexed and a little alarmed. It would not help their investigation if the very people they were observing were also observing them—and, what was more, discussing them. They must be more discreet with their investigations.

Mrs. Bartholomew, still standing in her drawing-room door, said, "Mrs. Wickham is by far the worst of the gossips here, Lady Montfort; I can assure you of that. And as for 'forming attachments,' that young woman is hardly beyond reproach." They walked together into the drawing room, to be welcomed by Mrs. Haldane, who patted the place next to her in direct invitation to Lady Montfort. And Clementine was immediately aware that the group was a little less tense than they had been yesterday. *Perhaps now that Miss Jekyll has left, and their competition concluded, they are falling back into the comfortable pattern found particularly among old friends.* She took her place next to Mrs. Haldane and accepted a cup of tea and a thinly sliced cress sandwich.

"Please tell me about your society, Mrs. Haldane; I understand from Mr. Urquhart you are the founder. When did you decide to start the Hyde Rose Society?"

Mrs. Haldane set down her teacup in its saucer on the side table next to the sofa they were sitting on, and turned her full attention to her. "I do hope I can persuade you into joining our group, Lady Montfort," she said. "It would be such an honor." And receiving no immediate response, she continued, "Well, we founded our society in the year dear King Edward came to the throne in 1901. It's hard to believe we have been going strong for thirteen years, isn't it, Amelia?" She turned to her friend, who nodded as she bit into a scone heavily laden with jam.

"Actually, it was Amelia and I who founded the society together that spring. We were in her pretty garden and she told me that she was trying to produce a tea rose of perfect pink."

Mrs. Lovell's well-upholstered shoulders shook with good-natured laughter. "And I am still trying to accomplish that, Maud. It is not really the success of producing a perfect rose, it is the process of trying to do so that I find the most rewarding aspect of rose breeding," she explained, wiping jam off her upper lip with her napkin. "It is such an absorbing hobby."

"You are very close, Amelia, very close." Mrs. Haldane patted her friend's hand. "Our next member to join us was Rupert Bartholomew. We met him through the Royal Horticultural Society." Her eyes misted a little at the memory. "Dear Rupert was so enthusiastic to join us. Do you remember how serious our first meetings were, Amelia? He would set us such tasks. And whenever he could spare the time he helped us write up our bylaws and set ourselves up so that we would be recognized

146

by the Royal Horticultural Society and become a proper organization with licenses and everything." She nodded proudly, and Mrs. Bartholomew left her chair by the window and took one next to Mrs. Lovell. "Of course Rupert was still a bachelor then, struggling to understand the business of breeding roses. It wasn't until two years later that he met our dearest Albertine. Where was that, dear, it was in France, wasn't it?"

"Yes, it was in France. Rupert came to visit the Barbier brothers; my two uncles. He wanted to plant a rose garden of old Bourbon Roses. That is how I met him." Mrs. Bartholomew smiled and shook her head in the pleasant recollection of old memories. "All those many wonderful years ago."

The group threatened to turn a little weepy at this point; Mrs. Haldane produced a delicate lace handkerchief, and Mrs. Lovell cleared her throat. Mrs. Bartholomew, whose eyes had filled with tears as she recalled her first meeting with her husband, patted Mrs. Haldane's hand in a rallying sort of way. Clementine recalled them to task with tactful determination.

"But what a simply beautiful rose he created. Golden Girl, such a very pretty name." She looked in turn to each of the women sitting in front of her and wondered which of them was Mr. Bartholomew's golden girl. Was it his wife, the dear friends Mrs. Lovell and Mrs. Haldane, or was it the young woman with the yellow curls upstairs in her room with a headache?

"And Mr. Bartholomew's other rose, what a perfectly pristine white: no hint of pink or yellow, such a difficult thing to achieve. Mrs. Bartholomew, is it really without a name? I expect you will come up with something quite lovely." Mrs. Bartholomew turned a brilliant smile on Clementine and her eyes, which had clouded with tears, brightened, making her look in that moment quite incredibly beautiful.

"Thank you, Lady Montfort, how generous of you to compliment the white rose. Golden Girl is a ravishing rose, but the white is my favorite too." *What a pleasant change,* thought Clementine, *to meet such appreciation in a wife for her husband's efforts. What a contrast to Mrs. Wickham's cruel little barbs to her husband and Mrs. Haldane's woebegone passivity.*

"In fact," Mrs. Bartholomew went on, "the five of us . . ." Having completely regained her composure she nodded to Mrs. Lovell, Mrs. Haldane, and Mr. Urquhart, who had finished fussing over his tea and was now enjoying an apricot jam tart cut into tiny pieces, and then she twisted in her chair to look for Mr. Wickham, who at this hour of the day was usually rustling through the evening newspapers to glean more news of the war in Europe. But neither of the Wickhams was taking tea with them today. "Well, anyway, all of the Hyde Rose Society are going to put their heads together to help me with a name for the white rose. We have to come up with something *ravissant,* don't we?" She looked around the group and was answered by a trill of happy laughter from Mrs. Haldane and smiles from Mrs. Lovell.

They are really quite nice when they are not quarreling in competition, thought Clementine, as Mr. Urquhart piped up, "We might even consult Henry Bennett, perhaps?" and when they laughed and exclaimed, "On no account," he good-naturedly joined in the merriment.

"And when did you join the society, Mr. Urquhart?" Clementine asked, keeping careful track of the chronology of their membership.

Mrs. Bartholomew said, "Why, the year Cicero won the Epsom Derby, of course! Rupert made a packet on that race. And afterwards . . ." She turned to Mr. Urquhart, who willingly took up the story.

"Afterwards Rupert invited me to dinner to celebrate, and that was when he suggested I join forces with all the leddies here. Of course my health was better in those days, easily nine years ago now." He shook his head at distant but happy memories.

"And then Mr. Wickham joined you," Clementine prompted, her eyes on Mrs. Lovell's face. She was rewarded for her vigilance by Mrs. Lovell's rather resigned nod at the mention of Mr. Wickham.

"Yes, Clive joined us the year afterwards. He wrote a formal letter of application and of course we were delighted to increase our number, especially to include a man of his experience. Clive has kept us to task all these years. Otherwise we might forget ourselves and have too much fun," said Mrs. Lovell. She smiled as she said this, and Mrs. Haldane fluttered in evident embarrassment.

Aha! I thought so, Clementine thought. *Mr. Wickham is not really part of this group of old friends at all.*

"And, Mrs. Bartholomew?" she said, turning back to Albertine, who was sipping tea. "Surely you will take your husband's place in the society."

The Frenchwoman shook her head to a chorus of "Of course she will" from the group.

"I am afraid not, Lady Montfort, although I have come to regard the tea rose a little more favorably thanks to the Hyde Society, and of course I will always visit my friends here, especially for their annual rose symposium. But now Rupert has gone I will return to my family in France and help them with the business of introducing new plant specimens into Europe from the Orient." Amid sighs and protestations she shook her head as she smiled at her old friends.

"Dear Albertine," said Mrs. Haldane, "you are *almost* one of us—and will always be an honorary member." Which Clementine thought surprising as it clearly stated that Mrs. Bartholomew was the wife of an erstwhile society member and not formally recognized as part of the group yet. Was there jealousy here toward the wife of her old friend?

Chapter Twelve

Mrs. Jackson returned from her meeting with Mr. Stafford in time to help Lady Montfort dress for dinner. As she began the business of putting up her ladyship's hair she recounted her conversation with Mr. Evans without revealing his unpleasant behavior.

"I think we are on the right track, Jackson; it is evident that Mr. Haldane believed he had reason to hate Mr. Bartholomew. Everything we have learned from Mrs. Haldane's guests is borne out by the butler. Now, did you ask Mr. Evans where everyone was on the morning that Mr. Bartholomew was in the dining room eating all the kedgeree?"

"I did, m'lady. And he obligingly wrote up a list for me almost immediately—but he asks that we remember that it was nearly six months ago and we are relying on his memory."

"Yes, I understand. Will you read it to me, please?"

Mrs. Jackson put down the hairbrush, pulled a single page from her pocket written closely in a schoolboy hand, and read aloud.

"'The servants were all about their work as usual. Mrs. Walker the housekeeper was supervising the maids as they put the house to rights and took up breakfast trays to Mrs. Haldane, Mr. Urquhart, and Mrs. Wickham. Mrs. Haldane's maid was with her mistress. The cook and her kitchen maids were of course all downstairs, and only the butler and Charles, the footman, were in attendance upstairs.

" 'Mr. Bartholomew ate breakfast alone in the dining room at eight o'clock, waited on by the first footman and the butler. Mr. Evans left the dining room at one point, he can't remember at what time, to fetch fresh coffee. Mr. Bartholomew finished his first plate of kedgeree and then helped himself to a second. Halfway through he complained of stomach pains and said something about indigestion. He mentioned as much to Charles, who reported this at the inquest. Mr. Bartholomew only ate a little of his second helping of kedgeree but he drank two cups of coffee, both of them poured by Charles from the fresh pot brought up by the butler. Mr. Bartholomew left the dining room at a quarter to nine and said he was going to 'walk it off.'

"At nine o'clock Mrs. Lovell joined Mr. Wickham in the dining room and they had their breakfast together. They arrived in the dining room some fifteen minutes after Mr. Bartholomew left for his morning walk. Mr. Wickham ate bacon and eggs and drank tea. Mrs. Lovell drank two cups of coffee, from the same pot enjoyed by Mr. Bartholomew, and ate a substantial breakfast of bacon, eggs, and toast. There was no kedgeree left, the butler remembered Mrs. Lovell remarking on it. Mr. Evans was quite sure that the remains of Mr. Bartholomew's breakfast had been removed to the kitchen when he left the dining room well before Mrs. Lovell and Mr. Wickham came down to their breakfast. The leftover kedgeree on Mr. Bartholomew's plate was scraped into the scullery slop bucket for the pigs. Mr. Evans was clear on that point because after Mrs. Armitage was accused of accidentally poisoning Mrs. Bartholomew he made a point of checking with the scullery maid."

"How very thorough of him," murmured her ladyship.

"What about Mr. Haldane, did he join them? Where did he eat his breakfast?"

Mrs. Jackson put the butler's page of notes back in her pocket and picked up the hairbrush. "In Manchester, m'lady. He had spent the week at his manufactory—he has a service flat near to his office where he stays when he is there on business. So it seems he was nowhere near the house on the morning that Mr. Bartholomew died. Mr. Haldane left the house four days before Mrs. Haldane's friends arrived, so he had no opportunity to see any of them. He returned to the house at half past eleven on the morning that Mr. Bartholomew died, just half an hour before Mr. Bartholomew was found in the orangery."

"Mr. Haldane was not in the house?" Lady Montfort turned her head, scattering hairpins in all directions, and Mrs. Jackson bent down to pick them up off the floor.

"Don't worry about those, Jackson, use some more . . . here . . . there are plenty of them." She swept her hand across the surface of the dressing table and pushed some toward her. *She is annoyed that Mr. Haldane was not in the house when Mr. Bartholomew was poisoned,* thought Mrs. Jackson.

"So, Mr. Haldane could not have poisoned the kedgeree if he wasn't in the house."

"Perhaps he was, though, m'lady. Perhaps he came to the house earlier, unobserved, and hid somewhere and then poisoned the kedgeree when no one was around to see him do it. Before staging his return to the house at about the time Mr. Bartholomew died."

"My goodness, Jackson, where do you come up with these astonishing ideas? You are quite right, of course, he might have done it that way."

"It was not me, m'lady, who came up with that one, it was Mr. Stafford. I visited the orangery with him while you were taking tea. The building is a good distance from the house, but it has been kept locked up ever since the death of Mr. Bartholomew. The head gardener only goes in there to water the trees and sweep up a bit. Mr. Haldane says no one must go in there at all, ever again. Except of course for the gardeners." Lady Montfort turned her head so quickly to look at her housekeeper that hairpins went flying again.

"*Really*, Jackson? So Mr. Haldane has forbidden entry into the orangery and it has been kept locked up all this time." Her ladyship's face expressed only the greatest hope that Mr. Haldane was culpable in some way. And Mrs. Jackson felt the slightest little jab of concern that her ladyship's thinking might be prejudiced against Mr. Haldane.

"Mr. Stafford has Mr. Clark, the head gardener's key and his permission to visit it, m'lady. He told Mr. Clark that he needs to create a view of the new lake from the orangery. Perhaps you would like to walk down there tomorrow morning, after breakfast?"

"Yes, I would, Jackson. Let us both take breakfast together downstairs and then we can walk down to the orangery. And now when you have finished my hair I must go down to dinner. Are you planning on joining us?" There was a momentary silence before Mrs. Jackson said that under the circumstances she thought not.

"I have told the butler that I will not join you all for dinner, if that is all right with you, m'lady. I would like to write up my notes of the happenings today." After her busy day with Mrs. Haldane's guests and her servants, Mrs. Jackson felt quite worn out. The thought of a quiet meal in her room and a good book was irresistible.

To say that any meal eaten in this house is a pleasant experience would be a colossal inaccuracy, thought Clementine. Mrs.

Haldane had attempted to seat her guests around the table in some sort of semblance of precedence. And Clementine, to her dismay, found herself on her host's right, with Mr. Wickham on her left. Mrs. Wickham had sent an apology that she would not join them for dinner as she was a little under the weather, and Mr. Urquhart, who obviously had experience of eating dinner with Mr. Haldane, was taking a light dinner on a tray in his room.

Conversation was stilted, perhaps because of their host's pre-occupied presence at the top of the table and the diners' reliance on the Englishman's favorite topic for any uncomfortable social event: the weather. Clementine noticed with frank relief that any talk of war was evidently taboo. Her main concern was that Althea had now arrived safely home, and she would assume that she had, unless she heard otherwise from her husband.

As the remains of a splendid summer pudding were taken away and Mrs. Haldane rose to her feet to invite the women to the Salon Vert so that Mr. Haldane and Mr. Wickham might enjoy their port, her husband left his place at the head of the table and said abruptly, "My dear, a moment if you please," and left the dining room through the door that gave access to the back stairs.

A tense, but obedient, Mrs. Haldane said she would meet her guests in the Salon Vert, and Mrs. Lovell, Mrs. Bartholomew, and Clementine left the room by the door leading into the hall.

"I wonder what *he* wants," Mrs. Lovell said and hesitated as if she would go back to join her friend. And from the other end of the corridor between the green-baize door to the back stairs and the service door to the dining room the aggressive tones of Mr. Haldane could be heard berating his wife.

The women hurried away to the salon, Mrs. Bartholomew

stern-faced and grim, and Mrs. Lovell casting a look over her shoulder that expressed her silent concern for her friend. Neither of them said a word, but Clementine suspected that when Mrs. Haldane joined them in the salon she would be a nervous and stuttering wreck. And so she was.

"Roger will not be joining us after port," she said to Clementine, as if she felt the need to justify her husband's absence. "He is extremely b-busy at the moment."

"How about a nice game of bridge?" ventured Clementine, hoping against hope that they all knew how to play what had become her favorite game. She was to be disappointed.

"I am most terribly sorry, but I don't play, and I don't think Albertine particularly enjoys cards." Mrs. Haldane was almost tearful at having to deny a countess an evening of the fashionable card game. "You must forgive us, Lady Montfort, we are so very provincial."

Dinner with the uncouth Mr. Haldane had evidently been too much for Mrs. Bartholomew. "If you don't mind," she said, "I will retire early; it has been a long day and somewhat tiring." Mrs. Haldane immediately rushed to console: "Of course we understand, how very th-th-thoughtless of us, it must be so hard to be here so soon after . . ."

But with her customary poise Mrs. Bartholomew said apologies were completely unnecessary, that she had been made to feel most welcome by the rosarians. She wished them all a pleasant evening and left the three of them alone together.

"Poor Albertine," said Mrs. Lovell. "Rupert's death has been a terrible blow to her; she struggles with the loss daily and selflessly still insists on contributing to the society, so I am afraid we selfishly forget she grieves most sadly for Rupert. Maud dear, why don't you play for us?"

But Mrs. Haldane, usually so compliant and eager to please her friends, said perhaps not, she was too tired tonight. And

Clementine, remembering the unkindness she had suffered at her husband's hands last night and his continued bullying outside the dining room, felt a moment of furious outrage toward the monster this poor woman was married to.

They sat on together as an hour ticked away and until all small talk among them was exhausted, and then to Clementine's relief, as she was practically nodding off her in her chair, Mrs. Haldane and Mrs. Lovell decided to call it a night.

As they rose to their feet to say good night and Mrs. Haldane dismissed the footman, there came a tremendous commotion from inside the conservatory. The heavy outer door to the terrace was thrown back with a tremendous bang and what sounded like a herd of large animals began crashing around among the wicker chairs in the center of the glass room. Clementine ran to the closed double doors to the conservatory and looked through its glazed panes into the half-dark of the room. She could just discern the figure of a woman collapsed among the disarranged furniture.

Mrs. Lovell was the first to push past her to open the door, crying out as she did so, "What on earth?" in her deep voice, loud with alarm.

For there, collapsed among the tipped-over chairs, was a disheveled Mrs. Wickham, her golden curls in tangled disarray. "Help me," Mrs. Wickham cried out as she tried to struggle to her feet, looking over her shoulder back into the night through the open conservatory door. "Oh please . . . help me." And she slumped forward into Mrs. Lovell's arms, howling like a terrified child.

"What has happened to you, Dorothy?" There was no answer from the sobbing Mrs. Wickham as she took shelter in Mrs. Lovell's embrace. "For heaven's sake, dear, stop crying and tell me what has happened." But Mrs. Wickham's sobs only became more desperate, and to Clementine's ears they sounded like the hysterical cries of a woman on the edge of losing reason.

Mrs. Lovell, still supporting the young woman in her arms, said, "Ring for the footman so he can help us get her into the salon." Despite her solid build and broad shoulders it was clear that she was having some difficulty in keeping Mrs. Wickham upright. "Come on now, Dorothy, you managed to run in here, surely if I help you, you can walk into the salon. We can't stay out here in the dark."

Mrs. Haldane, standing close enough for Clementine to see her expression, caught her eye and looked away, clearly humiliated by this display of hysteria in her conservatory. "What can have happened to her?" Clementine asked and was astounded to hear Mrs. Haldane say under her breath, "She has got herself into some scrape or other, I expect. She is *incorrigible*."

"Maud!" Mrs. Lovell's voice, uncharacteristically sharp with impatience, brought Mrs. Haldane to her senses. "Will you please call for the footman—now?"

Clementine reached out a hand and switched on the overhead electric light and the scene before them leaped into detail in its glare: Mrs. Haldane surrounded by overturned chairs and scattered cushions with her hand over her mouth and Mrs. Lovell bent awkwardly and holding in her arms what might have been taken, at first glance, as a bundle of last week's washing, until Mrs. Wickham lifted a dirty, tear-stained face from under the lee of Mrs. Lovell's shoulder.

"You had better ask him to bring some brandy too, Mrs. Haldane." It was quite evident to Clementine that Mrs. Wickham's plight was a good deal more serious than a mere scrape.

"No! Do not call anyone . . . anyone at all!" Mrs. Wickham's alarm was so great and her appearance so disturbing that Mrs. Haldane, who had been standing stock-still, her face blank with astonishment, was roused to action. "I will go to the drawing room and bring brandy myself."

"And I will help you take her into the salon, Mrs. Lovell." Clementine slipped her arm around the young woman's waist as Mrs. Lovell disengaged Mrs. Wickham's arms from around her neck and turned the still sobbing young woman to support her left side. With Mrs. Wickham slumped between them they managed to get her through the conservatory door and into the salon.

"Maud, please put down that cushion. I can manage now. Just go and get some brandy," Mrs. Lovell commanded as she sat the distressed young woman down in a corner of the sofa.

For the first time since Mrs. Wickham had crashed into their evening they were able to completely take in the extent of her alarming disarray.

Her hair was tangled and halfway down her back, her tear-stained face was blotched and bruised, and the lacy bodice of her evening dress torn to reveal livid red marks on the exposed fair skin of her neck and back.

Mrs. Lovell almost recoiled from this desperate sight before she recovered her sense of compassion. She turned to Clementine. "The poor thing is quite horribly hurt. Oh my goodness, would you just look at her dress? Quickly, Lady Montfort, I think she is going to faint!"

Clementine pushed forward an ottoman and carefully lifted the young woman's legs up onto it so that she did not pitch forward onto the floor. She noticed that her pale blue satin shoes were scuffed and dirty and that as she slumped back against the sofa cushions, the remains of what had once been both an expensive and lovely necklace was dangling from her neck, still dropping the occasional pearl onto her lap. Despite the still warmth of the night she was shivering, and Clementine heard her teeth chattering as Mrs. Wickham turned her eyes, dark with fear, to the door leading into the conservatory as if she believed that at any moment someone would come bursting in on them.

"You are safe, Mrs. Wickham. It's all right now, you are quite safe," Clementine said, trying to reassure the frightened young woman, and then to Mrs. Lovell: "She is in shock, her hands are like ice." Clementine chafed Mrs. Wickham's limp hands and looked across the room to Mrs. Haldane, who had returned with a brandy decanter and glasses on a tray.

"Wrap her in this," Mrs. Haldane said as she slipped her evening shawl from her shoulders, and Clementine draped the heavy length of embroidered silk around Mrs. Wickham's shivering shoulders, covering the ragged tear at the neck of her evening dress and the ugly marks on her back that were already darkening to bruises.

Mrs. Haldane took the stopper out of the decanter and with an unsteady hand started to lift it from the tray. Clementine crossed the room and took it from her, taking the opportunity to say, "Whatever happened to her out there involved considerable violence. I think you should ask your butler and footman to search the grounds." Which caused Mrs. Haldane's eyes to widen in alarm as she cast a look of utter dismay toward the immobile figure on the sofa. "Perhaps now, Mrs. Haldane, before it is too late?" Clementine pursued. "Mrs. Wickham has clearly been the victim of a vicious attack."

Mrs. Lovell waved Clementine over and took the brandy glass from her in her right hand, slipping her left arm behind Mrs. Wickham's shoulders. Mrs. Wickham winced as she was helped to sit forward. "Take a tiny sip, my dear, just a little one. There you are, now. Poor thing, she is so cold. Come on, another sip—that's the girl. There now, that's better." Although Mrs. Lovell's tone was solicitous, Clementine noticed that her expression was speculative as she coaxed the young woman to drink the brandy. Mrs. Wickham sipped, coughed, sipped again, and then lifted her tear-streaked and dirty face. "Yes, yes, much better, her color is not quite as bad." Mrs. Lovell cupped Mrs. Wickham's hands around the brandy glass. "There, sip that slowly, and now, my dear, you had better tell us what happened."

There was a considerable pause as they waited for Mrs. Wickham to bring herself under enough control that she could speak. Eventually she lifted her head and glanced again toward the conservatory before she began.

"I was attacked," Mrs. Wickham said and dipped her head to weep some more.

"So it would seem, but who attacked you?" Mrs. Lovell looked over the young woman's bowed head to Mrs. Haldane, her eyebrows raised, her head inclined.

"I saw no one, no one at all," cried the girl in great distress, and Mrs. Lovell shook her head at Mrs. Haldane, not in disagreement, thought Clementine, but in incredulity.

"So you were outside *alone* in the garden when this happened?" Mrs. Lovell asked and glanced up again to Mrs. Haldane.

Mrs. Wickham must have caught some of the disbelief in her voice because she said in a low, reluctant voice, "I was walking alone in the garden—and then someone, I don't know who, came up behind me and I was thrown down on the floor." The brandy had restored a little color to her face, but her pupils were still dilated with fear. *This young woman has had the most terrible time of it,* thought Clementine, *and these two are still behaving like cross spinster aunts as if she has done something foolish.*

"Are you quite sure you did not see who it was, Dorothy?"

She might as well have said, "Oh really, you must take me for a complete fool," thought Clementine as the expression on Mrs. Lovell's concerned face turned from sympathy to evident disbelief. *Does this young woman make a habit of wandering the grounds alone at night?* was all Clementine could arrive at, judging by Mrs. Lovell's doubtful expression.

"It wasn't . . . ?" Mrs. Lovell started to ask and then compressed her lips in tight disapproval. She turned her head to Mrs. Haldane, who was still rooted to the spot by the brandy decanter. "She is clearly frightened out of her wits and most horribly hurt . . ." she said to her friend, who nodded her concern. "I can't imagine what can have happened . . . she has certainly been given a very bad time of it. Perhaps we had better call Dr. Arbuthnot?"

"No!" cried Mrs. Wickham. "There is no need, I will be all right in a moment, I am not *that* hurt." And Mrs. Lovell nodded her understanding. "If you think you do not need a doctor, Dorothy, then we will not call one."

Clementine remembered Mrs. Haldane's initial reaction to Mrs. Wickham's distress, that she was "incorrigible," until the extent of her hurt and fear were made apparent.

They are not surprised she was outside alone in the garden at this hour of night, she realized, *but they are as horrified as I am by her appearance and what has evidently happened to her.*

"What did you see, dear?" Mrs. Haldane finally asked, her face expressing concern—possibly to what she might be told.

"It was dark; I couldn't see. They came up from behind." And to Clementine's surprise, Mrs. Haldane's tense face relaxed and she quickly looked away.

"They? How many were there?" Mrs. Lovell asked, pulling back from the young woman so she could look into her face.

"Just one, I think. I couldn't tell. He, she, they—I don't know." Her voice was so hoarse from her earlier bout of hysteria that Mrs. Wickham could now speak only in the barest whisper. "I couldn't see anything. But someone threw something over my head and knocked me to the floor. I raised my head to cry out for help and I was struck and kicked, hard, several times, so I lay as quiet as I could, facedown on the floor."

There were exclamations of shock from both Mrs. Haldane and Mrs. Lovell, all expressions of disbelief now gone.

"But did you hear anything?" Clementine could not contain herself; Mrs. Lovell and Mrs. Haldane were asking all the wrong questions.

"Yes, I heard footsteps running away." Mrs. Wickham bent her head and tears slid from the corners of her eyes onto the silk cushions of the sofa.

"Light footsteps, heavy footsteps? Do you think it was more than one person?" Clementine pursued.

Mrs. Wickham lifted her head and gazed at her vacantly for a moment. "No, it was just one person; my head was wrapped up in my shawl. That is all I know." She lifted a hand to wipe away the tears; her eyes were glazing with exhaustion.

"And where were you when this happened?" Clementine asked, and Mrs. Wickham muttered indistinctly, "I was in the garden—near to the shrubbery."

Judging by the genuinely puzzled expression on Mrs. Lovell's face, it was clear that she was now taking Mrs. Wickham's unknown attacker quite seriously. *Why on earth had she doubted the veracity of her story before?* Clementine wondered, and consciously transferred her attention from the victim on the sofa to the two older women in the room.

"Could she have surprised some burglars on the grounds?" Mrs. Lovell turned to her friend, who was sitting silently in a chair by the door.

Mrs. Haldane lifted her head and looked straight into her friend's face. "Yes," she faltered, and then as if more certain: "Of course, Amelia, that is what probably happened. She evidently surprised intruders. Oh, poor Dorothy, how frightened you must have been." Mrs. Haldane looked almost relieved, grateful even, that perhaps Mrs. Wickham had come across a group of house burglars.

What sort of idiocy is this? Clementine asked herself in exasperation as she observed this exchange. Had Mrs. Haldane guessed who might have harmed this young woman and was hoping perhaps that the victim had not recognized her attacker? Her mind rapidly replayed the events of the night from the moment Mrs. Wickham had burst into the conservatory, scattering chairs and calling out for help. Did Mrs. Haldane believe it might have been her husband who had gone out into the night and found the lonely Mrs. Wickham and forced his attentions on her and when she resisted had done this? She heard Mrs. Haldane's wretched cries of the night before as she stared across the salon at the anxious face of her hostess. *I really must pull myself together and pay attention to what is actually going on here and not give way to drama.*

"I will ring for Evans to take the menservants to look around outside," said Mrs. Haldane.

"No, do not ring for *anyone*." Mrs. Wickham for the first time spoke without hesitation, her voice surprisingly firm, and she pulled out her handkerchief and dried her wet cheeks; the brandy had evidently helped her to pull herself together.

"But why were you alone outside at this time of night, Mrs. Wickham?" Clementine asked, trying to sound concerned as she remembered the pert behavior of this young woman earlier that day when she had felt the need to point out Mrs. Jackson's unchaperoned trip to the orangery in the broad light of day with an old family friend. She saw Mrs. Lovell's arm close protectively around the young woman's shoulders, as if she need not answer this intrusive question.

Mrs. Wickham blew her nose on her handkerchief. It was quite clear she was thinking carefully about how best to answer this question.

"I went for a walk in the grounds before bed to clear my head. It is such a warm night and my room felt rather stuffy."

"And where did you go? Tell us exactly," Clementine pursued.

"Through the shrubbery to the croquet lawn and back again . . . to the rose garden, which is where I was attacked."

"You were attacked in the rose garden?" Clementine asked.

There was no answer from Mrs. Wickham—she had started to cry again.

"And you saw no one, no one at all," Mrs. Lovell interrupted with this statement, making Clementine wonder if the kindly Mrs. Lovell was forestalling more answers to nosy questions.

"Someone came up behind me and threw something over my head and pushed me to the ground."

"There you are—she ran into intruders!" Mrs. Lovell turned to Mrs. Haldane, who nodded.

Mrs. Wickham is changing her story, Clementine thought. *Why is she so reluctant to say where she was?*

"I am ringing for the butler now; of course we must investigate, dear." Mrs. Haldane's hand was already on the bell pull.

Evans responded to Mrs. Haldane's summons almost immediately. "Mrs. Wickham ran into some intruders outside in the garden, Evans, please take Charles and the hall boy out to check as quickly as you can. I think it would be a good idea to search thoroughly throughout the grounds and not just the gardens." Mrs. Haldane's voice was firm and, for the first time since Clementine had come to the house, she was very much in control. "And you had better tell Mr. Haldane what has happened."

The butler looked across to Mrs. Wickham on her sofa as if he was trying to ascertain the exact level of her distress and its possible causes.

"Certainly, madam, but Mr. Haldane is working in his study and expressly forbade us to interrupt him; perhaps I should investigate first and then report back to him?"

Mrs. Lovell's voice rang out from the sofa: "Evans, you must tell Mr. Haldane what has happened immediately and then find Mr. Wickham and ask him to come to us here." She glanced at Clementine and said, more to herself than to her, "If he is capable of giving her comfort, poor little thing." She gently smoothed Mrs. Wickham's tangled hair and eased her back into the cushions of the sofa, displaying, thought Clementine, genuine compassion toward the young woman whose face was still slack with shock.

The butler bowed his head in acknowledgment of his quest and left the room. Mrs. Haldane, having judged it was safe to leave Mrs. Wickham sipping her brandy on the sofa, joined her friend on the other side of the room where they discussed in hushed tones the increasing numbers of men who were tramping the countryside looking for work.

"They turn up at the kitchen door and ask if they can cut wood for a free meal . . ." Mrs. Haldane reported with considerable resentment. "The other day Reverend Price told me that several men had come to the vicarage asking for food in return for a day's labor. He said one of them was a giant of a man, practically dressed in rags."

Clementine bent over the back of Mrs. Wickham's sofa and asked as matter-of-factly as she could, "So your attacker knew who you were, Mrs. Wickham?"

Surprised, the young woman lifted her head and before she could stop herself said, "Yes."

"Not a tramp, then?" Clementine asked.

"I don't know, it might have been. No, probably not."

"But your attacker was a man?" Clementine watched the young woman's careful expression as she weighed up the significance of her question.

"All I know is that whoever it was was strong enough to throw me to the ground, and when I lifted my head . . . hit and kicked me with considerable force."

But earlier you said you were pushed to the floor, so you can't have been in the garden, Clementine remembered.

From across the salon the murmured voices of Mrs. Haldane and Mrs. Lovell could still be heard discussing the problems of lawless vagrants wandering the countryside.

". . . And they tramp from village to village to steal food or beg at cottage doors and terrorize women . . ." Mrs. Lovell poured herself another brandy.

"They should put them all in the workhouse . . ." Mrs. Haldane added, her pale blue eyes wide with indignation.

Clementine had no intention of joining this unenlightened conversation about the plight of the indigent. There was clearly no more information to be had from Mrs. Wickham who, having finished her brandy, was now half asleep in her corner of the sofa.

She walked through the open door into the conservatory and switched off the electric light. Closing the outer door to the terrace, she stood and watched through its glass-paned walls the lights bobbing around on the lawn and in the shrubbery. Mr. Evans and the menservants were searching the grounds, but she guessed they would find no one out there.

If Mrs. Wickham had taken dinner in her room and then gone for a solitary evening stroll in the pleasant night air before turning in, then why was she dressed in a beautiful and expensive evening dress and wearing satin shoes? Clementine, watching the activity outside, remained immersed in her

TESSA ARLEN

thoughts. Mrs. Wickham's account of what had happened to her was not completely accurate. But someone had attacked her and it was unlikely that it had been a tramp. Men who had no work, no home, and little to eat did not ramble through country-house gardens and attack and rob defenseless women, and if they found the courage to do so would have taken her expensive necklace from her, not broken it, spraying pearls in all directions.

The subdued murmur of female voices in the salon was interrupted by Mr. Haldane as he burst into the room, a cigar clamped between his teeth and his face brick-red from generous libations of port following his roast beef at dinner. He glared around the room as he growled questions at the three women sitting together in silence.

Concealed in the unlit conservatory, behind the stout trunk of a young date palm, Clementine drew near to the salon door so she could hear what was being said without revealing her presence. She had no wish to be in the same room as her host because she did not trust herself to speak civilly to him.

Mr. Haldane's unrelenting questions continued for a few more moments, and having extracted answers from a now defiant Mrs. Wickham, stammering apologies from his anxious wife, and cold silence from a distant Mrs. Lovell, he left to supervise a thorough search of the grounds. Clementine, watching from the conservatory, saw him erupt from the entrance to his house armed with a stout stick, with a bull terrier at his heels, looking for all the world like a well-heeled version of Bill Sikes.

Almost as soon as Mr. Haldane left, Mr. Wickham arrived—he had evidently not yet retired for the night. Without saying a word, he extended his arm to his wife and escorted her from the room.

Clementine, sure that the detestable element had departed,

returned to the salon. "They won't find anyone out there," she said. "Any interloper will have run off long before now."

"Important to make a show of strength, just in case, I suppose," Mrs. Lovell said, her voice grudging, as if she understood the need to turn out the house in a search and yet also knew it was pointless to do so.

"Poor Dorothy, she was shaking like a leaf. Whoever she ran into, it was a horrid experience for her," was Mrs. Haldane's only contribution.

"And we will never know who it was," Mrs. Lovell replied as she walked over to the tray on the table and poured herself another tot of brandy. She lifted it with an inquiring look at Clementine, who nodded, and she poured her a glass, obviously knowing better than to ask Mrs. Haldane, who did not even drink wine with her dinner.

Clementine took the glass and sipped the old brandy. It warmed a path down her throat, tight with disgust at the discourteous behavior of both Wickham and Haldane to their wives. *I would rather make hats for a living than try to share a life with either of those vile men,* she thought as she pondered the fate of Mrs. Wickham, Mrs. Haldane, and other women imprisoned in marriage to men who did not care for them. She tilted the glass and finished her brandy—enjoying the heat it created in the center of her chest.

Mr. Haldane returned to inform them that the grounds of the house appeared to be empty and that tomorrow he would report the incident to the police. He addressed the three of them as if they were dim-witted.

"She must have come across a tramp; the countryside is full of riffraff looking for a free meal at the scullery door or a chicken to steal. Now, ladies, please, no more little walks in the moonlight." He barked out a contemptuous laugh and left as abruptly as he had arrived.

Violent things happen in this man's house to his guests and he trots out these implausible reasons as if none of us has a brain in our heads, thought Clementine. And she wondered again why Mrs. Wickham, who had chosen to eat her dinner in her room, had worn not only an elaborate evening gown but also a necklace of pearls around her neck for a solitary stroll in the garden.

She suddenly felt very tired and yearned for the quiet of her room. She got to her feet and said good night, and as she left the room she heard Mrs. Lovell say to her friend, "I have some arnica upstairs, Maud, let's go and do something with that wrist you sprained pruning your roses."

"It was quite the strangest thing I have ever encountered, Jackson." Clementine reported the bizarre events of her evening to her housekeeper as Mrs. Jackson concentrated on the twenty-two buttons at the back of Clementine's evening dress.

"Did anyone ask Mrs. Wickham why she was outside alone at that time of night, m'lady?"

"Yes, I did, but I don't think Mrs. Wickham answered truthfully. I think she was worried that someone might find out what she had been up to; she did not want anyone to come into the salon, not even the footman. Mrs. Haldane said Mrs. Wickham was 'incorrigible' and I had the distinct impression that neither she nor Mrs. Lovell seemed to think that her being outside alone at night was out of the ordinary. Mrs. Wickham certainly didn't want anyone investigating outside for a culprit."

"It all seems very odd, m'lady," Mrs. Jackson said automatically as she concentrated on the last button.

"Yes, it was very strange behavior. Even though Mrs. Lovell and Mrs. Haldane initially did not appear to be surprised that she had been outside alone at night, they were quite shaken by what had happened to her, and quite worried by it, too. There is always a reason for peculiar behavior among a group of people who have lost one of their close friends to violent death." Clementine, now in her nightgown and dressing gown, climbed up onto her bed and sat with her back supported by a bank of feather pillows.

"Jackson, please make yourself comfortable so we may examine these strange events together. If I tell you my impressions perhaps you can quiz me into thinking more deeply about what happened. My head is in such a whirl, I am sure that I am missing something about the awful things that happened in this miserable house this evening."

Mrs. Jackson sat down in the chair at the foot of the bed, and Clementine closed her eyes, the better to visualize bizarre events as she spoke.

"After a disastrously uncivilized dinner, I was quite ready to say good night. It was all so very heavy-going. At the end of this miserable meal, Mr. Haldane called his wife to one side outside the dining-room door and, within listening distance of her friends, scolded and criticized her so thoroughly that she was cast quite low all evening. The man is a complete lout."

Mrs. Jackson shook her head at the behavior of uncouth men.

"Mr. Wickham stayed with Mr. Haldane in the dining room after dinner—I find his behavior to his wife quite petulant and ungracious as well. I have no idea where Mr. Wickham spent the rest of his evening after port, for he did not appear until much later on, when he was called down to see to his very distressed wife."

Mrs. Jackson remained silent as Clementine went forward in recounting the events of her evening.

"Moments after we had gathered in the salon, Mrs. Bartholomew, looking quite exhausted, poor woman, retired for the night. So there was Mrs. Lovell, Mrs. Haldane, and myself left in the Salon Vert as they *insist* on calling it—why are the aspiring classes so precious? We were on the brink of retiring, too, when Mrs. Wickham came bursting into the conservatory." She quickly recounted Mrs. Wickham's arrival and the subsequent conversations that followed.

"Ask away, Jackson. I can see you are bristling with questions."

"Certainly, m'lady. You say that Mrs. Lovell and Mrs. Haldane did not seem surprised that Mrs. Wickham had been out in the grounds at night, alone."

"No, they did not. Initially, that is. You remember I mentioned Mrs. Haldane's expression 'incorrigible'? Well, it was her first reaction when we found Mrs. Wickham in the conservatory. Then of course we got the poor thing inside and we could see how terribly hurt she was. And even though Mrs. Lovell was kind to the very distressed Mrs. Wickham, she was certainly questioning the truth of what she was hearing. And then both Mrs. Lovell and Mrs. Haldane seemed to have a complete change of heart when I asked Mrs. Wickham if she was sure she had not recognized her attacker, and just like that," she waved her hand in the air, "they both decided that she had been attacked by a tramp. Odd, very odd. Looking back on it all, nothing about the conversation between the three of them seemed right, somehow."

"Then may I pose some questions to you now, m'lady? Perhaps they will help clarify a little?"

"What? Oh yes, that's a good idea. Fire away, Jackson."

"Why do you think she was outside in the garden after ten o'clock at night, m'lady?"

"We know that she had eaten her dinner upstairs alone in her room and then she said she went for a walk to clear her head, but she was dressed in a very expensive and lovely evening dress and her jewelry . . . and now I come to think of it, she was wearing flowers in her hair. No woman dresses like that when she plans to spend an evening in her room, alone, with dinner on a tray."

"The flowers in her hair, were they roses from the garden she was walking in, perhaps?"

"No, it was a spray of little white flowers, they smelled quite delicious." She saw an *aha* expression light up her housekeeper's eyes.

"So she was outside to meet someone then, m'lady?"

"Yes, I think Mrs. Wickham went to meet a gentleman, someone she had arranged an assignation with. She either came across someone else, who maliciously attacked her, or the person she was meeting quarreled with her and did that to her. Or she met the man she had arranged to meet, and was discovered by her husband, or perhaps someone else. Of course she *might* have been attacked by a tramp, but that seems a bit farfetched to me. Tramps are not that bold. They are much more likely to attack someone walking along a lonely country road—to rob them."

"But who was she there to meet, m'lady, was it someone from inside the house, do you think?"

"She wanted to impress whomever she was meeting, so I do not imagine for one moment it was her husband, but we must check up on everyone's whereabouts, Jackson. And we also need to find out where Mr. Wickham was after dinner because maybe it was simply a matter of him discovering her with another man. Mr. Urquhart did tell us that Mr. Wickham got very angry over the Mr. Bartholomew business. It all seems rather sordid, and hole-in-the-corner, to my mind.

"When Mrs. Wickham had calmed down a little and Mrs. Haldane and Mrs. Lovell were talking among themselves, I had the opportunity to ask Mrs. Wickham if she thought the person who had attacked her knew who she was. And before she could think she said yes. I think I find that one of the most significant things about everything that happened this evening. Mrs. Wickham did not recognize her attacker, or she said she did not, but she said she thought the attacker recognized her. Of course how would she know a thing like that? I mean, really *know* it? I think she gave an instinctive and honest response to my question. The only truthful answer she gave all evening. I can't decide if this might mean that the person she went to meet attacked her and she is too frightened to tell us who he is, or that it was her husband who discovered her and punished her in that terrible way and she does not want to admit it." She tucked her bare feet under the coverlet and realized how tired she was. She glanced at the clock on the mantel. it was well after one o'clock.

"Where did Mrs. Wickham say she was when she went outside, m'lady?" Mrs. Jackson got up from her chair by the bed and found her notebook and pencil.

"First she said she had walked to the croquet lawn through the shrubbery and back, and then she sort of added that she had walked on to the rose garden. Both places are at opposite ends of the gardens. I think she was lying about where she was."

"Yes, I think so too, m'lady. Where else could she have been?"

"If she was not in the rose garden or the shrubbery . . ." A moment of introspection and then Clementine laughed. "Jackson, this is just like a guessing game—like charades or consequences. Mrs. Wickham met someone by appointment in a very beautiful evening dress . . . Good heavens, I have just remembered the lace hem of her gown had picked up some dusty cobwebs and little bits of dried leaf. So where had she been? Where would she have picked up cobwebs and dead leaves? It was a place she did not want to admit to being in, since she lied about it. She also said she had been knocked to the *floor,* not the ground."

"Do you think it was one of the buildings in the garden, then, m'lady?" Mrs. Jackson looked up from making notes in her book.

"Yes, I do." Clementine mentally ran through various structures in the gardens that afforded the seclusion of a meeting place and that might have a leafy floor and cobwebby corners. "She might have been in the rose arbor, the summer house, or perhaps she was in a potting shed . . . Oh, for heaven's sake, it was the orangery." Clementine clapped her hands together, threw back her head, and laughed in delight. "She had a little sprig of *orange* blossom in her hair. As if she had broken it off a nearby tree and tucked it behind one ear . . . for her romantic tryst." And looking across at her housekeeper she realized that Mrs. Jackson had guessed the orangery several minutes ago.

"I think you are right, m'lady, the orangery was unlocked this evening for the first time since Mr. Bartholomew was found there."

"And, I am sure the orangery is perfect for assignations: it is far from the house and completely private. But it was a strange rendezvous because her lovely gown was ripped at the neck, and there were bruises on her shoulders and back. She was most certainly attacked or treated very roughly, but was that done by the man she met there?" Clementine remembered seeing Mr. Haldane marching from his house with a stick over his shoulder. *Was this the first time he had gone out into the grounds of his house that night? Is this why his wife had looked so uneasy as she stood in the salon and had leaped so enthusiastically on the idea that a tramp had attacked Mrs. Wickham?*

She looked at her housekeeper, whose eyes were fixed intently on her face as she nodded her encouragement. "First thing tomorrow morning we must investigate the orangery,

Jackson. It is more than just coincidence that Mrs. Wickham was attacked in the very place that Mr. Bartholomew died, surely? And we must find out where Mr. Haldane and Mr. Wickham were at the time she was attacked. But why on earth would she choose to spend time in the orangery after what happened there earlier this year?"

Chapter Thirteen

At nine o'clock on the following morning, Lady Montfort and Mrs. Jackson walked down to the dining room together for breakfast. They were alone in the sunny room, as Mr. Haldane liked to eat his breakfast at an early hour and Mrs. Haldane's guests were taking breakfast in their rooms, the footman informed them.

"Any news of the man loitering in the grounds last night?" asked Lady Montfort.

"Not a sign, m'lady. We searched for nearly an hour and found no one."

"Then we will assume it is safe to venture out into the gardens," Lady Montfort added, and the young man said yes indeed it was certainly safe to venture out today.

Mrs. Jackson had lain awake for several hours in the night, deep in thought well into the small hours. She had heard the Bishop's Hever church clock sound the nightly hour across the fields and woodland that separated Hyde Castle from the village. She wondered if somewhere under the protective covering of a hedgerow a gentleman of the road slept in a dry ditch, lying low after the commotion he had caused at the castle. Somehow she doubted it; if there were tramps in the neighborhood none of them had been skulking in Hyde Castle's gardens earlier that night.

She had turned restlessly in her bed, her mind questing for reasons as to whom Mrs. Wickham, dressed in her most lovely dress, had walked to meet in the quiet secrecy of the orangery. And if she had gone to the orangery for a romantic appointment, how had she known that it was no longer locked up, or, more relevant, how had the man she was to meet there known that the orangery was open? As the early August dawn began to break she drifted off, to wake after two hours of deep sleep, unrefreshed and fuzzy-headed but with some sort of an answer to her question.

Mrs. Wickham might not have known that the orangery was unlocked. But she had certainly been told by the man she was to meet there that it was. And the only people who knew that the orangery was open were the head gardener, Mr. Clark; Mr. Stafford; and, because she had been with him when Mr. Stafford had told her that he had the key, Mr. Evans. This realization had brought Mrs. Jackson upright in her untidy bed to stare across her fancy bedroom at the little silver clock ticking away the minutes on the writing bureau at six o'clock in the morning. Within the half hour she was up, washed, dressed, and sitting at her dressing table with her notebook.

Mrs. Wickham had certainly not gone to the orangery to meet Mr. Clark. Mrs. Jackson had seen the head gardener only from a distance, albeit one that did not prevent her from noticing that he was a bent old man, with surely no interest whatsoever in the business of secret meetings. Perhaps Mrs. Wickham had an admirer who was staying somewhere locally, but since neither Bishop's Hever nor four-miles-distant Old Netherford had an inn or public house that put up guests, then she must assume for the time being that Mrs. Wickham's assignation had been with someone closer to home. She wrote three names in her notebook.

Her mind went back to the talk Miss Jekyll had given to the Hyde Rose Society about harmony of colors for herbaceous borders on their first evening at the castle. She remembered that Mrs. Wickham had spent quite some time in animated conversation with Mr. Stafford. Her behavior had been playful and, Mrs. Jackson's mouth came down at the corners in disapproval, inappropriate for a married woman. But surely there was nothing of the ladies' man about her friend. He would no more meet a married woman in the orangery than plant a garden with hybrid tea roses. But Mrs. Wickham, although not exactly pretty, had a pert manner and an energetic flirtatiousness about her that often appealed to a certain type. She sat hunched forward in her chair, her forehead wrinkled in concentration. *And Mr. Evans is quite definitely that type of man,* she thought as she remembered his devious behavior yesterday afternoon when he had led her into the covered walkway in such a sly fashion.

Mrs. Wickham went out last night dressed in her finery to meet someone in the orangery, a man to be precise, and to the best of Mrs. Jackson's knowledge the only men who knew that the building was accessible were:

1. *Mr. Evans*
2. *Mr. Stafford*
3. *Mr. Clark (unlikely)*

But who could have attacked her—if it was not the man she was meeting? However much Mrs. Jackson could picture Mr. Evans making a romantic assignation with Mrs. Wickham, she simply could not imagine him being violent—even if he did not get what he wanted. Mr. Evans was an opportunist, not a brute. She picked up her pencil and wrote the names of the two people staying in the house who had retired to their rooms for the night: Mr. Urquhart and Mrs. Bartholomew. Next she wrote Mr. Wickham.

And then, because he was the only person in the house who knew the orangery was open, she wrote Mr. Evans. But she did not, or could not find it in herself to write the name Mr. Stafford. After a moment's pause she added a fifth name to the list: Mr. Haldane. And then she stared down at the names on the paper:

1. *Mr. Urquhart*
2. *Mrs. Bartholomew*
3. *Mr. Wickham*
4. *Mr. Evans*
5. *Mr. Haldane*

And then finally, because this was, after all, an investigation and she knew she must, she reluctantly wrote Mr. Stafford's name.

Sitting next to Lady Montfort as they ate their breakfast, she ran over the four names of the men in the house that Mrs. Wickham might have gone to meet in the orangery. She discarded all of them except for Mr. Evans and Mr. Haldane. She took a sip of her strong Darjeeling tea. Mr. Evans's florid charm and ornate manners might very well appeal to a coquette like Mrs. Wickham.

The thought that she'd had yesterday, as she stood in the covered passageway with the butler, came into her mind again: the reason why there were no young women working in the house was because Mrs. Haldane or her housekeeper, Mrs. Walker, had the wit not to tempt the butler's weakness by hiring young women servants. It was not because Mr. Bartholomew was untrustworthy with young and pretty women servants, as intimated by Mr. Urquhart; it was probably because Mr. Evans was.

She sighed and hoped that she had this right, hoped she was not being as silly as Mrs. Wickham evidently was in her judgment of men. Her sigh must have been an audible one, because on looking up she saw Lady Montfort's brows were up in interrogation.

"Something just occurred to you, Jackson?" she asked in a low voice.

And she answered, "Possibly, m'lady, I am not quite sure."

"Good, then when we are finished here we shall enjoy a little after-breakfast stroll on this particularly lovely summer day, so you may deliberate further."

Mrs. Jackson chewed absentmindedly on a mouthful of breakfast, seeing in her mind only the open door of the orangery on a moonlit night and the tall, broad-shouldered figure of the butler as he walked up the steps, smoothing his hair with the palm of his hand as he did so.

How on earth could Mrs. Wickham possibly be interested in the attentions of this apology of a butler? A man as unsavory as Mr. Evans? It was preposterous.

Hold on a moment, she thought. *Just because she dresses in expensive clothes and swans around all day long doing nothing does not make her a lady.* No lady would run around outside in the dark of night with someone other than her husband. An image of one of Lady Montfort's friends who had done just that crept into her head. *Well all right then,* she thought, *no real lady would be* caught *running around outside at the dead of night with someone other than her husband.*

And was she only supposing it must be Mr. Evans because she couldn't bear the thought that Mr. Stafford might find a nincompoop like Mrs. Wickham attractive? Before she could stop herself she saw again Mr. Stafford walking up the steps, in the moonlight, to the open door of the orangery. She felt her cheeks flush and reminded herself to keep a cool head. *That is exactly what the trouble is with these investigations,* she thought. *They always turn up facts that are unsavory and make you wish you hadn't started snooping around in the first place.*

For the sake of this investigation she must be willing to accept that Mrs. Wickham intended to meet either of these two men. But what was far more to the point, *who* in the house had attacked her? Was it her husband, her host, the recently made widow, the elderly bachelor, a jealous butler, or the man she found herself very pleased to spend time with?

She had lost her appetite for her breakfast. She put down her knife and fork and patted her mouth with her napkin and looked across at her ladyship to see if she was ready to go to the orangery.

"What a perfectly beautiful morning. I think it is going to be a hot day." Clementine adjusted her hat brim against a bright morning sun as they stepped out of the terrace door and crossed a lawn still shining with dew. "Really, Jackson, the grounds are quite superbly kept, top marks to Mrs. Haldane's head gardener. Shall we go by way of the rose garden?" She noticed that her housekeeper was still preoccupied, as she seemed barely aware of the beauties of the day, and certainly no gasp of appreciation escaped her as they walked along ranks of late roses in their well-manicured beds.

"Mmm, yes, what a pity. Lots of hybrid teas. I have to say I dislike their stiffness, and there is a distinctly garish hue to some of them. But I do approve of the overall design of the garden beds. And look at that very pretty rustic summer house at the far end of this rose arch, taken as a whole it is really quite charming." She chattered on, aware that her housekeeper was immersed in her own inner conversation as they walked down the central path of the garden under a continuous tunnel of shockingly pink roses.

She is on to something, Clementine thought. *What a keen brain.* And wondered if she should tell her housekeeper about her humiliating experience the night before last when she had tiptoed along a corridor at two o'clock in the morning to eavesdrop on Mrs. Haldane's cries of misery in the company of her husband. *No, no need at all. No need to completely throw in the towel and tell her everything. She would never understand my behavior, any more than I can forgive myself for it.*

"So we are to meet Mr. Stafford in the orangery to hear what he has learned from the two young gardeners who found Mr. Bartholomew?"

Mrs. Jackson came out of her reverie and said, "Yes, m'lady, he said he would meet us there at ten o'clock."

"Since we are a little early, let us stand here and look at the lovely view from this pretty summerhouse; it will be quite breathtaking when the lake is completed. How clever he is."

"Yes, m'lady."

"Now we have a minute to ourselves, Jackson, tell me what occurred to you at breakfast."

"Most certainly, m'lady, but might I have a few more minutes to think some more on it? It is an idea only half thought out." Her housekeeper's voice was distant and preoccupied and there was a frown on her face as she stared across the lawns at Mr. Stafford's crater.

"By all means, Jackson, by all means. Oh look, there is Mr. Stafford now, walking up the rise toward us. There, he has just waved, he has spotted us. So let's walk on to meet him." And, turning, she beheld her housekeeper's cool stare as she watched Mr. Stafford coming up the steps, two at a time, from the lower lawn toward them.

Now for heaven's sake, thought Clementine, *why the frost? I thought these two were getting on splendidly when we went to the lake with Miss Jekyll yesterday.*

Mr. Stafford took off his hat as he came up the steps. "Good morning, m'lady, Mrs. Jackson." Clementine watched her housekeeper nod rather stiffly as she returned his greeting. Which caused Mr. Stafford to look slightly puzzled, but being the steady sort of man he was, he preceded them, without a word, up the path to the orangery.

"What a lovely building—what graceful proportions." Clementine wished most fervently that her husband's forebears had had the intelligence to build an orangery in the grounds of their house. This one was particularly elegant. The orangery was a tall one-story glass-paned building with a large glass dome. Its proportions were perfect, the seven graceful floor-to-ceiling single Palladian windows spaced regularly across its stone front took up the entire south wall. The center window had a pair of double doors as an entrance. In front of the building was a wide flagstone terrace so that in summer the citrus trees could be wheeled to stand in front of the orangery, and then taken back inside during the cold winter months where they would produce a bountiful crop of oranges, lemons, and limes.

The sun shone brightly on the glass dome and roof of the house, lighting the line of dark-leaved trees within. In front of the building's terrace was a formal herb garden. The sweet fragrance of thyme that edged its chamomile paths and the stronger, more pungent scent of rosemary and lavender in the last flush of bloom perfumed the warm morning air.

"Delightful," murmured Clementine, glancing at the upright figure of her housekeeper pacing alongside her with her chin up and her eyes on Mr. Stafford's back.

"How did you manage to get a key?" she asked Mr. Stafford as they stopped outside the double doors of the building.

"I asked the head gardener if I might have one for a few days. I told him that I want to create a view of the lake from the orangery. He was a little reluctant until I explained my reason. Mr. Haldane has been very clear that the orangery not be left open," he said as he turned at the entrance. "Look, Lady Montfort, you see if we remove those trees over there"—he pointed to an overgrown group of ash trees on the far side of the herb garden—"anyone standing in the orangery or on its steps, right here, will have a view across the herb garden and down onto the new lake."

"Oh really? How frightfully clever of you, Mr. Stafford. Of course I can't see what you mean until you remove the trees, but I am sure we are looking in the right direction." Clementine felt just the slightest tension building between her companions and was anxious for it not to take hold. It was bad enough having to pick her way among such a volatile group in the house; surely out here with her two friends she might relax and enjoy a pleasant break in her morning?

"Was the orangery locked up last night, Mr. Stafford?" Mrs. Jackson's voice was polite but formal.

"No, I had an appointment in the village and was running late after we met here, and I simply forgot to lock the door." He reached out his hand and opened the door, standing back to allow them both to enter the lofty interior crowded with trees that scented the air with the last of their blossoms.

"An appointment in the *village*?" Mrs. Jackson's voice was a little sharp-edged. Clementine thought she sounded like her husband's maiden aunt questioning the veracity of a schoolboy nephew.

Mr. Stafford did not answer her, but a small frown deepened the lines between his eyes.

"What a delicious scent!" cried Clementine, trying to distract from the animosity in Mrs. Jackson's voice and chilly expression. "Actually, in the warmth of this glass room, it is almost overpowering."

"Yes, that is why the windows in the roof are open to provide air circulation, otherwise it would be too hot in here for citrus; they should have been wheeled outside for the summer, not left in here. They are not a subtropical species, but Mediterranean in their temperament." He laughed and glanced at the housekeeper, who made no response.

Clementine decided to nip any conversation that criticized temperament of any kind in the bud. "Did you tell Mrs. Jackson that you had a chance to talk to the two gardeners who found Mr. Bartholomew?" she asked.

"Yes, I brought up the subject with both Peter Wainwright and Johnny Masters. It was young Johnny who found him. He's only about fourteen, but a decent boy and he works hard. One of his jobs is to sweep up and water the trees in here and pick up any fallen fruit so they don't stain the floor."

Clementine looked down; the floor was beautifully tiled in a Moorish pattern and the huge pots that the trees were standing in were glazed in a similar design. The tall, silent room was magnificent. She shuddered to think that a man had come in here to die.

"Where was Mr. Bartholomew? Where did Johnny find him?"

"Over here." Mr. Stafford walked to the far side of the room to a corner where, concealed behind a large lime tree, were a collection of taps fixed to the walls connected to some neatly coiled garden hoses. In the dusty corner were stray dried leaves, curled, brittle, and browned with age.

"Poor man," Clementine said, thinking how much he must have suffered as he crawled across this beautiful floor to die. "Was he trying to get to water, perhaps?" she added, looking at the hoses attached to the wall.

Mrs. Jackson said nothing.

"I am sure he was. Mr. Wainwright was outside weeding the herb garden later that morning when he heard Johnny's cries of shock—they were so loud they brought him in at the run. When he came in he found Johnny on his knees about here. And Mr. Bartholomew was lying about there." He paced the area, pointing to the tiled floor. "Mr. Wainwright sent Johnny for help and stayed here to try and revive Mr. Bartholomew, although he guessed almost immediately that he was dead. Mr. Haldane had just arrived back at the house from Manchester and it was he who summoned the doctor. No one was allowed in here until Dr. Arbuthnot came."

"Did Mr. Haldane come into the orangery when he was told of Mr. Bartholomew's death?"

"After he had telephoned for Dr. Arbuthnot, Mr. Haldane came down here and saw for himself that Mr. Bartholomew was dead. And he waited outside, along with Mr. Wainwright, for the doctor."

Mrs. Jackson had listened attentively to all of this and now she turned and walked to the nearest window to look out into the herb garden. "What is that?" she asked, pointing. "There by the side of the path on the left. Do you see? It looks to me"—Mrs. Jackson turned to look at Mr. Stafford—"as if it is a shawl."

"So it is!" cried Clementine. "What keen eyesight you have, Jackson." And the three of them walked outside.

Mr. Stafford bent over and picked up a white lacy evening shawl and held it up. It was a very fine shawl indeed, as light as the froth on whipped cream before it begins to thicken. And caught in the lace were stray leaves and bits of broken twig.

"Did you know that Mrs. Wickham was accosted last night at about ten o'clock when she went for a stroll in the garden, Mr. Stafford? She said someone threw something over her head and pushed her to the floor." Mrs. Jackson's voice was without any expression whatsoever. Mr. Stafford stood quite still, with the shawl in his hands.

"Yes, everyone has heard about it, Mrs. Jackson, from the scullery to the potting-shed." He held the shawl out to them. "Do you recognize it as belonging to Mrs. Wickham?"

Clementine took it and said, "I don't know but it will be easy to find out."

"What on earth was she doing out here at night?" he asked, his hands on his hips as he stared thoughtfully at Mrs. Jackson.

"She was possibly here to meet someone. Even though everyone knows the orangery has been locked for several months, that is until yesterday afternoon and evening, of course." Mrs. Jackson's voice was quite even, although she did not look at Mr. Stafford as she answered his question, but gazed off into the middle distance of the herb garden.

"Ah yes, I see now. Someone let it be known that the orangery was open." Mr. Stafford's face was solemn. "The only people who knew it was open were her ladyship, you, me, and Mr. Evans, and of course old Mr. Clark, but since he rarely bothers to talk to anyone I doubt he is our culprit. Is Mrs. Wickham often to be found wandering the grounds alone at night?" His voice was light and there was the beginning of a smile on his face.

"We do not know about Mrs. Wickham's habits," said Mrs. Jackson, finally returning her gaze from the center of the garden to the steps up to the orangery. "But she said when she came into the house last night, after her attack, that she had been strolling either in the shrubbery or the rose garden. She couldn't seem to make up her mind which."

"When she was actually in the orangery, do you mean? Waiting to meet someone in the orangery? And in your polite and thorough way you are trying to work out who that might have been." He sighed in what seemed to be exasperation and

Clementine realized that she was witnessing a falling-out between her housekeeper and Mr. Stafford.

"Or, even more interesting," said Mrs. Jackson, looking down her nose at the herb garden's beds—anywhere but at Mr. Stafford, "who it might have been who came up behind her, threw her shawl over her head, and then pushed her down onto the floor of the orangery before running away."

"What an exciting evening you must have all had," Mr. Stafford said, folding his arms across his chest. Clementine couldn't bear it any longer. This was quite ridiculous; what was Jackson driving at?

"Actually it was I who had the exciting evening; Mrs. Jackson had retired early. I was downstairs when Mrs. Wickham came rushing into the conservatory, sobbing that she had been attacked. As Mrs. Jackson says, Mrs. Lovell and Mrs. Haldane seemed to believe that she was out in the garden to meet someone. The attack, on the other hand, was supposed to have been made by a tramp, who had wandered willy-nilly into the grounds." Clementine laughed, anything to soften the polite exchange that had just taken place between the two of them. *Why on earth is Jackson being so accusatory?*

"I think Mrs. Wickham met someone here in the orangery. There were dried leaves and bits of cobweb on the hem of her gown and a little sprig of orange blossom in her hair. She said her attacker came up behind her, threw her shawl up over her head, pushed her to the floor, and ran off; hardly the action of an admirer. I suppose that when she picked herself up and started to run for the house she dropped her shawl in the herb garden. It all seems quite straightforward to me." She realized that she was overdoing her explanations and that Mrs. Jackson appeared not to be listening.

"So Mrs. Wickham came here to meet one person and was surprised by another. The first was probably an admirer, and perhaps the other might have been the man or woman who murdered Mr. Bartholomew, or perhaps it was her husband who surprised her. I can't imagine why anyone could think otherwise." Mr. Stafford made his statement matter-of-factly enough but he was still looking at Mrs. Jackson.

"Good heavens above, you are most probably right." Clementine was grateful for his quick mind and his willingness to rise above the palpable strain that was building between him and her housekeeper. *Did Jackson actually believe that it might have been Mr. Stafford who met Mrs. Wickham here last night?*

"And the next question one would ask oneself is: Who was the man that came to meet Mrs. Wickham?" Mrs. Jackson, looking a little less tense, asked the question of the fountain in the middle of the herb garden.

"You mean Mr. Evans, don't you?" Mr. Stafford was laughing now. "For, undoubtedly, it was the butler. Mr. Evans is known in the village as Dennis the Dandy and he is particularly partial to attractive young women—a fact I am quite sure *you* are aware of." Ernest Stafford's eyes were resting on Mrs. Jackson's face with an inquiring expression, inviting her to see the funny side of it all.

"Good grief, Dennis the Dandy—how priceless." Clementine's laugh sounded a little forced and she glanced at her housekeeper. "All along it was the butler!"

"Yes, it must have been, m'lady." To Clementine's relief, Mrs. Jackson smiled, a wholehearted beam that swept away all earlier traces of suspicion. "He is *actually* called Dennis the Dandy in the village?"

"Yes," said Mr. Stafford. "Everyone locks up their pretty daughters when Mr. Evans goes down to the village for a pint on a Friday night. Why, Mrs. Jackson, you surely didn't think it was me that the femme fatale of Hyde Castle was meeting in the orangery?" He had stopped laughing, and Mrs. Jackson blushed and then quickly recovered herself: "No, Mr. Stafford, I didn't for one moment imagine it could be you . . ."

And Clementine, heartily relieved that this little matter had been cleared up between them, thought to herself that when her housekeeper lied, she did it with such composure.

Chapter Fourteen

"Now then, Jackson, we must plan our next steps," Clementine said as they walked back to the house after saying goodbye to Mr. Stafford, who had made quite a business of locking up the orangery before they left. "We shall assume for the time being that Mrs. Wickham went to the orangery to meet Mr. Evans. So what we must discover now is who attacked her. And to do that we need to find out several things.

"Did Mr. Haldane leave the house last night after he had finished drinking port in the dining room with Mr. Wickham? Or did Mr. Wickham slip out of the house to follow his wife to the orangery after he left the dining room? Both Mr. Haldane and Mr. Wickham are high on our list of suspects, Jackson. And we probably need to check up on Mrs. Bartholomew and Mr. Urquhart as well. Would you be prepared to see if you can find out if anyone belowstairs might help us with these questions? Without your alerting Mr. Evans that we suspect him of hobnobbing with Mrs. Wickham, that is. And I will have a little chat with Mrs. Wickham about her visit to the orangery. She must be quite desperate for affection if she goes running off to meet Mr. Evans in the grounds at night. What did Mr. Stafford say the villagers called him, Randy Dennis?"

Mrs. Jackson's head whipped around and she looked quite

horrified for a moment. And then she stopped in the drive and looked down at her feet, half in embarrassment and half in delight, and laughed. "It's Dennis the *Dandy,* m'lady, though your name for him is very apt," she said when she had caught her breath.

"Yes, I imagine it probably is," Clementine said and the two of them stood in the early morning sunshine to enjoy their joke together.

But what Clementine did not say, as they walked on, shaking their heads at the oddities of the human race, was that she found the household at Hyde Castle more and more baffling each day. It was beyond her to imagine that a woman from a respectable family would want to involve herself with a butler. Clementine was not a prude or a snob—far from it. And in the circles she moved in she was aware that every so often the daughter or wife of an aristocrat did occasionally lose her reason completely and run off with a servant. In the past it was usually a groom who accompanied some lonely and despairing wife, or spinster daughter, on her morning ride and gave her the friendship and attention the poor thing so desperately needed, to lure her into running from hearth and home. But a butler was rather scraping the bottom of a barrel, she thought. Butlers were usually men of senior years, obsequious in manner and often more rigid in their thinking than the gentlemen they served.

Clementine tried to recall what Mr. Evans looked like, and in doing so remembered the assessing look he had given Mrs. Wickham last night when he had been called into the salon by Mrs. Haldane and instructed to mount a search of the grounds. *Yes, of course it was the butler that Mrs. Wickham went to meet. His assessing glance as he took in Mrs. Wickham's dishevelment had said it all.* She had probably been attacked as she had waited in the orangery for him to arrive. If that was how it had happened, what a surprise it must have been for him to find her sitting on the sofa in a state of complete disarray and sobbing on Mrs. Lovell's shoulder after she had failed to turn up for their meeting.

She did not share these thoughts with Mrs. Jackson. Since she suspected that the revelation that Mr. Evans was flirting with a guest in his mistress's house, once the amusement of Mr. Stafford's account of the butler's habits had worn off, had evidently embarrassed her proper housekeeper, who had remained silent throughout their walk back to the house.

Clementine tapped on the door of Mrs. Wickham's room an hour before luncheon and was bidden to enter. Its occupant was dressed and sitting in a chair by the window, a book open on her lap. A book she had hastily picked up to indicate that she had been busily reading when she had been interrupted, Clementine noticed, because it was upside down.

"Just popped in to see how you were doing, Mrs. Wickham, and to give you this." She did not offer the shawl that she was holding in her left hand; she held out a little flask of lavender water. "Lavender water is such a pleasant scent to help steady the nerves after a nasty shock. I do hope you have recovered, somewhat." She sat down unbidden in the chair on the other side of the fireplace and let the shawl drop into her lap. She noticed that Mrs. Wickham's eyes had fastened themselves on it as soon as she had walked into the room. *Poor thing, she looks quite desperately scared,* she thought, without any pity, for she was here to help.

"Good morning, Lady Montfort," the young woman said. Her eyes were pink either from lack of sleep or weeping, or both. A small flair of anger lit Clementine's stomach for whoever had hurt this harmless but very self-absorbed young woman. She drew a breath and made herself notice that Mrs. Wickham's hair was beautifully dressed and her morning dress impeccable. *Good for you,* she thought, *no need to completely give up because your married life is so without love that you have to go looking for it in places that ultimately disappoint.*

She looked around the room. It was clear that when Mrs. Haldane's friends came to stay, they always occupied the same rooms. This room was almost claustrophobic in clutter that had probably accumulated over many visits. There were pattern books from fashion houses strewn on the bed and on the tops of tables; over a chair in the corner were draped samples of richly patterned dress fabric. Some skeins of embroidery silk were dumped down on another chair by the window. And evidently Mrs. Wickham was a reader, for books were everywhere. She glanced at the titles of several of them on the table next to her. *Her Knight Errant,* by Polly Perkins, had a bookmark poking out about two-thirds of the way through, but there was also a copy of *Guinevere's Lover* and one of *Love Itself,* both by Elinor Glyn. *Aha,* she thought, *she likes her novels to be on the racy side.* She was surprised that Mrs. Wickham kept her more unseemly reading matter out in the open like this and not locked away. Miss Glyn's books were not considered suitable reading for gentlewomen. She set her bottle of lavender water down on the table next to Elinor Glyn's clandestinely popular best sellers.

"Thank you, Lady Montfort, how very kind of you," Mrs. Wickham faltered, as she accepted that Lady Montfort was here to stay for a while. Her voice had broken a little on the acknowledged kindness. *Oh dear,* thought Clementine, feeling a little guilty, *this is going to be only too easy.*

"I only hope you were not too badly hurt last night?"

"Just bruises, Lady Montfort, nothing more serious." The young woman's face was pale and Clementine noticed that she held her upper body quite still, as if any movement might be painful. Again she remembered seeing Mr. Haldane striding from the house, holding his stout stick in his hand.

"Yes, a little arnica will perhaps help with the bruising. I think I might have some. . . ."

"Mrs. Lovell . . . was most kind." Silence, her eyes still on the shawl the young woman was evidently waiting.

"As you can see, I found your shawl. You dropped it in the herb garden when you were running from the orangery." She kept her eyes on the young woman's face and saw it redden. *Fair-haired women always blush so easily,* she thought, as she watched Dorothy Wickham's eyes widen.

"But I wasn't in the orangery," she said a little too defiantly. Clementine wanted to cry out, "Tosh," but she bit her tongue, there was no need to be derisive.

"Oh, you weren't? How very strange, because that is where we found it." Clementine left the young woman to wonder if Evans had already snitched. "My dear Mrs. Wickham, I am only interested in knowing what happened when you were at-tacked. Why you were in the orangery is absolutely none of my business, and I wouldn't dream of asking you about it. But I would like you please to tell me, as clearly as you can, exactly what happened when your attacker came upon you." Clemen-tine had already decided that a direct approach was the best way with this young woman, and was relying on her social status and her mature years to intimidate the younger woman into revealing the truth of the goings-on last night.

Mrs. Wickham bent her head and started to weep, hoping perhaps that, like Mrs. Lovell, Lady Montfort would rush to soothe and make things right. Clementine sat her out, and after a while said in a kind but firm voice, "When you are ready . . ."

Mrs. Wickham sat up a little straighter in her chair.

"Yes, I was in the orangery. It was the first time it had been opened since Rupert's death. He was such a good friend . . . I wanted . . . I wanted to spend some time there, where he died."

How awfully morbid of you, thought Clementine, *when he died so horribly.* She waited.

"I heard a movement in the back of the room behind the trees, and I turned. I thought I saw someone standing at the far end of the row of trees. I called out. But no one answered, and I thought perhaps the moonlight and the shadows had made me imagine that someone was there. I turned back toward the door and then before I knew it someone pulled my shawl up over my head and I was pushed down onto the floor. I lifted my head to cry for help and that is when he kicked me, hit me. Before he ran away."

"You say he . . ."

"I imagine it was a man. But I saw no one, as I said."

Clementine nodded. "That must have been very frightening for you," she said gently. "Did this person say anything?"

"No." Her face was pale with anxiety, making her eyes look even more pink and strained.

"You think it was not a tramp, then?"

Mrs. Wickham shook her head.

"Last night you said that you definitely thought this person knew who you were; why is that, if you did not see who it was?"

"I was very frightened as I lay on the floor. I did not dare lift my head, but when I heard the footsteps disappear into the night, I had the distinct feeling that it had been someone I knew." In the comforting light of day, sitting safely in her room, she spoke with complete conviction.

"And do you think your attacker was already there when you arrived?"

"Yes, they must have been, otherwise I would have seen them come through the door. I was facing the door with my back to the trees."

"When whoever attacked you left, what did you do next?"

"I was very frightened but not too badly injured. I got up and untangled my head from my shawl. I couldn't be sure if my attacker had actually left the building or the area. So I went outside and looked around."

"And once outside?"

"I stood on the path for a moment or two and then I'm afraid my nerve broke. I couldn't tell if anyone was in the shadows watching me. I was so frightened I would be attacked again. So I ran as fast as I could, across the herb garden and the lawn, back toward the house. I crossed the drive and the upper lawn to the terrace—the conservatory was the first door I came to." She was out of breath but she was no longer crying, and she was, it seemed to Clementine, rather excited by telling her story. Clementine thought that if she asked Mrs. Wickham anything at this point she would willingly supply the answer.

"Did you see anyone at all on your way back to the house, Mrs. Wickham? Anyone at all, please be frank with me, this will go no further but it is very important."

It occurred to Clementine that Mrs. Wickham was bored to tears in a house full of people far older than herself, all studiously engrossed in their roses. *She livens her empty hours by playing games, poor little ninny.*

"Yes, I thought I saw someone walking up the drive ahead of me. It wasn't anyone I recognized—it might have been my attacker I suppose. It was a fleeting impression, a dark figure among dark shadows lit only by the moon." Clementine had the strangest feeling that she was quoting from one of the romantic novels she enjoyed reading.

She decided to take a risk. "Oh, I am sure that it was Evans, the butler," she said in a voice as smooth as milk. And Mrs. Wickham half rose from her chair in a panic.

"Den . . . Evans . . . ?" she cried out, and then, hearing how loud her voice sounded, she turned away in case she said anything she might regret.

"Ah, so you think it might have been the butler who attacked you?" persisted Clementine.

"No, most definitely not—it cannot have been. It was someone else."

"Then perhaps it was Mr. Evans whom you had arranged to meet in the orangery, Mrs. Wickham? Please tell me if it was, otherwise he might be wrongly accused of attacking you."

"Yes, it was Mr. Evans I was waiting to meet in the orangery, but he certainly did not attack me," Mrs. Wickham said rather melodramatically as she lifted her chin and shook her golden curls. And then she heard herself and her face fell. "But no one must ever know, Lady Montfort. Mr. Wickham . . . my husband . . ."

It was like bullying a kitten and Clementine felt instantly ashamed of herself. *There is no need to be unkind and make her uneasy even if she is a dangerous little troublemaker,* she reminded herself, and added, "I simply can't imagine how Mr. Wickham will find out, my dear, for I most certainly will not tell him. There is nothing for you to fear from me. And I think you have been a very brave and courageous young woman for being so candid with me."

"I promise you, Lady Montfort, there was no harm in what I was doing in the orangery. No harm at all. And I would be grateful, truly grateful if you would not tell *anyone* that I was there to meet Mr. Evans." For the first time, Mrs. Wickham expressed herself without a trace of self-conscious emotion. "Mr. Evans has been a very good friend to me," she said, her voice low, "and it would be wrong to get him into trouble with his employers."

"You have nothing to worry about, Mrs. Wickham." She smiled in what she hoped was a reassuring way. After all, if this young woman was in love with a butler, then that was entirely her affair. "As I said, it is not my business whom you are involved with."

"It is not what you think it is." Dorothy flared up a little now that she was sure her secret was safe. "No one could possibly understand that Mr. Evans and I have genuine feelings for each other."

Chapter Fifteen

Mrs. Jackson went looking for Lady Montfort and found her in her room, standing by the window.

"Ah, Jackson, come on in. I just had my little talk with Mrs. Wickham about her encounter last night, the poor silly creature. She admitted to having been in the orangery. Her attacker was there when she arrived, she thinks, standing behind the trees. He sprang on her from behind, pulled her shawl over her head, pushed her down onto the floor, and hit her a couple of times before running off."

"So she didn't recognize him, m'lady."

"No, she had no idea whom it might have been, she was taken by surprise, which was probably the attacker's plan. What is more, she admitted that she had been there to meet Mr. Evans. I reassured her it would go no further." Her ladyship looked not in the slightest bit embarrassed that she had immediately passed this information on to her.

"It seems that the person who attacked Mrs. Wickham was there for some other purpose than to surprise her with Mr. Evans, then, m'lady. So it might have been the other way around, Mrs. Wickham surprised whoever was already in the orangery when she arrived."

"Yes, it would seem so. And anyway I can't imagine

Mr. Wickham lurking behind the trees in the orangery just to surprise his wife, can you? Wouldn't he have waited for the lover to come along too, and then have the satisfaction of surprising them both? But you can never tell with men. But Mr. Wickham might have been lurking in the orangery for some other purpose entirely. Did you perhaps have any luck with your inquiries belowstairs?"

"Yes I did, m'lady."

Mrs. Jackson had spent a long and frustrating forty minutes in the laundry room with Mrs. Walker before she could return to Lady Montfort with the news that Mr. Wickham had left the dining room after port and cigars with Mr. Haldane. *This is the reason I avoid gossip and small talk,* she said to herself. For she'd had to listen to every mundane detail of life belowstairs at Hyde Castle and every tortuous opinion the upper servants held on the misfortunes of older men who marry younger wives before she could slip in the one question she wanted the answer to.

"However, m'lady, Mr. Haldane did leave his study between the time he left the dining room and the time Mrs. Wickham came back to the salon after she was attacked. The housekeeper told me herself. There are two telephones in the house. One is in Mr. Haldane's study and the other one is by the green-baize door to the back stairs. Unfortunately, Mr. Haldane threw his office telephone across the room a few days ago and it is no longer in working order." She paused to enjoy her ladyship's hearty peal of laughter. "So until the instrument can be repaired, Mr. Haldane has to leave his study and use the telephone by the door to the back stairs. The housekeeper saw him, not long after he and Mr. Wickham left the dining room, and she said he stayed on the telephone for quite some time, she could hear him quite clearly giving instructions to the managing director of his factory."

"And Mr. Wickham?"

"After Mr. Wickham left the dining room he told the footman that he had some letters to write and went into the library. Charles took him coffee whilst he was in there. And he was still there when Charles went to find him to come and attend to his wife." The servants' hall had been seething with gossip and speculation about the attack made on Mrs. Wickham that gathering information about who was where had been simple enough.

"Wonderful, Jackson, simply wonderful." Lady Montfort jumped up out of her chair and clapped her hands together. "So either Haldane or Wickham could have gone outside to the orangery."

"But none of the servants saw either Mr. Haldane or Mr. Wickham leave the house after dinner, m'lady."

"Are you quite sure, Jackson?"

Mrs. Jackson was more than a little irritated considering the patience it had taken to pump this information out of Mrs. Walker without her realizing she was informing on her employer, and it had taken even longer to wring these facts from the footman regarding Mr. Wickham's movements.

"Yes, m'lady, quite sure. The attack on Mrs. Wickham has been the talk of the servants' hall all morning long."

"But Mr. Haldane despises the rosarians; why would he ask Mr. Wickham to stay in the dining room to drink port with him?"

"I am afraid I don't know, m'lady. But the housekeeper was quite clear that they drank their port together, then Mr. Wickham went to the library and Mr. Haldane to the telephone room." She also did not add that Mrs. Walker was scrupulous in her detail. Mrs. Jackson could attest to that, having had to listen to every single one of Mrs. Wickham's faults listed by that avid gossip.

"But how would she know the goings-on upstairs at that time of night, I wonder?"

Only perfect training and steadfast commitment to convention mastered the sharpness in Mrs. Jackson's voice. "The footman, Charles, made a full report to the entire servants' hall later that evening as they all speculated on who could have done such a thing to Mrs. Wickham, m'lady, since none of them believe the tramp story. And he said quite specifically that Mr. Wickham was in the library all evening after Mr. Haldane moved from the dining room to his study. And then Mrs. Walker saw Mr. Haldane in the little glass-fronted telephone room and instructed Charles to take in coffee to him in the study the moment he had finished, which was well after the time Mrs. Wickham returned to the house. Later on when the butler informed Mr. Haldane of Mrs. Wickham's attack he had drunk the entire pot. I think, m'lady, we can safely say that until he went to search the grounds Mr. Haldane was in the house."

She watched her ladyship mull this one over and understood why she was so annoyed at this fresh information—her two most favorite suspects had alibis. "Mr. Wickham could have climbed out of the library window, Jackson."

"Yes, I suppose he could, m'lady."

"We should check to see if there are footprints or something in the flower bed under the library window."

"Yes, m'lady, we might do that." Mrs. Jackson wondered if perhaps she was overtired, as her night had been a sleepless one and inspecting flower beds was something she had every intention of avoiding.

"And Mr. Haldane could have cut his telephone call short and gone to the orangery without being observed by any of the servants."

Mrs. Jackson understood that Lady Montfort was hoping

that it was either Mr. Haldane or Mr. Wickham who had attacked Mrs. Wickham in the orangery and that she was linking the identity of the attacker directly to the person who had murdered Mr. Bartholomew.

"As you said earlier, m'lady, it would be uncharacteristic of Mr. Wickham to attack his wife if he found her with . . . another man. He would more than likely confront her and send her back to the house." There was a long silence as her ladyship considered alternatives.

"You are right, Jackson. But I am still puzzled by Mr. Haldane's movements." *But surely there weren't any movements?* Mrs. Jackson tried not to sigh. She was quite aware that Lady Montfort had formed a complete antipathy to Mr. Haldane. Whenever he came into the room she could see by her ladyship's face how offended she was, even though she was careful never to express her dislike; there is much to be read by the straight back and the averted profile.

"That leaves Mr. Urquhart and Mrs. Bartholomew, and possibly Mr. Haldane and Mr. Wickham as the only people who do not have an alibi for the time of the attack. Did you by any chance manage to find out what the other two were up to?" Lady Montfort looked around for her notebook and Mrs. Jackson got up from her chair and brought it over to her from the table.

"A housemaid took up a pot of hot chocolate to Mrs. Bartholomew ten minutes after she left the salon last night. She said that Mrs. Bartholomew was deeply asleep in her bed. She left the pot on the bedside table and it was still there, untouched, this morning when she went to clean the room. And apparently Mr. Urquhart was reading a book when his valet took him his late-night cup of peppermint tea and three pieces of shortbread."

"Both of them could have left their rooms after the servants left them, Jackson. But I can't see either of them running off to the orangery for some reason or other and then attacking Mrs. Wickham. Oh, this is so frustrating."

Mrs. Jackson felt she needed a break from being the amateur detective's trusted assistant and the bearer of bad tidings.

"Will you be joining the company for luncheon, m'lady?"

"Oh yes, I most certainly will. Goodness only knows what fun that will be. And I think you should come too, Jackson, it is important to mingle with our fellow guests and suspects."

Chapter Sixteen

As Clementine and Mrs. Jackson went down to luncheon she was immediately aware of a considerable to-do coming from the Salon Vert.

"Listen to that racket, Jackson, sounds like another catastrophe has occurred at Hyde Castle," she said to her housekeeper as they reached the bottom of the stairs and stood looking into the room. "Mr. Haldane is no doubt haranguing his guests with more information on war in Europe. What can have happened now?"

Mr. Haldane was standing in the middle of the salon, and standing in a cluster around him, their faces incredulous with shock, were the rosarians. The exclamations from the women and the wails of protest from Mr. Urquhart were so loud that Clementine and Mrs. Jackson arrived in their midst without being observed, and it was only when Clementine lightly touched Mrs. Lovell on the arm to gain her attention that she was given an explanation as to what all the commotion was about.

"Germany has declared war on Russia and at the same time has mobilized its forces to invade Luxembourg," Mrs. Lovell said.

"It's a disaster," cried Mr. Urquhart. "The world has gone mad."

"Germany has declared war on *both* countries?" Clementine could not believe her ears. "Surely not both. But if Germany intends to occupy Luxembourg, it can only be because . . ." She felt her heart leap into her throat.

"Germany will sweep through Luxembourg into Belgium. The French are quite ready for them; they were anticipating as much and they are completely prepared," Mr. Haldane announced, his eyes shining with avarice.

"But has Germany declared war on France?" asked Clementine, trying to stay calm. *Could this really be happening?* She saw Haldane's red face, bloated with too much rich food and port, dangerously deepen in hue with the excitement of his news; she heard his bellicose roar and, in a higher register, the fussy, nervous twittering of Mr. Urquhart. She turned away from the group and went to stand by the window, as far away from them all as she could get. Her chest felt tight and hard, and she could hardly breathe. She reached out a hand to open the window; it was far too hot in the room.

"Allow me, Lady Montfort." Mrs. Bartholomew extended a hand and pushed down on the handle of the casement window. Cool air poured into the room and Clementine took in a long, slow breath. The two women stood side-by-side in silence, looking out at the glorious afternoon, peaceful in the sunlight; the song of a lark soaring in the sky above drowned out by the racket that was still going on behind them.

"Let me get you a glass of water," Mrs. Bartholomew said. "Charles . . . bring . . ." The clamor in the room lifted in volume, all words indistinguishable, but above the buzz of shrill excitement, it was Mr. Haldane's voice that rode above all. Clementine's ears started to ring and her palms felt clammy and cold. Her family was European. Her daughter was married to a Frenchman.

"Here, m'lady, sit down," It was Mrs. Jackson standing at her elbow; a steady hand on her upper arm, she tugged a small armchair around so that it was facing away from the crowd in the room and gently sat her down in it.

"Is she going to faint?" Mrs. Bartholomew asked the question in an incurious tone of voice, as if she was inquiring after the well-being of a complete stranger, but she put a firm hand on Clementine's shoulder, as if to anchor her to her seat.

"No, I don't think so; she will be all right in a minute." Clementine heard her housekeeper's cool voice and struggled to maintain calm. All she could think of was her daughter, her sweet daughter and her lovely babies sitting in her beautiful house in Paris, and the German army marching across the Belgian border. Her head swam. No, it couldn't possibly happen, surely the French army would never let Germany invade?

"Is she ill?" Mrs. Bartholomew's voice interrupted Clementine's inner vision of battles along the Belgian border with France.

"No, she will be quite all right in a moment, *thank you*, Mrs. Bartholomew."

"It's this talk of war . . . these men are so aggressive, so excited. It is a shock, though, for Germany to declare war on Russia . . ."

"My daughter . . ." Clementine sipped water brought to her by the footman and summoned the energy to be coherent. "My eldest daughter lives in France; she is married to a Frenchman."

"Oh really, that is interesting, but where does she live?"

"In Paris."

"Ah yes, that's unfortunate . . ." A pragmatic response without sentiment or fuss. No Frenchwoman worth her salt would commiserate with anyone lucky enough to find himself living in Paris. *Yes it is, because if the German army successfully crosses Belgium into France, they would be in Paris within a day.*

"The Belgian army is tiny and disastrously ill equipped, it can never hold the German army back . . ." Mr. Haldane's exultant voice reached their ears.

"You can almost hear him counting up the millions he is going to make," Mrs. Bartholomew said, echoing Clementine's thoughts almost to the word.

"I don't understand." Clementine looked up at Mrs. Bartholomew. "When did all this happen? Has Germany actually declared war on France?"

"No, but they might as well have, for they mobilized their army and are now in occupation of Luxembourg. But it is evident what their intentions are: they have decided that they will go to war both with Russia and France." The Frenchwoman standing next to her was so quiet and her voice so low as she announced that her country was on the brink of war, that Clementine could hardly hear her. She needed more information. Looking over her shoulder, she caught the eye of the sensible Mrs. Lovell, who moved away from the group to join them by the window.

"Mrs. Lovell, you are so much better informed than I. What do you know; is this fact or speculation?"

"Early this morning Germany seized the main railway station in Luxembourg. From what I read in *The Times*, the German chief of staff, General Schlieffen, has apparently had his armies ready for over a week. When the German army took Luxembourg, King Albert of the Belgians made it clear that Belgium will remain neutral and he is forbidding access to either Germany or France. The German chancellor, Bethmann Hollweg, is saying there is no aggressive intent and that this is merely a precaution to secure the railways against a possible

French attack. And the French ambassador in London met with our Foreign Secretary and reminded him that the Treaty of London signed by the Great Powers guaranteed Luxembourg's neutrality. So if Germany makes a move to continue through Belgium to France . . ."

"We will declare war with Germany?" Clementine asked, and Mrs. Lovell shrugged her shoulders and lifted both her hands, palms upward.

"Perhaps, it is probably too soon to say. There are many in our government who are greatly opposed to our involvement in this mess. But Mr. Churchill ordered the grand fleet north to the Orkneys weeks ago. And France is asking us to secure the English Channel in case the German fleet move south to France. We are in a holding pattern right now, Lady Montfort. But it really doesn't look good. We must pray that we will not be drawn . . ."

"What are you saying?" Haldane rounded on them both. "We can't let the Germans get away with this kind of bullying. If they invade Belgium to get to France of course we will declare war. To do otherwise would be preposterous." Haldane's eyes were bulging and he waved his cigar in Mrs. Lovell's plainly disapproving face. "Schlieffen has been planning this for months . . . years probably. They will whip through Belgium and into France before you can say Jack-bloody-Robinson. And we will be the ones who will have to stop them." He stood straddling his hearth rug, brows down; a bad impersonation of John Bull guarding the shores of England.

And you will make a fortune out of equipping our army for war, with your nasty tins of beef. And our young men will have to go and fight. And my son will be among the first to be sent.

Her son, Harry, and all the young men he had grown up with would go to war if Germany invaded Belgium. Their country would empty of newly trained officers all eagerly rushing off to do their bit, because that was what young men did. They put on uniforms and rallied to the flag, fully under the impression that what they were doing was heroic. She would not let herself think about the thousands who would die or return home maimed and scarred from the terrible waste that would take place on the battlefield. And then to make things worse she realized that her son would not march off to war, he would fly. She felt cold and quite uncomfortably clammy and carefully raised her glass to her dry lips and took a sip of water before looking up at Mrs. Jackson standing protectively between her and Mr. Haldane; her housekeeper's face was particularly severe.

"It will be all right, m'lady," Mrs. Jackson said. "Lady Verity will come home to Iyntwood with her little boys and I am quite sure that Lady Althea is already there. Our prime minister will not let us be pulled into this mess, he is not a rash man. By the time the family goes north for the grouse shooting this will all have sorted itself out." Clementine knew that she was being reassured, but she was in no mood to be lulled into a false sense of security.

"You are very kind to try to bolster my spirits, Jackson," she said. "But if Germany invades Belgium I somehow think Englishmen will not be shooting grouse—there will be no Glorious Twelfth this year, certainly not in the north of England and Scotland."

"I do not think I will join our host for luncheon," said Mr. Urquhart to Mrs. Jackson as Mrs. Haldane invited her guests into the dining room. "Come, my dear, we will ask Charles to bring us a little something on a tray." Mrs. Jackson was gratified to see that Mrs. Bartholomew, hitherto rather distant with her ladyship, had formed a Franco-British alliance with her and was busy asking questions of whom the eldest Talbot daughter was married to and just how many hectares of vineyards the Comte de Lamballe owned in the Loire. And her ladyship, with her customary self-discipline and perfect manners, was doing her best to soothe Mrs. Bartholomew's anxiety about her country being invaded by Germany. It seemed her ladyship was in good company and so she followed Mr. Urquhart into the conservatory.

"Oh my goodness me, what a tempest in a teapot. Come, my dear, sit down and make yerself comfortable. No one will interrupt us, the conservatory is rarely used except by me." Mr. Urquhart gestured to her to close the salon doors and sank down into the deepest wicker chair with the most cushions.

"No war then, Mr. Urquhart?"

"My dear Edith, I seriously doubt it. Our Foreign Secretary, Sir Edward Grey, will sort this out in no time at all. We are not interested in war with Germany. Now if it were France, that would be a different matter entirely. France has been our enemy in Europe since time in memoriam. And I believe that she is just as eager for war with Germany as Germany is with her. France will never forgive the Germans for taking Alsace-Lorraine from them in the last war."

"The last war?"

"The Franco-Prussian War, or the War of 1870 as it is often called. I was just a young man then, of course. I expect the French are lined up on the other side of the Belgian border, waiting for the first opportunity to get at the German army."

"So we will declare war on whichever one of them invades Belgium first?"

"Perhaps, and in that case, my money is on war with France." His eyes twinkled approvingly at her quick grasp of the situation.

"Now, Edith, I insist, no more talk of war. What have you been doing with yourself this morning?"

She told him of her stroll in the gardens with Lady Montfort, and how beautiful the rose garden was.

He turned to the table on his right and lifted a scrapbook that was sitting there onto his lap and pulled his cashmere shawl tightly around his shoulders, even though the conservatory thermometer was standing at an oppressive seventy-two degrees and Mrs. Jackson's forehead was beginning to feel quite damp. He opened the scrapbook to display a carefully composed watercolor painting of his beloved rose Cupid, no doubt done by Mrs. Haldane.

"I do hope you didn't encounter a nasty tramp in the garden while you were out strolling." If his words sounded a little malicious, there was no indication that he was being so from the playful manner in which he patted the cushion of the chair next to him in invitation, thought Mrs. Jackson, as she obediently sat down.

"We encountered no one at all, Mr. Urquhart, it is quite a beautiful morning and the gardens are very pretty."

"Finley, please call me Finley, everyone does. I did not see the naughty little Mrs. Wickham among us just now." He closed his book and looked at her expectantly, and she realized that he wanted to talk about Mrs. Wickham's attack, so she said nothing and waited.

"So, I sadly missed the fun last night," he prompted, and she complied with a minimum of detail: "I wasn't in the salon when she came back to the house, I had already retired for the night. It doesn't sound as if she was too badly hurt but she must have been very frightened."

"Oh no, Dorothy is made of much sterner stuff than we might suppose. But those moonlight walks of hers will be her undoing, and the poor woman certainly doesn't deserve to bump into some gentleman-of-the-road when she was hoping for a more pleasant encounter." He was referring to Mrs. Wickham's alleged attacker, she realized, and politely listened as Mr. Urquhart twittered on about the dangers of the unemployed tramping the country to find work. When his concern for the safety of the villagers, the gardeners, and the neighboring farmers and their daughters had been thoroughly expressed, she asked a question guaranteed to seize his interest.

"You think she went to meet someone?" She wondered if the household knew of Mrs. Wickham's interest in the Hyde Castle butler.

The elderly man settled his spectacles more firmly on his nose and smiled at her, his eyes gleaming with interest.

"My dear, let us not waste our time wondering who the new light of her life is today; tomorrow it will be someone else. Mrs. W. enjoys variety and can be counted on to surprise us with the array of different men whose company she enjoys. Poor Clive, we all knew when he married a much younger woman his would be a difficult life. Then we met Dorothy and it simply confirmed our suspicions that when an older man falls in love with a much younger woman, just how blinkered they can be about little things like suitability and ultimately the real reason why a much younger woman would consider allying herself to a man no longer in his prime."

Mrs. Jackson had been through all this an hour or so ago downstairs. But Mr. Urquhart was far better informed than even the most indiscreet of ladies' maids.

"Money?" she hazarded the obvious guess.

"Yes, unfortunately, you are probably right. Dottie is very well heeled, you know. And Clive lost his money in the American railway crash."

Mrs. Wickham was the one with the money? This was indeed news. *What on earth is the attraction in a husband who is*

217

fussy and correcting and, in addition, has no money? she wondered, and wasted no time in asking the impertinent question of Mr. Urquhart.

"That is what we are all asking ourselves. Of course Clive has a position in society from a reasonably well-connected family; the Wickhams have been in Berkshire for many, many generations, whereas poor Dottie comes from trade. Her father owned draper shops and a cotton mill and left her a tidy sum, I can tell you—and she was his only child. So their marriage gave Dorothy status and it gave Clive the money he needed to breed those terrifying tea roses in those blinding colors."

And it was back to the old man's favorite topic: the hybrid tea rose.

As he happily enumerated all Mr. Wickham's faults as a rose breeder—as if this were the one reason why his wife was no longer interested in him—Mrs. Jackson, left alone with her thoughts, wondered why Mrs. Wickham with all her money would choose to remain married to the irritable Mr. Wickham and then make the Hyde Castle butler the object of her affections. Which brought her around to speculate on who had attacked Mrs. Wickham in the orangery.

It is far too hot to think in this room, she thought, *and it is too late to go in to luncheon. I will ask for a tray to be sent to me upstairs.* She put her hands on the arms of her chair preparatory to standing up, but Mr. Urquhart pinned her with a particularly determined look as he enumerated the many faults of Mr. Wickham's roses, and she knew it would be poorly mannered to leave the conservatory too abruptly. She must wait until he had at least finished with his favorite subject and prayed that the end would not be too long in coming. If she remained seated, though, she would certainly drop off, so she got to her feet and, nodding in agreement to whatever Mr. Urquhart was saying, she wandered over to a small library in the corner of the conservatory. It was an informal collection of books on horticulture and the cultivation of roses. As she glanced along its shelves she noticed that every so often a novel, possibly left behind by a visitor to the house, had been picked up and slotted into the bookshelves at random. *Henderson's Dictionary of Rose Cultivars* was nestled between *Love Will Find a Way*, by Polly Perkins, and *Wildflowers in Britain*, by Geoffrey Grigson. And farther along, to her delight, she found another castoff—probably from Mrs. Wickham: *Romancing the Nymph*, by Adelaide Peabody, was rubbing shoulders with *Delights of the Hedgerow*, and on its other side was *Reproduction of the Deciduous Species*. Smiling as her eyes traveled along the titles of other books, her eye was caught by a word that made her pulse leap and all drowsiness completely disappear. Gold letters on a leather spine announced: *A Toxicology of Plants from Exotic Climes*, by E. M. Phipps.

A toxicology? Isn't that the study of poison? This might very well be an interesting book to read. She pulled it out with some difficulty as it was tightly wedged and the humidity of the room had slightly warped the cover. As she opened the book she was aware that Mr. Urquhart had stopped babbling about tea roses and had joined her at the bookshelf.

"Looking for something to read, Edith? Now what do you have there?" His voice was close to her ear and she froze. "Hmm, *A Toxicology of Plants from Exotic Climes*, an interesting title. I am unfamiliar with the author, but quite a handy piece of writing to have in a conservatory." Finley took the book from her. "I didn't know you were interested in the subtropical genus, my dear," he said, his eyes lively with interest as he thumbed through the introduction, and Mrs. Jackson sat down in a nearby chair and waited patiently for him to finish his inspection.

"Ah yes, Nerium, such pretty leaves and fruit. Deeply

poisonous of course, there must be one in every conservatory in England. What nice illustrations." Her interest piqued, she reached out to take the book from him. But he laughed and moved away. "Aha, now here's an interesting plant: Persea americana. Hardly what we would call an exotic species, though. Ah, it is only the seed that is actually toxic, interesting . . ." He turned a page and then looked up. "Here is Charles with my luncheon." And he popped the book back into her lap and walked to the heavy door into the salon. He struggled to get the heavy door open a crack before Charles came to his aid.

"Bring it in here, Charles. What have you brought me? Oh how nice, a lovely little pot of Turkish coffee, and you have had the sense to bring lots of sugar, and two delicious fairy cakes and some shortbread. Set the tray down there."

And the elderly man settled himself in his favorite chair to enjoy his luncheon, leaving Mrs. Jackson to return to the book and stare at a slip of paper that had fluttered out of it when Mr. Urquhart had tossed the toxicology back into her lap. It was a list written in well-formed handwriting of what appeared to be plants: digitalis, laburnum, oleander, castor bean, belladonna, aconitum, tobacco. A line had been drawn through all the names listed except for castor bean and oleander.

Chapter Seventeen

Clementine found herself engaged in another walk directly after luncheon. Throughout the meal, Mrs. Bartholomew's earlier composure had rapidly eroded to fretfulness at the endless speculation that the German army, having successfully secured Luxembourg, would no doubt continue on through Belgium to France and invade, according to Mr. Haldane, probably the day after next. She had been preoccupied when she went in to luncheon and her uneasiness had turned to outright panic the more Mr. Haldane talked about the importance of Britain's preparedness for the coming war.

Sensing Mrs. Bartholomew's increasing anxiety, Mrs. Lovell had suggested that they take a walk past the new lake and onward to the edge of the property and then through the woodland to the very picturesque village of Bishop's Hever and back.

"It is a delightful walk and will get us out of the house and away from all this aggressive talk of war," Mrs. Lovell said as they left Mrs. Haldane working on a watercolor painting of Mrs. Lovell's rose in the company of a meek Mrs. Wickham busy with some embroidery. She turned to Clementine and said in what she no doubt imagined to be a low tone, but which carried quite clearly, "Poor Albertine's family live in Orléans, you know; she must be worried to death."

"But of course I am anxious, Amélie—Orléans is within a day's march of Paris." Albertine's accent was far more pronounced now that she had lost her customary self-possession. Her often serious expression had deepened and a frown creased her smooth forehead. "I cannot stay 'ere. I must return to Orléans before any travel becomes impossible. I must write to my brother this evening so we can make the necessary arrangements. Did you 'ear what Roger was saying about U-boats in the English Channel? Oh, why did I not return last month?" Clementine momentarily expected Mrs. Bartholomew to wring her hands as they walked down the lawn.

"My dear Albertine, I think you might be overreacting just a little. You must try not to worry," Mrs. Lovell declared but without much conviction. "I have absolute faith in our prime minister, Mr. Asquith; he will steer us through these choppy waters, I am quite convinced of it." At this, Clementine had to look away. *If any of these people, who spoke with such conviction that their government would find a way out of this mess, sat down to dinner with Herbert Asquith they would not be quite so ready to put their future in his hands.* She remembered a recent dinner party where the gentleman had drunk an entire bottle of wine by the time the fish course was completed.

Mrs. Bartholomew's rising agitation was making it difficult for Clementine to maintain sangfroid. *If war breaks out in the next few days surely Etienne will have the sense to send Verity and the children to the safety of their estates in the Loire Valley if she cannot come to us?* Verity was probably packing at this moment, and Clementine resolved that as soon as they returned to the house she would instruct Mrs. Jackson to do the same.

"I understand your concern, Mrs. Bartholomew," she said to the distraught younger woman walking at her side. "Perhaps you might inquire about a crossing to France as soon as we get back to the house."

"I most certainly will. But what will I do if the German army invades before I can get back to Orléans?"

"The French army will be ready for them, my dear, and we English will go to their aid. The German army is no match at all for the combined forces of Britain and France. But for now, I believe exercise is the best cure for nerves." This was said in the sort of voice that rallied even the most faint-hearted, and Clementine smiled her approval of Mrs. Lovell's no-nonsense attitude.

They walked on, stopping to exclaim at Mr. Stafford's excavation. And Clementine, in order to distract Mrs. Bartholomew, found herself enjoying a pleasant conversation with her about her husband, whom she evidently had cared for despite, if Mr. Urquhart was to be believed, his many failings.

"Some of my happiest times have been on plant-collecting trips to the Orient, Lady Montfort. I often wished that Rupert would come with us, but he was not a man who easily tolerated discomfort. And of course we spent many uncomfortable nights in camp when the rain poured down for hours." She laughed. "So he always stayed here when I went with my brother on our trips. He was very fond of Maud, and in her gentle way she kept him busy and he did not get into trouble. For my husband, you see, enjoyed the company of women and they always found him irresistible." Mrs. Bartholomew laughed, and Clementine thought her attitude toward her husband and marriage quite charmingly typical of the French.

Why is it, she thought, *that Frenchwomen are so practical where their husbands are concerned?* Her understanding was that French wives treated their husbands like children: they fussed over them, organized their lives, and then ushered them off to their mistresses every afternoon. No wonder her more amorous friends borrowed the expression *cinq à sept* for their pursuit of afternoon pleasure. In England, romantic arrangements outside of marriage were never referred to—ever. That sort of thing was kept firmly under wraps in an English marriage. Whereas she understood from Verity that the French were far more open about affairs of the heart. *Vive la différence,* she thought as she listened to Albertine talking about her husband's flirtations as if he were a naughty little boy.

There is nothing more relaxing than a walk in the English countryside on a fine day, and as Mrs. Lovell had promised, the winding path through the leafy beech woods, with its dappled shade and sudden sun-filled views over the Chiltern Hills, to the little village of Bishop's Hever proved just the thing to restore spirits and lift the mood. Clementine felt a strong desire to be on the other side of those hills, sitting on the lawn with her husband to enjoy tea outside, and Althea recounting her latest travels. *We will go home this evening,* she thought. *I must be with my family now.* And with this determination in mind, turned to follow Mrs. Lovell back to Hyde Castle.

"There now, I am really looking forward to my tea," Mrs. Lovell said when they came within sight of the house. "Oh look, how charming. Maud has arranged tea on the lawn. Let's hope that Finley has left us something to eat; I am quite hungry."

Mrs. Jackson had taken the plant toxicology and the list up to her room and hidden them in her suitcase, and then pushed it under her bed. Unsure what to do next, she had spent the following two hours pacing up and down the lawn, waiting for her ladyship to return from her walk. She was relying on Lady Montfort to go up to her room to change her dress and wash her hands before tea, so she was frustrated to discover that when she walked up the lawn in the company of Mrs. Lovell and Mrs. Bartholomew, she obviously had no intention of doing either. She sat herself down next to Mr. Urquhart and teased him about catching cold on the lawn and ate a good few egg-and-cress sandwiches before enjoying a large slice of fruitcake.

Unable to contain her impatience enough even to drink a cup of tea, Mrs. Jackson covered her impatience by helping the inefficient Mrs. Haldane pour tea, and because she could neither sit down nor stand still, she made herself useful offering cake and sandwiches to the gathering under the trees on the edge of the lawn, getting in the way of the footman and the butler and causing them great irritation.

Finally everyone drifted off to busy themselves in the privacy of their rooms as they waited for the next gargantuan meal to be presented to them. And Lady Montfort got to her feet and announced that she had some letters to write.

Once she had gained the sanctuary of their rooms Lady Montfort said, "I've been thinking things through, Jackson, and I really believe we are wasting our time here. Really I do. And I am worried that we might very well be embroiled in all this nastiness in Europe and be at war by the end of the week. Perhaps we should go home tomorrow morning. I will let Mrs. Haldane know when we go down to dinner. I am sure she will . . ."

She turned and caught sight of her housekeeper's face and stopped in midsentence.

"Now I can tell by the expression on your face that you have found something."

"Yes indeed I have, m'lady. If you will excuse me for a moment I will go and fetch it."

She was back almost immediately, clutching her plant toxicology in one hand and almost brandishing the list in the other. She waited until Lady Montfort had taken off her hat and washed her hands in the washbasin, and when she had seated herself Mrs. Jackson handed her first the volume on poisonous plants and then the list.

"A list and a book. Which comes first?" Lady Montfort opened the book and then looked up at her.

"I found the book in the small library in the conservatory, and inside it was the list."

A short silence and then her ladyship said, "No, we will not be returning to Iyntwood tomorrow, Jackson. Not after this monumental discovery."

"Do you think it is significant, m'lady?"

"I most certainly do. Quickly let us send a note to Mr. Stafford, he is down by his lake with a crew of workmen. Tell Charles to take it to him immediately." She got up and scribbled on a sheet of paper at her writing desk, so full of intention that she didn't even bother to sit down.

"There now, by the time Charles has run down to Mr. Stafford to summon him to the orangery, we will have had time to look up all the plants on the list in this very useful little book. So when we meet with Mr. Stafford we will not be completely ignorant and he can help us go forward to the next step of this investigation. Well done, Jackson. How on earth did you come across it?"

"I think it would be more accurate to say that it came across me, m'lady. I was browsing among the bookshelves in the conservatory—and there it was."

Chapter Eighteen

Mrs. Jackson was silent as she and Lady Montfort walked back to the orangery to meet Mr. Stafford. In the peaceful serenity of this exquisite late-summer afternoon it was unimaginable that their country might be on the brink of war. The solid stone castle standing squarely in its grounds presided over a world lit by that particularly golden luminosity peculiar to the northern European hour before sunset in late summer. As evening approached, the air began to cool, accentuating the scent of flowers that filled the tranquil gardens. *It is what Mr. Stafford calls the golden hour,* Mrs. Jackson thought; *there is something so enchanting about this time of day.*

They turned at the bottom of the herbaceous border and rounded a tall yew hedge that enclosed the entrance to the herb garden surrounding the orangery. The garden was alive with butterflies: Red Admirals and Purple Emperors fluttered like live jewels among the rosy red flowers of thyme and the deep-amethyst stalks of lavender in the slanting golden rays of the late-afternoon sun. The scent of crushed chamomile underfoot and the pungent nip of mint were balm to the troubled heart, and Mrs. Jackson slowed her pace and thought how beautiful the English countryside was, with its narrow country lanes flanked by hedges of flowering hawthorn with wildflowers crowding their verges and ditches. *We can't go to war, we can't involve ourselves in Europe's madness,* she said to herself as they crossed the chamomile lawn and walked up the steps to the entrance of the orangery, where Mr. Stafford was waiting for them.

Looking up from the herb garden to see him standing there, his hat in his hands as he watched them cross the lawn to meet him, she wondered how on earth she could have been so foolish as to imagine that he would arrange a covert meeting with someone like Mrs. Wickham. She remembered how suspicious she had been of him yesterday and felt awkward and embarrassed. *I practically accused him,* she said to herself. *What was I thinking?* And immediately she gave herself some advice: *You have your life and he has his, and they are quite separate. So don't go and get all fanciful and make a complete fool of yourself.*

"Good afternoon, Mr. Stafford, so sorry to drag you up here again, but we need to consult with you." Lady Montfort practically ran up the steps to him.

"Good afternoon, m'lady, Mrs. Jackson." The sun shone down on his bared head, lighting up the clean lines of his face and making his clear eyes shine with what Mrs. Jackson took for amusement as he nodded to her, an inquiring expression on his face as if he were saying, *What will she come up with this afternoon?* But the warmth of his expression assured her that whatever she had in mind he was game for, and she found herself smiling back as she looked up at him standing there on the top step.

"We have found, or rather Mrs. Jackson has found, something very interesting and we need your horticulturalist's opinion." *How resilient she is,* thought Mrs. Jackson in admiration that her ladyship had quite recovered from her panic about war and her determination less than an hour ago that they pack up and go home.

"Let's go inside," Mr. Stafford said as he opened the door, and they walked into the silent and still world of the orangery with its solemn procession of trees smelling so deliciously of blossom and that particularly stringent odor of potting soil, common in all buildings that house plants.

Lady Montfort handed the book and its attendant list over and then stood, hands at her sides, face expectant, and waited. And Mrs. Jackson stood equally as hopeful, but could not help but notice what a nice shape Mr. Stafford's head was as he bent it to look down at the list.

"Ah yes, I see. It is certainly a list of poisonous plants. And a very interesting one because it seems to fall into several categories: the British hedgerow and garden variety and then the temperate, tropic, or subtropic variety, and all by itself this reference to the tobacco plant. Do you believe it might have a bearing on Mr. Bartholomew's death, Lady Montfort?"

"I do hope so, Mr. Stafford. Actually Mrs. Jackson was talking to Mr. Urquhart in the conservatory when she found this little volume among some books there . . . and inside it was . . ." Lady Montfort glanced about for Mrs. Jackson to chime in with her account, but she had wandered off into the far corner of the orangery and, having slipped behind the lime tree at the end, was poking about among the coiled hoses and the dried-up leaves in the recess of the wall.

"What was it Mr. Urquhart said to you about the book, Mrs. Jackson . . . Jackson?"

"If you would excuse me, m'lady, for just a moment." Mrs. Jackson stepped to one side of a coiled hose so she was no longer blocking her light from the windows on the south side of the building. She lifted an arm and pulled back a thickly leafed lime branch and a beam of sunlight shone at her feet as she gently stirred a cobwebby pile of dead leaves trapped behind the hose with the toe of her shoe. And there among the brown and gray pile of plant debris came a flash of brilliant cobalt blue. With an exclamation of satisfaction Mrs. Jackson crouched down on the floor, pulled a handkerchief from her pocket and, using the utmost care, lifted something out of the pile of leaves, and even though she wanted to cry out, *Would you believe what I have just found?* she made herself walk out from behind the screen of trees at a sedate pace to her two companions standing on the tiled floor, waiting for her to join them.

Lady Montfort took one look at her face and said, "Have you found what you were looking for?" and then laughed. "Of course you have. Look at her, Mr. Stafford, she looks quite triumphant. Please don't keep us in suspense, Jackson."

Mrs. Jackson opened her hand and there, lying in the clean folds of her handkerchief, was a narrow, blue-glass bottle, the kind used in chemist's shops all over England. It was three inches tall with ridged sides and a grubby printed label, slightly lifting at the corners, stuck on its flat front. On it were the words "An Aid to Digestion" written in a fine copperplate hand in fading ink. The stopper of the bottle, was missing. Lady Montfort carefully lifted the bottle, still wrapped in the handkerchief, out of Mrs. Jackson's hand and raised it to her nostrils. She waved it back and forth under her nose as she cautiously sniffed the air above its open mouth and then she said, "Ginger? Yes, I think I smell ginger." She handed it to Mr. Stafford and Mrs. Jackson in turn. "Do not inhale any of the powder when you sniff," she said, and Mrs. Jackson remembered reading in the plant toxicology that ground castor beans could be damaging to the lungs if their powder was inhaled. The two of them obediently lowered their heads as they wafted the blue bottle under their noses as if they were savoring the bouquet of a fine and delicate wine.

"Yes, ginger." Mrs. Jackson could hardly conceal her disappointment. She had expected to find something of great importance. For surely that was what the unidentified person hiding in the orangery last night had been searching for, before he was interrupted by the arrival of the lovelorn Mrs. Wickham? But apparently all she had found was a bottle of digestive powders that the agonized Mr. Bartholomew had taken in an attempt to soothe his burning stomach as he lay dying in this building five months ago.

Mr. Stafford took the bottle back from her. "Yes, there is ginger," he said, and then: "Perhaps a little peppermint, but there is something else too, something sweet and powdery like vanilla—is vanilla used as an aid to indigestion?"

"I have no idea," said Lady Montfort, "but I know who would: Mr. Urquhart has his own little pharmacopoeia that he refers to, to nurse his delicate system." Lady Montfort turned to Mrs. Jackson. "I think you have found something important, Jackson, we just don't know how it all fits together, quite just yet. But what made you look for it?"

"There is at least half of the bottle's contents left . . ." Mr. Stafford said as he held it up to the direct light. "D'you see? And the printed part of the label says 'Fisk & Able' and an address just off the Burlington Arcade in Cork Street in London. D'you know what I think?" His voice was almost loud in the quiet room and his face was flushed with excitement. "I think we should have the stuff in this bottle analyzed. Because even though the powders inside look and smell innocuous enough, they could very well have been put there to mask the taste and smell of poison. And perhaps . . ." He held the list up in his left hand, with his right holding the little blue bottle shining in the sunlight, which reminded Mrs. Jackson of the illustration of the apothecary in her copy of *Romeo and Juliet*.

"'Put this in any liquid thing you will, /And drink it off; and, if you had the strength/ Of twenty men, it would dispatch you straight,'" she quoted.

"Absolutely, Jackson, how right you are," said Lady Montfort, beaming at her, and Mr. Stafford said in his forthright way, "Why, Mrs. Jackson, you never cease to astonish and amaze me."

"And me," said Lady Montfort, "for it is very possible she has found out the How of it all. Oh do be careful not to get any of that stuff on your hands, Mr. Stafford. And let us be careful not to touch the bottle itself . . . the police might want to test it later for fingerprints."

Mr. Stafford took the bottle, which was still wrapped up carefully like a precious thing in Mrs. Jackson's handkerchief. "If there is castor bean powder in this nasty little blue bottle, just one grain could be lethal—enough to kill several men— and the contents of this bottle, if they contain such a poison, could eliminate an entire village." Mr. Stafford's face was grim as he turned to Mrs. Jackson, who was deep in thought.

"Perhaps no one poisoned Mr. Bartholomew's breakfast," she said. "Perhaps Mr. Bartholomew ate some of the kedgeree, and because he ate so much his stomach started to complain so he took out his bottle of digestive powders and sprinkled some on his breakfast. He was halfway through his second plate when the poison began to work. Feeling unwell, he got up from the dining-room table and went outside for a walk, hoping that the fresh air would restore him, which it sadly failed to do."

"And he was found two hours later in the orangery by Johnny," put in Mr. Stafford, staring at Mrs. Jackson with such unmistakable awe that she had to look away.

Lady Montfort's voice was breathless with excitement as she conjured up Mr. Bartholomew's last moments: "He came into the orangery perhaps to find water. He pulls out his digestive powders because now he is in considerable pain and can only think of one thing that might help him."

"And it is the very thing that is killing him, poor chap," Mr. Stafford joined in. "As he falls to the floor the bottle flies out of his hand and lands up against the wall behind the hoses."

"And over the months, bits of debris and dust are swept carelessly over the bottle and cover it, until it is found by this clever woman." Lady Montfort's voice was jubilant and she looked as if she were about to embrace her housekeeper.

"And that is what the person who attacked Mrs. Wickham was looking for when he heard that the orangery was open for the first time in months. He was looking for the bottle of poison, as it had evidently not been found on Mr. Bartholomew's person when his body was discovered," Mrs. Jackson finished, and all three of them stared at one another, horrified by the wicked simplicity of what might conceivably have occurred.

"It could have happened at *any time* after the murderer had doctored the digestive powders," put in Lady Montfort, and Mrs. Jackson smiled because she knew exactly what her ladyship was thinking.

"What on earth made you think to look in the corner?"

"I think it was finding the list in the book, m'lady. It seemed as if it was an invitation to seriously consider that Mr. Bartholomew was maliciously poisoned. Then I wondered what Mrs. Wickham's attacker had been doing in the orangery before she interrupted him. Mrs. Wickham said she was standing in the orangery and someone came up behind her from behind the trees. As we were standing here I thought that he must have been searching for something that might incriminate him, something Mr. Bartholomew had dropped before he died. And of course it was this bottle of digestive powders. Ever since the day of the murder the orangery has been locked up—now everyone who was in the house on the day Mr. Bartholomew died is gathered here together again and the orangery is open for the first time since March. It was the murderer's opportunity to retrieve the one thing that pointed to Mr. Bartholomew being murdered. If Mrs. Wickham had not come in here and practically bumped into the murderer he would have found his bottle, broken it up, and then scattered the pieces. If there is poison in here," she waved the bottle, "then we know *how* Mr. Bartholomew was poisoned, and it only remains for us to determine who wrote that list." She was slightly out of breath after what was for her a long speech, her face glowing with pride. Mr. Stafford could hardly take his eyes off her.

"Very logical reasoning, Jackson." Lady Montfort was ready for action. "Mr. Stafford, I think we need to enlist your help. If you will take this little bottle to your cottage and empty some of the contents into a container and send it with a letter to Messrs. Fisk & Able asking them for an analysis, that would be most helpful. If you can get to the post office first thing tomorrow morning it will reach London by late-afternoon post. Wait a moment—what time is the last post at Bishop's Hever, is it half past seven, tonight? Sometimes these little village post offices only have five or six deliveries a day."

"Then I had better hurry. If I miss the last post I can catch the early-morning post at half past eight and it should reach London for the midday delivery."

"We must keep some of the contents intact in the blue bottle, Mr. Stafford," Mrs. Jackson added her instructions. "After all, we might be damaging evidence that the police will need later."

"How long do you imagine it will take Fisk & Able to determine if there is poison in the bottle?" Lady Montfort asked. "If we declare on Germany, then all of us will naturally disperse to our homes." Mrs. Jackson noticed that all the gaiety and excitement of discovery had disappeared and understood her ladyship's concern that they were running out of time.

"I will stress the urgency of it, Lady Montfort. It will not take them long to ascertain if the contents of a powder they have made up has been adulterated with another substance. Of course, identifying that substance might take longer."

"Oh dear," said Mrs. Jackson. "How I wish I had found that list and bottle earlier."

"I can certainly ask them to *test* for a poison, Mrs. Jackson, and there is a telephone at the post office I can use to make sure they are prompt to do so when they receive the package," said Mr. Stafford.

"How would they test for poison?" Mrs. Jackson asked.

"I believe a mouse is considered an adequate enough test."

"Well I suppose a dead mouse is a small price to pay." Her long-held belief that rodents and small animals should restrict themselves from venturing into pantries and larders far overrode any squeamishness she might have had about this small sacrifice.

"If they find one of the poisons on the list in that bottle, then all we have to do is identify who wrote the list and we will have our murderer." Eyes agleam, Lady Montfort saw a triumphant conclusion within their grasp.

She always makes it sound so simple, thought Mrs. Jackson, *and then there we are wondering if we are going to be shot or poisoned or hit over the head.*

Lady Montfort's attitude had changed considerably from the woman who had wanted to pack up and call it a day; she was in full take-charge form. "Jackson, would you be willing to help me find handwriting specimens from everyone who was staying here when Mr. Bartholomew died? I can get Mr. Urquhart to show me his scrapbook, and I already have a sample of Mrs. Haldane's writing from her letter inviting us here, but if you would identify the handwriting of the rest of the people staying in the house when Mr. Bartholomew died, then I think our work here will be practically done." Lady Montfort was so charged-up with what they must do next that she was pacing up and down, her mind hopping from one task to the next.

"I have seen Mrs. Walker's handwriting; it is of the old-fashioned, round-hand style, nothing like the beautifully formed copperplate on the list, and the butler's handwriting is almost illegible." She looked again at the list. "Perhaps after dinner I could pop into Mr. Haldane's study while he and Mr. Wickham are drinking port in the dining room."

"Thank you, Jackson; this business of identifying handwriting is not a very pleasant task, I wouldn't want you to do something that made you feel uncomfortable." And then, not waiting to ascertain the true level of Mrs. Jackson's possible discomfort, she breezed on with her own tasks.

"I will tackle Mr. Urquhart on the subject of digestive powders and suppliers and whether he did or did not advise Mr. Bartholomew on cures for stomach disorders. He probably knows who this Fisk & Able are."

Mrs. Jackson hesitated. Unlike her ladyship, she did not enjoy the company of the elderly Scotsman; she found him neither amusing nor diverting and thought him watchful in his quiet, covert way. And, in her opinion, his finicky and fastidious preoccupation with his health was unnatural in a man. Her expression must have communicated this because her ladyship went on: "Yes, I know, Jackson, I must tread very carefully indeed. Because even though he appears to be frail and harmless, it does not take brute strength to poison someone. And Mr. Urquhart has no alibi for last night when Mrs. Wickham was attacked."

"Neither does Mrs. Bartholomew," pointed out Mr. Stafford. "And they say that poison is a woman's weapon." He laughed when both ladies turned offended faces toward him and held up his hands in the age-old gesture of defense.

"In my experience, Mr. Stafford, most women are capable of doing anything a man can do, and I am sure there are many men who would have no compunction in resorting to using the cowardly weapon of poison," said Lady Montfort, and a thoroughly chastened Mr. Stafford tucked the blue bottle in his waistcoat pocket and, putting on his hat, said he would send word to them the moment he heard from Fisk & Able.

Chapter Nineteen

Clementine barely had enough time to throw on her evening dress in time for dinner, and when Mrs. Jackson had put up her hair and then retired to her room to change into her best black bombazine silk dress, they both went down the stairs at the double so as not to be late.

"I find it very strange that there might be someone sitting at the dining table who does not flinch from dropping poison into good, honest food, m'lady," Mrs. Jackson said to her ladyship as they joined the throng who swept into the dining room in a great herd, and sat down wherever they found themselves—leaving Mrs. Jackson and Clementine standing uncertainly at the top of the table.

If this is the way we go about conducting ourselves when war threatens, then civilized manners will certainly take a beating if we actually go to war. Momentarily stunned by the company's complete disregard for the order of precedence, Clementine remembered that she was to quiz Mr. Urquhart on Mr. Bartholomew's digestive powders and whipped down the length of the table as if she were competing in a game of musical chairs, and plonked herself down between Mrs. Haldane and Mr. Urquhart. She noticed Mr. Haldane was seated at the far end of the table, deep in conversation with Mr. Wickham and cheerfully ignoring his wife's other guests, which caused Clementine a silent harrumph about the mannerless people she found herself among. Then she became aware of a soft Edinburgh accent complaining gently in her ear and turned her attention to the elderly man on her right.

"I simply cannot abide listening to another evening of aggressive bluster from our host," Mr. Urquhart said, sipping a glass of water. "It is all quite unsettling. I do not imagine for one moment that I will be able to eat anything at all." He flapped his hand at the torchon of foie gras being offered by the footman and shook his head. "No, Charles, I cannot possibly eat that fatty liver, please take it away. Just bring me a nice floury potato, that is all I can possibly manage."

"I am not sure I have an appetite for my dinner either." Clementine exhibited a delicate little shiver of distaste. "I feel quite . . . put off."

"Oh dear me, Leddy Montfort, there is no need to suffer." He took a little pillbox from his pocket and placed it next to her plate. "Of all the nostrums that I have come across to keep my poor frail body tottering forward, I count on this one more than any other. It never lets me down; a simple compound of dandelion, artichoke, and fennel. Place it under your tongue and let it dissolve; there is only the merest bitterness to its flavor, and I can assure you, your appetite will return immediately. Of course it is too late for me to rely on such a simple remedy. My system has been in an uproar ever since Dorothy was attacked in the garden last night." He closed his eyes and lifted a hand to his brow at the horror of it.

Clementine reached for the enameled pillbox and as she did so happened to catch the eye of her housekeeper sitting across the table. To her consternation, Mrs. Jackson stared intently at her and gave the briefest but the most emphatic shake of her head.

Clementine withdrew her hand as if there had been a scorpion sitting on the white damask tablecloth. *What am I thinking?* All this talk of war had made her heedless. *Take whatever is in that pretty enamel box and I might be thrashing in agony on the dining-room floor in minutes, with this gentle old man administering all sorts of terrifying poisons in the guise of helping to "balance my delicate system."* She took a steadying sip of wine.

Her mind settled and she decided that she might take the pill, palm it, and then drop it under the table. She smiled at her housekeeper and nodded to reassure that she understood her concern and opened the lid of the pillbox.

Inside were several small tablets the color of mud. She tipped one out into her palm and, taking her glass of water in her right hand, pretended to swallow the tablet and took a sip of water. She dropped her left hand onto her lap and carefully tipped her palm to empty the tablet into her napkin. "Thank you, Mr. Urquhart, how kind of you."

"Do not mention it, my dear Leddy Montfort, you will feel as right as ninepence momentarily."

The footman served Mr. Urquhart his potato and he carefully speared a morsel with his fork in evident distaste.

"Have you heard if the seeds of the vanilla pod are efficacious for digestion?" Clementine's tone was casual, disinterested even; just a polite inquiry. But she was alert for a reaction.

"Vanilla?" He looked up at her as if she were joking with him. "Hmm, vanilla you say; whoever told you that, I wonder? It *was* used in ancient times to restore a more stable mood in hysterical women." His laugh was indulgent. "But not as a digestive aid, to my scant knowledge. It is primarily used as a pleasant flavor in cakes and biscuits. But I promise you that if you take the appropriate herbal remedies before you eat any meal, you will extend your life well into your nineties. Look at me, still going strong at seventy-five, and my doctor gave up on me years ago and said I would never make old bones." His kindly eyes were so benign behind his spectacles that Clementine didn't for one moment think she might be sitting next to a poisoner.

"Do you make up your own prescriptions?" she asked.

"Good heavens no, but Fisk & Able have been making wonderful compounds to aid digestion for decades now, and they are most efficacious. Poor Rupert was always an excessive overeater and suffered tremendously from indigestion as he went into his middle years, but not since I put him onto the powders from Fisk & Able."

Powders from Fisk & Able! Mr. Urquhart had recommended that Mr. Bartholomew take powders from Fisk & Able! She felt a momentary gallop of excitement and laid down her fork so that he could not see her hand trembling in excitement.

"Powders?" Clementine's heart rate had picked up considerably. "Why not tablets?"

Mr. Urquhart laughed. "Because he was quite unable to take any medicine in tablet form, no matter how many glasses of water he chased it down with, he took herbal powders dissolved in warm water. Mr. Able made them especially for him."

"I should get something similar for Lord Montfort." She did not feel the slightest remorse at assigning chronic indigestion to her husband, who never took medicine of any kind.

"Slippery elm, ginger, and a little peppermint is what I recommended for Rupert; simple enough to soothe the system of the heartiest overindulger." He smiled at her and took another tiny bite of potato. "And how is your appetite now, Leddy Montfort?"

"Quite restored," Clementine said as she turned to take a slice of succulent lamb offered by the butler, and wondered if the brown tablet on her lap contained one of the poisons on the list they had found in the plant toxicology and might, as Mr. Stafford had suggested, wipe out an entire village.

After dinner Mrs. Haldane and her guests left the dining room to Mr. Haldane and settled themselves in the Salon Vert for the rest of the evening.

"Would you play for us, dear Maud?" asked Finley, and the good-natured Mrs. Haldane took her seat at the pianoforte and beckoned Mrs. Wickham to her side to sing. Clementine noticed that Mrs. Wickham moved a little less stiffly. She obediently rose and made her way to the piano and Mr. Evans took up his position in waiting by the salon door. *She seems a good deal more recovered; the resilience of the young!* Clementine had been conscious of the butler all evening, as he had waited on them at dinner, and twice she had looked to see if she could detect any perceivable interaction between Mrs. Wickham and Mr. Evans. But the butler was quite punctilious in his duties and Mrs. Wickham ate her food in docile silence, every so often turning to Mr. Haldane on her left to be lectured on munitions.

Clementine had never particularly enjoyed listening to young women sing; amateur singers rarely had a voice worth listening to, being often off-key, nasal in their intonation, or worst of all shrill and shrieking. But as Mrs. Haldane played the simple melodies of old English folk songs, she was quite pleased to listen to Mrs. Wickham. The young woman had a naturally pleasant voice and the sentimental love songs were a delightful change from the Schubert's lieder she so often had to endure from the daughters of her friends. The butler evidently enjoyed them too, for the expression on his face softened a little and she noticed that his left foot gently tapped in time to the songs.

Mrs. Lovell was sitting on the sofa next to Mrs. Bartholomew, reading a list of names that she had come up with for Mr. Bartholomew's unnamed tea rose. His wife's face bore all the hallmarks of a woman who had been pushed well beyond her limits by the Hyde Rose Society over the naming of his white rose. Every so often she would nod politely, but her large, dark eyes were somber and she was clearly off in a world of her own.

Mr. Wickham, seated in a corner, was reading through the evening newspapers, each sporting bold headlines declaring the imminent invasion by the German army assembling along the Belgium border. GERMANY DECLARES WAR ON RUSSIA AND PREPARES TO INVADE FRANCE, blared one headline. THE SWORD IS FORCED INTO OUR HAND, says the Kaiser, and DECLARES WAR ON RUSSIA AND FRANCE, proclaimed another. Every so often, to everyone's annoyance, but most of all his wife's, Mr. Wickham would read out a report, cutting across her pretty voice with his petulant exclamations: ". . . crowds are beginning to gather outside Buckingham Palace—fat lot of good that will do them, why can't people stay quietly in their homes?" he announced with distaste. "And it says here that despite being on the brink of war, holidaymakers celebrated Bank Holiday Monday in all the south-coast towns . . . extraordinary behavior. I think perhaps we should say our goodbyes to you tomorrow, Maud; thank goodness we are not planning on going anywhere by train . . ." With every pronouncement, Mrs. Bartholomew exhibited more anxiety about her return to France.

"Je dois partir demain," she said, and Clementine noticed that her hands were holding on to each other so tightly that her knuckles were quite white.

"Perhaps you should make a telephone call to the stationmaster at Waterloo and reserve a place on the boat-train,

Mrs. Bartholomew," she suggested, and the lady nodded her head in agreement.

As Mrs. Wickham's last song, "Early One Morning," came to an end, she turned from the piano and groped for her handkerchief, and Maud said in her gentle voice, "Now now, Dorothy, it is just a song, dear."

"It is such a sad one though; deception is the cruelest of betrayals," Mrs. Wickham said and subsided on the sofa next to Finley to help him search through his embroidery silks for violet blue.

Clementine got to her feet. "I have been admiring your orchids, Mrs. Haldane, you must have been collecting for years." She stopped briefly in the middle of the room by Mrs. Haldane, who, having left the piano, was now seated before her painted composition of Mr. Bartholomew's white rose, which was standing before her on a little table, its petals glowing a pure pearl white against a swathe of blue silk. Mrs. Haldane smiled her tired smile.

"Thank you, Lady Montfort, my orchids are the work of the past fifteen years. But it is my head gardener who is responsible for their vigorous health."

Seeking an excuse to explore the room where her housekeeper had found the plant toxicology and the list, Clementine said she would take Mrs. Jackson for a turn or two around the conservatory to show her the orchids. The two of them slowly walked the considerable length of the conservatory's humid interior, stopping to admire different varieties of palm and enjoying the fragile beauty of the orchids grouped throughout.

"What a collection," Clementine said rather enviously. "Look at that glorious thing; it looks as if it has a cat's face—do you see, Jackson, like little whiskers? I expect this is an incredibly rare collection."

"Isn't this a castor plant?" Mrs. Jackson stopped in front of a large, heavy-leafed specimen in a green glazed pot towering up into the glass ceiling.

"Castor bean . . . Wait a moment, what does our toxicology have to say? Perhaps it will help us identify it." Mrs. Jackson pulled the slim leather-bound volume from her pocket, and Clementine consulted its index and turned to the right page. "Ah yes . . . 'Latin name *Ricinus communis*: leaves and stems are a dark reddish purple or bronze.' And look, do you see the fruit in the illustration?" She tilted the book for Mrs. Jackson to see the glossy color plate of *Ricinus communis,* with a detailed inset illustration of the flowers and their fruit. They both looked up at the small tree.

"This one isn't flowering, but it describes the fruit as 'spiny, greenish (to reddish purple) containing large, oval, shiny, beanlike, highly poisonous seeds with variable brownish mottling.'" Around the base of the tree some round conkerlike pods had dried and Mrs. Jackson bent down and picked one up. "Ah yes, m'lady, here are the beans." She split the dry pod and emptied the beans out into her mistress's hand.

"Aren't they pretty, Jackson? Yes, this is definitely a castor-bean plant." She turned to her housekeeper, her face lit with the pleasure she evidently felt that they had made a discovery. "Oh my dear Leddy Montfort and Edith, please do not play with the seeds, however pretty they are." Mr. Urquhart was regarding them from the doorway of the salon. His round, plum-velvet pillbox hat had slipped a little to one side, giving him a monkeylike appearance, and his eyes glistened with interest behind his spectacles. *My goodness,* thought Clementine, *all he needs is a barrel organ.*

"Such a lovely specimen of the castor-bean plant," Clementine exclaimed, dropping her hand with the book closed to her side.

"And such deadly fruit," twinkled Mr. Urquhart. "One of those beans in your hand could do quite serious damage."

"Good heavens," cried Clementine and hastily dropped the beans onto the floor, making the old man laugh and reassure her that they must be dried and ground to powder before they were truly harmful. "Do you see how much he knows, Jackson?" Clementine whispered under her breath.

"But it is not as dangerous as the deadly *Cicuta maculata,* which causes death within fifteen minutes. Oh, no need to worry, there is none in this pretty conservatory and the plant thrives only in North America."

"How much you know, Mr. Urquhart." Clementine's laugh was more than just a little shaky.

"But if we are looking for the queen of poison, in my opinion this beautiful white Nerium reigns supreme." He walked over to the far corner of the conservatory where there was a superb specimen, standing easily twelve to fourteen feet, with slender, elongated silvery-green leaves and clusters of pristine white flowers. "The oleander, a delicious plant with that soft powdery aroma of mmm . . ." He wrinkled his nose and inhaled the fragrance from a cluster of white flowers closest to him.

"Vanilla," whispered Mrs. Jackson almost reverently as she bent her head to a panicle of flowers and inhaled. "How . . . how . . . lovely!"

"But do not touch it, my dear Edith. Not even a petal or a leaf. Every part of this lovely shrub is poisonous—deadly poisonous. And if you were to break off a branch, the sap might irritate your skin quite unpleasantly. And please refrain from inhaling its scent too deeply, even that is sometimes an irritant. I am afraid it is true that many beautiful trees and flowers from other parts of the world are most toxic."

"Yes," said Clementine, gathering her wits. "But aren't both belladonna and the lovely aconite poisonous too, and both of them grow in our gardens and country hedgerows."

"Just as you say, Leddy Montfort. Atropa belladonna, or deadly nightshade as it is commonly known—'beautiful leddy' of course is the translation of 'belladonna'—is quite deadly. The juice of the berry was used by leddies a hundred years ago. A little drop was placed in the eye to dilate the pupils, an effect considered to be both attractive and seductive."

"Oh really? I had no idea, how fascinating." Clementine marveled at the extent of his knowledge, feeling as she did so quite unnerved. If only he would come out from under the shade of the oleander, as the half-light made him look quite menacing.

"Oh yes, belladonna has many uses, the poison was used in ancient times on the tips of arrows. And then, conversely, it was used in medicine to cure stomach ulcers, a fascinating plant indeed and extremely poisonous. Most plant toxins have both an efficacious and a dangerous side to them, Leddy Montfort. Digitalis is a perfect example. The delightful foxglove flowering on the edges of our woodland can be used to treat a weak-heart condition, as well as to stop the heart completely, depending on the amount that is administered and of course for what reason."

Standing in the shadow of the towering trees and shrubs, there was something almost malevolent about the round-shouldered old man, frail though he appeared to be. His cashmere shawl had slipped off his shoulders and the embroidery on his buff waistcoat looked like an illustration of the very plants he was talking about: embroidered vines twined around clusters of dark red berries, and star-shaped flowers with yellow centers drooped their delicate pale-blue heads. The electric light hanging overhead in the roof of the conservatory shone down on him through the branches of the oleander shrub and caught the polished lenses of his spectacles.

They gleamed like mirrors, making him look like a large insect standing under the tree.

"So much edifying folklore surrounds the lovely belladonna and aconite," the old man continued, every word precise and clear. "In the past, witches were believed to use a mixture of belladonna, opium poppy, aconite, and hemlock in an ointment, which they applied to help them fly to gatherings with other witches. I often wondered if they physically flew, or merely joined with their sisters in a flight of the mind. Some of these wonderful old plants can produce vivid hallucinations, d'ye understand? But perhaps we are far more enchanted with the image of these outcast women, astride their brooms— or maybe seated on the backs of toads, flitting through the night sky."

Clementine's laugh was forced and she felt a tremendous desire to fly away herself, as far as she could get from this strange little man with his shining insectlike spectacles and his sinister knowledge of poisonous plants. "I think we should go and help Mrs. Lovell and Mrs. Bartholomew choose names for Mr. Bartholomew's rose," she said to stop this unnerving conversation. "Are you feeling creative, Mr. Urquhart? I think Mrs. Bartholomew is anxious to name her husband's rose before she returns to France."

"Don't waste your energy, my dear Leddy Montfort." The elderly man stepped forward out of the shadows and into the light and Clementine felt almost reassured by the normalcy of his appearance now that she could see his eyes behind the lenses of his spectacles.

"I think it would be fun," she said gaily. "We can make it into a parlor game, lighten the mood a little with all this talk of war."

"Yes, let's treat it like a parlor game, for I promise you, dear Albertine has already decided what name she will give to

Rupert's pretty rose. I can quite assure you of that." And with all the courtesy of the late-Victorian gentleman, he gently herded them out of the conservatory and back into the salon, where the company was arguing over an appropriate name for Mr. Bartholomew's rose.

"Leddies, leddies, please—I thought war had already broken out. What are we trying to accomplish here?" he cried as he preceded Clementine and Mrs. Jackson into the salon and stood in front of Mrs. Lovell and Mrs. Bartholomew, who dropped their eyes and apologized.

"We are trying to decide," Mrs. Lovell said quickly, before she could be interrupted, "the best name for Rupert's white rose." And Mrs. Bartholomew folded her hands in her lap and compressed her lips.

She doesn't want them to be involved, Clementine realized. *And I don't blame her one little bit. This has nothing to do with them at all, it was her husband who bred this rose, after all.*

Mrs. Haldane put down her paintbrush and came over to join them. "Why don't we name it after a bird? Rupert so loved birds. What about *White Dove,* the dove of peace?"

"Not for a rose," said Mrs. Bartholomew very firmly.

Over in the far corner, Mr. Wickham sighed and put down the paper. "Make a list," he ordered. "And then Albertine should choose—*but* we must agree with her choice if she wishes the rose to be registered with the Royal Horticultural Society, it says so in our bylaws."

"Oh, but I have an idea," Clementine put in. "Let us each take a slip of paper and write down the name that we think would best suit the rose. Why, we could make a game of it. If Mrs. Haldane were to put the rose in the middle of the table, here, we could each come up with our best choice and write it down. Then we each draw one and try to guess who chose the name. Perhaps this way Mrs. Bartholomew will find the name she is looking for."

"What a wonderful, wonderful idea!" Mrs. Haldane looked quite pretty as her face lit up with a smile of genuine pleasure. She had been so low-spirited and quiet these past few days that Clementine was quite convinced she was suffering still from her husband's brutality to her three nights ago.

Mrs. Lovell, their practical leader, took charge. "Gather round in a circle, that's it. A game will help shake us out of the doldrums." When Mrs. Lovell smiled, her large plain face was most attractive, but tonight, to Clementine's mind, her toothy smile was unnerving. *I simply must get a grip on myself,* thought Clementine; *all that sinister talk in the conservatory about poison has completely unnerved me.*

Mr. Urquhart smiled. "And if we can't come to an agreement through Leddy Montfort's parlor game, we might ask the celebrated rosarian Henry Bennett for his suggestions." And Mrs. Haldane and Mrs. Lovell burst out laughing as they looked at each other. The suggestion of a parlor game had eased the tension and restored good humor all around and Clementine felt less tense and almost lost the feeling that she must be on her guard.

"Henry Bennett advised Finley on how to best breed his pretty Cupid, didn't he, Finley?" said Mrs. Lovell, and she and Mrs. Haldane giggled like naughty schoolgirls teasing their schoolmaster.

"Yes, my dear leddies, he most certainly did. Dear Mr. Bennett gave me very precise instructions, which I followed to the letter. Laugh all ye wish, it was indeed a celestial intervention and a most useful one, too." His smile was benevolent as he gazed at them both, neither discomfited nor annoyed by their laughter.

Clementine decided she needed to know a little more. "I don't understand," she said, looking for clarification.

"There is a sphere, another physical world, where those who have gone on to the next life enter, and it is on this plane that we can converse with them," the old man explained.

My goodness, thought Clementine, *he is quite serious*. What an eccentric Mr. Urquhart was, with his tea-time cakes, his herbal remedies, and his knowledge of roses, plant poisons, and the occult. Now that he was indulging his friends' teasing his interest in the spirit world, she had quite forgotten how disturbed she had felt in the conservatory. But evidently Mrs. Jackson had not. She now spoke out with marked disapproval.

"I don't believe in that sort of thing," she said rather primly, looking down her nose. "If those who have gone before can indeed communicate with us, I don't think we should stir things up and bother them. It is wrong to interfere with things we don't completely understand."

Was this her circumspect housekeeper who barely uttered a word of opinion unless it was strongly sought? *Making discoveries has certainly brought Edith Jackson out of her shell.* Clementine realized that she enjoyed hearing her housekeeper's inner monologue.

"I am inclined to agree with you, Edith," said Mrs. Lovell. "But Finley only calls on people who have done good things, and his questions are quite benign."

An argument broke out between them all on the rights and wrongs of contacting the world of the dearly departed, until Clementine interrupted them.

"I have a wonderful name for Mr. Bartholomew's exquisite rose," she said. "Shall we all write up our suggestions?"

And Mrs. Haldane obediently searched for pencils and cut strips of paper from her sketch pad.

"I will just spectate, if I may." Mr. Urquhart took two tiny white pills from a gold box. He caught Clementine's eye and said, "Peppermint," in a faint voice and she nodded her commiseration.

"One slip of paper each," Mrs. Haldane said as she handed out paper and pencils. "Edith, please come and sit by me. You will have to help me, I am sure I shall never think of anything. I am such a dunce at parlor games."

They settled down in a circle around a table on which Mrs. Wickham had placed an empty basket for their slips of paper, together with the china-blue pot in which grew the sturdy stems, leaves, and blooms of Mr. Bartholomew's white rose. Even Mr. Wickham came over to join them, saying officiously, "We only write the name of the rose. Nothing else, otherwise it might give the game away."

Clementine had not expected them to participate quite so thoroughly as the Hyde Rose Society's chatter died down. They sat and thought, bit the ends of their pencils, and then concentrated in earnest. The minutes ticked by; the mantel clock chimed a silvery peel and six pencils scratched away on paper.

"Have we all written something? We must fold our papers exactly in half and put them in the basket. No, Maud, just in half, that's the way," commanded Mr. Wickham. "And I will give it a good shake." He picked up the basket and passed it for their offerings. He reminded Clementine of a terrier: every movement was brisk, and if they didn't comply with his exact wishes they might be given a little nip.

"Dear Albertine, even if you don't choose my name, I will not mind at all." Mrs. Haldane hastened to assure her friend that there would be no hard feelings and Mrs. Bartholomew gave her hand an affectionate squeeze and murmured her thanks.

"It is, after all, just a little game to pass the time," said

Mrs. Lovell, as if to convince herself that they would not all fall out again if a winner was not chosen from their suggestions.

Mrs. Bartholomew put her hand into the basket. "What do I do now?" she asked Clementine.

"Draw one out and then read what is written there, and we will try to guess who named the rose."

"What fun!" cried Mrs. Wickham, her girlish spirits quite restored. She smiled at her husband but he turned his head away. *What a miserable little worm he is,* thought Clementine. *Why does he always seek to put her in her place?*

Mrs. Bartholomew plucked out a folded paper and opened it. She laughed. "'Pure Justice.' Well, this is Clive's choice most certainly. You completely gave it away with your 'Justice' reference, Clive." Clementine glanced at the paper as it was thrown down on the table. *It is true that people's handwriting accurately represents their character,* she thought. Mr. Wickham's handwriting was tight and small with an aggressive dash at the end of the word *justice.*

Mr. Wickham said, "I think it is a good name, it would do justice to Rupert's hard work." As usual his tone was tetchy, and Mrs. Bartholomew shot an almost scornful look in his direction.

"I will pick one next," said Mrs. Lovell. "Let me see, what do I have? 'The Pearl.' Oh dear, of course I can guess who—because it is mine. How silly, I have picked my own name." Mrs. Jackson craned her neck to look at the slip of paper, and Clementine glanced down at Mrs. Lovell's hand holding the paper next to her. Her writing was well formed, upright, and even. *Yes,* thought Clementine, *just one look at the handwriting is enough to guess who has written it, but it is nothing like that on the list of poisonous plants.*

"Mrs. Jackson's turn," said Clementine.

"'White Hart,'" read out Mrs. Jackson as she looked around

her, and her eyes came to rest on Mrs. Wickham, who was sim-pering and looking coy.

"Dorothy, you just gave yourself away, my dear. Of course 'White Hart' is yours." Mrs. Lovell patted Dorothy's arm as if she had done something clever. And Clementine picked up the discarded slip and looked at the ornate, immature hand. *Not your handwriting on the list, then, Mrs. Wickham,* she thought, and said as she looked across at the young woman, "I think that is a beautiful name for a white rose, Mrs. Wickham, espe-cially since you have spelled it h-a-r-t, most suitable."

Mr. Wickham put his hand into the basket next. "Hmm, hard to say who could have come up with this one. " 'Rupert's Pride.' Let me think now. Well, it is either Lady Montfort, Albertine, Mrs. Jackson, or Maud. I say Mrs. Jackson."

"Wrong." said Mrs. Jackson and cast a brief look at the slip of paper in his hand.

"Well, I know it's not Maud, so I am guessing Albertine." Albertine shook her head.

"Well then, it is Lady Montfort." Mr. Wickham turned to her with a fussy little bow of his head.

"Yes it is mine. I think 'Rupert's Pride' is a wonderful name. I hope you decide to use it, Mrs. Bartholomew."

Mrs. Bartholomew returned to them from her thoughts and said, "Don't you English say that pride comes before a fall?"

There was a shocked silence at this remark, but the French-woman either was not aware of her faux pas or didn't care. *She has been in a strange mood today,* thought Clementine, *unset-tled out of her usual composure, and almost aggressive about the naming of her husband's rose.*

"Now there are just two slips left," said Mrs. Lovell. "Both Lady Montfort and Maud should pull them out at the same time."

They both opened their slips of paper and Clementine

laughed as she read hers. But Mrs. Haldane sat staring at her paper, a small frown gathering. And then she looked around at them all. "I don't understand," she said, holding out her slip, and Mrs. Jackson neatly took it from her.

"Albertine, why did you write your own name? Why would Rupert put your name to his rose?" Mrs. Haldane asked, her perplexity etched on her face in a deep frown, her voice quite sharp.

And why wouldn't he? Why wouldn't he name his rose after his lovely wife? Clementine asked herself. Mrs. Jackson handed the slip of paper to her. Mrs. Bartholomew had written her Christian name, ALBERTINE, in even capital letters, almost as if she were shouting it. And of course there was no way to identify if her handwriting matched that used to write the list of poisons.

The slip of paper Clementine had drawn read "The Dove," and it lay in her lap, in the pretty feminine handwriting of Mrs. Haldane, with its round-hand scrolls, loops, and curls: the handwriting that had been on her letter inviting Clementine to come to her rose symposium.

"Albertine, why would you name Rupert's rose after yourself?" cried Mrs. Haldane again. And Mrs. Lovell rushed in to say, "I think Rupert would have wanted his last rose named after his wife and Albertine is a perfect name for a white rose." She had reached out her hand to her friend, who was half out of her chair, her accusing face turned to Mrs. Bartholomew. "Albertine means noble and . . ."

"I am not sure he would . . ." said Mrs. Wickham, and Clementine saw there were tears standing in her eyes.

"And *I* am quite sure he would *not*," Mrs. Haldane's voice held no hint of her usual appeasement or apology; she was expressing herself almost angrily. *It is staggering,* thought Clementine, *that this mild-mannered woman could be so vehement.* Mrs. Haldane's eyes were angry and hard, and her lips clamped so tightly that she sounded as if she were talking through her teeth. *Well, it seems to me,* thought Clementine, *that we need not ask what sort of relationship Mrs. Haldane and Mrs. Wickham had with the late Mr. Bartholomew.* Their outrage that he might have preferred to name his rose after his wife had most certainly upset them both prodigiously.

"My dear Maud, of course the rose should bear my name. It must be named after its creator." For the first time since she had heard that her country might be in danger from a German invasion, Mrs. Bartholomew looked at ease and quite sure of herself.

"Its creator?" said Mrs. Wickham, tears spilling from her eyes.

"Yes, it was I who developed this rose, not Rupert."

And all the good-natured humor of the evening evaporated in an instant, as the group of rosarians exclaimed in horror and asked Mr. Bartholomew's wife exactly what she could possibly mean.

Clementine watched Mrs. Bartholomew shrug her shoulders in that wonderfully Gallic way that expresses impatience and distaste and a certain disregard for what others think.

"It is quite simple, really. Rupert loved roses, and so desperately wanted to create a rose of his own. Unfortunately, he was often rather muddled in his approach. So I helped him. I helped him to develop Golden Girl, which made him very happy. But it was I and I alone who spent two years creating my white rose: *Rosa Albertine.* It is quite simple, what is there to understand?" Again that dismissive little shrug, as if she was quite indifferent to the uproar she was causing.

"Are you saying that Rupert lied to us?" Mr. Wickham had a most censorious expression on his face; he had picked up a pencil and was beating a rapid little tattoo on the table with it, as if he were trying to decide whether to convict or not.

"Well, Clive, I think that is rather an unfortunate thing to say. I know that he took the credit for Golden Girl, and since I did not mind, what was the harm in that? But did he actually tell you that he had bred this white rose? I am quite sure he did not!"

"Are you saying that he would have *told us* that the rose you created was his?" cried Mrs. Lovell, not quite as distressed at this information as were her fellow rose breeders. She turned to Mrs. Haldane and said, "Would he have actually lied to us? Of course he would, I always told you he was a vain and ridiculously silly man, and now we have proof." Clementine did not find it surprising that Mrs. Lovell had such a low opinion of the erstwhile Mr. Bartholomew. In that moment it came to her that Mrs. Lovell had never been in love with Mr. Bartholomew or even merely attracted to him. But she might very well have been jealous of Mrs. Haldane's romantic inclinations toward him. As Mrs. Jackson had observed, Mrs. Lovell was very protective of Mrs. Haldane—motherly in her concern for her well-being—and when Mr. Haldane was in proximity quite assertively so. *That's it exactly,* thought Clementine. *She was not jealous that her friend was infatuated with a man that she herself was attracted to, she was jealous of their close relationship. She felt excluded.* The charismatic Mr. Bartholomew must have been a considerable distraction in the close friendship between the two women.

"I do not know what Rupert would have done or said to you about this rose. As you know, he came to show you the rose when I was in China. And then of course he died." Mrs. Bartholomew turned her face away, and a tear rolled out of the corner of her eye. "Ah," she said as she dashed the tear away, and it was a deeply broken and drawn-out sound, "all I wish to do now is return to my family. There is no reason for me to be here in this country any longer now that Rupert has gone."

Despite what was her obvious jealousy over the naming of

the white rose, Mrs. Haldane could not bear to see Albertine hurt. She jumped to her feet and put her arms around her, bending over her from behind the sofa, a lock of her faded blond hair hanging down over the Frenchwoman's shoulder. "Albertine, of course you should name your rose. We are just so terribly surprised. Please forgive us for making you justify yourself." She lifted her head and looked around the room to her friends. "Of course we understand. You were such a good wife to Rupert. The rose is Albertine. A lovely name for *your* beautiful rose."

Aha, thought Clementine, *she does not mind that this is Albertine's rose. She does not care that Mr. Bartholomew bamboozled all of them by pretending he knew how to breed roses. She simply could not bear the idea that if he had created this rose he would wish to name it after his wife and not Mrs. Roger Haldane.*

There were murmurs of dissent at this statement; Mrs. Wickham cried out that she was convinced the rose could only have been bred by Rupert and no one else, and Mrs. Lovell shushed her quite briskly.

Mr. Wickham took control. "We must abide by our bylaws. If the rose was Bartholomew's—and since he implied it was and is not here to tell us otherwise—it must legally be considered one bred by a member of our society." Which caused everyone to start talking at once.

Clementine turned her elegant head to Mrs. Jackson with her eyebrows ever so slightly raised. Having created this stormy interlude between the members of the Hyde Rose Society, she judged it best that they leave them to it. She nodded to the door and they murmured unheard good-nights before they left the Hyde Rose Society standing in the middle of the room, each one shouting down the other. But before she left, Mrs. Jackson, the perfect paid companion, turned at the door, returned to the little table, and swept up all the little slips of paper littering the table into a basket that she took with her from the room.

As they crossed the hall they came upon Mr. Haldane, who was marching across it toward the salon waving a late edition of the *Evening News* in his hand. "Germany has declared war on France!" he cried, his newspaper held aloft. "The German army has crossed the border at last—they have invaded Belgium." He waved his paper at them most aggressively. "And, what is more, if the Germans don't clear out of Belgium, we will declare war on them!"

Chapter Twenty

It was one o'clock in the morning. Mrs. Jackson, eyes tired and desperate to close, was sitting next to Lady Montfort in her bedroom as they assembled their carefully gathered clues in an attempt to discover which one of his friends had poisoned Mr. Bartholomew.

Before them on the table was a large square of white paper and in the middle was the list of seven poisonous plants. And arranged in clockwise fashion around the list were the slips of paper that had garnered handwriting samples from all the rosarians except those of Mr. Urquhart and Mrs. Bartholomew. Under each slip was written the name identifying the penmanship of its owner. And then off to one side there was a longer list of names of everyone staying in the house, including those who worked downstairs. Mrs. Jackson carefully drew a line through all the servants belowstairs. "None of their handwriting matches that on the list," she said. "And one of the housemaids and the scullery maid can neither read nor write, and the other maids' handwriting looks like a spider crawled across the page."

"So now, Jackson, we have three names left on our list: Mrs. Bartholomew, Mr. Haldane, and Mr. Urquhart. Strange that you could not find a specimen of Mr. Haldane's handwriting in his study, isn't it?" said Lady Montfort.

"He has an Imperial typewriter, m'lady. Perhaps he uses that for his correspondence."

Mrs. Jackson had let herself into the study after dinner while Mr. Haldane was still in the dining room, waited on by Mr. Evans. It had been an awful moment for her, tiptoeing around in the half-dark in a room that reeked of cigar smoke, which reminded her that she was trespassing in a very male preserve. The wastepaper basket was empty, but search as she might she could find no evidence of Mr. Haldane's handwriting. In desperation she had tried the drawers of the large mahogany desk, even though it was counter to her years of training as a servant and her natural self-respect to do so. She was almost grateful that all the drawers and cupboards in both desk and filing cabinet were locked.

"And I looked for Mr. Urquhart's scrapbook. It is no longer in the conservatory; he must have taken it up to his room." Mrs. Jackson wrinkled her nose in concentration. "I did catch a glimpse as he turned pages. His handwriting looked similar, evenly spaced copperplate, but at that distance I could not be sure." She had no intention of violating the privacy of either Mr. Urquhart's or Mrs. Bartholomew's rooms. "So the list of poisons could have been written by one of three people in this house, or maybe none of them at all." It had occurred to her, although she would never dream of saying so as she was sure her ladyship was aware of this too, that the list could be as old as the book, written years ago by someone who had nothing whatsoever to do with the Haldane household.

"I can't imagine that Mrs. Bartholomew would murder her husband; she appears to be quite devastated by his death." This remark caused Mrs. Jackson considerable alarm; surely where murder was concerned everyone was suspect until he or she

was proven innocent. And after all, husbands and wives murdered each other all the time, if they didn't there would be very
little to report in the more sensational daily newspapers. But
she also kept this thought to herself.

"The only one of them who appears to have no knowledge
of plants whatsoever is Mr. Haldane, m'lady. Mr. Urquhart
has a considerable knowledge of both plants and poisons, and
Mrs. Bartholomew is a horticulturalist, so she would probably
know how to concoct poison from a plant."

Lady Montfort did not acknowledge this reasoning. She was
staring at the list of seven deadly plants with a frown on her
face. Her fingers tapped rhythmically on the edge of the table,
her lips pursed in thought.

"I have the strongest feeling that Mr. Urquhart knew what
we were up to in the conservatory. Don't you, Jackson?" She
looked up, her eyes tired but her face still determined that they
reason as much as they could tonight before they had any information on the contents of the blue bottle from Fisk & Able.

Mrs. Jackson acknowledged that she thought so, too. She had
formed an even greater distaste for the elderly bachelor ever
since he had instructed them on poison as he stood underneath
the white-flowering oleander, his queen of poisons. She did not
think it mattered that they did not know whether castor bean
or oleander had been put into Mr. Bartholomew's bottle of
digestive powders, just so long as it was either of them. And
supposing Fisk & Able replied that the bottle contained only
slippery elm, ginger, and peppermint?

She fell into a brooding silence. *We have to leave tomorrow,*
she thought, *we can't stay here if we declare war on Germany.
His lordship will come over here and get his wife himself if she
doesn't return home.*

In her view, everything pointed to Mr. Urquhart: his knowledge of poison, his continual administration of pills, tablets,

and powders, and the fact that the elderly gentleman had kindly advised Mr. Bartholomew on powders from Fisk & Able to help him with his indigestion. Mrs. Jackson had been particularly repelled by the unattractive expression on the old man's face as he had instructed them about witches because, coming as she did from Lancashire, which throughout the ages had been a witch-infested county, she despised such things and found his dabbling in the occult disturbing. It was not only a decidedly morbid activity but also a very un-Christian one and it offended Mrs. Jackson's deeply Anglican sense of right and wrong, tenets by which she lived. It was *right* to go to church on Sunday and sing hymns, and to say one's prayers if one remembered to at night. But it was *wrong* to try to contact those who had gone before, as it smacked of witchcraft and devil worship.

She sighed. "I am convinced it was Mr. Urquhart, m'lady. Everything points to him. But there is no motive I can perceive, unless he was driven by jealousy and wanted to eliminate his competitor, Mr. Bartholomew, in the production of the perfect rose."

"Well if he did bump off Mr. Bartholomew, he was barking up the wrong rosebush." Lady Montfort looked extremely tired and her voice was a little too terse. "Because evidently it was Mrs. Bartholomew who developed both those roses. What a joke they all are. That will teach them all to be so competitive with each other. Their best tea rose was not even bred by one of them. Perhaps that is why Mr. Urquhart poisoned Mr. Bartholomew—because he was a liar and a fake." She leaned back in her chair and closed her eyes.

"I know you do not agree with me, Jackson, but I am convinced it was Mr. Haldane. He has a marked and unhealthy jealousy of his wife, who was clearly devoted to Mr. Bartholomew.

Look at the way she carried on when she thought the white rose might be named after Mrs. Bartholomew. I know she was hoping Mr. Bartholomew would name his rose 'Maud Haldane.' And then when she was told that he had not bred the rose, but that his wife had, she didn't mind in the least if Mrs. Bartholomew gave the rose her own name. So it would seem Mr. Haldane had all the motive in the world to have eliminated Mr. Bartholomew. There are so many reasons, actually, I can barely count them." But she lifted a hand with her forefinger extended and proceeded to do just that: "One, to get Bartholomew away from his wife, who was clearly in love with him. Two," her middle finger joined her forefinger, "so that he can secure a lucrative government contract for his Haldane's Hearty Stew now that Bartholomew's Bully Beef is in disarray, and three," she waved the appropriate number of fingers in the air, "his conservatory is stocked full of poisonous plants. There is a plant toxicology *and* a list of seven poisonous plants, *two* of which—two of the most poisonous ones—are growing in his conservatory and are on the list. And not only that, he only has to have a meal or two with poor Mr. Urquhart to see that the man is a perfect victim to be framed for murder by poison with all his little potions, tablets, and powders. And then there is the way that he intervened when Mr. Bartholomew died and got a doctor to write the death certificate for food poisoning from the kedgeree at breakfast. And of course he got rid of the cook, which was his greatest mistake, because here we are, investigating." *She has run out of fingers now that she has so many reasons to incriminate a man she has disliked since we got here,* thought Mrs. Jackson.

"Good heavens above, he even made sure that there was fish on the menu for breakfast on the day his friend died. Don't let's forget that, Jackson." She was so evidently convinced of her theory that she was waving her right hand in the air as if it held all the proof in the world that Mr. Haldane had painstakingly doctored Mr. Bartholomew's digestive powders.

Mrs. Jackson lowered her eyes. She could not argue with any of this, but it just felt so wrong. Mr. Haldane was more than likely quite capable of murdering Mr. Bartholomew. But by poison? It just didn't fit the man's personality. If he had strangled, stabbed, or shot Mr. Bartholomew, it would have been far more in keeping with the type of man he was. Her ladyship could be so emphatic sometimes. She sighed again.

"And one last thing, of course," Lady Montfort said. "Whilst Mr. Bartholomew was sprinkling poison on his breakfast kedgeree, Mr. Haldane had the perfect alibi: he was up in Manchester." She stopped at the look on her housekeeper's face. "I am so sorry, Jackson, I must be awfully tired. I can tell you have a theory, please tell me what it is."

"I think, m'lady, that everything you have said rings true. All are incontrovertible facts and I agree with every one of them. But it is important that we identify the handwriting on this list."

"But Mr. Haldane has all the motive in the world, whereas the other two do not."

Mrs. Jackson did not sigh a third time, as to do so would be disrespectful, but she did certainly believe that Lady Montfort was prejudiced and was entirely grateful when she called their deliberations to a halt, at least until they had had more information from Mr. Stafford.

In the broad light of day, with the birds singing in the trees and puffy white clouds scudding across a soft blue summer sky, it was almost impossible to believe that they might be on the verge of discovering the identity of a cold-blooded poisoner, Clementine thought as she looked out of the window next morning. *And it is quite amazing really,* she thought, *how a few hours of sleep put everything into proportion.*

After luncheon they judged that hopefully Mr. Stafford would have had an opportunity to talk to either Mr. Fisk or Mr. Able and that it would do both of them good to go for a walk in the fresh air and discover if this was indeed the case. Clementine was feeling particularly buoyed up because Mr. Urquhart had agreed to show her his fascinating scrapbook on the evolution of the hybrid tea rose at tea time, which would give them the opportunity either to eliminate him from their list of suspects or to identify him as the murderer. Now everything hinged on the contents of the blue bottle.

"After I left you I went home and transferred some of the powders in the bottle to a clean meat-paste jar and was just in time to catch the last post before the post office closed yesterday evening, so it arrived in London by the midday post today. I went back to the post office half an hour ago and used the telephone there to confirm receipt." Mr. Stafford addressed them both, as they sat on benches in the summer house, each of them hanging on to his every word. Mrs. Jackson was convinced she knew what he would say next and, judging by the smile on her face, so did her ladyship, but they listened in polite silence as Mr. Stafford enjoyed the business of relaying his news.

"Mr. Fisk said that as soon as they received the powders they knew exactly what compound they were looking at. As you had already surmised, there was slippery elm, ginger, and a little peppermint, in powder form, that they made especially for Mr. Bartholomew. And they also confirmed that something else had been added to it. But what it was exactly, he was unable to tell me. He offered to send the powder off to a chemist in London who would be able to analyze the contents and give us a clear idea of what exactly had been added to the digestive powders. And we are talking about poison here," he added, grinning as he watched their very serious faces light up in innocent pleasure. "Because Mr. Fisk conducted an experiment with the bottle's contents on a white mouse, purchased expressly for the test—his bill will be sent on to me—and the mouse died almost immediately with a barely visible dose from the contents of the bottle."

Lady Montfort, with a look of pure joy on her face, said, "He was poisoned then." The smile vanished. "Oh that poor man, what agony he must have been in. Who on earth could be so callously cruel and so terribly wicked to do something like that?"

"Someone with very clear intentions, someone unscrupulous, and someone with only their own interests at heart . . . and someone very dangerous," Mr. Stafford answered promptly, his face as grim as that of Mrs. Jackson. These grave words spoken so seriously had their effect.

"Jackson, we must wind this matter up as quickly as we can. If Lord Montfort found out that I had taken you to stay in the house of a poisoner, he would never forgive me," Lady Montfort said at last.

"I don't think either of you should eat or drink anything at all in that house." Mr. Stafford's voice was somber and he looked at Mrs. Jackson with great concern. "Perhaps now would be a good time for you to turn this over to the Market Wingley police. Colonel Valentine could continue this investigation for you, since we have undoubted proof that Mr. Bartholomew was murdered by poison."

Mrs. Jackson nodded her agreement. The thought of the elderly bachelor dropping belladonna into her afternoon cup of tea and then sitting there watching her behind his shiny spectacles as she died an agonizing death sprang immediately to the forefront of her mind. She looked at her ladyship, who had reached into the pocket of her skirt and drawn out the list of poisons.

"It would not take us a moment to decipher whose writing this is, and then we will have a full explanation for Colonel Valentine," she said rather wistfully, and Mrs. Jackson understood that handing the matter over to the constabulary would most certainly not be her decision at this stage.

"We have not quite finished with the How, Jackson," her ladyship continued. "Mr. Bartholomew had a bottle of what he believed were simple digestive powders. He overate at breakfast and sprinkled the powders on his kedgeree hoping to ease his discomfort. But *how* did the murderer put poison into his digestive powders?"

Mrs. Jackson couldn't stand it any longer and forgot herself enough to interrupt her ladyship, not that she seemed to mind. "I think the murderer must have given Mr. Bartholomew a bottle of powders that had already been tampered with, m'lady. Someone who knew he suffered from indigestion and had recommended Fisk & Able's remedies. And since Mr. Urquhart recommended the powders, Mr. Bartholomew would have been quite happy to have accepted a bottle of them from him." She did not look at her ladyship as she said this, because she knew who Lady Montfort's favorite suspect was, and to put forward an alternative might be perceived as contrary and, worse still, disrespectful.

"Mrs. Jackson thinks it is Mr. Urquhart and will tell you why," Lady Montfort said to Mr. Stafford. So Mrs. Jackson explained her belief that it was Mr. Urquhart who was their culprit and not Mr. Haldane. She was clear and gave her reasoning in detail, with Mr. Stafford interrupting only to ask the occasional question. At the end of her considerable speech, Mr. Stafford threw back his head and laughed.

"Well, that's quite astonishing," he said. "What has become of that silent and very circumspect woman who always discouraged gossip and never recounted the business of others?" he said with evident admiration and not a little pride.

"She has become a detective," said Lady Montfort with equal pride. "Even if she isn't always willing at first to divulge her thinking, when she does, it is always worth waiting for."

Mrs. Jackson looked quizzical at this point and her ladyship smiled.

"But she is being polite, you see, for I have another theory. My favorite suspect is Mr. Haldane," and Lady Montfort trotted out all her theories to back up her suspicions.

At the end of it, Mr. Stafford must have realized that his being there was not just to relate the story about the mouse that had died but in some way to adjudicate their thinking. He started to shake his head.

"So you are both working on the same theory that whoever put the poison in the bottle went searching for it in the orangery and bumped into Mrs. Wickham?" he asked.

And they answered that they were.

"Because if that is the case, Mr. Haldane did not have to wait for the orangery to be unlocked before he went on his search for the poison bottle; it was he who had told the head gardener to lock up the orangery. And Mr. Clark told me when he gave me the key that on no account was I to mislay it as it was the only copy in his keeping. Mr. Haldane had the other."

Lady Montfort's groan was rather histrionic as she rose to her feet. If she had cursed and kicked a small pot of pink geraniums, standing dangerously in her way, across the summer house, Mrs. Jackson would not have been in the least surprised. She turned her head away so as not to witness her ladyship's downfall and also to conceal the look of triumph she could feel threatening to make itself seen. After inspecting the view of the surrounding gardens for defects, she glanced down at her hands in her lap and then stole a glance at Mr. Stafford. He was watching her. Then the lines at the corners of his eyes deepened. He was laughing *at* her. *He knows that I have solved it,* she said to herself, feeling a wave of such great happiness engulf her that she almost laughed with delight.

"I am guilty of being pigheaded," Lady Montfort said. "I suppose I really wanted it to be Mr. Haldane because I dislike the man and I really like Mr. Urquhart. He reminds me of my uncle, who was an elderly bachelor fascinated by Eastern religions and most eccentric in his ways, especially about observing particular Hindu holidays and religious rituals. But unlike Mr. Urquhart, he loved to travel and was extraordinarily knowledgeable about Moghul history. Ah well . . ." She turned to acknowledge the larger thinking of her housekeeper, but Mrs. Jackson was still admiring the view and sat there as faraway from them in thought as if she had risen to her feet and walked away.

Lady Montfort and Mr. Stafford sat politely waiting for her to return to them. After a few moments she did. And she felt at that moment as if they had all three of them missed the point of their inquiry altogether.

"But why have we not included Mrs. Bartholomew on our list of suspects?" she asked.

"Because she was miles away when her husband died," said Mr. Stafford.

"And she was such a good wife to him, almost like a mother. Everyone says so. Everyone says that when Mrs. Bartholomew was with him, Mr. Bartholomew behaved himself, especially, of course, where other women were concerned. But most of all she looked after him. She even worked on developing his roses for him." Evidently Lady Montfort found it rather touching that Mrs. Bartholomew had cared so much for her husband that she'd even helped him with his roses. "That sort of kindness is selfless; I had a governess when I was young who always did my French conjugation for me, the kindest of women who could not bear to watch me squirming in my chair over the future tense of the verb *être*."

"But is that real love, m'lady?" Mrs. Jackson asked. "When you keep on rescuing someone? I can understand that a governess might want to do that for a child, m'lady. But we are talking about a married couple. Doesn't that sort of love—if you can call it love—end up being a real burden to the one who always makes it right for the other?"

"Well, I suppose it might . . . I don't think I would want to be married to a man who always needed propping up."

Mrs. Jackson smiled at this, as Lord Montfort propped up the better part of two counties in England.

"Why don't you have a sample of her handwriting?" Mr. Stafford asked.

They went over the game they had played to suggest the name of the rose.

"Well, I think it is a double coup to Mrs. Jackson," Stafford said. "All you need is a sample of her handwriting to prove she wrote the list or that Mr. Urquhart did. Whoever wrote it is the killer."

"But she was so fond of her husband!" cried Lady Montfort.

"Yes, that is what we have been told by everyone, m'lady." Mrs. Jackson couldn't imagine being shackled to someone for the rest of her life, let alone someone as spoiled as Mr. Bartholomew. "Sounds to me like she was a nanny to a very spoiled, self-indulgent, and selfish man; she even had to pretend it was his rose she had worked so hard to develop. And she was in a very strange mood last night when she announced that the white rose was not his but hers, and that it should not only be named after her but registered under her name as the breeder. And how much could she really have cared for her husband if he was always running after other women?"

Here was the conundrum, she realized. It was apparently considered quite normal for men and women of the aristocracy to indulge in clandestine affairs with one another's mates. The late King Edward had made it fashionable to indulge in a bit of hanky-panky; at least it was certainly portrayed that way in London's music halls. And then of course they all had far too much empty time on their hands. But what about the respectable middle classes with their love of doilies, putting-the-milk-in-first and other rather painful refinements—did they carry-on with one another's wives? If Mr. Wickham and Mr. Haldane were examples of the male attitude to erring wives, it was certainly something that upset them very much. Men like Mr. Haldane appeared to believe that a wife was her husband's property with a duty to ensure that his home was welcoming and comfortable and where his needs were considered above all others. She sighed; a truly happy marriage was a rarity, it seemed.

"I can't imagine that Mrs. Bartholomew was happy in her marriage. Mr. Bartholomew sounded like a right babby." Her Lancashire pronunciation came through in her contempt. And both Mr. Stafford and Lady Montfort laughed. "Is it possible for a woman to divorce her husband because she is not happy with him, m'lady?"

"I don't know if she could, but I rather think that she would not," said Lady Montfort. "Of course it *is* done, but rarely, and if they are people with land and assets then it is quite a business and inevitably means that they are ostracized from good society. There is such a thing as not letting down the side after all; we must set an example, you see. I mean where would we all be if we just gave up on marriage? But I am not sure about people like the Haldanes and the Bartholomews; I am not familiar with the new middle-class attitude to these things."

"And if a woman has no money of her own and her husband is rich?" asked Mr. Stafford.

"She probably does not divorce him. A man may divorce his wife for adultery, but apparently it is much more difficult for a woman to divorce a man for straying outside of marriage; she has to have other reasons which she must prove, such as cruelty or desertion. Divorce is a sordid business and I am not familiar with the law. But Mrs. Jackson is right to suspect Mrs. Bartholomew," replied Lady Montfort.

Mr. Stafford brought his hands palms-down on his knees to emphasize what he said next: "So if she had no money of her own and wanted to be rid of a rich but annoying husband, she might poison him."

Chapter Twenty-one

Mrs. Jackson realized later that morning that she must talk to Hyde Castle's butler. As much as she found his inappropriate behavior unsettling, she needed to ask Mr. Evan's permission to speak to the footman Charles. She finally hunted him down in the silver pantry and as he rose to his feet with a polishing cloth in his right hand, she half bowed her head in acknowledgement of the many constraints there were on his time.

"Please don't let me disturb you, Mr. Evans," she said as he started to take off his apron and sleeve protectors. "I have a question that I am hoping you will help me find the answer to. No please, I think we can stay here." She didn't want to be spirited off to the alleyway next to the dairy again.

He pulled out a chair for her and she sat down at the table, and he resumed his seat.

"How can I be of help?" he said with commendable sincerity. "Are you any closer to determining how Mr. Bartholomew died?" His concern was quite genuine, she thought.

"Would it be all right for me to talk to Charles?" she asked, knowing how important it was to observe protocol about these things; to avoid causing muddles.

"How would you phrase your question, Mrs. Jackson?"

"Well, I would ask him if he had happened to notice whether

Mr. Bartholomew took out a little blue medicine bottle at breakfast on the day that the gentleman died. It contained digestive powders and apparently he either drank it mixed in water or in his tea, or even sprinkled it on his kedgeree." After a moment's consideration the butler gave his permission. And suggested that he stay in the room with them, so that Charles did not feel awkward being questioned by a guest's companion.

As soon as Charles was ushered into the butler's pantry it was quite clear to Mrs. Jackson from the footman's manner that he was uncomfortable. She decided that speed and clarity were of the essence in dealing with the young man's unease; hedging about would make him even more nervous.

"Charles, on the morning that Mr. Bartholomew ate his breakfast kedgeree . . ." The footman's eyes shifted, and Mrs. Jackson felt a little stir of anticipation. He knew something. She continued, "You waited on him, didn't you?" A brief nod and the young man licked his lips. "Did he at any time take out a little glass bottle and . . ." Relief was quite apparent in the young footman's face. Quite evidently he was used to powders and pills being consumed at mealtimes in this house.

"No, madam, not that I could see. But he often took digestive powders for his indigestion."

"But not on the morning that he died?" She noticed that all tension had left the young man's face. Charles was quite willing to answer her question about the little blue bottle. *Why the initial anxiety then, what did he think I was going to ask him?*

"Did you see him use his digestive powders that morning—maybe he sprinkled them on his kedgeree?" she asked.

"I'm afraid I just don't remember, madam. Mr. Evans left to bring up some more coffee and I was busy sweeping up the rice and fish that Mr. Bartholomew had spilled on the sideboard—so he might have sprinkled something on his breakfast, but if he did I did not see him do it."

"But would you have thought it strange if Mr. Bartholomew had produced a bottle of digestive powders and sprinkled it on his kedgeree?" she asked.

He shook his head.

"And what was the color of the bottle he kept his digestive powders in?"

"It was a blue glass bottle, ma'am, a little medicine bottle."

Mrs. Jackson nodded and felt the immense relief that comes when something we suspect is proved.

"Thank you so much, Charles. There is no need for me to ask you not to repeat our conversation, is there?"

The young man came to full attention. "Wouldn't dream of it, ma'am; anything to help clear up the business of Mrs. Armitage's wrongful dismissal. You can count on me." His face was red with the earnestness of his statement.

Downstairs in the green salon, Clementine was witnessing a storm among the Hyde rosarians, which had been building since yesterday evening and was now threatening to break. She had been sitting in the Salon Vert with a book when Mrs. Lovell, Mrs. Haldane, and Mrs. Wickham returned from a stroll in the gardens where, apparently, Mrs. Wickham had confided that Mr. Bartholomew had talked to her privately about the name he would give to his white rose, and not once had he mentioned his wife as its creator or as someone he would name his rose after.

They were now sitting in the salon like a trio of flustered hens and after more discussion and argument had gone to consult with Mr. Urquhart in his quiet corner of the conservatory.

When they had finished their discussion with Mr. Urquhart and he, in some consternation, had relayed his concern directly to Mr. Wickham, Clementine decided to go upstairs and consult with Mrs. Jackson.

"Mrs. Haldane is pulling rank as chairwoman of the Hyde Rose Society, which does not include as its members Mrs. Wickham or Mrs. Bartholomew. They are going to convene a formal meeting—at which Mr. Urquhart, as secretary and treasurer, will take the minutes." Mrs. Jackson turned from restoring order to her ladyship's chest of drawers.

"And they are going to decide according to their bylaws whether to accept the name of 'Albertine' for Mr. Bartholomew's rose. Because once they have decided on a name, the rose will be registered as a hybrid tea rose and be given a little metal tag with a number on it, and the name of the breeder of course, which this group all fully accept is Mr. Bartholomew and not his wife. I had no idea how seriously these amateur societies took themselves."

"If Mrs. Haldane, Mrs. Lovell, and Mr. Wickham are dead against naming the rose Albertine, m'lady, then you can be quite sure that Mr. Urquhart will have no choice but to accept it, because it will come down to a vote." She closed the drawer.

"Yes, that's right, and what is more, if we are around and about we might be able to take a quick look at Mr. Urquhart's handwriting in his minute book."

Clementine suspected the society would sequester themselves away from ears and eyes, as surely they did not want a strong-minded and determined Mrs. Bartholomew to intervene and make trouble. *How sneaky they are,* she thought. *It is quite incredible that they would make such a fuss about the naming of a rose.* And they were obviously not in the slightest convinced that Albertine should even be considered as the rightful producer of the lovely white rose. *No wonder she was so annoyed with them last night; she knew that they would not believe her.*

"Cat's among the pigeons now, m'lady, and it's a good thing, when emotions are stirred; people show their true hand."

"Yes, you are right, and the three ladies in question are rather steamed up."

"And Mr. Urquhart?"

"Mr. Urquhart only said that the entire episode is very disturbing to his system."

Clementine went back down to the salon just as the Hyde Rose Society left to meet in the privacy of the drawing room. Their meeting did not take long. They returned just as the butler started the ritual of bringing in the silver kettle, teapot, sugar basin, and milk jug and setting them in order on a white tea cloth. When all was ready, Charles appeared with plates of sandwiches, a cake stand with a pretty sugar cake, and chaffing dishes with anchovy toast and hot scones. As the Hyde Rose Society filed into the room, a vigilant Clementine noticed that Mrs. Bartholomew, who had been sitting alone in the conservatory, looked up at their faces as if trying to gauge how the meeting had gone. To Clementine's interested eyes Mrs. Haldane was looking unusually flushed, Mrs. Lovell upset and embarrassed, and Mr. Urquhart as unconcerned as ever.

Mr. Wickham was saying loudly, "I will make arrangements to register the rose under the name Rupert's White Dove, and then we can be done with this business." He brushed past Mrs. Jackson, who was holding the door open for the footman, and Mrs. Haldane, catching sight of Clementine's cold expression, wailed.

"Oh dear Lady Montfort, I truly hope this little contretemps will not put you off joining our society." And Clementine, who had no intention of joining in the first place, said "Not at all, Mrs. Haldane, not at all."

"Unfortunately we have had to vote against Mrs. Bartholomew naming the rose. She is not a member of the society and according to our bylaws may not..." Mrs. Lovell trailed off, looking rather ashamed. And Mr. Urquhart, trying to juggle his shawl, the book of bylaws, and his minutes book, started to interrupt a little pettishly and then, overcome by the burden he was carrying, dropped his shawl to the ground. Mrs. Jackson was across the room to help him.

"Ah, Edith, thank you, my dear. Such a lot to carry and I am ... Oh dearie me." Mrs. Jackson had dropped both books and Mr. Urquhart's pen on the floor. "Not to worry, at least the inkwell did not take a tumble, and it is always easy to mend a nib. Thank you, my dear Edith, so kind of you. Would you mind carrying them for me? I should take them up to my room immediately."

And as Mrs. Jackson followed the elderly man out of the room, she caught Clementine's eye and shook her head. Mr. Urquhart had not written the list of poisonous plants that had fallen out of the plant toxicology.

Lady Montfort met Mrs. Jackson at the foot of the stairs as she came down from Mr. Urquhart's room.

"Well, Jackson, not his writing, then?"

"Most certainly not, m'lady, his writing is completely different, very sprawling really. I simply can't believe that he is not our murderer." She felt not only tired but thoroughly irritated.

"Come on, Jackson, brisk walk in the grounds, I can't bear the thought of taking tea with these people. Let's walk to Bishop's Hever and back, that will give the Rose Society time to deal with a very angry Mrs. Bartholomew. If anything has convinced me never to join a society, this afternoon's little charade certainly has. The pettiness of people who form groups, make up rules, and then fuss over them is completely beyond me."

And off they went into a pretty afternoon with a freshening breeze, and the clouds scudding away to the south. The sky was darkening to the north and the far horizon was the color of dull pewter.

"Storm coming in," announced Mrs. Jackson in the triumphant voice the English always adopt in the face of bad weather.

"I know we have given up on Mr. Haldane as our suspect, but I went to the post bag a moment ago to include my letter to Lord Montfort to reassure him that we will leave tomorrow. and there was Mr. Haldane filling the bag with letters of his own. He most certainly did not write that list of poisons, his handwriting is quite ill formed; such a pity." And Mrs. Jackson marveled that when her ladyship admitted final defeat, she did so with grace and good humor.

They walked on in silence together, opening the gate at the edge of the gardens that took them out to the footpath to the beech woods.

"Let's play a game, Jackson. Let us imagine all the ways that Mrs. Bartholomew introduced poison into a bottle of her husband's digestive powders, and made sure that he dosed himself from that particular bottle when she had been gone nearly three months."

"Perhaps he had had no need of the powders until then, m'lady," suggested Mrs. Jackson, to be sternly corrected.

"Mr. Urquhart says Mr. Bartholomew *customarily* suffered from indigestion due to his overindulging at the meal table and that he took these powders often. And you said that Charles was used to seeing Mr. Bartholomew's blue bottle at breakfast time. So we must assume for the moment that this was a new bottle he had opened that morning. If Mrs. Bartholomew is our culprit, how did she organize that part?"

Mrs. Jackson thought about this, but the list of plant poisons was bothering her and kept diverting her concentration back to it. She tried to remember the order in which the poisonous plants were listed.

Foxglove was the first one. What was the second? Ah yes, laburnum. She kept on until she thought she had all the plants on the list. She was counting on her fingers. What was the last one? She couldn't for the life of her remember.

They came to the stile at the entrance to the beech woods. Lady Montfort bunched up her skirt and climbed over, leaving Mrs. Jackson on the path staring down at buttercups growing along its grassy edge.

"Jackson?"

She looked up. There was her ladyship standing on the other side of the stile with a particularly inquisitive look on her face.

"I'm sorry, m'lady, I was woolgathering," she explained and then lifted her skirt clear of her boots to climb onto the first board of the stile. "What was the last poison on the list, m'lady, can you remember?"

Lady Montfort started to reach into her pocket for the list she carried with her wherever they went. "No, m'lady, before you look at it, would you try to remember?"

"Tobacco? No, it was . . . monkshood."

"I think it was written as aconitum, m'lady, and . . . what number was it?"

"Were there seven plants on the list?"

Mrs. Jackson turned to answer and then stood quite still, her eyes wide, her hand halfway up to her mouth. She saw the list with its even copperplate handwriting quite clearly in her mind. "Yes, there were seven items on the list." And then she was struck with another image, one that made her next question overloud in the still afternoon air. "Do you remember Frauline Bertholde, m'lady?"

282

Her ladyship frowned. *Of course she thinks I have gone stark-staring mad,* Mrs. Jackson thought as her heartbeat picked up. She felt almost breathless with excitement. Frauline Berthold had been employed as governess to both Lady Verity and Lady Althea to teach them German and French. She had been a pleasant enough woman, continually at war with the Talbot nanny who believed in fresh air, whereas the frauline suffered terribly from drafts and the cold. A good instructor though, because she had taught the Talbot girls well; they were fluent in both languages.

"Frauline Berthold? Jackson, what can you be talking about?"

"The frauline loved to make up lists, m'lady. She put them up on the servants' hall notice board all the time." Mrs. Jackson remembered seeing the board and on it a neat strip of paper with a list of instructions about the menu for the children's supper: one meal for each day of the week to be served promptly at six o'clock in the nursery.

"The number seven, m'lady. On the Continent they write 'seven' with a little horizontal bar on the stem of the seven to distinguish it from one,' Mr. Hollyoak told me. "Because when they write the number one, they give it that little peak at the top of the stroke like a cap."

"Do they really? How odd of them. I am sorry, Jackson, I simply don't understand . . ."

"The list of poisons, m'lady. I am quite sure that the last and seventh plant on the list was written in the Continental style, the way the frauline did it and the way Mrs. Bartholomew would do it."

"Well for heaven's sake. How on earth did that just pop into your head? We must have read that list dozens of times."

"Yes, m'lady, but we were always more interested in the plants listed. Not the numbering of them. Until now I couldn't even remember how many were on the list until I started trying to put them in order. Let's take a look at the way the number seven is written on that list, m'lady." Lady Montfort pulled it from her pocket:

1. *Digitalis*
2. *Laburnum*
3. *Oleander*
4. *Castor bean*
5. *Belladonna*
6. *Aconitum*
7. *Tobacco*

Twenty minutes later they were still on either side of the fence, her ladyship seated on the top board of the stile with her feet on the middle board, too consumed with the excitement of their discovery to continue with their walk.

Lady Montfort was recounting how often they had gone over the list. Even shared it with Mr. Stafford, and he had not noticed the way that the number seven had been written.

"It just goes to show you, m'lady," Mrs. Jackson said, "that sometimes the simplest thing is sitting in front of you trying to make itself known and is stubbornly ignored." She was of course speaking of her own neglectful observations.

"Mrs. Bartholomew must have spent a long time planning how to poison her husband so that she would not be here when it happened. She must have worked on that list of poisonous plants quite diligently and selected the poison that ended up in his digestive powders for a very good reason. No doubt hoping that if someone discovered her husband had died from poison, then blame would be cast on either Mr. Urquhart, with his fascination with herb lore and cure-alls and his desperate determination to breed the better rose, or Mr. Wickham and Mr. Haldane, who as jealous husbands would want to get rid of Mr. Bartholomew. And of course every single poison on the list was available either in the conservatory or in the grounds, except of course for tobacco."

"There were two things she could count on when she went away on her planting trips," said Mrs. Jackson. "One that he ate too much and the other that he—"

"—indulged in the other deadly sin, Jackson, lust thereby provoking the men in this house."

Mrs. Jackson looked away; sometimes her ladyship was perhaps a little too outright. "So she poisoned his digestive powders, knowing that he would use them at the breakfast table when he had overindulged at dinner the night before."

"And then she went off to China with her brother and whilst she was away he poisoned himself." Lady Montfort stared at the list in her hands.

"And when she came back, m'lady, the only thing she had to worry about was where was the bottle of poison that she had sent him? It had not been found on his person or among the personal effects that were sent to her when she came home to mourn his passing." Mrs. Jackson, standing among golden buttercups in her dark blue dress, was looking positively radiant.

"So she comes to the house to see if she can locate the bottle in the orangery where he had died. Perhaps she believed, as we do, that he would try to dose himself with the powders to alleviate the pain he was in from the poison.

"And when she gets here she discovers that Mr. Haldane has had the orangery locked up ever since her husband's death. How frustrating for her that must have been. And then the other night she discovered that it was open. Oh my goodness, Jackson, I was the one who told her. Or at least Mrs. Wickham did. It was when Mrs. Wickham came in from the garden and reported to me that you and Mr. Stafford were walking in the orangery garden. She was reporting on what she thought was your . . . your . . . meeting Mr. Stafford in the garden without a chaperone." Mrs. Jackson's face looked so shocked that Clementine laughed. "I know, Jackson, sinners always point fingers at others for the sins they commit themselves, as the Reverend Bottomley-Jones is fond of saying. Mrs. Bartholomew was standing in the hall when Mrs. Wickham made her moral objection to your visit to the orangery alone with a gentleman. Effectively announcing that the orangery was now open. After dinner Mrs. Bartholomew says that she will retire for the night. She pretends she is asleep when the maid brings her hot drink, and then gets up and, under cover of darkness, runs to the orangery to search for the bottle."

Mrs. Jackson was nodding in a vague sort of way, but her eyes were fixed on the floor as she listened to Lady Montfort sum up the sequence of events.

"But how did she get the poison to him, m'lady? How did she get the poison to him from China at a time when she could be sure that he had run out of his digestive powders and that he would dose himself from the poisoned bottle before she came back to England?"

"Well, she must have known how long it took for him to get through a full bottle of the powders. Oh for heaven's sake, it can't be another simple little fact waving away at us from the sidelines as we imagine all sorts of complicated arrangements, can it? Did she post it to him, Jackson?" And as her housekeeper's head came up from contemplating the flowers around her feet her face broke into a smile. "Yes, she did. Of course she did, she posted it from China, from Shanghai, the port city of China, when she arrived."

"Surely someone at Hyde Castle would remember him receiving a parcel, m'lady. Surely someone will remember? If they do, then perhaps that is all the proof we need."

But her ladyship was shaking her head and looking doleful.

"No, Jackson, it is not enough. Where is the paper, where is the string, where is the canceled postage, where is the proof? Who saw him open the package and heard him say: 'Here are the digestive powders that my wife forgot to give me before she left. Now, where's that dish of kedgeree?'"

"How on earth will we discover that, m'lady, without announcing that we have only come here to prove that Mrs. Bartholomew poisoned her husband five months ago?" A large drop of rain fell on Mrs. Jackson's hand and another on her cheek.

"Oh my goodness, Jackson, we have to run for it, otherwise we will be soaked. What possessed us not to check the barometer before we left the house?"

Lady Montfort swung her legs over the top board of the stile and jumped down onto the path and they broke into a run. As they came up the lawn at a fast pelt the sky darkened and the wind picked up. They had just reached the terrace when the sky opened up and the rain came down in a heavy deluge.

"Dear leddies, dear leddies, come in. Oh my goodness, are ye soaking wet? You poor things, come in here and take off your wet shoes. You are just in time, we were about to send out Charles with an umbrella for you both. I am sure your beautiful dress is quite ruined, Leddy Montfort."

Chapter Twenty-two

"There is absolutely no need to make a fuss, Finley; they are a little damp, that is all." Mrs. Lovell came forward. "My goodness me, what athletes you are, the pair of you. We watched you racing up the lawn; we were quite sure you would be caught in the downpour."

"I told Charles to come out to you with the umbrella," cried Mrs. Haldane, and on cue there was Charles coming into the room with a large black umbrella.

"No need, Charles." Mr. Urquhart waved him away. "What these poor leddies need is their tea." Mr. Urquhart was quite ready to take over this part of their recovery. "I do hope you can toast them some tea cakes. And tell the cook to make sure that the butter is tempered for their scones."

How could we possibly have imagined that this little elflike man doctored his friend's bottle of digestive powders, knowing that he would die in agony? thought Clementine, feeling guilty. *But he has this way of looking at you as if he knows exactly what you are thinking that is most perturbing.* That afternoon in the conservatory when he had lectured them on plant poisons had almost convinced her that he might have been their villain.

And almost immediately she felt regret that it would not be Mr. Haldane who would be arrested. *I suppose it is too much to hope for that someone as brutal and uncouth to his wife as that man could be taken away for murder.* Mrs. Haldane would then be free to live here for the rest of her life in the company of her kind friend Mrs. Lovell, dabbling in watercolors and dreaming of inventing a beautiful tea rose and calling it the White Dove of Peace. If only the poor creature had half as much pluck as Mrs. Bartholomew.

She looked around the room and her gaze fastened upon fussy Mr. Wickham, who might find the courage to poison someone but was far more content to correct and chide his wife for her silliness with men who did not merit any decent woman's interest.

Mrs. Haldane, Mrs. Wickham, and Mrs. Bartholomew. All three unhappily married women had dealt with their loveless lives in such different ways. *Do most women feel they have no choice in their ill-fated marriages? Do they suffer in silence, accept their loveless state, and seek distractions, or do they resort to empty love affairs—or, in desperation, turn to poison?* She realized in that moment how supremely lucky she was in her marriage. Her husband not only offered her respect but he accepted her for precisely who she was. She felt a momentary pang of longing for the quiet of Iyntwood and her garden in the company of her husband. How much of their quiet pleasant life would change if their country went to war? She resolutely pushed the thought away. There was much to be done in the next few hours.

She glanced around the room. The meeting to correct Mrs. Bartholomew's attempt to appropriate her husband's rose had brought the members of the Hyde Rose Society together, united in their determination to protect the deceased Mr. Bartholomew. Whatever his faults, they were all loyal to their fellow rosarian, she realized. Perhaps they sensed that his wife hated him. Her gaze rested finally upon Mrs. Bartholomew as she coolly announced to the group that she had secured a place on a boat leaving the Port of Dover for Calais tomorrow afternoon and would say goodbye to them all after breakfast tomorrow.

Oh good heavens! Clementine nearly sprang to her feet in agitation. *We don't have much time left. We have to get this all sewn up.* Her suppressed alarm had communicated itself to Mrs. Jackson, who was looking at her across the salon: her eyes were gleaming with intention, her face was flushed from her run, and her hair was standing out in pretty little curls and spirals around her face. *How beautiful she is when she makes discoveries,* Clementine thought. She beckoned Charles over to her.

"Charles, please deliver this note to Mr. Stafford immediately; if he is not in the garden, take it to him in the village," she said as she handed the note she had just written.

"Meet you in the orangery at six o'clock. Eureka."

It was a breathless and still slightly damp Clementine and Mrs. Jackson who met a puzzled Mr. Stafford.

"No, Jackson, never mind about interrupting, you just go ahead and tell it all. Such a clear, well-organized brain," Clementine said to Mr. Stafford.

And Mrs. Jackson recounted. She recounted everything briskly, without repeating herself, without stopping for breath, and in her admirably succinct way. She recounted everything from A to Z and from 1 to 7.

"There now," Clementine said when Mrs. Jackson had finished and had then patiently answered a question or two from Stafford. "What do you think about that?"

"It is quite astonishing—quite astonishingly clever. But how will you prove it, Lady Montfort?"

"I have a plan for that which I will share with you in a minute.

Mrs. Bartholomew is off to France tomorrow and with the way things are in Europe might disappear without a trace from France to China or anywhere in the world. So we have to be quick. Will you, Mr. Stafford, now that you have the entire story, please drive over to Market Wingley to Colonel Valentine, the chief constable there? His address is written down on this paper. Please present my compliments and tell him what we have discovered. Then ask him to drive over to Hyde Hall after dinner. Say at about ten o'clock? Tell him I think I can guarantee that Mrs. Bartholomew will be quite ready to confess to the murder of her husband."

Mr. Stafford said he would, but then he became uneasy. "What are you planning to do? he asked her. "Do you have a plan?"

She saw him look at Mrs. Jackson. *I am sure he thinks she is more levelheaded than I am,* Clementine thought, and then she realized from his look that this was far from what he was thinking. No doubt Mr. Stafford's unease was for their safety in "flushing out" Mrs. Bartholomew, a poisoner with everything to lose. But his greatest concern, Clementine realized, was evidently for Mrs. Jackson, standing in front of him with her gray eyes shining with the zeal of a woman on a mission and her lovely russet hair still damp from their walk in the rain to the orangery.

Oh it can't possibly be true, can it? Clementine thought as she saw his look of pride and . . . yes, it was delight on his face. He was staring at Mrs. Jackson as if she were the Holy Grail.

Of course he is entranced by this remarkable woman, she thought as she realized that she was probably going to lose her housekeeper, and her friend and companion. *Ah well, so be it. If Jackson has the same regard for Mr. Stafford as he evidently does for her, then it will be a perfect match. Perfect. But this must all wait until later.*

"Mrs. Jackson and I must go back to the house now. After dinner I am going to persuade Mr. Urquhart to help me play a game. I am quite sure he will do everything he can to help me. And then we will see exactly how Mrs. Bartholomew conducts herself. With a bit of luck you will be waiting in the wings with Colonel Valentine to hear her confession. I would suggest that you bring Colonel Valentine into the conservatory by the terrace door, so he will be able to hear everything that takes place in the salon when I set my trap for Mrs. Bartholomew. It is vital that no one knows you are there. Please make sure that Colonel Valentine has everything he needs to make an arrest."

And as the two of them left the orangery, the last thing they could hear over the rain as it started to hammer down on the glass roof was Mr. Stafford calling out to them to be very, very careful because people and animals are most dangerous when they feel cornered.

"What is it exactly that you have in mind, m'lady?" Mrs. Jackson asked as she helped Lady Montfort change for dinner. She had become very adept at the complicated business of dressing her ladyship, closing the many hooks and eyes and buttons on her lovely dresses and then sweeping her hair into a glossy fold at the nape of her neck. She searched for evening gloves and then snapped the catch of her ladyship's diamond necklace about her neck.

"A little dressing-up tonight, Jackson, just for the occasion. I don't want to overdo things, but I am in the mood to celebrate. How long have we been here now?"

"Four nights I think it is, m'lady. There now, that's very nice." She smoothed down the neckline of Lady Montfort's elegant garnet-red gown and stepped back to admire her. Of all the women she had ever seen dressed for dinner, no one looked more elegant and lovely than her ladyship. Her clothes were beautiful without being ornate, she never wore too much jewelry, and she moved with such unhurried grace that she made everything she wore look marvelous.

"I will just go and change my dress, and I should be ready in a moment, m'lady," she said.

"Put that list somewhere very safe, Jackson, we must be very careful not to lose it."

There was no sign of Mr. Haldane when they went down to dinner. So though the numbers were uneven at the table, at least dinner was a comparatively civilized affair. Clementine didn't bother to wait and see if they were attempting an order of precedence, she merely went and sat herself down next to Mr. Urquhart, who clearly appreciated the effort she had taken to dress so splendidly.

"I do hope you will join our little society, Leddy Montfort, both you and dear Edith. You will both be a credit to us, I can assure you."

They chattered away, the best of friends, and toward the end of the meal Lady Montfort put her head a little closer to Mr. Urquhart's as she suggested that they might for once play a little after dinner.

"Dancing, do you have in mind?" He was patently not an enthusiast.

"Why no, Mr. Urquhart, I thought perhaps we might have a séance. I am fascinated by the business of talking to someone who has crossed over to the spirit world."

His bright little eyes fastened themselves on her face and he smiled. And she once again experienced that uncanny feeling that he knew exactly what she was thinking.

"Ye know, do ye not, Leddy Montforrt," his Scots accent

was a good deal more pronounced, "that we highlanders are blessed wi' the second saight?"

"So I have heard, Mr. Urquhart."

"Eh, enough of the 'mister,' wi' ye. Once and fer all, will ye please call me Finley?" He twinkled at her most flirtatiously and she twinkled right back and said, "Well, Finley, I think it would be a nice idea to ask Mr. Bartholomew what name *he* has in mind for his white rose, don't you?"

Chapter Twenty-three

Clementine breathed a sigh of relief when Mrs. Haldane suggested that Mr. Wickham and Mr. Urquhart join them in the salon after dinner rather than drink port alone together in the dining room.

"Of course we would love to, Maud, just like old times." Mr. Wickham bowed his head courteously to her. Having put Mrs. Bartholomew in her place at the Hyde Rose Society meeting, and excluded his wife from any decision she might venture to make on the Bartholomew rose, Mr. Wickham had established male superiority once again. He was determinedly masculine, invincibly in charge, and stubbornly unmovable, thought Clementine as he led the way out of the dining room. Women might try to make ridiculous and emotional demands and stray from what convention demanded, but Mr. Wickham would bring them to heel. She wondered why some men had to work so terribly hard to establish their rule over womankind. His condescending smile and his little swagger as he bowed them into the salon was almost as detestable as Mr. Haldane's bluster and bullying.

Horrified as she was that Mrs. Bartholomew had resorted to poisoning her husband to be free of him, she did rather wish that Mrs. Haldane might exhibit more backbone. In Clementine's experience, most bullies backed down if they were confronted. *What would Mr. Haldane do if his wife stopped cowering and asserted herself?* she wondered as she caught Mr. Urquhart's eye, to remind him of their plan.

"Gather round, leddies and Clive, it is a rare chilly and wet night for August. And the spirit world has much to share with us," Mr. Urquhart said as they settled themselves in the comfort of the salon. And seeing Mr. Wickham open his mouth to object, he had the sense to add, "Leddy Montfort and Edith have particularly expressed an interest in communing with the spirit world." And that was that; their aristocratic guest must not be disappointed.

Mr. Urquhart bossed Charles about over the placement of a round pedestal table with an intricately inlaid top in tulip wood and ebony, and when four chairs were placed around it he opened a flat carved box on its surface.

"Oh, Finley," said Mrs. Lovell playfully in her scolding voice, as if she objected to joining the séance, but Clementine noticed that she was too comfortably sedated with trout almandine, a fricassee of chicken in truffles, tender escalopes of veal, and several glasses of wine to care about the impropriety of a séance.

"You are quite hopeless, Finley," said Mrs. Haldane, giggling like a naughty schoolgirl. And in a whisper to Clementine: "He knows that Clive disapproves. What do you have in mind, Lady Montfort?"

"I am rather hoping he is going to introduce me to the world on the other side," Clementine replied.

"I am not quite sure I believe in what Finley calls the spheres," said Mrs. Haldane, "but he only invites benevolent spirits."

"Though we did once have a very angry Indian from Calcutta sneak in at one time. He frightened poor Finley quite terribly," added Mrs. Lovell, her plump shoulders shaking with merriment.

"Sit ye down there, Leddy Montforrt." Mr. Urquhart had become almost flamboyantly Gaelic. "Now, where is dear Edith?"

"Oh, she will be with us directly."

"Prepare the room, Maud. And, Charles, be off wi ye. We will ring when we want our coffee," Mr. Urquhart commanded, and Mrs. Haldane rustled around the room switching off electric lights, much to Mr. Wickham's annoyance as he tried to read his newspaper by the light of a candelabra in a far corner of the room. His wife, forbidden to involve herself in such a pagan activity, was drawn like a moth to the flame of endless possibilities, none of them real in this world but hopefully revealing. She came as close to the table as she dared and sat down with her eyes fixed on its inlaid design.

Mr. Urquhart dealt out glossy white cards, each bearing a letter of the alphabet in order, in a ring around the table's edge, followed by the numbers one to ten. Finally, he completed the circle with three cards: Yes, No, and Farewell, one after the other with the same efficient precision.

In the center of the table he carefully set down a large, heart-shaped wooden board made of walnut and inlaid with mother-of-pearl. There was a small hole at the pointed end of the heart and it moved smoothly and easily across the table's surface on delicately turned little wooden castors.

"We will not indulge ourselves in automatic writing tonight, Leddy Montfort. But we will ask questions. And since I sense it is a propitious night to engage the spirit world, we will also receive answers. The moon is nearing its fullness and standing in Capricorn, a most practical and forthright sign, and if you were to ask me more on the subject I would say that Capricorn can sometimes possess a particularly hardheaded and distinctly avaricious cruelty. But to continue: if you will gather round, we will begin."

There was a rustle of silk as Mrs. Haldane and Mrs. Lovell joined Clementine at the table. Mr. Urquhart seated himself and nodded them all to their places. "That's it, we are all sitting at the cardinal points: North, South, East, and West."

Mrs. Bartholomew started a conversation with Mr. Wickham about train times from Market Wingley to Marylebone station. And Mr. Urquhart closed his eyes. The candelabra on the table behind him flickered in a draft from the door into the hall and caught the diamonds in Lady Montfort's ears in a thousand flashes of brilliant light. Mrs. Haldane said, "Ooh," and shivered.

"Place the tips of the fingers of both your hands lightly on the planchette and raise your arms off the table. Now we will relax, clear our minds of chatter and speculation, and wait."

There was silence in the room. Clementine could hear Mrs. Lovell breathing heavily on her right, and felt Mrs. Haldane's cold dry fingers next to hers on the wooden planchette. She noticed that they had all obediently closed their eyes. Mr. Urquhart, sitting across from her, looked more like an organ-grinder's monkey than ever. As if he had heard her thoughts, his bright little eyes snapped open and he looked at her across the table. She submissively lowered her eyes and concentrated.

Charles had been told to wait until they rang for him for coffee. She hoped that in that time Mrs. Jackson would come in through the door and be ready when they had finished their discourse with the spirit world.

She took a slow breath, relaxed her shoulders, and consciously lifted her spine so that her arms were lifted lightly above her wrists. She felt like a pianist preparing to play one of those

modern sonatas, something melancholic and atmospheric by
Debussy or Satie.

The silence deepened; it was so quiet in the room that the
rustle of Clive's newspaper was clearly audible as he turned
pages. She blocked out the sound of every whispering page. As
if in response to her concentration, the rain redoubled its efforts
and drummed down on the conservatory roof, clearly audible
as the doors were open from the salon into the conservatory,
and was it Clementine's imagination or was there the delicate,
vanilla scent of oleander in the air?

She concentrated her thoughts forward to the table before
her with all her might. And when Mr. Urquhart spoke, she
startled so much that the planchette shifted a little under her
fingertips.

"O spirit world, send us word that you are with us tonight,"
Finley said. His voice was astonishingly normal. *I would have
thought he would have become even more Celtic in his outward
dealings with the other world,* thought Clementine with interest.

"Send us a sign that you are with us. Send us a sign that you
will commune with us."

Another long silence, and just when Clementine thought her
wrists would break under the strain, the planchette came to life
under her fingertips. *Yes, it really has come to life, how astonishing.* The planchette stirred a little and moved two inches
northward and then drifted westward before stopping.

"Is anybody there?" Mr. Urquhart asked, and after the slightest pause, as if it had no intention of keeping them waiting, the
planchette took off across the table to the Yes card.

Extraordinary, such a definite and forceful move.

"Ah . . ." Mr. Urquhart breathed. "Welcome, spirit. Do ye
wish to speak to anyone here?"

A moment and that was all it was before the planchette took
off again and glided across the table, this time south toward

Clementine. Pointed end forward, it stopped at the card directly in front of her.

"A." A little cry from Mrs. Wickham, sitting as usual on the edge of things.

Through half-closed lids Clementine saw Mrs. Haldane lift her head and open her eyes wide. "Oh my good heavens," she whispered as Clementine felt the planchette vibrate underneath their fingertips.

Cool and clear, Mr. Urquhart spoke again.

"Spirit, is there anyone you wish to talk to in this room?"

A-L-B, the planchette spelled as it flew back and forth across the table's surface, E-R-T-I-N-E.

"You have a message for Albertine?" Mr. Urquhart said this loudly and Clementine peeked and saw him glance over to the other side of the room.

"But this is *encroyable,* and in the worst possible taste. You should be ashamed of yourself, Finley, at your age," Mrs. Bartholomew answered, but she stood up from her chair and put her empty port glass down on the table.

"Do you wish to speak to Albertine?" Mr. Urquhart continued his conversation with the spirit.

And the planchette danced across the table's surface and pointed over and over again to Yes.

Mrs. Lovell was breathing so heavily that Clementine had to open her eyes and look at her to make sure she was not in some distress. But the woman was leaning forward, a frown on her face and her eyes open and bulging in intense concentration.

"Albertine, dear, he wants to talk to you. He has a message for you," Mrs. Haldane called out.

"Albertine," Mr. Urquhart said. "Ask the spirit for your message."

And from across the room a weary voice said, "Who are you talking to, Finley?"

"Someone from the spirit world who says he has a message for Albertine, my dear. He has a message for you."

Silence from Mrs. Bartholomew. The planchette did not move.

And then, galvanized, it began to zigzag back and forth across the table, pointing to each letter in turn:

T-H-E N-A-M-E O-F T-H-E R-O-S-E.

"Do you have a name for the rose?" Mr. Urquhart asked, and then he cried out across the room, "Albertine, he has the name for the rose. What did I tell you? Ask and ye shall receive." The door opened and Clementine felt a draft from the hall as someone slipped into the room.

All Clementine's senses were alert. There was a rustle of silk as Mrs. Bartholomew walked across from the other side of the room to stand indecisively in its middle.

O-L-E-A-N-D-E-R.

"Oh-lee-and-der? What on earth . . . ?" said Mrs. Lovell under her breath. "Doesn't make sense."

But Mrs. Haldane was quicker. "Oleander," she said loudly. "It is the name of a shrub, I believe." But the spoken name brought Mrs. Bartholomew to the table far quicker than it was thought possible for a woman to move in a darkened room full of furniture.

"What did you just say, Maud?" she said as she came up to the table.

The planchette, as if invigorated by the sound of her voice, started its zigzag dance again.

O-L-E-A-N-D-E-R, O-L-E-A-N-D-E-R, O-L-E-A-N-D-E-R.

"Oleander," repeated Mrs. Haldane.

"Why is it saying that?" Mrs. Bartholomew's voice was shrill in the silent room.

"Perhaps it is the name Mr. Bartholomew wants us to give the rose," said Finley.

303

"But it is not suitable." Her accent was strong, thick with mistrust and suspicion. "No one would call a rose a name like that."

A-L-B-E-R-T-I-N-E, spelled the planchette; it was skimming easily now as if it were flying through the air and not across the surface of a prosaic drawing-room table. T-E-L-L T-H-E-M A-B-O-U-T O-L-E-A-N-D-E-R. And Finley spoke the words aloud for those not quick enough to keep up with the planchette's rapid movements.

"What is going on 'ere?" Mrs. Bartholomew cried, and there was sharp anger in her voice. "What are you trying to do?"

"The spirit has spoken, Albertine. It says you should tell us about Oleander." Finley's voice was heavy and somnolent, as if he were talking in his sleep.

The planchette made seventeen more movements, each of them swift and definite.

O-L-E-A-N-D-E-R A-N-D M-U-R-D-E-R it spelled, and then it flew off the table onto the floor.

There was a cry of alarm from Mrs. Haldane, who leaped to her feet as she stared in horror at Mrs. Bartholomew. "Albertine . . . what have you done?" she cried.

In answer, Albertine brought her foot crashing down on the planchette, shattering it into pieces.

"That is what I have to say to you and your cheap tricks!" she cried. But Mr. Urquhart, showing just the whites of his eyes, had reared back and was sitting with his head tilted to one side. And out of the little man's mouth came a voice far deeper in tone than he normally used.

"Albertine. Tell them about the Oleander. Tell them . . . set yourself free and tell them you gave poison to Rupert." Finley's shoulders slumped. And Clementine, trembling with excitement and fear—*this silly game had gone too far*—was halfway out of her seat. Mrs. Haldane sank down onto the floor amid the wreckage of the broken planchette, sobbing. "He *was* poisoned, he was *poisoned*. I knew it all along. And you"—she stared up at Mr. Bartholomew's murderer with horror—"you did it. You did it because you couldn't stand that we all loved him and you didn't."

And Mrs. Lovell cried out "Oh dear God, what is happening? Can it be true?"

Mrs. Bartholomew, her face scarlet with rage, poured forth a torrent of French. *"Comment osez-vous essayer de me piéger, vous petit crapaud,"* and swung back her arm and fetched Finley such a clout that Clementine winced at the sound of his poor old head hitting the wooden frame of the chair. And as she struggled with her schoolgirl French for a translation, Mr. Wickham came across the room and clamped a firm hand on Albertine's wrist.

"Albertine, have you lost your wits? For God's sake, get a grip on yourself."

And Clementine heard herself saying, "Just tell us about the oleander, Mrs. Bartholomew. You ground it up and put it in his digestive powders, didn't you?" Another cry from Mrs. Lovell, and Mrs. Haldane sobbed even louder.

"I was in China when he died," shouted Albertine, struggling in Mr. Wickham's strong grip: he had her by her arms from behind. She bent forward and tried to shake herself free. "Let me go; I was in China."

Mrs. Jackson's slender person stepped forward from the darkness of the room into the candlelight; in her black dress with her pale skin she looked almost like a manifestation from the spirit world herself. She placed three bright patches of color on the table in front of her.

"Proof, Mrs. Bartholomew, that you sent poison to your husband from Shanghai."

Mrs. Lovell bent over the table and said, "They are stamps from China."

And, to Clementine's complete and utter relief, there on the table were three patches of bright color embellished with flowers, birds, and Chinese characters.

Mrs. Bartholomew lifted a face draining of color to look at Mrs. Jackson. "How?" she cried. "How did you find out that I sent it from Shanghai?"

Mr. Urquhart lifted his head from the back of his chair and said, "Because Rupert told us, Albertine. He said you poisoned him."

Mrs. Wickham, who had been sitting with narrowed eyes watching this exchange, stood up. "Albertine, you most certainly did kill Rupert, you were so jealous of his love for me that you killed him. I hope you hang."

"You are a complete fool, Dorothy, almost as stupid and selfish as Rupert!" cried Albertine, her eyes wild and her hair unravelling from the tidy coil at the nape at her neck. "He was a child, a stupid, indolent, selfish child. He had no idea of love, of loyalty!" And with a cry of anger Mrs. Bartholomew broke free of Mr. Wickham and threw herself forward to the table and the stamps lying on its surface. But Mrs. Jackson was too quick for her; she swiped the bright patches of color up from the table and put her hands behind her back. And as Mrs. Bartholomew sprang toward Mrs. Jackson she was halted only by a voice that cut across the room: "Albertine Bartholomew. You are charged with the murder of your husband, Rupert Bartholomew, on the third of March, 1914 . . ." and two burly constables lifted her clear off her feet.

A tall, gray-haired man stood among them, accompanied by Mr. Stafford, who was looking not only a little white about the gills but quite shaken to see the group of people sitting in the half-dark with Mrs. Jackson standing in their midst clutching three sticky Shanghai postage stamps in her hand.

"Sit down here, Maud, and please stop crying, it will just give you a headache. I think you need a little brandy." Mrs. Lovell took a weeping Mrs. Haldane away from the table and sat her down with her arm around her shoulders.

"I loved Rupert, Amelia, he was the kindest . . . most kindest of men." Mrs. Haldane wailed like a brokenhearted child.

Mrs. Jackson went to the bell pull and rang for Charles.

"Charles," she said, smiling at the footman; all evening he had been looking particularly hang-dog but now he brightened up. "That went very well, but I am afraid we cannot give you your stamps back because they will be needed. Now would you light a fire and bring some brandy in here, please? And some coffee—hot, mind—with lots of sugar, and sandwiches. And then be on hand for Colonel Valentine so you may tell him about the package that came for Mr. Bartholomew the day before he died, the one that came from China." She turned to the chief constable, who was standing in the middle of the room, with his two constables supporting a now silent Mrs. Bartholomew.

"You see, Colonel Valentine, Charles collects stamps and he steamed the stamps off the package addressed to Mr. Bartholomew from his wife. I am afraid the brown wrapping paper bearing the address, written in Mrs. Bartholomew's hand, has long since gone. But I am sure that Mr. Stafford has already given you the little blue bottle and if you look at the frank on the stamps with a magnifying glass, you might be able to discern the date." And then she modestly stepped to one side.

Mr. Stafford came across the room to her.

"That was remarkable playacting. Who put Mr. Urquhart up to it? Was it Lady Montfort? I was quite taken in." He added in an undertone, "And what about the stamps? Where did you come up with them?"

"Charles is a philatelist; his aunt proudly told me of the fact when I had tea belowstairs. You see, we guessed that Mrs. Bartholomew had posted the poisoned digestive powders to her husband from China. Shanghai, to be exact. I had a conversation with Mr. Evans about postal deliveries that day, and he told me that it was Charles's job to distribute the post when it came. When he questioned him, the poor boy completely broke down. He said he had seen the Shanghai stamps on a small package addressed to Mr. Bartholomew, and he couldn't help himself. He steamed them off the parcel before he gave it to him. I hope Mr. Evans does not sack him for taking them."

"No one surely loses their job for taking three stamps?" Mr. Stafford's voice was incredulous, and Mrs. Jackson smiled.

"Servants must not take things that don't belong to them," she said simply. "It is the code we work by. In this case, his taking the stamps was of immeasurable help in forcing a confession from Mrs. Bartholomew; it looks to me as if she will admit to the murder of her husband."

A white-faced Mrs. Bartholomew was standing upright between two policemen, her face rigid with anger. She did not look particularly cooperative.

"Her fingerprints will be all over the bottle anyway," said Mr. Stafford.

"Very luckily we did not need to rely on modern police methods," said Mrs. Jackson—her eyes were still alight with the excitement of it all.

Lady Montfort, having finished talking to Colonel Valentine, came across the room and sat down in the chair she had occupied for the séance. She still looked very upset, Mrs. Jackson thought. As Charles returned through the door with a tray of glasses and brandy, she went over to him and filled a glass, then went back to her ladyship.

"You look rather shaken up, m'lady; perhaps this will revive you," she said as she handed her a glass with a little brandy and then directed Charles to administer refreshments to the stunned group of rosarians who were standing in a dazed bunch on the other side of the room as far away from Mr. Urquhart and Lady Montfort as they could get.

"Was that playacting, Lady Montfort?" Mrs. Jackson noticed that Mr. Stafford couldn't take his eyes off the elderly man who had wrapped his cashmere shawl around his shoulders and was now sitting by the fire crackling in the hearth, his pale eyes gazing deeply into the flames, like a very tired old wizard.

"It was certainly not playacting, my lad." Mr. Urquhart turned his head and frowned at Mr. Stafford. "It was the spirit of my friend Rupert Bartholomew. I felt his presence quite strongly, the poor man."

Colonel Valentine had turned away from Albertine, who was now being escorted out of the room between two policemen. In the hallway they came across an outraged Mr. Haldane, who burst past them into the room, shouting at his wife.

"Maud, what the ruddy hell is going on in this house? Policemen? Are you mad? Where are they taking Albertine?"

"You need to calm down, Roger," said Mrs. Haldane, lifting her head from taking a sizable sip of brandy. "The police have just arrested Albertine for Rupert's murder. I should watch what you say if I were you, dear, otherwise you might find yourself up on a charge of obstructing the course of justice." Mr. Wickham nodded agreement. "Yes, she is right, Roger, I would keep quiet if I were you."

Mr. Haldane laughed. "Whether she murdered her husband or not is quite immaterial. There are other, more important matters on hand." He had taken center stage in the room, and his squat, toadlike body clad in his evening clothes looked macabre and out of place among the dainty tables and lacy cloths.

"Our prime minister has given Germany twenty-four hours to withdraw its army from Belgium. Otherwise we go to war."

Chapter Twenty-four

Colonel Valentine quietly closed the door to the library. Charles had lit a fire in the grate and had left coffee and sandwiches on a table.

"Thank you so much for driving over here at such a late hour, Colonel Valentine. I was so worried that you would not make it in time, and then we would have had to deal with a very angry woman without your constables." Clementine sank down in a chair by the fire. She still had brandy in her glass, but she seemed completely unaware that she even had a glass in her hand. She shook her head to Jackson's offered cup of coffee. "Now, how can I help you?"

Colonel Valentine cleared his throat and looked at his notes. "Well, Mr. Stafford was very clear about what you had discovered. He did not mention the séance, of course, just that you hoped with the aid of a parlor game to trick Mrs. Bartholomew into a confession, which was evidently successful from what I heard in the conservatory."

"Ah, so you were there all the time, you heard the entire thing."

"Yes, we arrived just as you were all finishing your dinner and were sitting in the conservatory from the moment Mr. Urquhart set up his Ouija game or whatever it is."

Clementine nodded, though she was not terribly sure that it should be referred to as a game. She was still trying to understand the events in the salon after dinner.

"Did Mrs. Bartholomew make a full confession to you?" Mr. Stafford asked.

"Yes, she did. She wanted her husband out of the way so she could return to France and marry the man she was in love with. It's always the same when a woman murders her husband: there is usually another man." Mrs. Jackson smiled at this, but said nothing.

"Of course there is money involved, too. Mrs. Bartholomew inherited everything her husband owned on his death. She admitted this to us, but she seemed a good deal more agitated about a rose. I expect that will all come out later."

"I can explain that to you, Colonel Valentine. You see, she had bred a very beautiful rose for her husband, which he claimed to be his own. Quite a lovely specimen for a hybrid tea rose. And she simply wanted him to acknowledge that she had created it and that it carry her name: Rosa Albertine. I think in her mind, poisoning her husband was justification for his stealing her rose." After days of watching men badger and belittle their wives, Clementine's voice expressed not a tinge of regret for what had taken place in Hyde Castle five months ago.

Mr. Stafford stirred in his chair and said, "Surely a woman doesn't poison her husband simply because he denies her the right to name a rose she created after herself." He looked most uneasy.

"It is surprising what will drive a woman to murder, Mr. Stafford," Mrs. Jackson said.

"Well, my business here is done," said Colonel Valentine. "We will ask Fisk & Able to make sure that the chemical analysis of the digestive powders is made available to us. Mr. Stafford has given us the original bottle with its contents and they will be tested for Mrs. Bartholomew's fingerprints. I will certainly do all I can to keep your good name out of this, Lady Montfort." He nodded at Stafford and Mrs. Jackson, assuring them that he would do his best to keep them out of it, too.

"Thank you, Colonel Valentine. I am sure Lord Montfort will be heartily grateful to you." Clementine took a sip of brandy.

The three of them sat on in the library. Mr. Stafford, who had missed his dinner, ate an entire plate of sandwiches; Clementine had another brandy; and Mrs. Jackson sipped some particularly delicious Turkish coffee.

"May I ask you about the séance, m'lady?" Mrs. Jackson asked, and Mr. Stafford dusted off his hands with a napkin and said that he, too, was curious.

"It all sounded so real from the conservatory," he said. "I thought old Colonel Valentine was going to have a fit. All we could hear, of course, was that high, thin Scots voice spelling out the words. It was quite eerie."

"I asked Mr. Urquhart, at dinner, if he would help me set up one of his Ouija sessions. By the way, he does not like that word at all. You see he completely believes in the other side, as he calls it. And you know something?" She laughed, a little embarrassed. "I know this sounds almost ludicrous, but I do think that Mr. Urquhart is blessed with some sort of Celtic 'sight,' as they call it. Do you remember the lecture he gave us in the conservatory, Jackson? When he told us all about poisonous plants and their many uses?"

Mrs. Jackson nodded. "Yes, m'lady, it was quite unnerving; I was convinced he was the murderer and was playing some sort of game with us."

"You see, I think he sensed something was off about

Mr. Bartholomew's death right from the start. He told me that he had guessed that it was not accidental food poisoning. He said, 'I knew it would just be a matter of time before it all came out, and then you and Edith arrived and I sensed that you were here to solve the mystery surrounding his death.' So you see, it was quite easy for me to tell him that I wanted to force a confession. I did not need to say from whom, and he did not ask me."

"So it was Lady Montfort moving the board around." Mr. Stafford's face lost its tight look and he laughed in relief. "With Mr. Urquhart's cooperation?"

"Yes, I did guide the board, but Mr. Urquhart was not cooperating with me, other than to set up the séance." Clementine hesitated. "After Mr. Urquhart 'got through' to the other side, I took over and guided the planchette to spell out that the spirit had a message for Albertine and that the rose should be named Oleander—which was a lucky guess, of course, because she might just as easily have used ground castor bean. But . . ." She laughed again and took another sip of brandy. "Really I must have had a little too much wine at dinner. I could have sworn that the whole thing took off from there. Perhaps Mr. Urquhart was guiding the planchette, but there was a moment when it actually seemed to move itself. It felt almost electrifying."

"What about when he went into a trance, m'lady? That was awful." Mrs. Jackson turned to Mr. Stafford. "You didn't see it, but it was actually quite disturbing. He collapsed back in his chair, his eyes rolled back in his head, and this strange voice came out of him. It was a horrible moment." She shivered.

"It was unearthly, that's how it felt to me; even standing in the conservatory with two burly constables breathing heavily and pouring sweat in the heat of that room, it sounded otherworldly. What an act." Mr. Stafford laughed, but it was an uneasy laugh.

"But you see," Clementine finished her brandy and set down

her glass, "I don't think it was an act. I truly believe that Mr. Urquhart, funny little man that he is, with his toasted tea cakes and his hypochondria, actually in that moment went into some sort of trancelike state. I have seen holy men do something of the sort in India. Auto-suggestion? Quite possibly, but it was his voice from another world that completely did for Mrs. Bartholomew."

She looked at the clock on the chimney piece. "Good grief, look at the time. Let us go upstairs, Jackson, and pack up our things. It is nearly midnight and when we wake up tomorrow morning, if the German army has not retreated from Belgium, we will no doubt be at war. And if that is the case, it would be better for us to be at Iyntwood than in Mr. Haldane's house."

On the morning that England declared war on Germany, Mrs. Jackson was grateful that they had at least had time to enjoy a decent breakfast, before Mr. Haldane roared the expected news across the dining room. The sound of his voice had certainly galvanized her ladyship into action; she had never seen her say her goodbyes before with such purpose and speed.

"Well, thank goodness that is over, Jackson," she said as they settled themselves in the hushed comfort of the Iyntwood Daimler and bowled out through the grandiose entrance gates, leaving the entire Hyde Rose Society grouped together on the steps of the castle's baronial entrance—waving them off with energetic enthusiasm. "The drama of the last few days has left me feeling quite drained. But it was awfully sweet of them all to turn up for breakfast to say goodbye. Even Mr. Urquhart deigned to eat his toast and marmalade in the dining room. He didn't look in the least bit bothered by that terrific smack on the head that Mrs. Bartholomew gave him last night."

"Some of those frail-looking elderly men are very resilient, m'lady. I must say, though, it was very nice of them to turn out at such an early hour. I don't think anyone can have slept very well last night, what with Mrs. Bartholomew's arrest for murder, and knowing that we would probably wake up to find ourselves at war. I can hardly take it in myself."

"Yes, I can't quite believe our country is at war either. One moment we were thinking how unpleasant the Austrians were being toward Serbia and then the next thing is we are all at war." They both brooded on the fate of their world, until Lady Montfort rallied them both, saying that there was no point in dwelling on something they were powerless to change.

"It was awfully nice of them to join us for breakfast, wasn't it?" she said. "But I think that serving kedgeree was rather a macabre touch; who on earth thought that was a good idea? They are such strange people."

Nothing could have persuaded Mrs. Jackson to eat even a forkful of kedgeree, but she had thoroughly enjoyed Hyde Castle's wonderful sausages—she had treated herself to two this morning and had jotted down the name of the pork butcher in Market Wingley who made them. "The kedgeree was Mr. Evans' idea, m'lady. I rather think he was making a point to Mr. and Mrs. Haldane and he is about to make another one as well." She was rather curious to see her ladyship's reaction to yet another unorthodox outcome in the Haldane household.

"Oh really, Jackson, what does Evans have in mind? He is certainly a bit of an oddity."

"Well, his bags are packed, m'lady. He told me this morning when I went belowstairs to say goodbye that he could no longer continue to work for a man as unpleasant as Mr. Haldane, and now that Mrs. Armitage's name has been cleared he will be handing in his notice." This morning in the servants' hall she had almost changed her opinion about Mr. Evans. He had behaved most honorably over the business of Mrs. Armitage.

"Evans is leaving Hyde Castle? Very sensible of him, too; where is he going?"

"To America, m'lady; he has had an offer to act in a film they are making over there. He says England has had its day and that there is all the opportunity in the world in America for a man with his skills."

Lady Montfort laughed. "Yes, I imagine he would do quite well in America in pictures. He has a very large way of being, not a quality best suited in a butler, but one that might do very well in the cinema. So he is abandoning Mrs. Wickham; she doesn't seem to have much luck where love is concerned."

"I think she is well out of that one, m'lady, I would not have said that Mrs. Wickham and Mr. Evans had a future together, they are too much alike. And Mrs. Wickham, it seems, is often attracted to the wrong type of man." She smiled. "It's a knack she has," she added with dismissive Lancastrian practicality.

Her housekeeper was looking particularly bonny this morning despite their few hours of rest. Clementine wondered if she dare pursue the subject of Mr. Stafford, whose clearly expressed admiration for her housekeeper's role in this investigation last night had been nothing short of worshipful.

No, she thought, *this is not your business, and if she wants to confide in you, she will.* But part of her couldn't resist saying, "What a good friend Mr. Stafford has turned out to be throughout this business—so generous with his time and so very helpful. I invited him over to Iyntwood so he can see how well his design for the new rose garden turned out, and he said he would pop over next week."

To her delight, she noticed that Mrs. Jackson's usual equanimity disappeared completely as she turned her head and carefully inspected the side of the road and the hedgerows. Her fair skin flushed pink as she said, "Yes, so he said this morning. Hyde Castle will most likely be his last commission for a while; he suspects that this war will change a lot of things."

This morning? My goodness, she was up early!

"Yes, I am afraid you are probably right, Jackson. War will change everything."

Could it really be possible? The enormity of it hit Clementine again, even though it was impossible to imagine war on a morning like this with the sun beaming down on meadows full of peacefully grazing cows. Clementine, tired and grateful to be returning home, felt a lump rise in the base of her throat. In the coming months their lives would no doubt be turned upside down by a conflict that involved the most prosperous countries in Europe; a war of such unimaginable industrial magnitude that it would probably not take them long to understand how harmful to their world it would be. The country would empty of young men as sons, brothers, husbands, and lovers would march off to do their duty in that carefree way young men often displayed at the prospect of the glories of battle. Mr. Haldane and men like him would grow still richer, and most certainly nothing would ever be the same again.

She looked down at the envelope in her lap that had been put by her plate at the breakfast table. The Montfort crest announced that it was from her husband. She opened it and pulled out a single sheet of paper. Written in familiar handwriting were the words: "Darling Clemmy, Althea arrived home yesterday, as did Harry, and Verity arrives with the children tomorrow. Darling, please," and then a two-word poem: "Come Home."

Author's Note

I have run Lady Montfort and Edith Jackson's investigation into the death of Rupert Bartholomew as closely as I can to coincide with the events in Europe as the days counted down from July 23, 1914—when Emperor Franz Joseph delivered an ultimatum to Serbia in response to the assassination of his nephew and heir, Archduke Franz Ferdinand, in Sarajevo—to Britain's declaration of war with Germany on August 4, 1914. They were thirteen very uncertain days, which led to a world war so destructive and catastrophic that when it ended, on November 11, 1918, of the 65,038,810 men who fought in it, on both sides, 8,528,831 were dead, 21,189,154 wounded, and 7,750,919 prisoners or missing in action. It was referred to as the war to end all wars.

On a lighter note, there was no Hyde Rose Society, but in the leisured days in England before WWI, those with money and time on their hands had many interesting and diverse hobbies. I do not particularly admire the hybrid tea rose so enthusiastically created by the member of the Hyde Rose Society, and I like to imagine that Miss Gertrude Jekyll would not have recommended the use of them in her garden schemes. I am sure she would have stuck to the old roses that are also mentioned in *A Death by Any Other Name.* Here is a little more information about the redoubtable Miss Jekyll.

Gertrude Jekyll (1843–1932)

What is one to say about June, the time of perfect young summer, the fulfillment of the promise of the earlier months, and with as yet no sign to remind one that its fresh young beauty will ever fade.

—GERTRUDE JEKYLL

Miss Jekyll created some four hundred gardens in Britain, Europe, and America; her influence on garden design has been pervasive to this day. She spent most of her life in Surrey, England, latterly at her beautiful home Munstead Wood, Godalming. She ran a garden center there and bred many beautiful varieties of plants. Some of her gardens have been faithfully restored, wholly or partly, and are open to the public. The Godalming Museum has many of her notebooks and copies of her garden drawings, (compiled and sorted by members of the Surrey Gardens Trust); the original drawings are in the University of California, Berkeley.

Miss Jekyll's books about gardening are widely read in modern editions; much has been written about her by others. She contributed over a thousand articles to *Country Life, The Garden,* and other magazines. She was also a talented painter, photographer, designer, and craftswoman and was much influenced by Arts & Crafts principles. Her brother, Walter, was a friend of the author Robert Louis Stevenson; it is thought that his name may have been borrowed for the title of Stevenson's *The Strange Case of Dr. Jekyll and Mr. Hyde.* The family historian, Gertrude Jekyll, is well known for her association with the English architect Sir Edwin Lutyens; she collaborated with him on gardens for many of his houses.

For more information and a guide to her many books please visit: http://gertrudejekyll.co.uk/shop.

E. AURORA

1/18 - 15 (12/17)
10/19 - 18 (8/18)